Known to millions as the agony aunt from Granada Television's *This Morning* programme, Denise Robertson has worked extensively on television and radio and as a national newspaper journalist. Beginning with *The Land of Lost Content* in 1984, which won the Constable Trophy for Fiction, she has published 18 successful novels, including the best-selling *Beloved People* trilogy. She lives near Sunderland with her husband and an assortment of dogs.

The second volume in
The Beloved People
trilogy

DENISE ROBERTSON

Strength for the Morning

This edition published in the United Kingdom in 2004 by Little Books Ltd,
73 Campden Hill Towers, 112 Notting Hill Gate
London W11 3QW

First published by Constable 1992

Text copyright © Denise Robertson 2004

The moral right of the author has been asserted

A CIP catalogue record for this book is available from
the British Library

ISBN: 1 904435 35 1

Printed and bound by CPI Bookmarque, Croydon

BOOK ONE

1

June 1939

Diana Brenton steered her dark-green Lanchester carefully into Chester Square and came to a halt outside the Colvilles' town house. She had been a qualified driver for only four months, and London's traffic was still intimidating. All the same, she must get as much practice as possible. If there was to be war she must be prepared. She had told Loelia Colville, her childhood friend, 'I mean to drive an ambulance,' and had seen disapproval in Loelia's eyes, but it did not move her. If Hitler made war, he would do it from the air. There would be terrible carnage and everyone must do their bit.

She stepped from the car and looked at the stately Chester Square houses. Impossible to imagine them razed to the ground, but she had seen on newsreels what the German air force had done in Spain. She collected her bag from the passenger seat, tucked her hair into her hat and mounted the steps.

It was a relief to be out of the car, but there was no escape from the heat. The leaves of the plane-trees were drooping and so were those of the geraniums in the window-boxes. As she waited for Loelia's door to open she put a hand to the nape of her neck and felt moisture at her hairline. Trust God to send trying weather in the midst of a crisis.

A moment later a uniformed maid was welcoming her into the hall and Loelia was hanging over the banister on the first landing.

'Do come up, Di. I'm fearfully perplexed about the Adares' party next week. The Kents will be there, and you know Marina: eight feet tall and slim as a willow. She makes me feel like a dumpy little pillar-box.' As Diana mounted the stairs she thought how bizarre life could be at times. They were digging slit trenches in Kensington Gardens, barrage balloons floated obscenely over London's parks, even restaurants had given way to panic and sandbagged their windows... and she and Loelia were about to discuss party clothes, as though how you looked on an evening out were still the most important subject under the sun.

For the next hour they considered and tossed aside Worth and Schiaparelli, Hartnell and Molyneux, most of them condemned because of their length. This year of 1939 was the Year of the Leg, and for women of fashion, hemlines must be seventeen inches above the ground. 'It's useless,' Loelia said at last, snatching up a *peignoir*. 'I shall have to buy something ready-made; there's no time now to order anything decent.' She looked the picture of misery, her plump little face with its hint of double chin sunk on her chest. Her red hair was twisted in plaits around her ears and wisps had come adrift with every change of outfit. She tried desperately to tuck them in, and then sighed. 'I must have a cigarette. I feel positively *distrait*.'

Diana accepted a Black Russian from Loelia's platinum case and they inhaled in companionable silence for a moment.

'How is Howard?' Loelia asked, eventually. 'Henry says he's sorry for politicians at the moment, having to decide between re-arming and appeasement and those dreadful Irishmen intent on blowing people up.'

'You know Howard,' Diana said easily, holding a shocking-pink Schiaparelli jacket against her and turning from side to side to see her reflection. 'He doesn't say much. He's at the House of Commons so often nowadays, and preoccupied when he's at home. He should have resigned his seat after Munich, because he's needed in Belgate. That's why we go north this afternoon; he also has a constituency meeting at the weekend.'

'Henry and I are coming to Yorkshire for the grouse. Perhaps we could come over to you for a day or two? It's aeons since I saw Durham – not since Rupert's twelfth birthday, if I remember correctly. How is my godson, by the way? Still itching for war?'

Diana blew a cloud of smoke into the air and then let out the last of it in a perfect, round smoke-ring. 'My first-born son, your godson, eats, sleeps and dreams RAF, and of course now that we have advertisements and recruiting drives, it feeds the fever. Pamela is just as bad, but with her it's air-raid precautions. *Wavering sound, go to ground. Steady blast, raiders past* – every time she hears anything remotely resembling a siren she chants that ghastly doggerel over and over again. I can bear the threat of war, but civil defence is too much.'

'I know,' Loelia said, sympathetically, as a maid arrived with coffee and tiny almond biscuits on a tray. 'But we mustn't let it interfere. It'll probably come to nothing in the end.'

She poured two cups and handed one to Diana.

'Queen Mary is up to her tricks again. She went to the Carstairs-Laceys' last month and a snuff-box caught her eye. "What an exquisite little snuff-box. I wish I had enamel of that shade of green in my own collection!" Sybil ignored her, of course, knowing what she's like, so Q.M. repeated it, on and on, until Sybil said, "Perhaps Your Majesty would allow me to present it to you?" She demurred, but she took it just the same. The old scrounger! And smoking like a chimney into the bargain. Still, these must be worrying times for her, with all her German relatives, and the King needing support. The last thing he needs is a crisis.'

England had been living with the threat of war for more than a year. People fretted and speculated; young women enrolled for first-aid courses; and Savile Row tailors toiled over uniforms for new and youthful officers. But the parties went on unabated, uncertainty adding an edge to the gaiety.

'I shall go home to Valesworth if there's a war,' Loelia said, stubbing out her cigarette and inserting a fresh one into her onyx holder. 'Henry says he can manage alone here, as long as the children are safe. And Max will go at once, probably to active service. He's a captain in the Terriers now, you know. Laura says she'll take the children back to America if the worst happens. Poor Max. But he would never leave England – not in a crisis.'

Diana tried to look merely politely interested, but as usual felt a little flutter of self-consciousness at the mention of Loelia's brother, Max, and his American wife. She saw that Loelia was watching her, and turned away to put out her cigarette. She was never sure if Loelia knew about her affair with Max. It seemed a lifetime, now, since he had been her lover when she was a girl newly married to Howard: since he had cast her off when she was carrying his child, and married an American heiress. Howard had not only forgiven her, he had kept her secret and treated Pamela, Max's child, like his own. For all she cared, thought Diana fiercely, Max and his American wife could disappear in a puff of smoke. All the same… it would be just like Laura to scuttle off if there was danger. She was the type who took to her bed at the least excuse; how could she face up to a war?

'I must go,' Diana said, getting to her feet. 'Howard expects to be home by one.'

Loelia accompanied her down to the hail and kissed her fondly. 'You'll be back for Ascot, won't you?' She heaved a theatrical sigh. 'Let's have fun this season, Di – before we're too old, or done down by Herr Hitler. The news is so depressing. It makes me quite morose.'

But even as the door closed on Diana Brenton, her lifelong friend was scampering back upstairs to make a momentous decision: whether to wear the grey or the beige for lunch at Hatchetts in Piccadilly.

Howard Brenton paused on Westminster Bridge and looked downriver. Behind him towered Big Ben and the turrets of the Palace of Westminster. He leaned on the parapet, watching the comings and goings on the waterway, and thought of the grey-faced men he had left behind in the lobby of the House of Commons. They were all showing the strain of the last few months, Government and Opposition members alike. Hitler was still pursuing the line that if Britain kept her nose out of his business, he would keep his nose out of hers, but only fools believed him now.

Gloom overhung chamber and committee rooms. Outside, in the country at large, life appeared to go on as usual. The Season was in full swing: the Derby, Ascot, the Fourth of June at Eton, Goodwood and Cowes. Shipping companies were even reporting a cruising boom. How nice it would be simply to sail away from it all, but he must stay put for a while. Those who knew talked not of 'if' but 'when'.

A strong campaign was being waged in and out of Parliament for Winston Churchill and Anthony Eden to be invited into the Cabinet. To many, Churchill was a pugnacious individual who lived for war: a turncoat who smoked cigars in bed and tippled brandy. There were some who still condemned him for his championing of the ex-King during the abdication crisis. Churchill was in his sixties now, past his best, a shadow of the brilliant youth he once had been. But who else was there to stand firm?

The German press campaign against Britain had a new, gloating note about it, but Emerald Cunard continued to entertain Herr von Ribbentrop, the German ambassador.

Last week, at the Colvilles', Howard had heard a man vow that the Hitler regime was on the point of collapse, the German army untrained and bootless, and their tanks made of cardboard. 'Eat, drink and be merry, for all will be well,' was the message of the uninitiated. But preparations were under way to protect London in the event of air-warfare, and to evacuate children from all major cities. Notices had appeared in the paper: *Those who wish to get out should go to any of the stations announced as evacuation centres... they should take their gas masks and only small hand luggage... take some food for the journey and a rug or blanket. No domestic animals can be taken. No one can choose his destination. Householders will be required by the billeting officers to receive refugees up to the limit of one person per habitable room in the house.* The citizens of Britain were now being referred to as refugees! Children were to be evacuated in school groups, and small children had to have identity labels attached to their clothing.

If war came, Howard would have to think what to do with Diana and the children. Their house in Durham was too near to the obvious target of the coalmines, and the house in London, of course, would be out of the question. Loelia would go to Valesworth; perhaps Diana could join her there?

Far down the river a siren hooted, and sea birds wheeled in the blue sky. It all looked so normal. Howard straightened up. He liked to walk for half an hour or so after leaving the House, but today he faced the long drive north with Diana. If they were to get home to the Scar before dark, there would be no time to spare.

Two girls passed him, chattering about Merle Oberon and *Wuthering Heights*, the latest film. 'I cried all the way home from the cinema,' one of them said happily. 'I can't wait to see it again. And that Laurence Olivier, ooh...' Howard found himself smiling foolishly long after they had passed from earshot. How wonderful to be young and have a head filled with nothing but celluloid dreams.

As he walked he began to look over his shoulder for a cruising cab. He would have two days in Durham – hardly enough time to see to the pits, let alone anything else. Thank God he had a good manager. Norman Stretton had come to him without experience of the mining industry or British manufacturing, but with an understanding of men. There had been peace in the Brenton collieries for the last nine months – ever since Munich, in fact. And though this was in part due to the men's preoccupation with the German threat, credit was due to Stretton for his tact and fair management.

'Cab, sir?' Howard had fallen into a reverie, but the cabbie had recognized a potential customer and slowed down anyway.

'Mount Street,' Howard said, sinking back into the leather seat. He thought of the miles between London and Durham, with Diana grinding the occasional gear or taking corners on the Great North Road on two wheels. She always gave out an anguished 'God!' when she made an error, and followed it up with 'Sorry'; though whether she was apologizing to him or the Almighty, Howard was never sure.

He felt a glow of satisfaction as he thought of his wife. Things had been rocky between them at first, owing to the affair with Max Dunane, but they were comfortable together now, both as lovers and companions. She was more beautiful than ever, in her thirty-sixth year: still striking, but without the old restlessness. How easily he might have lost her. Instead, he and Diana had grown closer – and he had Pamela, into the bargain. He had three sons and he loved them all, but with a daughter, you knew a closeness, an open affection you could not find with sons.

He began to fish in his pocket for coins, thinking as he did so that he must spend more time with Rupert, his eldest son. There had been such a bond between them once. The boy was sixteen now, and mad to fly aeroplanes. Howard closed his eyes, then, thinking of Hitler and his Axis and Joseph Stalin, poised to strike or embrace wherever he eventually chose. If Russia aligned with Germany...

'Here you are, sir,' the cabbie said and Howard stepped out onto the warm pavement, trying not to think of his son being swept up by war.

Frank Maguire was on his way to one of the pits owned by Howard Brenton, whistling as he walked, his belly full of fried bread and black pudding. He paused at the newsagents to buy five Capstan cigarettes and a *Daily Herald*. On a board outside the shop a newspaper bill said, *Mauretania nearly ready for maiden voyage*, and the front page of the paper showed the huge ship on the stocks in Liverpool. Frank felt a glow of pride in a British achievement as he went on his way.

In the kitchen he had just left, Anne, his wife, poured herself a cup of yellowing tea. Across the room Frank's precious wireless was silent, but she made no move to switch it on. She shirked the news broadcasts now, with their constant gloom and tales of wickedness across the Channel. Why England should bother about places like Poland and Czechoslovakia Anne couldn't imagine. She sipped her tea and thought about the future. If there was war, they would take Joe; he was nearly seventeen, and desperate to enlist. Up to now she had managed to terrorize him out of it, but if there was war...? She had never wanted the boy, God forgive her, but the moment he had been put into her arms she had known that she would kill for this child if she had to. With the others it was different; she loved them because they were hers – with the possible exception of Stella, who was devil-spawn if she ever saw it – but she did not feel any of them to be part of her, an extension of herself. Only Joe. Tears filled Anne's eyes as she thought of him going off to war, perhaps never to return.

She stood up hurriedly and began to clear the table. A couplet came into her head: *For men must work and women must weep...* Well, that was wrong for a start because most women, as far as she could see, had to weep and work at the same time.

In the nearby town of Sunderland, Anne's sister Esther was making her own preparations for war.

She still hoped Mr Chamberlain would produce another miracle, but her partner, Sammy Lansky, was scathing about the Prime Minister. 'He didn't bring anything back from Munich, Esther. Not a blind thing, except defeat and humiliation – he got that, all right.' No one seemed to support Chamberlain any more. Errand boys had ceased to whistle 'The Umbrella Man', and when people spoke of leadership it was Winston Churchill's name which sprang to their lips. Esther had laid in a store of material for black-out curtains, and sticky paper strips with which to pattern the windows of her precious semi-detached house. She worked hard in the business she shared with Sammy, and the house was the fruits of her labour. What she had seen of Spain on newsreels at the cinema had convinced her that if the German air force ever bombed England, there would be little or nothing left standing, but she meant to do what she could to preserve what was hers, Hitler or no Hitler.

Today, she and Sammy were preparing a bedroom in the Lansky home for the two young boys Emmanuel Lansky, Sammy's father, was taking from the stream of Jewish refugees fleeing out of Germany. Emmanuel Lansky had been the Belgate pawnbroker, driving over from Sunderland on Wednesdays and Fridays to open his lock-up shop there, and Esther had been a wide-eyed fifteen-year-old orphan with hardly a penny to her name. He had taken her under his wing, and helped her, and in the intervening years they had grown close. Esther grieved to see what was happening to him now, as he watched the Nazi shadow fall across Europe.

Every day the papers were full of fresh outrages against his fellow Jews. He worried about his dead wife's parents, elderly now and living in fear in Paris. If war came, would Hitler be content with Poland, or would he sweep on into Holland and Belgium and ultimately into France, as the Kaiser had done before him? Tales of the Nazi concentration camps which filtered out were almost unbelievable in their horror. The *News Chronicle* estimated that ten per cent of prisoners were dying, after appalling whippings and torture, and even *The Times* carried pathetic appeals in its small ads: *Help urgently needed for 64-year-old Jew. Good appearance, hard worker. Former manufacturer. Please help. Box B7432.*

For months Lansky had fretted over his inability to take children into his all-male household, and then Sammy had made the suggestion. 'We're doing well, father, Esther and I, making money hand over fist, with all this talk of war and more work about for everyone. Take two children, boys who need *shul*, and I'll pay for a *goyah* to look after them.' Sammy had winked then and leaned to his father. 'Perhaps you'll get your scholar, after all, papa. A *mentsh* instead of your *shmuck* of a son.'

Emmanuel had longed for Sammy to become a scholar and a teacher, but his son was an entrepreneur, with a string of shops and market stalls. When Sammy proposed taking the children, his father had nodded and fingered his beard. 'Promise me one thing, Samuel, if we take these poor boys: that they will be *my* boys, for the *yeshiva* only, not conscripts for your business empire.'

'I swear,' Sammy said solemnly and Esther, smiling indulgently, was glad to think that old Lansky would have youngsters to share his love of books and the Jewish law.

Now they were preparing a blue-and-white room, with a double desk and a bookcase and a splendid wind-up gramophone in a mahogany case. There were two beds, and a cushioned ottoman, and even two silver photograph frames to hold precious family portraits. As she worked, Esther imagined how it would be when Eli Cohen, who had charge of placing refugee children in Sunderland, knocked and ushered in two boys, tall youths, bespectacled probably, and sadly in need of cherishing. Sammy would clown about to make the boys feel at home, and they would begin to smile in spite of themselves. Emmanuel's eyes would mist over, and she herself would make sure they lacked for no creature comfort. It was the least she could do for homeless children.

She began to dust the dressing-table and chests, suddenly thinking of her own son. He would be a boy now, not a child, growing up somewhere with adoptive parents who loved him. *I did the right thing,* she thought. *I loved him enough to let him go.*

Downstairs again, they drank tea and ate toasted teacakes until the evening paper dropped through the letter box. The headlines were full of the King and Queen's visit to the World's Fair in America, but sandwiched between the gossip items was the stark announcement that the Dublin government had outlawed the IRA. More than thirty bombs had gone off in postboxes in cities around Britain, adding to the tension. Now Dublin had taken sides. Page two gave details of Nazi atrocities on Czech Jews, and Esther's heart ached at what Emmanuel would make of that. If the boys came soon, perhaps she could hide the paper before he read it.

At last Eli Cohen's knock came at the door. 'I'll go,' Esther said, but Emmanuel stayed her with an uplifted hand. 'I must welcome them, Esther.'

He threw his door wide, expecting to see two pale young men, but there were no boys. Only two teenage girls, one clutching a satchel, the other a shawl-wrapped bundle. Both faces were tear-stained, both pairs of eyes dark with apprehension.

'I'm sorry, Manny,' Eli said apologetically from behind them. 'The boys went first, and then the little girls. These two were left. Take them for tonight, since there's no one else with room. I'll find somewhere else for them in the morning.'

There was a moment of silence, and then the older girl, who Esther thought looked about fifteen, held out a hand to Emmanuel. 'Thank you,' she said in precise English. He was still dumbstruck, and she nudged her sister to life with an elbow. 'Thank you,' the younger girl whispered politely, despairingly, but her eyes said, *You don't want us. No one does.*

'They can come to me,' Esther said, moving forward, resisting the impulse to seize them and hug them tight. But Lansky had recovered his composure. '*Ni to far vus,*' he said. 'You are welcome.'

And then there was honey-cake and milk, and a general bustle, and Eli Cohen was slipping away with a relieved smile on his face. Only Sammy remained a picture of consternation. 'I said *boys*, Esther,' he repeated, when they were alone in the kitchen. 'Boys are easy. These are girls. *Oy vey!* Eli's done it now.'

The two girls sat in their belted raincoats, wolfing the honey-cake and milk that Sammy had fetched from the kitchen, until the younger girl's eyelids started to droop. Emmanuel offered her more food, but she shook her head. She spoke to her sister in German, of which all they could make out was the word *schlafen*.

'She means she wants to sleep,' Sammy said, and gathered their pathetic bundles for the journey upstairs. He turned back to the girls as he reached the door. '*Alles gut,*' he said in halting German. '*Alles gut* – all is well, young ladies.'

Old Lansky stayed downstairs, while Esther accompanied them to the room so carefully prepared for boys. 'Will he keep them?' she asked Sammy anxiously, when beds had been allotted and toilet arrangements made, and she and Sammy were back on the landing together.

'They'll stay for the time being,' Sammy said firmly, 'but in the long run I don't see how we could manage with them. It'll have to be boys.'

When Esther went back into the room she looked at the strained young faces. They must be near the age that she had been when she had come to the Lanskys for help. She remembered how she had felt then: afraid and despairing. She wished she knew their language, and sought desperately for the few words of Yiddish she had, but nothing suitable came to mind.

Suddenly she saw an ivory hairbrush protruding from the younger girl's satchel. On an impulse she seized it and, sitting on the bed, began to unpin the girl's braids and brush the long hair with slow, reassuring strokes.

The older girl watched her for a moment and then settled back on her pillows. 'It's going to be all right,' Esther said, and smiled and nodded in translation of her words. There were faint answering smiles as she got up, but when she moved to put out the light she saw alarm flare on both faces. Then Sammy appeared in the doorway, carrying a nightlight in a saucer. '*Schlafen*,' he said, when it was lit. And then, before he closed the door, '*Shalom*.'

2

June 1939

As Esther washed in icy water she thought of the days when she had been fire-*goyah* to the Lanskys. Emmanuel had found her a room in Hendon for three shillings a week, and a job as housekeeper to Philip Broderick. Dear, dearest Philip! She took a towel and held it to her face to dry it, closing her eyes against the soft folds, remembering the happiness she had found with him, the pain of losing him, and of their child, growing up somewhere, perhaps never knowing that he had been born out of love. But she didn't allow herself to think about the boy often and today was certainly not the time. The two German girls might be awake by now and needing her help. However well-meaning Sammy was, he was no substitute for a woman.

When she was dressed and had eaten toast and marmalade, she hurried down to the garage where her new black Hillman saloon was kept. Sammy called it her black beetle, but Esther was inordinately proud of it.

She ran it out onto the drive and looked back at her house. She owned a house and a new car: it seemed unbelievable. She locked up the garage, checked the front door again, and set off for the Lanskys.

Ruth and Naomi Guttman had come to Britain from their home in Hamburg on a *Kindertransport*. They had said goodbye to their parents at the huge station, where stone lions guarded the entrance and jackbooted SS guards searched their baggage for hidden valuables. Ruth's precious

violin was taken from her and Naomi's sandwiches ruth-
lessly separated in case paper money had been hidden in the
filling. All around them children were sobbing or turning
angrily from parents who they felt were abandoning them.
The girls' last glimpse of their mother was of her waving
through a cloud of steam.

A child in the carriage cried out, '*Mutti, mutti*!' and Naomi
clutched her sister's arm, wailing, 'I want to go back.'

Ruth shook her head. 'We have to go.'

Both girls had heard the Hitler youth singing as they
marched, singing of *Judenblut* – Jewish blood – and the
benefits to be gained if it was spilled. They had been taught
in school the theory of Germanic longheads which held that
Jewish skulls were several inches shorter, and so inferior.
When a Jewish boy had been called to the front of the class
so that the teacher could demonstrate, Ruth had known it
was time to go. But why did their parents not come, too?
The Guttmans' glassware business had been smashed on
Kristallnacht, along with 7,000 other Jewish concerns,
while fashionably dressed German women brought their
children to witness the orgy of destruction. By the end of
that purge, hundreds of synagogues had been burned, an
unknown number of Jews lay dead, and prudent parents
made plans to get their children to safety.

It had taken the Guttmans six months to get their daughters
onto a *Kindertransport*, clutching the precious passports
with a red letter 'J' on them to denote *Juden*. Around them,
children vomited with fear or wet themselves with confusion.
All they had to eat were biscuits, for neither of them liked
to eat the sandwiches the SS had fingered. They washed
them down with water, passing the bottle to other children
less well-provided for, until, at the Hook of Holland, Dutch
dockers brought them cheese and bread and jugs of milk.
Naomi would have refused them in case they were not
kosher, but an instinct for survival had arisen within the

fifteen-year-old Ruth. 'Eat,' she said fiercely, and began to cram the food into her own mouth.

They arrived at Harwich, dirty and tired, to board another train for Liverpool Street Station, there to be herded by volunteers into an assortment of cars and vans, and conveyed to a hall attached to a synagogue. One of the children had looked from the car window and seen a shop window full of copies of *Mein Kampf*, surrounding a picture of Hitler, the author. The boy cried out in fear, and nothing would convince him he was safe until a British policeman stepped forward to open the car door for them and smiled a welcome.

They spent two days and nights in London, while groups of children were gathered and despatched to cities and towns around Britain. 'You're going to Sunderland,' a woman told them at last, and a rabbi, in their own tongue, repeated their destination and told them not to be afraid.

They slept fitfully on that first night in Emmanuel Lansky's home, both of them huddled into one of the single beds. In the early hours, Sammy Lansky tiptoed into the room and looked at the two waxy faces: the older one set determinedly, the younger one tear-stained and vulnerable in the light of the nightlight guttering in its saucer. He lit another, placed it alongside the first, and vowed then that nothing more would harm them. For the first time in a long while, he went voluntarily in search of his *tefillin* and *tallis*, so that he might ask God's help in keeping his vow, before he went to bed.

Esther arrived in the morning to the smell of toast and coffee, and scrambled eggs bubbling gently in a pan. Sammy poured coffee for her and pushed forward the cup. 'Is everything all right?' she asked nervously.

Sammy's eyes rolled heavenward. 'It's a *she'alah*, Esther. He won't budge. They go - here, there, anywhere, but they're out. He's afraid, that's the trouble. What does he know of little girls?'

'They're not so little,' Esther said doubtfully. 'They must be thirteen or fourteen.'

'You know that, I know that, but the *mentsh* who is my father sees only babies – girl babies.'

'I'll talk to him,' Esther said.

'Talk!' Sammy threw up his hands. 'And I wish you *mazel*. I'd sooner try to move a mountain.'

That morning Howard Brenton drove himself down from the house he had built for Diana when they married. It was a long, stone mansion with myriad windows and a roof of green Westmorland slate set against the white blaze of limestone that gave the hill its name of the Scar. Below lay the village of Belgate and the pit, the deepest and richest of the three Brenton collieries. Throughout the Thirties it had been a struggle to keep men working, but Howard had managed it – unlike other coal-owners who laid off their men with less thought than they gave to the redundancy of their pit-ponies.

Since his father's death, he had also managed to improve conditions in Belgate. The infamous rubble-walled houses known as the Shacks had come down, and a pleasant terrace taken their place. There was piped water now; deaths from diphtheria had more than halved; and a scheme to do away with the privies and the night-soil men was in hand. In the meantime, Howard and his family grew richer by the day. In the House of Commons, he sat on the Conservative benches, but sometimes he found the ethics of socialism curiously appealing. 'From each according to his means, to each according to his needs' – it was not a bad doctrine by which to live.

As he neared the foot of the hill, Howard resolved to resign his seat in the House as soon as the war crisis was over, and leave politics to those who had a clearer idea of where they stood. He was forty-one years of age and he felt every day of it. He had served in the last war, his wounded knee troubled him still, and his cheek was scarred: surely that was enough for one man? He lifted his hands from the wheel for a second and slammed them down again. He wanted done with it all. He wanted time with his wife, and a chance to get to know his children better. Perhaps Hitler would cease his folly and the world would stop rocking and settle back on its axis. He would take Diana to Europe, then, and live like a lizard in the sun for a while. In the meantime he must do his best for the men who depended on him, not only in the pits but in the coke works and the factories and all the other enterprises that bore his name. His father had left him an empire, but sometimes it felt like a millstone.

As he drove into the colliery yard, he saw Frank Maguire coming out of the manager's office. The man had a son born on the same day as Rupert; they had drunk a toast to their heirs that day: their one moment of togetherness. Since then Maguire had been involved in every protest at the pit, every strike. But he was straightforward and he could sometimes crack a joke to ease tension. All in all, if there had to be an agitator in Belgate, Maguire was the one to be preferred.

Frank Maguire was a hewer, a lord of the pit, with a putter to take what he hewed from the face to the flat. They were both 'on piece', and they worked with might and main, sending the pony flying backwards and forwards through the narrow shaft, only an inch to spare either side. As he hewed, one thought preoccupied Frank: the long wait before he could open his gallon bottle of water and take the thick, damp jam sandwiches from his snap tin.

As they moved forward, laughing, talking occasionally, coughing as they inhaled dust, they would test the roof with their picks. A good roof, a safe roof, would ring like a bell.

A bad one would reverberate like a drum, and they would go quiet and take precautions against a roof-fall. Today, however, the picks rang a merry peal until it was snap time, and the jerking and crashing of tubs ceased for a while as they squatted in a refuge hole to eat. Bread and cold bacon for some, bread and dripping or bread and jam for others... unless their household had had a windfall, and then they had a mutton pie.

They were all naked except for their boots and pit drawers, but they leaned against the bleeding walls while the pump snorted and gurgled until sludge choked it up. They laughed a lot. If you knew that that day you might be found dead, mouth pressed full of dirt, crushed by a fall of stone, you tended to laugh while you could.

'Well, I can't wait for a war,' one wag said, mouth full of bread and saveloy. 'Nice little billet, three meals a day, nee pit, nee nagging. Roll on the *Blitzkrieg*, that's what I say.'

'It's no joke,' Frank said, thinking of yesterday's paper and what it said the Nazis were doing in Czechoslovakia.

'It's all right for thou, lad,' the man said, nodding at Frank. 'Thou'll get the parliamentary nomination when old Gaffney snuffs it, and live in London like a bloody lord. I wish I'd been a union man, but all I did was pay me subs.'

'And draw thy benefits, Billy. Thou's had more compen in the last three years than I've had hot dinners,' Frank retorted.

The wag grimaced and put his fingers into his armpit, as though to quell pain. There was a roar of laughter at his discomfiture, and then the deputy was rising from his kist and signalling a return to work.

Frank went back to his hewing, but his mind was on the remark his marrer had made about London. Gaffney was the Labour candidate for Belgate, which was the seat held by Howard Brenton. Gaffney was elderly and ailing, a man who had served the party well but should now be put out to grass. Frank would stand a good chance of the nomination when that time came – and if he got it he would sweep Brenton from the seat at the first opportunity. He thought of how sweet his victory would be, and when next he raised his pick to test the roof it rang for him like a peal of triumph.

Esther looked down from her eyrie high above the warehouse and office. There were two typists in the room below now, and a bookkeeper, and an office boy who brewed tea as black as liquorice, all the while whistling the hit tunes of the day.

Sometimes, when she reviewed the rise of Sammy Lansky's business, she could scarcely credit it. They had begun with £100, £50 the gift of Emmanuel Lansky, £50 her own hard-earned savings. At first it had been hand to mouth, a case of selling oranges bought cheaply here, some packet sago there. Then there had been the saga of the condensed milk; Sammy had bought an enormous quantity of sweetened tinned milk which a wholesaler could not shift. He had decided to change the labels – or rather, he had staggered from barrow to kitchen table with the crates while Esther changed the labels. They had called the new product 'Choice', and had reaped a large profit from it.

At first they had had a barrow, then a market stall. Now they had three stalls, two shops, and a thriving check-trading business which operated by giving vouchers to customers to shop at designated stores. The store paid to get the trade and the customer paid extra for the privilege of settling the bill by instalments.

Now, by her own standards, Esther Gulliver was rich. She was buying her house on a mortgage, she had a nice car, and could afford regular trips to the cinema or tea in town. Compared with her sister, Anne, she was lucky... except that Anne was surrounded by her children, and Esther could only conjure up a picture of how her own child might be.

She had worked for Philip Broderick for six years before they became lovers. At first she had pitied the small, mis-shapen man, but she had come to recognize the spirit and the sweetness behind his pale, tortured face. He had taught her to appreciate books, to understand the politics of the day, to realize that there was a country outside the county of Durham, and a world beyond that country.

Thanks to Philip, she read two newspapers each day and drank in details of national and world affairs, but it irked her that there was now no one with whom she could discuss what she learned. Anne's head was always too full of the ups and downs of family life to care – except about the possibility of war, and she could not discuss that in a rational manner. The looming crisis and its consequences for the Jewish race were too painful to chew over with the elder Lansky, and Sammy turned her every attempt at a real conversation into a comedy routine, with Esther as the straight man. At least, he always had done in the past. Today, when he took his place at the desk across from Esther's he seemed strangely subdued.

'What are we going to do with them, Esther? I went to their room before I left, and they were huddled together like two lambs awaiting slaughter. Eli Cohen is coming this morning to take them away – and to what? All the good houses, the places where they would be cared for, took their quota long ago. Only the Lanskys are left: an old man and a *shlemiel*. If there's war, I'll have to join the army, so even if papa changed his mind, who would see to them then?'

Esther would have been moved by Sammy's apparent misery if she had not known him so well. 'Why not come straight out with it, Sammy?' she said sweetly. 'You've decided that the girls are staying, and you want to know if I'll give an eye to them. True?'

Sammy was across to her in an instant, lifting her round the waist and whirling her a foot above the ground.

'What a pearl, what an *oytser* my Esther is! She even reads my mind!'

He set her down suddenly and looked at her. 'Marry me, Esther. Make a *mentsh* of me. Then we can adopt the two little sparrows and all live happily ever after.' His dark eyes were on her and Esther could not fathom the expression in them. Was he joking? He had been a twelve-year-old when she had come to light his father's Sabbath fire for the first time. Now she was thirty-two, and he was a businessman of twenty-nine with a string of *shikse* girlfriends and a reputation for high jinks that would kill his father if he ever heard of it.

Esther slapped him on the arm and turned away. 'I have trouble enough, thank you. But I will help with the girls – *if* they stay, that is. They have a chance to be gone by teatime and two nice young scholars in their place.'

Diana stood at the window of the morning-room to watch Howard's Daimler thread down towards Belgate. She had looked forward to coming north, to seeing her children again, but suddenly a whole day lay ahead of her, with no lunch at the Savoy, no tea with Loelia, no supper at the Embassy or Aro's, no circling a minute dance floor till midnight had come and gone. What was she going to do in a house set on a hill, run by an efficient cook-housekeeper and a large staff, with two of her children away at school and the other two in the nursery upstairs, preparing to learn about dinosaurs?

In the end she spent the day mooning around the house, inspecting Noel's guinea-pigs, the stables, the kitchen garden; gazing out from the Scar to the bleak prospect of Belgate below.

What would war do to the children who lived in that huddle of houses? Last month she had taken her own children to be kitted out with gas masks. Until then she had consoled herself with the thought that the gas masks might never be needed. Now she could not be sure. They had shuffled along wooden benches as their turn came nearer, and then she filled in five yellow cards for an implacable lady with a hat like a chamber-pot and an ARP band on her upper arm.

Diana had purposely turned the whole thing into an expedition, a joke – but then, suddenly, as the black rubber snout was fitted over Noel's face, his eyes had widened in terror and it had not seemed a joke at all. Another child had caught a whiff of his fear, and burst into tears as its mother tried to comfort it, her own voice thick with terror. They sat, one by one, while the fitter checked for size and tightened straps, and then they filed out, each clutching a brown carton that was suddenly a threat and not an acquisition.

Diana turned away, wishing Rupert were at home. She saw him so seldom that it would have been heaven to cosset him for two whole days. They could have gone walking, out beyond Belgate and across the fields. And she'd have got news of his friends, and told him about the Colvilles, and they would have been pals together.

When Howard arrived home she was waiting with a Martini. 'Prepared by your handmaiden. And don't ask me what my enigmatic expression means: it's meant to display utter rectitude. I'm being the good wife and mother, so there!'

She sat on the ottoman in his dressing-room while he bathed, carrying on a conversation through the open door.

'It's nice to get away from the House,' Howard said. As he lay in the warm water, it was as though his cares were dissolving away.

They ate well, chicken consommé, lamb chops with home-grown vegetables, and a delicious raspberry sorbet, all washed down with Diana's choice of wine. She was enjoying playing the courtesan tonight, choosing Howard's cigar, rolling it between her fingers and holding it to her ear to check its excellence, tempting him with sweetmeats and nuts and raisins. They had coffee in the drawing-room, looking out from the height of the Scar to the fields of Durham and the far off blue-grey strip that was the sea.

'This is heaven,' Diana said, kicking off her gold strap sandals and lighting one of the Black Russians she now favoured. 'A whole evening together and no terrible telephone to interrupt.'

'I'm sorry,' Howard said. 'The last few weeks have been hard on you.'

'I can bear it,' Diana said. 'But coming back here to Belgate makes me wonder if the whole thing isn't just a phoney crisis?'

Howard shook his head. 'They say Herr Hitler has told the British ambassador he prefers to make war now, when he's fifty, rather than when he's older. He means to conquer Europe, Diana: make no mistake. He wants a *Blitzkrieg* on Poland to blood his troops. After that…'

'The children must go to Valesworth if war comes,' Diana said. 'Lee agreed to take them ages ago, since Henry won't need her in London as you'll need me. Besides,' She paused, choosing her words carefully. 'I must do something, Howard. I can't just sit on my hands in the country while everyone else does something to help. It would drive me mad.'

Howard was opening his mouth to remonstrate and she hurried on. 'That's why I learned to drive in such a hurry. It wasn't because we lost Fox; it was because I knew drivers would be needed if there was war. I mean to drive an ambulance, Howard. I'm determined to do it, so please don't try to stop me.'

It was the old Diana, the fiery girl of years ago, before Max and motherhood had tamed her. For a moment the memory brought a smile to Howard's lips. But only for a moment.

'It's out of the question, Diana. If war comes, it will mean aerial bombardment – on London especially, if Hitler stays true to form. I can't resign now; it would be cowardice. But how could I concentrate in the House, as I must do, knowing you were careering around the streets during an air raid?'

Diana's fingers had begun to drum on the arm of her chair, but she made an effort to be placatory. 'If a bomb falls, Howard, it won't much matter whether I'm careering around the streets, as you put it, or sitting placidly in Mount Street playing Ludo.'

'Precisely. That's why I want you away from London altogether, in the country, with or without Loelia. And the children *must* be kept safe…'

He sounded worried and it took the edge off her irriation. 'I know how you feel – I really do, darling. But it's the children I'm thinking of. If this war drags on for any length of time, Rupert will join up. We both know that. Wild horses couldn't stop him once he's old enough. And if it were to end quickly, and not in our favour… we know what would happen to the children then. I have to do my bit, Howard. And *for* the children, not in spite of them. Please try to see it my way.'

'I am trying, but I want you safe – and besides, there's Belgate. Someone must be there to organize things. Hitler won't just strike at London; he'll strike at factories, at docks and railways, and at coalmines. Imagine Belgate unprepared, those clustered houses… I need someone here, Diana, someone I can trust, making arrangements, planning relief, keeping up morale.'

He had chosen the wrong argument. He knew it as soon as the words left his lips.

'You have someone here already, Howard: Norman Stretton. He's someone Belgate respects and trusts in a way they've never respected me. I don't understand them. I've tried, because I care about them; I didn't, but I do now. If I thought my being there would help I'd do it like a shot. But we both know I'd be of no real help, I'd merely irritate them. It's Stretton for Belgate, Howard, and me for the city, where I belong. Now, let's stop talking about the war and have a lovely evening.'

She put a record on the gramophone, a tune Howard had heard whistled in the London streets and issuing from his wireless when the Savoy Orpheans were broadcasting. It was 'Deep Purple', a haunting tune, romantic and intimate. After a while Diana stubbed out her cigarette and came to curl beside him on the sofa. Her turquoise dress, with its long, slashed sleeves, was high in front and fell almost to her waist at the back. When Howard put his arm round her, her flesh was cool and firm, and he felt a sudden longing to hold her naked in his arms.

Instead, he put up a hand and stroked the buoyant dark curls.

'Happy?' Diana said, arching her neck to look up at him.

'Very.' He kissed her then, and they did not draw apart until the record ended and the needle began to click over and over again.

'Take me to bed,' Diana said, but it was she who pulled him to his feet and led the way up the wide stairs.

Anne Maguire was longing for bed, too, so that she could lay her weary head on the pillow and forget her troubles. That night Joe had reiterated his determination to join up as soon as he could. 'I want to go in the Gunners, mam. Make a career of it.' His freckled face shone with anticipation, and Anne was torn between a fierce pride and an itch to box his ears.

She sat, feet on the fender, watching the dock to see what time Estelle, or 'Stella' as she now liked to be called, would show her face, remembering that day, all those years ago, when she had set out to seduce Frank Maguire. She had been nineteen then, running her father's drapery shop for him, cooking and cleaning in an attempt to take her dead mother's place. And she had been a lady, too: neat as a new pin, with nails like almond halves, and skin like a lily. Her hair had been dark – not touched with grey like now – and she had washed it every week with scented soap.

Frank Maguire had buzzed around her, but she had given him no encouragement. He had been a good-looking lad – still was – but he was a collier, and came from a large and feckless Catholic family. Anne had set her sights on a professional man, or someone in trade, if she had to make do. She looked down now at hands scarred and stained from peeling vegetables and cleaning up. The dreams you had when you were young and daft and confident that you could overcome anything, even a drunken father and a dying business!

In the end it was her father who died first and had taken the business with him, and she and Esther were pitched out into the street, with the creditors after them in full cry.

Poor little Esther, only fifteen and wet behind the ears. She had gone into service in the house on the Scar, until the Brentons, thought Anne bitterly, had taken advantage of her and she had had to flee for her life, only to fall into the clutches of a Jew-boy, and work for a cripple. Still, between them they had set her up with a house and a car, so it hadn't all been bad.

Anne had been due to go into service with the Brentons, too, but something in her had rebelled. So she had set about seducing Frank Maguire, claiming to be carrying his child after one painful encounter. He had stood by her, as she had known he would, and they had married in the Catholic church, and set up home in a hovel, with bits and pieces begged from all and sundry.

Anne sighed, and looked at the dock again. Where *was* Stella? Getting into trouble, likely, and who was Anne to criticize? She had had such plans… but then the pretended pregnancy she had dreamed up to get her way turned into a terrible reality. She had run up- and downstairs, drunk gin and prayed – really prayed – that the child would die in the womb. God had known best, though, as he always did. Joseph had come into the world smiling, and thrived ever since. She had looked at him, bloody in the doctor's hands, and fallen in love. And she had learned her lesson: to trust in God. In his good time He would elevate Frank to his proper place and bring down the Brentons. She might only be a convert to Catholicism, but she knew the power of God.

She reached to put a lump of coal on the fire, picturing Diana Brenton brought to her knees, begging in the gutter while the workers got their dues. Her exultation was cut short by the chime of the mantel clock. Half-past ten and that little bitch still roaming the streets! If Stella wasn't careful, she'd end up one day worn out and old before her time – and not with a good man like Frank Maguire, that was for sure!

Ten minutes later Frank came in, stooping through the door, smiling the slack smile of the ever-so-slightly tipsy. 'Hallo, pet. You've kept a good fire on, I see.' There were beads of sweat on his brow, and he opened the buttons at the neck and cuffs of his shirt before he sat down opposite her.

'Our Stella's not back,' Anne said accusingly.

Frank pursed his lips and shook his head.

'Well?' Anne demanded. 'What are you going to do about it?'

'Shall I go out and look for her, pet?'

'You might have to,' Anne said sharply. 'And you might have to hold me back when she does show up. Her time's ten o'clock, and *that's* an hour more than she should have. She thinks she can do as she likes; well, she'll learn she can't.'

Joe came in five minutes later, but not a cross word was said to him. Instead, Anne got to her feet to cut thick wedges from a fresh-baked stotty and smother it in butter from a dish swimming in a bowl of water to stop the butter from running away in the over-hot room.

'Our Stella's not in,' she said, when he was fed and wiping his mouth with the back of his hand. Joe sipped from his mug of tea and looked at the clock.

'She'll only be down Rosemary's,' he said, but Anne snorted at that suggestion.

'She's down some back lane, Joe, with some sackless lad. I can't stand any more disgrace, and I hope everyone knows that.' The men fell into an uneasy silence, remembering when Stella had been molested by Carter, the fruiterer, and the house had reverberated with the sound of Anne's wrath.

Frank was shrugging into his jacket to join Joe in a search, when his daughter came through the door, dark-blue eyes wild at the prospect of a clout from her mother, looking to Joe for protection, actually dodging behind him when Anne darted towards her. Her hair curled in ringlets on her forehead, her mouth trembled in apprehension, but there was still a defiant tilt to the blond head set on the slender neck. She looked beautiful, but abandoned.

'I've only been down Rosie's, honest, mam! We were looking at her film-star photos, that's all.' But there was a leaf caught in her hair and her skirt had a crumpled look. As Anne lifted her hand, Joe raised his arm to check it and Stella darted for the stairs.

'I'll swing for you, miss, before you're much older!' cried Anne. 'Either that, or you'll be in Gray's House.' That was the home where 'bad girls' went to give birth, and it had a well-deserved reputation for lack of charity. Stella did not reply, but when she was safe in the bedroom she shared with her sisters she shut the door and put out her tongue in the darkness. Tonight she had tasted power: the power of a man's yearning to possess her. And Bobby Smiles was not the only one that would slaver after her, for as long as she chose to let them.

She pulled her blouse, still-buttoned, over her head, then shed her skirt and vest, moving cautiously across the darlened room, past the beds where her sisters slept, pulling back the curtain to let in the moonlight. A mirror hung on the wall, next to a picture of Mary amid lilies. Estelle paused in front of it and raised her arms above her head so that her breasts moved up and out, taut and shapely, especially when she turned from side to side the better to see them.

She stood for a moment, enjoying the silhouette, feeling her power, thinking of all the pleasure that was to come. If there was war, she could escape – go far away, out of Durham. And war *was* coming! Bobby had shown her a cigarette card tonight: *How to avoid contamination by mustard gas*. If they were putting it on cigarette cards, it must be true. And when it came, she would be ready for it.

3

July 1939

Diana was awake when the maid brought the big, brass-railed tray into the bedroom and drew back the curtains. Beside her Howard slept soundly, and she would have liked to leave him sleeping, but today they had too much to do. And besides, this time all the children were at the Scar. She poured him a cup of tea, and then shook him gently. 'Come on, darling. Time to wake up.'

Howard stirred and stretched, and then a slow smile overtook his face. 'God, it's good to be back here again. You can almost feel the peace.'

Diana rather liked the ever-present rumble of hoofs and engines that filled the street outside the London house, but she nodded amicably. 'It's nice. Now sit up and I'll let you have a paper.'

They were folded neatly at the side of the tray; she gave him *The Times*, keeping the *Telegraph* for herself. It was the same gloomy picture in each paper: 2,000 Nazi guards had entered the free city of Danzig, and attacks on Poles were a regular occurrence. Losing Danzig would mean the Poles lost their access to the Baltic, and they did not intend to let the city go. Britain was pledged to come to Poland's aid if it had to defend itself, and Neville Chamberlain had reaffirmed that pledge in the House earlier in the month.

'It doesn't look good, does it?' Howard said.

But Diana was skimming the society pages. 'There's a picture of Loelia here, with Laura and two of the Kennedy girls. She was at school with Kathleen Kennedy.'

'Loelia?' Howard's mind was still on Danzig.

'No, silly, *Laura*. You know: Laura Dunane, Max's wife. She's never away from the American Embassy, according to Loelia.'

'Joe Kennedy is no friend of Britain,' Howard said, stroking out his paper. 'What is it they say at the Foreign Office? "I thought my daffodils were yellow until I saw Joe Kennedy".'

The American ambassador and his chic wife had a seemingly endless supply of handsome, charming children.The Kennedy men wore red carnations and wide, white smiles in the photograph, and Kathleen Kennedy was smiling, too, as befitted the girl who had stolen the heart of the heir to the Duke of Devonshire.

Will she marry Billy Hartington?' Diana asked.

'Shouldn't think so.' By now, Howard was deep in Danzig again but he raised his head to reply. 'The Cavendishes are Protestant to the core, and the Kennedys are rampant Catholics. They say that's why Joe Kennedy secretly dislikes the British: because of Ireland.'

'Why come here, then?' Diana did not expect an answer and she didn't get one, but by then she had come across a picture of the Queen, dazzling in a Norman Hartnell gown. The diminutive Queen was a month away from her thirty-ninth birthday, although she looked younger. However, she was making an effort to slim; she had ordered five courses to be served instead of six at Palace dinners, and she was trying to cut down her favourite meal: afternoon tea in the Scottish fashion. All this had come from Loelia, and was therefore gospel truth.

'I must slim,' Diana said, and Howard, tiring of Danzig, folded his paper to take her in his arms.

'You,' he said, kissing her firmly, 'are perfect as you are. Now, let me get out of bed.'

Diana smiled. She had diverted him from the grim news

of the day, and she was glad. She could hear the children stirring in their rooms, and she thought of breakfast, with all of them for once together around the table. She half-ran to the bathroom, shedding her nightdress as she went, anxious to enjoy her family while there was still time, before war clouds drifted over them. Would she have to send the little ones away? As she ran her bath, she contemplated evacuation and, finding even the thought unbearable, decided to postpone decision until it was forced upon her.

Howard came to speak to her through the bathroom door. 'I'm sorry I was so late, last night. What was Rupert having to say?'

'What does he ever have to say?' Diana replied. '"Aeroplane, aeroplane, aeroplane" – interspersed with "flying, flying, flying". Oh, and "lessons, lessons". That came in, too.'

'It's probably a phase,' Howard said but suddenly the water seemed cooler to Diana, the bath less of a cocoon.

She was the last one down to breakfast, and found Rupert and his father at the table, deep in conversation.

'I could have flying lessons now, couldn't I? There's no law against lessons at sixteen, is there?'

'I don't know,' Howard said. 'But if not, there should be. When you're seventeen I'll think about it. Now, help your brother with his egg, and stop being obsessive. How's Blaze?'

Usually mention of Rupert's gelding could divert him, but not today. 'If there's a national emergency they're going to put horses down,' he said gloomily. 'Forbes minor says his uncle told him. There are 40,000 horses in London, and when bombs fall the horses will go mad and stampede. So they're going to shoot them.'

'*Pas devant les enfants*,' Diana said, frowning. Ralph's eyes had grown round at the mention of shooting, and Noel was looking a little uncertain.

Only Pamela stayed serene. 'We can bring the horses here,

can't we, papa? Till it's all over, and then they can go home again?'

Rupert's eyes rolled. 'You are thick sometimes, Pammy. Forty thousand? We can only stable four, and that's tight.'

'I didn't mean here, exactly,' Pamela said defensively. She was nine years old, and did not like to be mocked. 'I just meant here in Durham. In the fields. We could do it, couldn't we, pa?'

'Perhaps,' Howard said, 'if we had to. But there isn't going to be a national emergency, and I'll thank you not to spread rumours, Rupert. Things are bad enough –' He had played into his son's hands.

'See!' Rupert said, triumphantly. 'You *do* think there's a crisis. In which case –'

'If you mention flying lessons I shall impale you on my fork and roast you alive,' Diana said, to giggles from all three children.

'Anyway,' Pamela went on. 'If you go to be a flyer, you'll have to learn to sleep without a light.'

The shot went home as she had known it would. 'I already do when I'm at school, fathead,' retorted Rupert. 'I just like having it here. I'm used to it... always have been.'

'That isn't true: about the horses, is it?' Diana asked Howard when a nurserymaid had collected the small boys and Rupert had chased a giggling Pamela up the stairs.

'I'm afraid it is,' Howard said. 'I don't know the details, but I know they foresee a problem with them. They've met with the RSPCA, and vets, and drivers of horse-drawn vehicles, to work out a plan. I don't think they'll shoot them, but they have to plan ahead. For everything. The children will leave London – that's all arranged. Horses are just one more item.'

Diana put her napkin to her mouth and pushed away her plate. 'My God, it's really going to happen, isn't it?' She wanted Howard to say, 'Of course not,' but he was silent.

*

For once, Anne Maguire was not thinking of the threat of war. She was too busy packing mutton pies into a cardboard box, and then inserting the box into the huge wicker basket out of which she could feed her family throughout the day. It was Saturday, the day of the Durham Miners' Gala, and families were trekking from all over the county to drink, and carouse, and talk, and cheer the political speeches of their leaders.

It was the zenith of Anne Maguire's year, their one family day out. Once she had the preparations over, she would enjoy every minute of it, from seeing the Belgate banner planted among the others to watching Frank take his place as a union official on the platform beside the Labour leaders. One day he would be a Member of Parliament, a leader himself, and Anne would make her weight felt then: by God, she would!

When the pies were packed, she turned to the stove, making butties with fried eggs, lining them up on the top of the range, shouting all the while for Stella to get her lazy bones out of bed. 'Have you died?' she called sarcastically, and received 'I wish I bloody had!' for her pains. If it hadn't been for the row of hungry faces around the kitchen table she would have run up the stairs and leathered Stella's legs. No one else in the house would have dared to back-answer their mother; even Frank was afraid of Anne's tongue. But Stella would meet her mother's gaze eyeball to eyeball. For years Anne had tried to gain the mastery of her, but it was useless. Now she simply prayed for the girl to make an early and sensible marriage and be someone else's responsibility.

The children queued at the sink to wash, and she inspected each one as they were done, checking behind ears and necks for tidemarks. At moments like this she was proud of her family, and amazed at the size of it. She looked at them:

Joe, Gerard, Angela, Theresa, David and Bernard. Only Stella was still missing, and she went to the foot of the stairs to shout for her again.

But Stella was halfway down the stairs, and Anne came to a sudden halt, aghast at the sight of her. 'Frank,' she said weakly, 'get out here and do something before I lose my reason.'

Stella had tied her blond curls up with an emerald ribbon, and her face, shorn of its fringe, was boldly painted, lips,eyes and cheeks. Even the fair brows were pencilled into a supercilious dark arch. She had on a knitted silk jumper through which her erect nipples could easily be seen. *She's a woman*, Anne thought, and felt first a shaft of fear and then a sharper shaft of jealousy.

'What's up?' Frank said apprehensively from behind her. Stella stayed on the middle stair, one leg in a high-heeled shoe provocatively out-thrust, one hand on her hip, the other clutching the banister.

'Where did you get them, that's what I want to know?' Anne said suddenly, her voice dropping as she reached forward to finger the hem of the skirt. It was gaberdine; it had cost money. But in the instant she raised her eyes to Stella, she knew that, however the outfit had been come by, she would be better off not knowing. 'Get upstairs,' she said wearily. 'Wash your face, and put something decent on, or else stop at home. That's all there is to it.'

For a moment Stella contemplated defiance. But the skirt and blouse had not been come by honestly, or at least not by means that her mother would consider honest. She had smuggled them out of the shop, telling herself that as they underpaid her and worked her to death into the bargain, it was fair dues. No chance of convincing Anne of that, though. She turned on her heel and mounted the stairs, moving as provocatively as she dared, expecting every minute to feel Anne's hand stinging her rump.

'Where'll she wind up?' Anne said to Frank. 'Just tell me, because what's in her doesn't come from my side.'

Frank had heard it all before and today was not a day to take offence. 'Blame it on me, pet,' he said equably. 'Now, where's this food you're on about? The cart'll be round anytime for you and the little'uns. Best get yourself fixed up. And, Annie Maguire, before you ask: you'll be the bestlooking lass in Durham the day.'

'There'll be people on the road,' Howard said as they entered Belgate. 'It's the Big Meeting today – all the Labour hierarchy up to make speeches.'

'Do they hate us?' Diana asked suddenly, in matter-of-fact tones. They were threading through the streets of Belgate now, on their way to see Howard's mother in Sunderland, and he negotiated a corner before he answered.

'I don't think they hate us, but they hate what we are. They think the land, and all on and beneath it, belongs to the people – or it should. Anyway, it's academic: they'll never achieve nationalization, more's the pity. They'd find out then what it really means to be responsible for other people's lives.'

'Would you like to be free of it?' Diana asked curiously.

'Sometimes. But sometimes I think the pit has me in its grip as surely as the meanest trapper-boy.'

Ahead of them people were marching three or four abreast along the road. Hearing the car, they moved to the side and turned to watch it. The men had children astride their shoulders or carried packs on their backs. Some of the women smiled. Others, recognizing the Brentons, lowered their eyes. One man raised his hand in a mock salute.

'Maguire.' Howard nodded acknowledgement.

'The agitator?' Diana asked.

'The union man. That's not necessarily the same thing.'

'They look happy,' Diana said, and there was a note almost of wonder in her tone. She was remembering a week or so ago, when she had gone with Henry and Loelia to the Eton–Harrow match. Harrow had beaten Eton for the first time in thirty-one years, the sun had shone to cele-brate, and grey top hats were doffed in wonder or despair, depending on whose side they were. But the women, in their floating garden-party frocks, had had the same air of delighted anticipation of a good day out as she saw now on the road.

Howard Brenton glanced out at the landscape as they crested a rise, and he saw the county spread out before him, the Pennines a dark backdrop in the west. Each year his men trekked to the ancient city of Durham to proclaim solidarity with their fellow miners, as they had done for years. Would they still be able to do it if there was invasion and alien government? Last week the Chancellor had announced new defence borrowings of £500 million, and every day it seemed there was a new reassuring pamphlet or statistic of preparedness. But had it all come too late?

The day before yesterday he had slipped into Westminster Abbey to pray for peace, like thousands of others were doing now day by day. A woman had been there, in Soldiers' Corner, kneeling on the dusty flagstones. There was nothing special about her. She wore black, with a patterned scarf at her neck and a single row of pearls. A black felt trilby covered her hair as she prayed, and she wept a little, to the consternation of a man near her who had only one arm and wore two medals on his breast. It was not until she rose to her feet that Howard realized she was Mrs Neville Chamberlain.

They were passing an open cart now, filled with women and small children and baskets of provisions, all on their way to their Gala. 'Let them enjoy their day,' Howard thought. 'And next year, and the next year, too, please God.'

*

Esther Gulliver had risen early, bolting her breakfast and whisking round her neat semi with a duster and vacuum-cleaner. Today, knowing that Sunderland would be quiet, with so many gone to Durham, she was off on a shopping expedition to buy things for the home, and one or two much-needed articles for Ruth and Naomi. Emmanuel was still determined the girls should leave at the first opportunity, but at least she could kit them out before they went. Until now they had managed with one or two things borrowed from her, but it couldn't go on.

She had expected the shops to be deserted, but at some counters women were standing two deep. They were buying, not in ones or twos, but in dozens: towels, sheets, blankets, pots and pans. They seemed to be buying in a frenzy, fingering the goods only for an instant before making their purchase. *They're hoarding!* Esther thought and felt the cold presence of war.

She scuttled away to Meng's and ordered coffee and biscuits while she reviewed her shopping list. She loved buying for her home, improving it, restocking it, but if there was war there would be shortages. On the other hand, if everyone raided the shops, they would create the very shortages they feared. And what about those who couldn't stock up? People like Anne, finding it hard to make ends meet day to day, never mind spending ahead? It wasn't fair. Esther could remember her own hard times too well not to feel for others.

They had been poor as church mice at home, she and Anne, with her father off drinking every night and the shop only taking coppers. Anne had been brave, then, and kind to her young sister in her own sharp way. *I would do more for her,* Esther thought, *if she would let me.*

She settled her Jenner's tailored sports hat more firmly on her head before she rose to go. It was gusty outside, and the hat had cost a guinea. She was gathering up gloves and bag when a shadow loomed over her.

'Miss Gulliver?'

She recognized the man at once as the solicitor who now handled Sammy's business.

'Mr Gilfillan,' Esther said. He was beaming down on her as though she was peaches and cream, but she had armoured herself against men when Philip died. You couldn't love like that twice; nor could you settle for less. On the other hand, it was nice to think someone admired her, and she smiled up at him from under the brim of her hat.

'I'm here with my sister…'He was nodding towards a pleasant-looking woman who was sitting with a child at a nearby table. 'She's come north to visit me. We were wondering if you'd care to join us?'

Suddenly Esther felt flustered. 'I'm sorry,' she said, trying to stand up, feeling the edge of the table in her way. 'I was just going – I've so much to do. Saturday's my only day for shopping.'

Gilfillan was putting a good face on it, but the disappointment showed. 'Another time, perhaps. Give my regards to Mr Lansky.'

Esther hardly drew breath until she was out in the street, making for the place where she had parked the Hillman. She couldn't account for her own agitation; Gilfillan was only a business acquaintance. If Sammy could see her now he would tease her and call her a goose. Suddenly she wanted to see Sammy, longed for the peace of the Lansky house, for Emmanuel's strength, Sammy's gaiety and –increasingly – the welcome the girls gave her whenever she arrived. She drove to the quiet street where they lived, and parked under the trees that bordered the pavement.

She had her own key to the house, which would be silent now for the Sabbath. She could make them tea and sit quietly, enjoying their contemplation, until darkness fell,and the Shabbos was over and Sammy bustling about like a cat on hot coals to get ready for an evening on the town. She loved the Sabbath: the flickering candles, the peace, the feeling of the family safe in the home amid the splendour of silver and crystal and snow-white linen.

This is my haven, she thought as she opened the door.

In Durham, Anne was feeling discontented. She had come for a day out, a respite from her responsibilities, but instead she was having to keep a constant watch on Stella, who was ready to sidle off with the first man who gave her the glad eye. Frank had gone about his union duties and would not reappear till the speeches were over, and Joe was tossing the drinks back with the other Belgate lads. There was only Anne to box ears, and keep the baby's finger from his nose, and make sure that David, who was set on drowning, didn't stray too near the river. Two hours ago the day had stretched ahead, a cornucopia of delights; now she was hoarse with shouting, her back ached, and she wanted to go home. But she was stuck here, in charge of the children and the precious hamper.

By the time the men reappeared, Anne was ready to do murder. Frank's face was alight with fervour: he was drunk on speeches and visions of one day owning the pit in which he now worked. But before he could communicate his feelings Anne intervened.

'Wipe that daft look off your face, Frank, and grab hold of these bairns. And you, Joe: find our Stella and fetch her back. Box her ears if you have to, but fetch her.' She turned back to Frank. 'No good'll come out of this, Frank. They're all too old now to be let loose, and I can't have eyes in the back of my head. Forget the pub; I want this lot seen to.'

Frank tended his children as best he could, trying to keep alight the dream that oratory had awakened in him. They spread out the food on the grassy river bank, and ate and drank; and the children quietened down once they were fed.

Anne closed her eyes, hearing the far-off laughter and the music of the fairground. She was almost dozing when Joe spoke up. 'Why don't we visit Auntie Mary and see her new baby?' She heard Frank tut-tutting the idea away; Frank's sister, Mary, had been a widow and housekeeper to the Brentons until she had fallen in with a drunken doctor and got herself pregnant. In her more generous moments Anne acknowledged that Mary and Patrick had married, eventually and respectably, but this was not a generous moment. She had had no wish to visit her sister-in-law, but she was not about to be tutted out of it.

'Why not?' she said, opening her eyes. 'We'll pack up here and we'll go. And then...' she paused for effect, 'you can get me and the bairns back on the cart, and you can go for a drink. A *drink*, Frank – not a barrel. Don't turn up at home legless, or there'll be hell on.'

They left their chattels in safe keeping with Frank's marrer and his wife, and set off through the winding streets to the grey stone house with the imposing brass plate: *Patrick Quinnell MB BS.*

Mary welcomed the Maguire family into her living-room, and let Anne take the tiny baby from its crib and hold it on her knee. Anne liked babies, and as far as she could see, this baby was not a patch on any of hers. She glanced complacently at her own brood, especially Gerard, who was destined for the priesthood, and then pronounced her nephew a 'grand little chap'.

'Did you get my letter?' she asked. 'We'd've come over sooner, but it's a long way.'

'He hasn't been christened yet,' Mary said. 'We'll fix a date while you're here, and then you can all come over for it. Pat will arrange it. We're calling him Benjamin Patrick Francis.'

They drank tea and ate wedges of ginger cake, spread around the room, a tidal wave of arms and legs and eager young faces. Mary and Anne shared the sofa, the baby between them. Frank and Patrick sat by the fire, their feet on the fender, gazing complacently at their offspring. Gerard browsed along the bookshelves while Angela and Theresa and David sat wide-eyed on the hearthrug, restraining the toddler, Bernard, whenever he strayed too near the fire.

Only Stella was uneasy, moving from room to room, plumbing the house in fifteen minutes and then announcing it was time to go home.

'What did you think of their place?' Frank asked, when at last they were safe outside again. There was a note of pride in his voice at his sister's achievement, and it annoyed Anne.

'I've seen the house before,' she said flatly.

Well, I know, but I mean, it's been done up a bit since then. She's made it... well, more like a proper home.'

'We could all make Palace Beautiful if we had the money, Frank. I had taste once.' Her tone implied that that was the one thing Mary lacked. 'But you have to cut your coat according to your cloth!'

Frank's face fell, and Anne's conscience pricked her. He was a good provider in his own way, and no man in Belgate pit worked harder. It was the shifts he lost on union business that brought them down, and she was not averse to those. She put out a hand and patted his arm, thinking she would find the 45 shillings to get him a new suit at Burtons before the end of the year.

'Mary's got a very nice house, Frank. They seem happy together.' She couldn't resist a final small barb. 'And at least he's made an honest woman of her.'

It was late evening when the Sabbath ended for the Lanskys. Esther shepherded the girls up to bed and drew the curtains in their bedroom. Already it was taking on a more feminine appearance. Sammy had brought in a handful of garden roses to fill a vase, and the girls had set out their few precious mementoes. Esther would have liked to pick up the photograph of their mother and father: a plump, smiling woman in a chair, hands folded in her lap, and a bearded man standing at the side, one hand tucked in his jacket, the other protectively on his wife's shoulder. But she was afraid to refer to it in case it reduced either girl to the tears she had seen more than once in the first days.

There was also the problem of language. She could understand them now, as far as their everyday needs were concerned, and Sammy was always coaching them in English, but it would still be impossible to handle any emotional conversation. She contented herself with sitting quietly while they completed their muttered prayers, and then smoothed the sheets over them. She stroked Ruth's hair and smiled as she said goodnight, and would have done the same to the younger girl if two arms had not come up suddenly and clasped her around the neck. She hugged the girl, so thin and slight in her arms, and then kissed her warmly. 'Goodnight, God bless.'

They slept in their own beds now, itself a sign of progress, but a light was still left burning, for both of them feared the dark. Esther was letting herself on to the landing when Sammy appeared, washed and shaved and ready for a Saturday evening out.

'They're not asleep, are they?' he said, preparing to open their door.

No, they're still awake. And where are you off to?'

He bent to kiss her on the temple. 'Mind your own business, Esther Gulliver. If you won't take pity on me, I must take what love I can find.' He rolled his eyes and patted his jacket above his heart to express pain.

'Get out,' Esther said, pushing him gently. 'Say your goodnights and don't disturb them too much.' But as she descended the stairs she could hear the girls chuckling and knew he was up to his tricks, and entertaining them. More English lessons, probably – but it would take more than improvement in language to win over old Lansky.

She found him perusing the evening paper. 'They are stopping Jews from entering Palestine – the British government. Do they not realize these people are refugees? Will they send…' He raised his eyes to indicate the girls on the upper floor. 'Will they send *them* back to what they came from? To murder?'

'Hush,' Esther said. 'You're doing your best. Things like this are beyond us. We can help the girls, though: *if* they stay.'

The old Jew held up a hand. 'No more, Esther, no more. I cannot deal with girls. I cannot even understand them. They will do better elsewhere.'

It was growing dusk as Stella Maguire made her way home. There had not been room for her on the cart with her mother, for many of the women who had walked to Durham in the morning had claimed a place for the return journey.

'I'll make me own way home,' she said and, when Anne would have set her face against it, Stella hastily agreed to come home with a group of older girls and one or two married women. 'Don't lose sight of her,' Anne said to one girl – but the guardian never got a chance to carry out her promise, for Stella melted away before the cart was out of sight.

Down a side street she outlined her mouth with her precious Tangee lipstick, and then trawled the streets of Durham looking for some excitement. But the men (and boys, too) were more interested in drink than in women that early in the evening. She knew which pub her father was in, and she made sure to give him a wide berth. At around eight o'clock, tired and bored, she decided she had better go home. A cart was leaving for Seaham and they offered her a lift halfway if she held a sleeping child on her knee.

When the cart put her down on Warden Law, Stella stood watching the sky grow red in the west, streaked just like the inside of a shell. It made her feel funny inside, seeing so much beauty. She was sick of Belgate: the dirt and grime of the pit and the dull, grey streets. Somewhere out there were exotic places like Hawaii and Mozambique and Copenhagen. She had only a sketchy idea of where they were, but they sounded wonderful.

Ahead of her she saw a horseman, seated motionless on his mount by the side of the road, also staring at the sky. The curious immobility of the figure intrigued her, but as she grew near she saw that it was only Rupert Brenton, the snob from the house on the Scar who would inherit the lot in the end without lifting a finger. Stella couldn't resist a dig as she passed him.

'What's the matter? Your neck got in a crick?' He wouldn't know who she was, and if he did there was nothing he could do about it.

But he didn't frown, or chide her impudence. He turned to smile at her, and then gestured towards the sunset with his crop.

'It's a plane: a Vickers Spitfire. It's got a 12-cylinder Merlin engine, liquid-cooled. They're keeping the horse-power secret, but it's incredibly fast.'

Stella tried to look interested and knowledgeable, noticing that he was not bad-looking and had nice dark hair with a hint of a curl. After another moment or two watching the plane, he raised his crop in salute to her, and trotted away. She watched him till he was out of sight, thinking that he would be a catch for someone one of these days.

He didn't really notice me, she admitted to herself, chagrined. Well, you never knew. One day she might make him.

4

Esther always called at the Lanskys' in the mornings now, before going on to the warehouse. Emmanuel was still adamant that another home should be found for Ruth and Naomi, and Eli Cohen was ever more apologetic: 'I'm trying, Manny – every day I try. Have patience!'

Lansky was courteous to the girls, but there was none of the indulgence he had shown Esther when she came to him. *He is afraid of getting fond of them,* Esther thought. *He's keeping up his guard, because he knows they must go elsewhere in the end.'*

Today she called out a greeting as she closed the front door, and went into the kitchen, where Emmanuel was busy with breakfast. She heard Sammy coming downstairs, and when he came into the kitchen behind her she sensed that he was tense.

'Good morning, Esther. Morning, papa.'

Lansky turned and handed Sammy a dish. 'The table is set. Call the girls.'

'They're already up, papa. And they have a surprise for you.' The girls came into the kitchen flushed and giggling. Ruth was still fastening the slide that held back her dark hair, and Naomi was tugging at the sleeves of a cardigan grown too short for her. They settled at the table and Naomi cleared her throat as Ruth drew a breath, looked at Sammy for reassurance, and then reached for the morning paper that lay beside Lansky's plate. She opened it at a centre page, cleared her throat and began to read.

'New Yorkers were stunned last night by the seventeen-year-old Judy Garland, playing Dorothy in Harold Mien's *Wizard of Oz*.' She paused, looked up at Sammy, who winked and nodded reassuringly, and then continued: 'Dorothy goes off to see the Wizard with a scarecrow, played by Ray Bolger, a tin man, played by Jack Haley, and a cowardly lion, Bert Lahr.' Her English was heavily accented, and she hesitated over many of the names, but it was still a triumph.

'See?' Sammy said, beaming, to his father, 'I promised you a scholar.' He turned to Naomi, anxious lest she felt left out. 'And you, Princess. You have a party piece, too.'

'Sammy!' Esther said warningly, for she had heard some of last night's English lesson. But Naomi had already begun.

'Johnny Macatootah's dead,' she recited obediently. 'He died last night in bed. He cut his throat with sunlight soap, Now Johnny Macatootah's dead.' She grinned engagingly and looked from one to another for praise.

Esther bit her lip and looked severely at Sammy, who had spent an hour teaching the rhyme to Naomi, parrot-fashion.

Sammy looked at his father, his eyes rolling as though conscience-stricken. Lansky surveyed them all solemnly, and then his chest began to heave. Esther was about to rebuke Sammy when she realized the old Jew was laughing: laughing so heartily that tears were running down his cheeks.

'That's my Samuel,' he said, wiping his eyes. 'Nothing by halves. He gives me not one scholar but two!'

'So?' Sammy said anxiously.

'So?' Emmanuel replied. He looked round the table for a moment. 'So who is Emmanuel Lansky to argue with so many scholars?'

'They can stay?' Sammy said.

'They can stay. And heaven help us all.'

But as Emmanuel Lansky looked first at Ruth and then

at Naomi, and saw them smile, he knew that beauty had entered into his home.

It felt strange to be in London in August, Diana thought, as she wandered through an uncharacteristically empty Selfridges. She was meeting Howard for lunch at the Embassy Club at one and was trying to kill time by shopping. All her friends had fled from London at the end of the season, and she would be gone, too, if it were not for the damned crisis which dragged on and on and tied Howard to the city. He had urged her to go with Lee to Valesworth, or north with the children, but a kind of tense anxiety gripped her now and made her want to stay near to the House, that fount of up-to-the-minute news.

As she went by cab from Oxford Street to the Embassy, a sudden desire for the Venetian Lido gripped her. To lie in the sun without thinking or worrying would be perfect bliss.

Howard was waiting when she entered the dining-room, standing up to greet her, smiling with his mouth but not his eyes. 'What's up?' she said, allowing the waiter to adjust her chair, laying down bag and gloves, and fixing her eyes on her husband's face.

Howard leaned towards her and spoke quietly. 'It'll be out by tonight, but I don't want it overheard now. Ribbentrop flew to Moscow this morning to sign a non-aggression pact with Stalin. That opens the way for Hitler to attack Poland while Stalin has a free hand with the Baltic States.'

'My God,' Diana said, feeling in her bag for her cigarette case. 'But that means – I thought we had a delegation in Russia discussing an alliance with them *against* Hitler?'

'We did. A joint Franco-British deal. And while the bear is talking with us, he's dealing with Hitler.'

'Are you sure it's true?' Diana said, accepting a light from Howard's gold lighter.

'It's true, all right. Apparently Molotov submitted a draft agreement to Ribbentrop four days ago.'

'What will it mean?' Diana asked.

'It means the last chance of peace is gone, I'm afraid.' Howard began to study the menu.

'I can't believe it.' Diana's eyes, too, raked the elaborate menu, but she saw nothing.

'It's true, darling. I've seen it coming for a long time. Think: once Hitler couldn't open his mouth without a tirade against Bolshevism. Then, all of a sudden, not a squeak. At the same time Stalin gets rid of his Jewish Foreign Minister, Litvinov, and replaces him with Molotov, a comparative unknown who has no record of anti-German sentiment.'

'And while all this is going on, England sleeps,' Diana said bitterly.

'No, that's unfair. We're prepared. But we do need more time. Now, enough of that - and, for God's sake, don't tell anyone! It'll be out by nightfall but until then… I think we'll have a bottle of something very special.'

'That's it then, mam.' Joseph's face was bright red and perspiring as he shovelled the last of the coal into the coalhouse and reached for the yard brush Anne proffered. Each month, winter and summer, their load of gleaming concessionary coal was tipped in the back street and had to be moved. Once Frank had done it; now it was Joe's task, to be rewarded with hot tea and thick white bread spread with beef dripping and sprinkled with salt. She loved this moment, across the kitchen table from her favourite son, seeing his face grimed with coal dust and smiling with the satisfaction of a job well done. It frightened her sometimes, the thought that she loved him so much.

He grinned at her now. 'Penny for 'em?'

'Worth more,' she said, reaching to refill his mug, noticing that, although he was not yet seventeen, his forearms were thick and corded with muscles that would have put many a full-grown man to shame. It seemed only yesterday that he had taken his first communion, accepting the wafer, the body of Christ, with eyes like organ-stops.

'Anything in the paper?' Joe nodded towards the daily paper folded on the arm of Frank's chair.

'Get washed and you can see for yourself,' Anne said. 'More bread?' There was a picture of the King looking grave on the front page of the paper and another of Churchill and Eden on an inside page, with an article saying they should be back in the Cabinet.

'Jimmy Forest's enlisted,' Joe said, as he washed. He spoke lightly but he did not meet her eye, which meant he was testing her.

'Good for him,' Anne said firmly. 'He's twenty-one. It's his privilege.'

'You don't have to be twenty-one.'

God, he was stubborn, Anne thought. When he was a little lad he had taken no for a telling, but now... She pushed aside the teapot and leaned towards him.

'Look, Joe, I will never, ever sign for you to join up. Not while there's all this talk about war. And your father won't sign for you, either, because he's more frightened of me than he is of Hitler. If you could get that through your thick skull we could all settle down and get on with things. You can join the TA when the time comes, but that's it – so let's hear no more of it.'

'What if every mother was like you?' Joe muttered, almost sullenly. 'What if every mother said "No"?'

'Then there'd be no wars,' Anne said sweetly. 'If every mother stood firm everywhere and said they didn't bring bairns into the world to be slaughtered, it'd be an end to it. So I'm making a start. Your father's always on about it only taking one good man to turn a tide; well, this good woman is putting her foot down. And if you bring the subject up again, I'll skelp you!'

It was almost home time and Esther was preparing the books to go off to the new accountant when she saw Sammy down below on the office floor. He looked up at her little glass eyrie and waved, but she could see that he was preoccupied. It couldn't be business. Everything was running like clockwork now: they had regular suppliers and new outlets; Gilfillan kept them straight legally; and on his advice they were turning the books over to an accountant. Sammy had grumbled a little, saying they would have to toe the line now if they were going legitimate, but Esther sensed he was really pleased at this gradual delegation of responsibility. She watched him now moving from desk to desk, having a word here, checking a document there. The girls in the office adored him; the office boy, a cheeky little so and so, would die for him. Sammy was good with people. But today he was looking decidedly grim.

She closed the last of the ledgers and sat back as his step sounded on the wooden stairs and he opened the door.

He didn't speak at first, just pulled a face.

'What's up?' she asked, and then, when he grimaced again, she rapped on the window and signalled that she would like tea and biscuits at the double. 'Now then,' she said, turning back.

'Stalin has signed a pact with Hitler. I first heard it on the wireless. Non-aggression, they say, but we all know what that means. It means he'll stand by while Hitler and Mussolini carve up Europe, then old Joe Stalin will get a few titbits as reward.'

'Not necessarily,' Esther said uneasily. 'It doesn't *have* to mean war.'

Sammy smiled grimly. 'It means there'll be war within the month, Esther. Within the week, for all I know. I'll be called up, and the fortunes of Lanver Products will be squarely on your shoulders.'

Esther would have argued but Sammy held up a hand.

'No *plaplen*, Esther: it's coming. What we have to do is work out what to do for the best here. I've known it for long enough, I suppose. I tried to shut it out – God won't do that to Sammy Lansky, I said. Not let him build up a business and then blow it all sky-high. But…' He shrugged. 'Anyway, you'll have Gilfillan for advice, and providing you don't drive him mad with passion he'll stand by you. The accountant will see to the financial side. He's the best we could've hired, so that's all right. And you know this business like the back of your hand. No, don't give me the modest little fire-*goyah* act. You've grown up since those days; we both have. I've seen you wheel and deal, and sack people when it was called for. There'll be extra complications of course, with a war-rationing, I should think, and shortages. But you'll cope.'

He reached out suddenly to touch her cheek. 'I know how brave you are, remember? I saw you give up the *boyt'shik'l* because you thought it was the right thing to do. You're a tigress, Esther – and if you don't know it already, you're about to find out.'

Esther felt like anything but a tigress at that minute. Apart from anything else, she couldn't imagine a day without Sammy, let alone months – perhaps even years. There had been a hundred years' war once; she could remember that from school. And what if he died? Men died in war. As if he sensed her terror, Sammy moved to put his arms around her.

'Cheer up. You know me: I may turn out to have flat feet. Or a hernia – they say that lets you off. And even if the army takes me, I'll get leave. I'll be the week-day soldier and come home every Shabbos to please papa.' He kissed her gently on the forehead and then set her firmly in her chair. 'Now,' he said briskly, 'clear up here, and we'll go home and talk in comfort.'

Emmanuel was waiting when they reached the house, his hat for once a little awry on his head, the buttons on his waistcoat slotted in places through the wrong buttonholes.

'Samuel, you must go to Paris,' he said. 'At once. We must get your grandparents out of there quickly. I have been thinking about it for days, but this news: Hitler will sweep through the low lands and on into France. Paris will fall...'

Esther interrupted. 'What about the Maginot Line?' Everyone knew about the impregnable Maginot Line of fortifications, built by the French after the last war to make sure the Germans could never again invade their country.

'*Pouf* to the Maginot Line,' Lansky said impatiently. 'Nothing will stop Hitler now – except, please God, the sea.' There was conviction in his tone, a certainty of doom. 'You must go now, Samuel. They are old; they cannot be uprooted in a moment. You must get them out now, while there's still time. *Gey leyf*!'

Sammy was shaking his head. 'I'll try, father, but I know them. Leave their precious house? *Folg mir a gang!*'

There was a sprinkling of stars when the men emerged from the cage.

'Nice calm night,' one said, but Frank had spotted the pit manager, Norman Stretton, in the yard: an unusual sight at night unless there was trouble. He came towards them now, a folded newspaper in his hands.

'Bad news, I'm afraid. Mr Stalin has made up his mind at last: he's thrown in his lot with the Axis.'

Someone let out a long, low whistle.

'So it's war,' Frank said.

'I should think so, Maguire. There may be some last-minute moves, but if Chamberlain keeps his word and Herr Hitler doesn't see sense...' He held out the paper. 'See for yourself.'

Frank's thoughts were sombre as he parted company with his mates one by one and walked on alone. Annie would take on now, and no mistake. And Joe would be drawn in... unless the war was over in a flash. But in his heart Frank knew that if a war was short it would only end one way: Hitler's way. England was unprepared. Worse than that, there were people in high places who had set their faces against war. There were even men in the Labour Party who would sell out for peace – not many of them, but one was too many. Thank God the Durham Miners' Association had always come out against Fascism. At least he could be proud of that.

He braced himself for Annie's railings when he entered the kitchen, but for once he had misjudged his wife. She was seated by the fire, her sewing in her lap. 'There's pannacalty in the oven,' she said quietly. Her eyes were red but there was no trace of tears. Frank bent to kiss her and this time, although she did not respond, she did not push him away, either.

'They're all in bed,' she said, as he shovelled the tasty bacon-and-onion-and-potato mixture into his mouth, wiping up the gravy with great wedges of homemade bread. 'Joe wanted a good night's sleep, and I sent our Stella up. I had to before I throttled her.' She sighed heavily. 'I tell you, Frank, if she's not a changeling I don't know what she is. She's pleased – *pleased* we're about to be plunged into war! "I'm tired of waiting," she says. 'There'll be some activity around here now." I don't know what she's expecting, but I know she's cracked.'

'She doesn't think,' Frank said soothingly. 'She's young and daft, and she doesn't think things through, that's all. Any road, who says our Joe'll go, even if there is war?'

'He'll go, Frank,' Anne said. 'All the Belgate lads'll go, you watch. They'll be mown down, but the lords an'

– 61 –

masters'll be all right. They'll have desk jobs, the Brentons and their like. Nice and safe. It's the way of the world, and you'll never change it.'

When Frank had bathed before the fire, they mounted the stairs and climbed into the creaking bed together, both heavy with sleep but wanting and needing closeness. He put a hand on her breast in the darkness and whispered against her ear, 'Is it all right?' They obeyed the time of the month now, for seven living bairns were more than enough.

'I think so,' she said and turned towards him, covering his mouth with hers, digging her fingers first into his arms and then his back as though in an effort to drive the forces of darkness away with the strength of their love.

It was midnight before Sammy was packed and ready for the drive to Dover. Esther had called off her trip to the pictures with David Gilfillan, and collected a bag from her own home so she could stay with Emmanuel and the girls until Sammy's return. 'That's a comfort to me, Esther. Not that he needs help; he's taking to the *girlt'shikls* like a duck to water. But he's in pain – not just about my grandparents, but for the whole Jewish race.'

Esther had made him sandwiches and filled a flask with tea against the long drive. 'You're good to me,' he said, kissing her cheek. 'If there's a war, you'll have to marry me and reform my character. I can't be shot with a bad conscience, Esther: it wouldn't be fair.'

'Fool,' she said, pushing him roughly. 'You can't even talk sense in a crisis.'

But if Sammy had asked her seriously, Esther might well have said 'yes' at that moment. And then Lansky was there, tears in his eyes, to kiss his boy and make him promise to be careful. The girls had been in bed long before, but now, suddenly, they appeared, shawls clutched around them on the half-landing. Sammy went up to them and Esther saw him embrace them and heard a hurried conversation. It was half in English or German, half in gabbled Yiddish, and she understood only two words: *Hilfe* which meant 'help' and *Mutti* which was 'mother'. There was also a word she had not heard before but which was now repeated: '*Mishpacha, mishpacha.*'

When Sammy came down to the hall his eyes were wet.

'They want me to bring their parents out,' he said quietly. 'Since I'm going across the water, they want me to go to Hamburg and bring back their family.' He gripped Esther's hands until she cried out in pain. 'Make them understand that I would if I could, Esther! For God's sake, make them see that.' And then he was gone, in a roar of engine and burr of tyres on the road, and nothing was left for her or Lansky to do but stand, arms linked, in the gateway until the tail-light disappeared from sight.

5

3 September 1939

There was a puff of white cloud over to the east, but otherwise the sky was a deep, unsullied blue as Frank Maguire climbed to the top of the Scar. Normally, on such a Sunday morning, freed from the pit, his black pudding and streaky bacon inside him, Frank would feel a deep contentment as he gazed out over Belgate, seeing signs of improvement here and there, thinking of what could be done when there was a Labour government and he, perhaps, a part of it.

But today was not a day for dreaming dreams. A nightmare was taking shape; he could see it every day in his newspaper or in the wireless reports. Ten days ago the King had cut short his holiday at Balmoral and returned to hold a crisis meeting of the Privy Council; now the Queen, too, had come home. The paper had shown her smiling graciously, but with lines of strain around her mouth. The Prime Minister had told the House: 'The peril of war is imminent, but I still go on hoping.' The House had given Chamberlain its backing in his stand against aggression, and when George Lansbury would have put the pacifist view some members rose and pointedly left the chamber. The people, lining the streets, broke into a rendition of 'Rule Britannia' as the Prime Minister passed on his return to Downing Street.

All this and more Frank had read of or heard on his radio, until sometimes he thought nostalgically of the days when he had been both ignorant and unconcerned, pressing his nose against Gulliver's shop window to catch sight of Anne behind the counter.

He sat down on the grass at last, plucking a juicy blade on which to chew, and looked over the Belgate rooftops until he found St Benedict's. Anne was there now, threading her rosary through her fingers. All over the country people were praying for peace. The King and his brothers had driven through sunlit streets to sink to their knees in Westminster Abbey, joined by men coming or going from work and women with shopping bags on their arms; but Hitler had still marched into Poland on Friday, and the British and French ambassadors had issued their ultimatums. Now the country was under a black-out order, the services had been mobilized and all men between the ages of eighteen and forty-one told to stand by for call-up. Even bairns were being uprooted and sent off God knew where, in case of air raids.

Frank put up a hand to wipe his eyes, misted with heat and emotion. When he opened them he saw a figure below him, at the foot of the hill, waving strenuously to attract his attention. It was Joe.

Frank got to his feet and began to hurry down. The boy was mouthing at him and gradually the words came dear: 'It's on the wireless, dad. They say, "Stand by for an announcement". You'd better come on home.'

Sammy Lansky heard the announcement on his own bedroom radio while he shaved at the wash-hand stand. He had been expecting it, so his face betrayed no sign of alarm. He flicked lather from the blade into the sink and carried on with his task. He had been back from Paris for only a few days, returning on a Channel packet that was running double shifts, shuttling back and forth across the sea, crowded to the rails with hollow-eyed refugees, returning holiday-makers and British expatriates carrying their golf clubs and tennis racquets with their luggage, mad to get home in case of war.

He had driven from Dover along congested roads filled with charabancs and cars taking evacuees to the safety of the countryside, many of them driven haphazardly by women who had applied in thousands over the previous few days for provisional driving-licences.

He had tried to telephone Esther, but the telephone lines, too, were overcrowded; and when he turned from the telephone box he saw a poster giving details of a bomb flung by an IRA cyclist in a Coventry street, which had killed five people and injured fifty in a dreadful taste of what might be to come. Dear God, surely taking on Germany was enough without the IRA.

He had returned to Britain with failure heavy upon him. At first Paris had seemed its old self: the chestnuts were in leaf on the boulevards, the pavement cafés were as crowded as ever, the women as elegant, the men ordering a *vin rouge* or a *bière de pression*, and taxi-drivers still using the Champs-Élysées as though it were a racing-track. But then he noticed the strained faces of the elegant women, the moroseness of the mood above the glasses of wine or beer; and not even the heat shimmering and dancing along the broad avenues could dispel the chill of fear that pervaded the beautiful city.

Except in 4, Avenue Collaigne, where his grandparents lived.

Sammy had cajoled, pleaded – in the end had ordered – his grandparents to pack and come away with him. They refused to listen, or even to take seriously the threat of German conquest. '*Ici c'est la France*,' his grandmother said indulgently, as though he were still a little boy who could not get his frontiers right. In the end, he had been forced to leave without them, their only concession to his fears being a promise to think again if war came. But at least he had found someone to keep a watch on them. Some of his friends had left Paris, for jobs elsewhere or to join the French Army. But Marc Luchaire was still working for the Paris *Daily Mail*, in the narrow rue du Sentier.

'I'll keep an eye on them, Sammy. Leave it to me. I can't guarantee their safety if the Boche come, but at least I'll keep you posted, that much I promise.'

It was small consolation, but better than nothing. Sammy returned to Sunderland, anxious to explain to everyone why he had come back alone. Ruth stilled his words with an upraised hand. 'We know,' she said in accented English. 'It is finished.'

And now there was war, and he would be in it. But the business must go on, for the sake of Esther and the girls, and because such businesses, servicing ordinary people as they did, would be needed to keep people fed. There was a lot to do before he signed up.

He thought of what dying might be like, in a foreign field with no one to say *kaddish* for him. And he thought of Esther, who would probably be married to Gilflllan by then, forgetting he had ever existed. It irritated him until he remembered how many beautiful little *shikses* would mourn him, and that brought a smile and a whistle to his lathered lips.

When he was finished he went downstairs to find his father, who was in his study, nose deep in a book. Lansky looked up as Sammy entered.

'Good morning! Have you seen the girls today? Esther is here, in the kitchen – feeding them again.' He shook his head. 'She wishes to make up for the years of famine with feasting. I respect her motives but I fear for their stomachs.' He was smiling at his own joke until he saw no answering smile on his son's face. 'What is it, Samuel?'

'They said on the wireless that they want us to stand by for an announcement, father. I think this must be it.'

*

As September began, Diana saw city clerks loading important papers on to vans which would take them to safety outside the capital, and London's churches filled with people needing to pray. She saw queues of men, old and young, waiting to register for military service. Some underground stations shut and services were cut, kerbs were painted white against a black-out, and sandbags appeared everywhere.

The evidence of impending war was so omnipresent that she could hardly believe her eyes when she opened her *Times* to read a letter from George Bernard Shaw telling people not to worry, for 'Hitler is under the powerful thumb of Stalin, whose interest in peace is overwhelming.' She hurled the paper into the waste-basket and set about casting on stitches for a pair of khaki socks with unaccustomed fingers. At least she could knit for soldiers – except that the loops proved as slippery as eels, and in the end she was driven back to *The Times*, to read advertisements offering houses or flats to let in 'safe' areas, or requesting 'country home for three pedigree corgis...'

Even the King made a concession to the times, driving to Downing Street for a meeting – the first time the monarch had paid anything but a social visit – because the Prime Minister felt he should not leave the telephone. The Duke of Windsor, calling himself a 'citizen of the world', sent Hitler a telegram urging him to avoid war. The reply came as the Germans bombed Warsaw; it said that if war broke out, it would be England's fault.

It was certainly *someone's* fault, Diana thought, as she saw confused little children being herded into railway stations for evacuation. More than three million people, mostly mothers and children, were moved in the course of a weekend. Under-fives travelled, often tearfully, in parties of fifty,

carrying whatever clothes and possessions they could manage. Their mothers were not allowed into the station to say
goodbye: an unnecessary piece of brutality that Diana
thought more befitted the Nazis than their opponents. She
was helping with the evacuation of the blind and patients
from London hospitals. They travelled in Green Line buses
converted into ambulances, and Diana found their obvious
fear terrible to behold.

She made two trips, and came home stony-faced. 'I don't
know who is to blame for this, Howard, but I hope they burn
in hell for it.' And her anger was not lessened by the sight of
queues of people outside veterinary surgeons, clutching
beloved pets which must be put down before hostilities began.
Thinking how easy it had been for her to make arrangements
for her children and animals, Diana felt ashamed.

On the night of Saturday 2 September, the House met in
emergency session, expecting the Prime Minister to
announce an ultimatum, but Chamberlain hung back until, as
Arthur Greenwood, Labour's acting leader, rose to speak, a
cry rang out from the Tory benches: 'Speak for England!'

As Greenwood demanded action, the Cabinet dithered,
but eventually the ultimatum was sent. A silent crowd had
waited in Downing Street for days now, watching the
comings and goings, hoping against hope for a smiling face
that would mean good news.

Loelia's call came just before eleven o'clock the following morning. 'I'll be terribly brief, Di. It's just to say I'm
expecting your brood any time you're ready. Laura has
gone to America and taken the children, and poor Max
feels he may never see them again. She was lucky to get a
passage – her father pulled strings. The boat trains are so
crowded they'll only take passengers, so there were hundreds
of people weeping at Victoria, and people tumbling out of
returning trains with all their worldly goods, according to
Henry. He went to meet his aunt; she's lived in Menton for

twenty years, poor thing! She may come to Valesworth, too. Thank God we have so much room. You and Howard must come down whenever you can and see the children. And me: I shall die with no parties, no season. No gossip! My God, Diana, I'll be completely cut off. You must ring me every day – twice, if there's something sensational.'

Diana did not wish to offend Lee, but neither did she wish to miss the news. She managed to put the phone down in time to hear the Prime Minister, speaking from Downing Street. His words were simple: 'This country is now at war with Germany.' It was 11.15, and outside the sun was shining.

A few minutes afterwards the sirens sounded. Howard heard them as he moved from his office in the House of Commons to the Chamber. Diana started up from the bureau where she had been writing to her sister-in-law, Caroline, and went to the window. People were standing still, looking up at the sky, but there was no obvious sign of an air raid.

When nothing happened, Diana sat down again and took up her pen, but it was almost impossible to concentrate on family news for a sister-in-law with whom she had so little in common. Caroline and her husband had been pro-Fascist, had extolled Herr Hitler's virtues and chided Churchill for his belligerence. What must they feel like now?

Howard was in the House three-quarters of an hour later to hear Chamberlain make a two-minute speech. 'We are ready,' he said, and the MP next to Howard let out a snort of disbelief. But Howard felt a strange calm, a sense that the shilly-shallying was over and the real business of defending peace could begin.

In Belgate, Anne Maguire was basting the joint when the fateful words were uttered. She closed the oven door and sat down in her chair, trying to work out her own reactions. She had expected to feel devastated when war actually came; she had feared she would go to pieces and rant and rave, or weep until she made herself ill. Instead she felt calm, even resolute. It was here, and like everything else that had ever happened to her, it would have to be faced up to and bested. Somehow, some way, she would keep Joe out of the army. She had always gloried in his health and strength, but now she wished with all her heart that he was a little bit crippled, or short-sighted, like other women's sons often were. And there would be no evacuation for her bairns. If they went, they all went together.

When Frank came in, with Joe behind him, he looked at his wife's face. 'It's war,' she said. He went to the pantry and brought out the stone jar of sarsaparilla. Joe brought glasses and filled them, and then Frank raised his glass. 'God bless England,' he said. 'And let's get the bugger over quick.'

It was not until the next day that they learned of Hitler's statement to his people, in which he branded the British as war-mongers and called down divine wrath upon them: *Gott strafe England.*

The Guttman girls sat quietly as the announcement of war came. When the Prime Minister finished and Lansky switched off the set, Naomi began to cry quietly. It was Sammy who bent to hear her words, and then vigorously shook his head. 'She says the Nazis will come here now,' he said to Esther, 'but I've told her "fat chance".' He turned back to Naomi and repeated his assurance. '*Folg mir a gang, Naomi liebchen. Folg mir a gang!*'

They ate their midday meal in almost complete silence. Even Sammy was subdued, and Esther could see that he was thinking of his grandparents. The Channel ports were choked with people fleeing in both directions. Schmelling, the pork butcher who had lived and worked in Sunderland for twenty years, had put up his shutters and fled the day after hooligans smashed his shop window and daubed 'Dirty Hun' on his door. He would not be the only one. Everyone's life was being disrupted. David Gilfillan had already registered for military service; if she could help him enjoy himself in the last few weeks of freedom, Esther thought, she must. It was her duty – but if she had had a choice she would've ended the affair. She respected Gilfillan, but she didn't love him.

She was clearing the table after tea when Lansky motioned her to come nearer to the wireless set. She set down the tray and took a seat as the King's familiar, halting tones came over the air waves. It was obviously a great effort for him to overcome his speech impediment and address his people, and Esther felt her throat convulse as the hesitant words began.

'For the second time in the lives of most of us, we are at war. Over and over again we have tried to find a peaceful way out of the differences between ourselves and those who are now our enemies. But it has been in vain.'

Suddenly she felt Lansky's hand on hers. 'Don't be afraid,' he said. 'We have each other and...' He nodded to the two girls, side by side on the sofa. 'God has given us the *kinderlach*. *Baruch hashem*: the Lord be praised.'

In Belgate, Anne clasped Frank's hand as they willed the King to find the words. He faltered sometimes, but then his voice gained strength.

'We have been forced into a conflict. For we are called, with our allies, to meet the challenge of a principle which, if it were to prevail, would be fatal to any civilized order in the world... It is to this high purpose that I now call my people at home and my peoples across the seas, who will make our cause their own. I ask them to stand calm and firm and united in this time of trial. The task will be hard.'

'He's speaking better,' Frank whispered and Anne nodded.

'They say it's her, the Queen. She stands by him and eggs him on. She's a good wife.'

'He's doing better,' Diana said. 'And he's being so gallant.' Outside, the streets of London were silent, everyone huddled around wireless sets, waiting for comfort and leadership.

'There may be dark days ahead, and war can no longer be confined to the battlefield. But we can only do the right as we see the right, and reverently commit our cause to God. If one and all we keep resolutely faithful to it, ready for whatever service or sacrifice it may demand, then, with God's help, we shall prevail. May He bless us and keep us all.'

Will it all be all right in the end?' Diana asked, when they had switched off.

'I think so,' Howard answered. 'Churchill and Eden are coming back, Winston to the Admiralty and Eden to the dominions. The PM had no choice. Besides, it makes sense, and he knows it. The Commonwealth will pitch in, and America will help where it can. In the end, Diana, right will prevail. It always does.'

She put down her glass and moved to kneel beside his chair. 'That's why I love you, Howard: you have such belief in ultimate good. No matter what life does to you, you still keep your faith.' They both knew what she meant. When she had betrayed him with Max Dunane, Howard had never been bitter, never despaired.

'You make me sound quite horribly upright,' he said. 'As for never being shaken... I'm rattled now. As long as Chamberlain stays as Prime Minister we won't get decision. We need Churchill and Eden – and Attlee, too. I trust that man.'

'How long will it take?' Diana asked, but Howard shook

his head. He knew she was wondering if the war would be over before Rupert was of military age.

'Don't think about it now,' he said. 'Let's think about what we must do with the cellar. Get rid of the horrid, musty smell for a start, don't you think?'

6

6 December 1939

At first it was only religion that the Guttman girls had in
common with their hosts, but as they became accustomed
to their surroundings and their English became less hesitant,
they shed their lost air. Ruth, the older girl, was tall and
handsome rather than pretty. Her hair was bushy and had to
be restrained with slides and kirby-grips. As she seized on
Emmanuel's books, and often joined him in his study,
Sammy turned his attention to her sister. Naomi was smaller
and thinner than Ruth, and a year younger: fourteen. Her
eyes were huge and deep-set, her cheeks pale and still
hollowed. But when she smiled, her beautiful face took on
a glow, and she smiled more with each day, except when
something reminded her of her parents.

'They will need a school,' Lansky had said. 'And other
girls and companionship. But first: the reading.' So, as the
weeks passed, they worked with Esther in the evenings,
Ruth soon striding ahead into Kipling and Shaw, Naomi
beginning with a school reader and smiling triumphantly
when she graduated to a proper book. Lansky took over
then, and the girls persevered in between giggling at the
way his bushy eyebrows twitched as they perused the text.
At the beginning of December they were enrolled in school.

Sammy had registered with the first batch of army
recruits. By the end of October he was gone, but he had put
the time to good use, preparing Esther to take over the
business, fitting out the Lansky cellar against air raids and

persuading Esther to move lock, stock and barrel to the Lansky house.

'See it my way, Esther. Am I going to he on my narrow little camp-beds under my thin, grey blanket, driving myself *meshuge* worrying about the old man and the girls in one house, you in another? Let me worry about one house, Esther – one bomb.' He had grinned then as she looked shocked. 'I have to think of these things. If you go up in smoke, that's my business gone.' He rolled his eyes. '*Oy vey*, the work that's gone into it, the tears, the sweat, the sacrifice – and the one person who can save it for me won't come where there's a cellar!'

She had laughed at his antics but had not said 'yes'. She loved her home with all her heart. Since Philip's death and the giving up of her child, she had channelled everything into nest-building. How could she throw dust-sheets over her precious furniture, turn off gas and water, and walk out: perhaps for years, certainly for months? And then she had seen the anxiety lurking behind Sammy's clowning, and relented.

'It means a lot to you, doesn't it?' she said. 'All right, but only till we see how things go.'

Sammy had kissed her then, and held her dose. 'You *oytser*, Esther. Now, if you can go a little bit further... He held his head back and beamed at her. 'If you can go so far as to say you'll marry me, then I will go off to war and finish it –' he slapped his hands together, '– just like that.'

Sometimes, when Sammy had made his mock proposals, Esther had thought she detected a gleam of sincerity in them. This time, though, she knew beyond doubt that he was joking, so she answered in a similar manner. 'You're far too good for a *nebuch* like me. Besides, I don't fancy joining a harem. Come back when you've done with all the others; then I might take you.'

'All right,' he said, with a final sigh. 'Be an *altemoyd*. See if I care.'

'I'll risk it,' Esther declared. 'There's worse things than being an old maid.'

Together they cleaned out the cellar, finding, in the process, a treasure of pickles and preserves laid down by Rachael Schiffman in her days as housekeeper. Sammy had become sentimental then. 'My Schiffy: what a *balabosta*, Esther. She brought me up, that woman. Cooked for me, cleaned for me, saw to it I stayed straight. Did she know I loved her?'

'Yes,' Esther said firmly. 'She knew and she was proud of you. Now, let's look at this lot. It could come in handy.'

They put down two rugs and then, because Sammy still thought it cold, he measured the floor and went off to buy a length of Turkey carpet and a thick underfelt. When it was down and the rugs placed on top, the place felt warmer straight away. But it did not end there; Sammy wired a bulb from the electricity supply on the floors above and hung it from a beam.

'You'll need lamps, too, Esther.' He grimaced. 'If it gets bad, the power may go. You'll need to keep water here – and change it regularly.' He could see her face falling as he spoke. 'Cheer up. You'll be safe down here.' He gestured towards the one source of daylight, the window in the area. 'I'm having shutters made for the window. They'll do as black-out, and protect against blast, too. And you'll have a wireless – you can run it from the plug in the back passage. We'll have bunks for sleeping, though I doubt you'll get the old man into one. He will sit in his chair, *davening* away, telling himself every silver lining has a black cloud. Still, with you and the *lieblings* around he can't get too low.'

Sammy left behind him a shelter that would have done for royalty and two very tearful girls. 'He'll be back,' Esther had said, trying hard not to show her distress. His car now stood at the kerb, looking strangely forlorn without its rakish driver, and when she passed Emmanuel's study once she was sure she could hear the sound of sobbing. If she didn't do something, she thought, they could lose everything they had gained in the last few weeks: the shadows had come back to the girls' eyes and Emmanuel looked a hundred.

The news out of Europe seemed set to break his heart. At Yom Kippur, the holiest day in the Jewish calendar, the Germans had imprisoned several thousand Jews in the synagogue at Bydgoszig and then refused them permission to use the lavatories. They were forced to use their prayer shawls, their precious *tallis*, to clean up the resultant mess. If diplomats of neutral nations were to be believed, hundreds of Polish Jews were shot every day or herded into ghettos under the eye of the Gestapo.

But Emmanuel couldn't be allowed to fret. Esther summoned them all to the dining-room and took up a stance by the fire.

'Now,' she said firmly. A lock of hair escaped from its Kirby-grip and fell over her eye, but she blew it back into place with an impatient puff. 'You love Sammy; I love Sammy. He's gone to fight a war so that we can all live happily ever after, and while he's away it's up to us to see that he doesn't lose by it. I'm going to run his business and I'm going to make a good job of it: you can depend on that. But if I come back every day to long faces, I'll lose my concentration. I need help: help in the house from you two, and help with decisions.' She looked directly at Lansky. 'Two heads are better than one. Anyone who loves Sammy will *work* for him, so that he doesn't come back to a *she'alah*. Now, do you help me or not?'

The girls had not taken in all the words, but the message had gone home. 'Yes,' Ruth said. 'Tell us what to do, please.'

Lansky stood up and came to take her in his arms. 'That is Queen Esther, as I told you long ago. We will all work together, so that Sammy will come back to find all is well.'

Esther leaned her head against the broad chest for a moment, hoping Lansky would not detect how terrified she was of what lay ahead, with not only a business, but three other people now dependent on her. *God help me,* she thought. *Don't let me let them down.*

Anne Maguire inspected shop windows anxiously every day, terrified that essential items would disappear. She was feeling flush because miners were getting a National War Wages advance: eightpence a shift for adults and fourpence for under-eighteens. She had three wage-earners now, and she was beginning to feel the benefit of it. When Frank remonstrated with her about hoarding groceries, she drew his attention to an item on an inside page of the paper, stating that titled ladies were stocking up with face-creams and cosmetics in case of war.

'If they can make sure they can feed their vanity, Frank, don't blame me for making sure I can feed my family.'

People said the war might go on for years – unless Hitler invaded at Easter, and then that would be the end of that! The black-out was depressing her, and the constant carping of Collie Lewis since he got to be a warden was enough to drive anyone to murder: '*Put that light out!*' Some people were using it as a catchphrase, but Anne didn't find it funny.

Frank had covered all the lights in the house with tins painted black, and with a hole in them to accommodate the flex. These made sure the beam of light pointed downwards and not towards any chinks there might be in the black-out. The black contraptions made for gloom, but at least it was safe.

A communal shelter had been erected at the end of the street: a smelly, red-brick tomb of a place, Anne thought the one time she looked in. Every second house in Trenchard Street had its own shelter, at the bottom of the garden. It looked like a mound of earth when the council men finished installing it. Frank and Joe mucked about with it then, putting in bunks for the children and a long bench with cushions on for her. The men would go off as soon as the siren went, Joe to his work as an ARP messenger, Frank to march up and down fields with his marrers, looking for parachutists. 'Though what you'll do with nowt but a broomstick between you, I do not know,' Anne told him. For her part, she learned the ARP drill off by heart: wailing sirens and short whistle blasts meant 'take cover'; hard rattles meant 'gas'; handbells meant 'gas danger over'; and the long, straight siren was the 'all clear'.

At first, cinemas and theatres were closed. When they reopened, Anne shunned them, fearing to be away from home when the Germans struck. After a few weeks, however, without a single air raid, the lure of Hollywood became irresistible once more. The first time the manager appeared in front of the screen to announce that the sirens had sounded, Anne had run home in panic. Nowadays, though, she sat tight, sucking Maltesers if she was lucky enough to have some, eyes like saucers as Bette Davis emoted in *Dark Victory*, or Leslie Howard glowed in *Escape to Happiness*. The cinemas were now full, as though the whole country had panicked and then, shame-faced, come back to normality. There were some good films, that autumn: *Stagecoach*, and *Goodbye, Mr Chips*, and *The Wizard of Oz* to which she took Angela and Theresa for a birthday treat. But her favourite film was *Wuthering Heights*, which sent her reeling home with eyes so swollen that at first Frank thought she had been attacked. 'Who was it, Annie? he shouted at her, and she wiped her nose and said 'Merle Oberon,' and burst into tears again. Nowadays, though, they wouldn't let her in unless she was carrying her gas mask, which meant she sat and fingered it all through the picture in case she left it behind.

*

At the end of October, Patrick Quinnell turned over his practice to an older doctor who had come out of retirement for the war, and went to work in the Emergency Hospital they had grafted onto the old one outside of Sunderland.

He had gone to the front in 1915, anxious to use his new skills as a surgeon to save lives. But the carnage of the First World War trenches had broken him. He had been a drunken failure on the night Emmanuel Lansky had prevailed on him to deliver Anne Maguire's first baby; there was no one else available, and he had brought the child into the world with hands that trembled, not with fear but with drink.

A grave-faced, fair-haired woman, Frank Maguire's sister, had carried out his commands quietly, and then, when the baby cried out, had reached to touch his hand and say 'Thank you.' Quinnell learned that her husband had been killed in the service of the Brenton family, who owned the Belgate pits, but he had never expected to see her again – until the day he reeled from a Durham public house and she was standing there in front of him. In that moment, his life took a turn for the better. They were friends for two years and lovers for six before Mary agreed to marry him. And then, as they drove from the church, she had told him she was pregnant.

Patrick was aghast. He had not wanted to bring children into a world that seemed determined to hurl itself into another conflict; but when his son was placed in his arms the unfocused eyes had seemed to fix on his, calm and reassuring. Patrick had looked around him and found the world not such a bad place after all. Thanks to sulphonamides, he was now able to treat many more infections in his patients. Venereal diseases, which had concerned him ever since he saw them escalate in the aftermath of the last war, were now showing a steady decline. There had been 42,000 cases in

1920; now in a year there were 18,000. Pneumonia and diphtheria still took a yearly toll, but inoculation and a pure water supply were decreasing the latter disease with every week that passed. Quinnell had now turned his attention to the high level of TB in his Durham practice, for the illness accounted for approximately a third of all deaths from disease among young adults.

It was caused in the main by appalling housing conditions, but the housing boom of the Thirties was going to make a difference. Four million new houses had been built in Britain since the end of the last war, and as those who could moved out of rented accommodation, so more room was made for those who could not afford to buy. For Patrick Quinnell, the whole picture had been more hopeful, until the shadow of Hitler marred his new-found delight. He left his Durham practice to go to war, in a way, once more.

'Your Mary can't stay in Durham on her own with that baby,' Anne said to Frank firmly. 'Not with Patrick working round the clock in Sunderland once the casualties start. She was good to us when we had nowt; we were sleeping on the floor till she bought us that bed – and it's still going strong.'

Frank smiled the smile of a naughty boy, then, and smacked his lips to remind her of all the goings-on the brass bed had seen. 'Never mind the mucky thoughts,' Anne said. 'Concentrate on your Mary and that canny little bairn.'

It made her broody to hold Mary's baby in her arms. She was resigned to having no more of her own – enough was as good as a feast. But it was nice to hold a clean-smelling little body, to feel the fuzz of hair against your cheek, or the nappy grow warm and moist under your hand. If Mary came to Belgate... well, you never knew what might happen. She might get war-work, and turn the bairn over to Anne, lock, stock and barrel.

'Well?' she asked Frank, in tones that demanded a prompt solution.

'Well?' Frank replied uneasily. 'I don't know where Mary can go.' He would take her in if it came to the push, but they'd need a shoehorn to get her in here. When the lads were all round the fire there was a forest of legs as it was.

The following day Esther came to tell them she had moved into Lansky's house.

'Left your own home?' Anne said, scandalized. 'After all you've spent on it? It'll go to rack and ruin – if it doesn't get bombed. An incendiary could hit it, and it'd be burned to the ground before a soul knew.' There had been a short film at the end of the *Pathe News* on how to deal with incendiaries, and Anne had watched it in horror. Now they had a stirrup-pump with thirty feet of hose, two pails of water, a bucket of sand, a long-handled scoop, and two grey blankets to damp down if necessary. It was to serve three homes, and they had all shared the cost – but Anne made sure it was kept in their own house.

She was buttering bread for Esther's tea when the glorious thought struck her: why couldn't Mary take Esther's house? It was no more than a mile from the Sunderland hospital, and no one could deny it was a little palace. Let Frank's sister and her fancy husband see what her sister had. That would show them!

'Tell you what,' she said, licking the knife clean and setting the bread on a plate. 'I just might be able to do you a favour about your house. You could let it to Mary. She'll pay, all right – and she needs it, our Es, to be near to her man. Remember, he's in Sunderland on war work now.' She didn't add: 'It's the least you can do,' but the words hung in the air.

Every fibre of Esther's being revolted at the thought of anyone, even a woman like Mary whom she knew and liked, getting their hands on her precious house. And a child: muddy boots on the Wilton carpet, sticky little hands to get at the Doulton figurines. Someone sleeping on her good spring mattress. No, it couldn't be allowed. But even as her heart said 'No', her brain said, 'Think about it.'

The war might go on for a long time. Lansky was ageing fast, and there was no realistic prospect of her being able to leave his house until the war was over and Sammy returned. That Sammy might not return could not even be contemplated. If her house was left empty and unlived-in for months or years, what would happen to it? In her mind's eye Esther saw her beloved sitting-room damp and mildewed, even covered in cobwebs like some dreadful scene from Great Expectations.

'I'll have to think it over,' she said, at last. 'But it'll probably be all right.' Anne sat back, satisfied, and began on the Belgate gossip. She listed the men who had gone off to war and the hardship endured by their families. 'Twenty-four shillings a week the wife gets, five bob for the first child and three bob for the second. And most of their men making £4 or more before they were called up. Brenton's giving them £1 a week; I suppose it's the least he can do. But it's the first time I've been glad that Frank's a pitman, and his job's reserved.'

Anne glowed with satisfaction as they sat down to their ham and pease pudding, until Esther asked after Estelle and reminded Anne of the cross the good Lord had seen fit to put upon her already over-burdened shoulders.

'She wants a job in a factory. "War work", she calls it, but the amount of muck she puts on her face it'd be more like the Follys Burrshare. "You stay where you are," I've told her. She says there's Canadians coming to the camp at Ryhope: all millionaires! It's not stars in that one's eyes, our Esther – it's pounds, shillings and pence. Tell me honestly, when I was her age...'

Esther wiped her mouth to gain time. She could not remember a time when Anne had not had an eye to the main chance, at whatever age.

'Don't let's talk about it anymore, Anne,' she said at last.

'You know it upsets you. Stella's going through a phase, that's all. And war's unsettling. I don't know how I'm going to keep the car going unless I get extra petrol for work. One gallon a week won't go far.'

'Is that the ration?'

'That's it,' Esther said. 'One gall per car per week.'

'What about those girls of yours?' Anne asked, trying to expunge the fact that Ruth and Naomi were Germans from her mind.

'They're lovely,' Esther said eagerly, leaning her elbows on the table.

'She's grown bonny,' Anne thought suddenly, seeing her sister's face soften as she spoke. Esther was plumper now, and had a good colour, and her hair suited her rolled up like that. 'How old are you now, our Es?' she asked, thinking what a sin it was that such a woman had never known a man.

'Thirty-two,' Esther said. 'What brought that on?'

'Wedding fever, I suppose,' Anne said. Poor Sally Balmer: two daughters rushing to wed before their lads go off. Think of the cost of that! There's weddings going on left, right and centre: "Marry in haste, repent in leisure" – but they don't think. There'll not half be a reckoning when this war's done.'

'You can't blame them,' Esther said. 'If they're in love and they're going to be separated, it stands to reason they'll marry first if they can.' Tonight she must say goodbye to David Gilfillan before he went off to war, and she was praying that he would not propose to her.

Diana had missed the children more than she would have imagined. She was used to being separated from them, but that had always been from choice. This was enforced separation. She knew they would be happy with Lee, and Valesworth was a wonderful place to be a child, almost as good as Barthorpe, her own childhood home; but she was going to miss a vital part of their growing up, and it hurt. Noel was six now and Ralph almost eight; Pamela was nine. How strange life was; Pamela was now living in her father's ancestral home, quite unawares.

She bought Christmas gifts in Harrods, spending lavishly in an effort to make up to the children for their banishment. *Damn Hitler*, she thought, 'and his whole bloody crew.'

It was dusk when she emerged, shaking her head at the doorman's offer of a cab. Her purchases were being delivered and she felt like walking. Lately she had walked more than ever before, noticing the changes taking place: the skies full of silver balloons, slit trenches in parks, people sitting on sandbags to eat their lunch. But most of all she noticed the absence of children. They had been spirited away as though by a Pied Piper, and London was the poorer for it.

By the time Diana reached Mount Street it was dark, unbelievably dark because the night was moonless. She had to grope the last few yards, and as she walked she suddenly realized how much the black-out had taken from her. She had always loved the hour after dusk, the moment when the lamps in the street sprang to life and the traffic diminished. Best of all had been the lighted windows, like cinema screens giving vivid pictures of other people's lives. A kitchen-maid gazing out into the area as though awaiting Sir Galahad; a mother reading to her children to fill in the time until papa came home; sometimes an old person, man or woman, dozing in a chair, blind to the world; once, at an upstairs window, a young girl braiding her hair. Now there were only blank exteriors, characterless houses without a chink of light.

She had tea by the fire with Rupert, who was in London for a few days, toasting their teacakes on a long brass fork as they had done sometimes for nursery tea. He was a handsome boy now, broad-shouldered and straight-backed.

'He's like Derry,' Diana thought, remembering her brother who had died in another war. One day Rupert would inherit the Durham pits, the factories, the whole panoply of Brenton wealth and power. What would he make of it?

'Cheer up,' Rupert said suddenly, pulling a browned teacake from the fork and passing it to be buttered. 'You look awfully down in the mouth. I'll tell you what: why don't we go out on the town tonight? Papa, too, if he comes home in time. If not, I'll escort you. Everything's open again; we could go to a show and then on to Quaglino's. I fancy Champagne and oysters and then steak bearnaise...'

'Delusions of grandeur!' Diana said, but all of a sudden the prospect was unbelievably appealing. Until Rupert said, in his wheedling way, 'Let's enjoy ourselves while I'm still around.' The remark chilled her.

That night in her room she decided to make a preliminary visit to Valesworth to check on her two youngest children, Pamela being still away at school. They would all be together for Christmas but she wanted to see them now, without delay.

She fretted in the train, longing to see their faces and hear what they hoped for when Father Christmas called.

'You've grown,' she told Ralph and swept Noel into her arms for a hug, before following Loelia into the Great Hall, where an eight-foot Christmas tree towered in the well of the stairs.

'It's like the old days,' Diana said, clasping her hands to her cheeks with delight. She was standing there, still starry-eyed, when a figure in uniform appeared in the door of the library. 'Hallo, Diana,' he said, and she saw that it was Max Dunane, holding out his hand in greeting.

As he raised her hand to his lips, Diana looked into his bland face, full of friendly concern for her, oblivious of the dreadful time when he had spurned her – even hinted the child she was carrying was not his. *You're a swine, Max,* she thought, but there was nothing else to do but smile and ask after his wife and children, safe now in the United States. She turned to Loelia, then, and remarked on her new bottle-green one-piece trouser suit.

'It's a siren suit, Di. They're all the rage: awfully warm and comfy. Nowhere for draughts to get in, but *très* difficult when you go to the lavatory. Still, one can't have everything. I do hope we can give you splendid meals while you're here. It's so fortunate that we have almost everything we need on the estate. All we've been short of is butter, but they're making it at Home Farm now, so that's all right.'

The two women went upstairs, side by side, listening to the chatter of their children down below, remembering their own nursery days. 'We were lucky, weren't we?' Loelia said, curling up on the day bed while Diana took off her coat and hat and repaired her make-up.

'We *are* lucky, Lee darling – having a place like this to retreat to. Howard is so worried about the Belgate women and children; if their men go to war, they'll have a struggle. He's told Stretton, his manager, to help them all.'

'Perhaps the war won't last long,' Loelia said, wrinkling her plump little face to express anguish.

'Howard thinks Churchill will be Prime Minister soon and lead a coalition – at least, that's what he hopes will happen,' Diana said.

'A coalition? Those never work. Besides, those Labour men are all pacifists.'

'No, they're not,' Diana said firmly. 'Howard is terribly keen on Attlee, and Ernest Bevin is a rough diamond but a patriot. Besides, Lee, we can't have elections in the middle of a war, and the Conservatives can't remain in office forever.'

'I don't see why not,' Loelia said, leading the way out of the bedroom. 'They have all the best people, after all.'

BOOK TWO

7

March 1940

Esther walked to the window and looked out at the quiet street. Last winter had been one of the worst for centuries: coal-carts and lorries had been unable to move on the icy roads; they had even had to queue for water when pipes froze. It had seemed as though nature was doing its best to intensify the hardship of war. And then spring had come, and Esther could not remember when she had appreciated it more. She was suddenly seized with longing for her own home, for the neat garden where the roses would have begun to bud. But she could not leave Emmanuel Lansky now - and even if she could, her home was not available. Mary was living there with Patrick and their son.

Esther put away longings for home, and hurried along the landing to rap on the girls' bedroom door. 'Ruth! Naomi! Time to get up.' There was an answering call, and she could already hear Emmanuel moving around his bedroom, so she went downstairs, collected papers and post from the lobby and milk from the step, and went on through to the kitchen.

Mercifully, the range was still alight, and Esther riddled it and set it to blaze up while she set the breakfast table. The girls were settled to their porridge and toast, and Lansky to his newspaper, before Esther had time to sort the letters. There were three in Sammy's familiar hand: one for his father, one for Esther, and one for Ruth, whose turn it was this time. She shared it with Naomi, both of them

chuckling at whatever was written. Lansky was smiling,
too, as he read his son's letter.

Esther had opened a letter from David Gilfillan.

*I am going overseas soon – I can't say when or
where, but I have forty-eight hours embarkation
leave. I am going to Hull to see my mother, and then
coming on to see you, if you will let me? Oh, Esther,
there is so much I have to say to you, and so little time.*

The letter was more emotional than Gilfillan's letters usually were, and that disturbed her. She looked at the date of
the letter and saw it was already three days old. So he would
be here today! She put it back in the envelope, and then
opened Sammy's letter in the hope of finding diversion.

Dearest, beloved Esther, it began, *the angel who is not
only saving this shmuck's business for him but lifting it to
hitherto undreamed-of heights.* She laughed aloud, her
tension over Gilfillan relieved.

'Sammy doesn't get any better,' she said, waving her
letter at Lansky before she read on.

*I am being posted to Manchester, or precious near. No
chance of leave yet, although I keep trying. Could you
come down on the train, Esther? I can always get out
for an hour, and we could confer face to face so much
better than by letter. I have some ideas on how you
can supplement supplies. Yours is the really important
war work: all I do here is gamble (do not tell the aged
pareñt) and polish my boots. Oh, for a crack at the
real enemy! I'm tired of fighting the sergeant-major.
Still, if you could come down and bring some nice
kosher tit-bits, I might survive till the armistice.
Seriously, if it's impossible I understand, but if you
could come a humble private will say kiddush for you.
I await your reply, your loving friend,
Pte Samuel Lansky.*

PS: Kiss the girls and the old man, and tell him I am behaving like the mentsh he always knew me to be. The fact I am at present on jankers is a miscarriage of justice.

She shared her letter with the girls, putting her arms around them. They nestled against her now; she had noticed that first in the tram-car a week ago, on their way home from the shops. *They are ready to be loved once more*, she thought, and wrote to Sammy that night to tell him.

He looks tired, Diana thought, as she glanced at Howard across the breakfast table. He was pale, and it made the scar stand out on his cheek. Aloud she said, 'More tea, darling?' Howard took his eyes from the paper to pass his cup and she heard the faint tinkle of cup on saucer as it trembled in his hand.

'What are they saying in *The Times*?' she asked, as she passed the cup back.

They're describing yesterday's debate,' Howard said, 'but they can't do it justice in print.'

The House of Commons had been electric, the Peers' Gallery crowded, the Strangers' Gallery packed with ambassadors and ministers from two-dozen nations. The reason for their interest was not only the debate on the ignominious flight of the British Expeditionary Force from Norway. In all probability, the fate of the British Prime Minister would be decided before their eyes, in the cockpit of the House.

When Neville Chamberlain rose to his feet a volley of boos and catcalls came from the Labour benches. 'He missed the bus! Resign! Resign!' Howard saw Chamberlain sway slightly, as though the abuse had been a blow, but then he rallied, praising the courage of soldiers, sailors and airmen even in retreat.

For nearly an hour he spoke, but it was in vain. Now the dissent came from the Tory benches, too, until, in the end, Leo Amery denounced him, borrowing words used by Cromwell two centuries before: 'You have sat too long for any good you have been doing. Depart, I say, and let us have done with you. In the name of God, go!' Amery pointed at Chamberlain as he spoke – and when Howard recounted the story to Diana she had felt the hair prickle on the back of her neck. Churchill tried to defend Chamberlain, but Lloyd George chided him: 'Don't allow yourself to be converted into an air-raid shelter to keep the splinters from your colleagues.' In the vote at the end, the Government's majority was reduced from over 200 to eighty-one. Some forty Tories, including former Cabinet members, voted against their leader. Others abstained.

'Do they think Chamberlain will go?' she asked Howard now.

He shook out another paper. 'They're speculating. Some still think Halifax will take over, but I can't see it. Attlee won't join a coalition unless it's led by Churchill, and without Attlee's support, Halifax couldn't function. Not properly. But I think Chamberlain still hopes to survive.'

'After that humiliation?' Diana was shocked. Amery had not been alone in his denunciation, and as Chamberlain had left the House, Harold Macmillan and other rebels had sung 'Rule Britannia', while still others chanted, 'Go! Go! Go!'

Howard glanced at his watch before he replied, 'To be fair to him, Diana, I think the man truly loves his country. If he thought it the right thing to do, he'd brave any humiliation. Still, in the end he'll *have* to go, and then it'll be up to Winston.'

'Will he be able to turn the tide?'

Howard was rising now, impatient to get back, and Diana walked with him to the hall.

'If he can't, no one can,' Howard said but there was no buoyancy in his tone.

She kissed him warmly before he opened the door. 'Try to get home tonight. I miss you. And we must talk about the children; we have to take them somewhere this summer. They're growing up, and we're missing it, Howard. They won't know us soon, unless we make an effort.'

Even as Diana spoke, her conscience pricked her. It was not from choice that Howard spent night after night out of his bed and away from his children.

When he had left, she dressed and set out for Harrods. On the surface little in the store seemed changed as she moved from department to department. Women were buying crazy new hats, primping from side to side in mirrors, many of them looking like facsimiles of Princess Marina, with their dark hair and the double row of pearls tight at the base of the neck. Fashion was changing, Diana thought: shoulders were widening, hats had an aggressive tilt to them, and everyone, it seemed, had adopted zip-fasteners. Skirts were straighter and bodices looser, and shoes were becoming positively clumsy. Every woman had a gas-mask case, even the whores in Piccadilly; suddenly they had become a fashion accessory, some covered to match coats, others in suede or gaberdine, a few in fur or lizard-skin. One or two shoppers, making direct for the food hall, wore the new siren suit with their hair done up in snoods or Mammy-style headscarves like Mrs Churchill. *We are girding ourselves up for war*, Diana thought, and resisted the temptation to buy more than she needed. Her momentary feeling of virtue was dissipated when she remembered Loelia's promise of game and food from the Dunane farms. Easy to hold back when you could see no prospect of deprivation.

She spent twenty minutes choosing a new lipstick. Make-up was subtler this year, and she approved of that. She bought one of the new high Hussar felt hats, laughing out loud at the sight of it perched on her head but liking it just the same. As she passed through to the evening-wear salon, a girl was twirling in the centre of the floor, a heavy green satin dress swirling around her. 'It's lovely, mummy, isn't it?' she was saying. 'May I have it?' Her mother nodded indulgently. If it had not been for the black-out curtains over the shop windows, Diana could have believed it was 1938 again and war despatched to limbo.

She was beginning to think about lunch when she felt a hand on her arm. 'Diana?'

It was Max Dunane, in his army greatcoat, a major's crown on his shoulder.

'Max! I thought you'd be beavering away in the War House.'

He had taken her arm and was moving her through the crowds. 'Have lunch with me,' he said. 'I have an hour or so, and I was simply wandering around here, wondering what I ought to buy. Take pity on me.'

A momentary flash of resentment came in Diana, and went. If war escalated, either of them might die.

They ate at a corner table, the hum of conversation and the clatter of cutlery forming a wall around them so that they could speak freely – at first about little things: the irritation of rationing, the pitfalls of the black-out, the idiocy of air-raid precautions. 'And what do you think of Lord Haw Haw?' Max asked her.

'Howard says he's a traitor,' Diana replied. 'But I find it hard to take him seriously. He was a Mosleyite, wasn't he? I hate the way he speaks through his nose: "Jairmany calling… jairmany calling!"'

'We think six million people are listening to him,' Max said. 'He may have a nasal voice, but he's clever. Most of what he says is simply propaganda: rubbish. But then he'll slip in some little snippet of genuine information that makes the whole thing seem credible.'

'Rupert is most impressed, but all the same he thinks someone should go over there and shoot him.'

'How is the boy? He's seventeen soon, isn't he? Lee said his birthday was coming up.'

'Yes, he's seventeen next month and mad about joining the air force. I can only pray it's all over before he reaches the right age. How do you think it looks?'

Max grimaced. 'Not good, I'm afraid. The French won't hold, if it comes to it. Hitler will take the Low Countries first, and then mop up France. After that...' He shrugged and looked down at his hands. When he raised his eyes Diana saw they were misted.

'She's a lovely girl.'

It took a moment for Diana to realize who he meant. Pamela?' She had to look away to hide her discomfiture. 'She's fine. Very much a daddy's girl...'

She had not meant to be hurtful, but as soon as the words were out she regretted them. Max saw her confusion and put out a hand to cover hers.

'No, don't be afraid to say it. If she loves Howard, I'm glad. He deserves it. I wasn't fair to you, Diana – or the child. Looking back, it's hard to believe I behaved as I did. Lately, with Laura and the children away, I've done a lot of thinking, and I don't much like my thoughts.'

Diana would have silenced him, but he wouldn't let her. 'I want to make it up to you, and Pamela, and Howard, too, if he'll let me. It's not that I don't love Laura – but there is more than an ocean between us. You and I were soulmates, Di...'

Max broke off and shook his head suddenly, and then his grip on her hand tightened. 'Have dinner with me tonight? Please! Howard, too, if he's free. We can talk about the old days – just the way we were a long time ago, before we had to grow up.'

Mary Quinnell sat upright in the passenger seat of the black Ford saloon, her hands clutching her handbag which contained the precious list of names and addresses. The driver glanced at her. 'All right?' he said, and she nodded. She had joined the Women's Voluntary Service as soon as she moved to Sunderland, anxious to do her bit in whatever way was possible. Today she had left her baby with Anne and was off on her first real mission: to visit children evacuated to the country. Tales were filtering back of homes where evacuees were not being welcomed, and this was fuelling parents' understandable reluctance to let their children go. Anne had been forthright. 'No bairn of mine's going out of my sight. I'll deal with air raids; Hitler, too, if he comes; but I want my bairns where I can see them.' But if the bombers came, as Patrick believed they would, Anne might have to change her mind.

According to the papers, half of the children evacuated in the first months of the war had returned home. Where mother and children had gone together, the fall-out had been even greater. There had been no German air onslaught as yet, and homesickness was a scourge. Apart from that, the charge of six shillings a week per child was beyond the means of many parents. Three and a half million people had evacuated danger areas at the start of the war: the biggest shift of population since the Great Plague of 1665, according to Patrick. Half of them were people going to bolt-holes in the country, either rented or with friends, but the rest were evacuated under the official scheme, and billeted on people who did not always want them.

This was the case at the first house Mary called at. 'Just get them out when you can,' the harassed householder told her. 'The language! And the fleas and the nits, not to mention certain little thieving ways. The family came to see them, did you know that? Arrived with a babe in arms, dumped it on me, and went straight off to the pub. No wonder the children are monsters!'

When she spoke alone with the children, the picture was

just as bleak. 'Take me home, missus, please! I'll do anything, I'll be good, but take us home – today!'

Fortunately, all the billets were not so ill-matched. Some of the children seemed to be thriving and some of the hosts genuinely pleased to have them.

Mary conferred with the WVS representative in the area, who was gloomy about the whole operation. 'Half of my mothers, more than half, if I'm honest, went back within weeks, taking their children with them. Never mind the bombs; they're terrified of the country: the quiet, the animals, so much fresh air! I dread to think what will happen when air raids really start. Those who've tried it once won't be persuaded to come back. The whole thing was rushed, and that's a fact.'

As Mary rode home she resolved that nothing – *nothing* – would ever persuade her to separate her family.

'Well, I'm not sure,' Anne said, turning her head this way and that. The permanent wave had cost twenty-five shillings, and Joe and Frank had paid for it between them. It was her first perm, and the corrugated waves and sausage curls both horrified and intrigued her.

'I like it,' Joe said stoutly.

'You look nice whichever way you've got your hair,' Frank said.

Anne seized on his words. 'You don't like it, then? You mean I look all right in spite of it?'

It was in vain for him to protest. She seized a comb and began an onslaught on the new hair-do.

'Wait till you hear about Gallagher,' Frank said in an effort to divert her. Anne stopped combing at once. Gallagher, the former Brenton agent at the pit, had systematically oppressed and robbed the men while old Charles Brenton had been alive. Howard Brenton had sacked him as soon as his father died, but bitter memories lingered.

'Well, go on,' Anne said. 'What about the sod?'

'I don't know the exact details,' Frank was spinning it out slightly, to get her going. 'But according to the lads, he's going to be the one to control food supplies.'

'The rations?' Anne said, round-eyed. 'What's it got to do with *him*?' She was the proud possessor of eight ration books, and was relishing the purchasing power.

'Nowt,' Frank said. 'But you know him: you can't keep that sort down. And that lad of his, Stanley, he's got a reserved occupation, so they say.'

Anne snorted. 'Reserved! Bloody conchie, that's what he is. Still, Gallagher or no Gallagher, we'll manage. One-and-tenpence-worth of meat each a week, and lamb only one and four a pound – we'll have meat coming out of our ears! And chickens and offal and sausage and meat pies for no coupons – not that we'll be knee-deep in chicken, the price it is. And we never had four ounces of butter before the war; chance'd be a fine thing there. Twelve ounces of sugar's ample, and so's the bacon allowance. I don't know what everyone's moaning about. Sally Liddle was nearly crying the other morning, and her man's lived on taties and bread as long as I've known her. It's not *us* I'm sorry for, Frank, it's them with a man in the services. They get paid so little...'

At that moment the door opened and Stella appeared. She was bright-eyed and dishevelled, her blouse open so far that it revealed her underpinnings, and her speech, when she said 'Hello', was definitely slurred.

'Where've you been?' Anne pounced – but then, realizing it was not yet six o'clock, 'Why aren't you at the shop?'

'Because I've left,' Stella said, advancing into the room on heels high enough to make her totter slightly.

'Left? *Left*?' Anne clutched a chair-back with one hand and put the other to her mouth.

'What d'you mean "left"?' Frank said. 'Tell your mother what you're talking about.'

'I've left the shop. I wasn't sacked; I put me notice in, and they said "Go now", so I did.' Stella was triumphant.

'I'll swing for her, Frank,' Anne said, her eyes rolling. I've said it before and I'll say it again: I will *hang* for her.' She advanced on her daughter and seized her by the shoulders, shaking her till Stella's blond hair waved like a flag. 'Why've you left? Why, why, *why*?'

'Because I've got a better job,' Stella said, squirming away, her elation deserting her.

'Where?' Frank said.

'In a factory. Twice as much as I'm getting now, and the chance of bonus.'

'I knew it,' Anne said, wearily. 'I said this war would get everybody in the end, and I was right. This proves it. We could keep her in hand when she worked down the street. Tell me how we're going to manage her now?'

Mary thanked the driver and stood at the gate until the car rounded the corner. A light was on in Esther's house – impossible to think of it as 'her' house – so Patrick must have collected Benjamin and be home. She closed the gate carefully behind her and walked up the path between the neat rows of daffodils. 'I'm back,' she called as she let herself in. The baby was asleep on the settee in the living-room, carefully covered with a rug, but she found Patrick seated at the kitchen table, a glass in his hand, a half-empty bottle of whisky in front of him.

The shock robbed Mary of words. He had not drunk alcohol since the bad old days. She wanted to move forward and smash the bottle to the floor, but she controlled herself. Instead she unpinned her hat, stuck the hatpins into the band and sat down opposite him.

'What's the matter, Pat?'

He shook his head vaguely and lifted the glass to his lips, not drinking. 'Put it down and tell me what's wrong.'

To her relief, Patrick lowered the glass to the table.

'We had a boy died today. Nineteen.'

Mary knew they had patients from an explosion aboard a munitions ship in the hospital: they had been extensively burned, and Patrick had expected them to die.

'That's sad,' she said. 'But drinking won't bring him back.'

'It helps *me*,' Patrick said, and she was frightened by the intensity of his words. 'It helps *me* to keep on walking and talking and mouthing platitudes. I wish I were dead!'

She was silent for a moment, and then she got to her feet. She fetched the sleeping baby from the next room and carried him into the kitchen, holding him so that his father could see his tranquil little face.

'You can't die, Pat,' she said matter-of-factly. 'You gave that right up when you brought a new life into the world. I know how you feel: you suffered through one war, and you feel you can't cope with another. But you can and you will. You lost a life today; you might save one tomorrow and the next day and the next. And you won't drink, and you'll use your skills, and when this war's over you'll know you've done your best. It's not much, but it's what most of us have to make do with. Now, hold this bairn and let me pour that whisky down the sink.'

She heard him cry out once as the spirit glug-glugged away, but it was a cry of anguish, of letting go, rather than a cry of abandonment. *He'll be all right*, she thought and turned back to put on the kettle for tea.

As the debate droned on, Howard looked at his watch. Eight o'clock – he had better telephone Diana and tell her he would not be home before midnight.

She took the call dressed in a housecoat, her make-up

already applied and her hair done. She meant to tell Howard that she had accepted Max's invitation on his behalf as well as her own, but somehow the words did not come. Instead she said, 'I'm dining out, darling. I'll tell you about it later. I'll be home before you... No, I won't wait up. But come as soon as you can – you haven't had a good night's sleep for ages.'

As Diana mounted the stairs to finish dressing, her legs felt suddenly shaky. Perhaps she shouldn't go out with Max? There was still time to call it off. She could give him sherry when he arrived and say it was impossible in Howard's absence. But by the time she reached her room she had made up her mind; the truth was that she enjoyed Max's company, even if she didn't know how to explain that to Howard. But she would never, ever, enter into a sexual relationship with Max. Not again.

Max looked strangely boyish in khaki, she thought, and he always had a story to tell, or a joke to relate, or a delicious item of gossip. It was really like having Loelia back again – someone to joke with, someone who knew her inside out. There couldn't be any harm in it as long as she kept her head. She was all ready, and a night out would do her good, especially if they could remember the old times at Barthorpe and Valesworth. There was no way she would ever again risk her marriage, but a little reminiscence could surely do no harm?

Esther was waiting in the hall when David Gilfillan came to collect her. He carried flowers wrapped in ribbon-trimmed florist's paper, and her heart sank a little at the look in his eyes, a mixture of both ardour and desperation.

They went first to the cinema to see Robert Donat in *Goodbye, Mr Chips*, and under the cover of darkness Esther felt him groping for her hand. Tomorrow he was going back to his unit, and then on to God knew where. She let him take it, and even squeezed his fingers in an attempt to give him comfort.

Afterwards, they found a dining-room in the Grand Hotel and ordered supper and wine.

'I'm going overseas, that's all I know, but it'll be France, I suppose.' David was twirling the stem of his glass between finger and thumb, the rest of his hand flat on the table.

'It may not be,' Esther offered, because she couldn't think of anything else to say. 'Perhaps you're going to the Middle East, or…' She tried to think of somewhere safe, so that she could banish the apprehension from his face. *He isn't cut out for war,* she thought. *He was meant to practise law somewhere, in the Lake District perhaps, or the Yorkshire Dales, and have a nice house and two children and a labrador and a family car.* Instead he was going into the unknown, with a few weeks of training behind him and his job kept open for him if he managed to return. Suddenly she wanted to mother him, to make him feel safe and comfortable for just a little while. But where? She had no house of her own now, and the Lansky home was out of the question. And then she remembered Sammy's flat: the bolt-hole he had kept for entertaining his girlfriends. He had asked her to keep an eye on it. She fished in her handbag and found the key. She would use the flat this once, in an emergency, but never again. They would have to find somewhere else – if there was another time.

'Let's go,' she said firmly. 'We'll have our coffee in a place I know.' He paid the bill and they went out into the cold, dark street and ran, hand in hand, for the sanctuary of his car.

Afterwards Esther asked herself again and again why she had done it. She had set him in a chair by the gas fire and brought him coffee on a tray. They talked of Garbo, and Gable, and Hollywood, and what America would do about the war. And then she locked the front door, and led him to Sammy's bed.

'Are you sure?' David asked, standing there, head bowed a little. Esther put a finger to his lips and then reached up to loosen his tie. They kissed like children at first: he uncertain, she swept up in memories of Philip. Philip smiling, Philip sleeping... How could she lie with another man?

And then she put out the light and they undressed, sometimes themselves, sometimes one another. When they touched, naked and shivering with the cold, he let out a cry and she felt his body harden against hers. 'I love you, Esther,' he said and she said, 'Yes, I know,' because she couldn't say she loved him, not with truth. Not yet. Perhaps she might with time. If they were given time.

She had to help him, guiding him into her, slowing him down when eagerness threatened to run away with him. And then, when he was moving rhythmically inside her, she tried to list what she knew about this man in her arms. He was decent and good: 'A *mentsh*,' Sammy had called him. He played golf, and went to the Presbyterian church on Sundays. His body was lean, and surprisingly strong, and his hair smelled of Lifebuoy soap. Philip's hair had been soft to the touch, his neck fragile, the bones of his torso fragile like a bird. *Oh Philip*, she thought, *would you understand me now?* And knew, even as David arched and cried out, that her one true love would have trusted her to do what must be done.

It was only when Gilfillan was sleeping beside her that she thought of consequences. There must *not* be a child. It was useless to think there couldn't be; there might. She slipped from the bed and tiptoed to the bathroom. If only she had the douching equipment she had used with Philip. She washed herself again and again in the hope that there was no trace of Gilfillan remaining inside her.

She prayed then, before crawling into the warm bed, carefully so as not to wake him. As she was falling asleep she had a brief moment of regret; if Gilfillan did not come back it might have been nice to think he had carried on his line... But it was only a momentary pang. He would come back – to think otherwise was out of the question. As she settled down for sleep she suddenly remembered Master Howard, back from the war all those years ago, with his little scar and the limp and the good looks of a film star: at least, that's what she had thought when she had been a child working in his house, and they had all known for certain that there would never be another war.

Diana and Max dined at the Ritz, to the tinkle of laughter and the discreet rattle of silver on porcelain. Above them was the magnificent ceiling, the waiters hovered as usual, the food was as exquisite as ever. *It could be ten years ago*, Diana thought, *when we were lovers and the world was at peace*.

As she ate her avocado mousse and sipped an excellent Chablis, she tried to remember how it had felt to be wild. It must have been exciting some of the time or she would not have done it, but all she could remember now was the pain of it, and the blessed relief when Howard had stood by her and made it all come right. That was why this *tête-à-tête* with Max was so harmless. She could *never* betray Howard, and that made her safe: as safe as houses. She could laugh with Max, or argue, or mourn the passing of their youth; she could give and receive news of Lee, and commiserate with him on his enforced bachelordom; but in the end she was Howard's wife, and glad of it.

If one or two of the other diners, people who knew her, looked at her and Max a little strangely, she ignored them. What did other people's opinions matter, when there was a war on and any of them likely to be blown to bits by next week?

As if he had read her thoughts, Max smiled at her. 'It's good that we met up, isn't it? With Lee banished to Valesworth and my darling wife scuttling to safety... well, they say old friends are the best, and they're right.' It was the nearest Max had come to condemning Laura, and Diana decided to treat the remark lightly – in fact to pretend she hadn't heard it.

'Isn't that Peggy Ashcroft over there, in the green hat?'

'I think so,' Max said. 'Who's the man?'

'Search me. He's rather gorgeous.'

A waiter stepped forward to refill their glasses. 'I mustn't be late back,' Max said, as the man moved away. 'There's another flap on – and of course everyone's waiting to see who will follow Chamberlain.'

'Strange to think he's gone.' Diana sounded almost regretful, and she saw surprise on Max's face. 'Oh, don't misunderstand: I want him out just as much as everyone else. But it seems as though all the old pillars are crumbling; the royals, the politicians, old families selling up – even countries are disappearing. I want something to stand still.'

'But not Chamberlain. The sooner he's out the better. I reckon his goose was cooked after that speech last month.

Hitler made a fool of him at Munich, and then Chamberlain says, "Hitler has missed the bus." Pompous ass. Hitler's getting ready to gobble up Europe. Missed the bus, indeed! Chamberlain couldn't be allowed to get away with that.'

Poor little man,' Diana said. 'What was it Lloyd George called him: "a good Lord Mayor of Birmingham in a bad year"? If there'd been no Hitler, he might have gone down to history as a not-half-bad PM. *C'est la vie!*' She pushed aside her plate. 'No more, I'm full. Howard says the last scene in the House was dreadful, with people baying like hounds and reminding Chamberlain of that "missed the bus" remark.'

'Who does Howard think the King will choose?'

'Churchill,' Diana said firmly. 'He says Attlee and Bevin will refuse to cooperate unless it's Winston.'

'Bloody cheek,' Max said gloomily. 'I don't see why colourless little Socialists should decide who governs Britain.'

'What does it matter?' Diana said. 'As long as we get the man we want, I don't care two pins. Now, have you any deep dark secrets of war to impart? I'm fearfully discreet.'

'Are you free tomorrow?' Max asked, laughing. 'I've got seats for *Dear Octopus* – or I can have, if you'd like to go. What about Howard?'

Diana sighed. 'I'll be lucky to see Howard at all, especially if nothing's decided by then. Ring me tomorrow. I may know something by then.'

She stood up, collected her wrap, and they began to thread their way towards the door. She knew people at other tables were looking. She saw a woman she knew slightly lean to her companion and whisper. Well, let them whisper if it enlivened their boring lives. She turned to Max, not bothering to lower her voice. 'Take those seats, Max, darling. I haven't seen a good play for ages. And we can dine first at Mount Street, if you like.'

They were out in the ornate hall now, and she was regretting her bravado, but it was too late to take it back. *I must put an end to this*, she thought as they walked together to the door onto Piccadilly. *I must and I will – as soon as there's something to be cheerful about. I'll sort it all out then.*

And she must find herself a job, too. Something worthwhile, something to make Howard proud of his wife. She had meant to drive an ambulance, but it seemed there was no need of such things. In fact, at times, you could almost believe the war was simply a bad dream.

*

Howard stood at the side of the lobby, watching the comings and goings. Something must break soon, for the news from Europe was disastrous. He saw Arthur Greenwood, Clement Attlee's deputy, come down the stairs, looking relieved, even smiling at colleagues as he passed. What did that mean? Ten minutes later, Howard knew.

Chamberlain had at last given way, advising the King to send for Churchill to form a government. Churchill would lead an all-party team to achieve victory; he would act as Minister of Defence as well as Prime Minister, and would bring some trade-union leaders into the government.

Howard went to a telephone and rang the Mount Street number. It was the parlourmaid who answered, a new and very young girl still nervous about answering the tele-phone. 'Can you tell your mistress I have some news for her?' Howard said.

The mistress isn't here, sir. She went out earlier. In a car with a gentleman, with red hair.'

Were they going to a restaurant?'

'I don't know, sir. Shall I ask if anyone knows where they are, sir?'

'No, thank you,' Howard said. 'I'll call again later.'

He put down the phone and made for the lobby. So: Diana was out on the town with Max Dunane. What, exactly, did *that* mean?

8

May 1940

Howard joined in the nation's sigh of relief when Churchill became Prime Minister. Now there would be a stand, even a counter-attack. But the *Blitzkrieg* which had overcome the Poles now took the Dutch and the Belgians, and then mowed through the French lines as though through grass.

Howard sat in the House as Churchill gave a sombre rallying call. 'I have nothing to offer but blood, toil, tears and sweat. We have before us an ordeal of the most grievous kind.'

People offered excuses for the success of the German advance. France had been betrayed by a fifth-column working within it; Germany had infinitely greater numbers of tanks; France had been swamped by German paratroopers. In fact, as far as Howard could see, French incompetence had been a greater threat than any fifth-column could have been. German airborne operations had been few, but the threat of German might descending from the air had been paralysing. And the Germans had not had more tanks; they had simply deployed those tanks they had more effectively, concentrating them on the point of breakthrough instead of along an extended front. Death rained down from Heinkels, Stukas and Messerschmitts. The French army could not move on roads that were clogged with refugees, nor could it blast them out of the way as the enemy did. As French civilians trudged south, the British Expeditionary Force fought its way to Dunkirk in the hope that the Royal Navy would be waiting for it there.

That same weekend Diana went down to see Rupert. She had not seen him since Easter, and the sight of him was a shock. He seemed to have grown up quite suddenly, losing the rounded contours of puberty, becoming almost lantern-jawed. Where there had been down in the holidays, now there was stubble; his hands were magically strong and capable; his voice deep and more authoritative. *Has all this happened overnight?* she thought. *Or did I simply not see it until now?*

They ate lunch in the Spaniard's Arms, making small talk about new clothes or sports equipment or the doings of family and friends. But all the while Diana was aware that something was brewing.

'We lost an old boy this week,' Rupert said at last. 'That makes two. Chastney minor at sea, and now Manners in France. I remember Manners: he was captain of rugger in my first year.' There was an almost accusing note in his voice, as though she was personally to blame for casualties.

'That's awful, darling,' she said. 'I feel so sorry for their families.'

'I expect they're proud,' Rupert said. 'They died for a just cause.' There was passion in his voice and a terrible, childlike anger. 'Hitler is running through Europe like a plague, mother: one country after another. We can't sit by while they take France, and then come on here.'

Diana tried to keep her voice level. 'Of course not, darling, but there are people to deal with that…' She was about to say, 'It doesn't involve you,' when she saw the scorn in his eyes and thought better of it. 'I know you want to help,' she said instead. 'I understand that; I even approve. But you're not David, you can't go out with a sling and take on Goliath. It's not that kind of war. Your father says it will be a war of equipment, not men. Not like Flanders or the Somme where they threw in men like missiles. If you really want to help, to make a difference, you'll work terribly hard for your Oxford, so that you're equipped to train. Wouldn't that make sense?'

'Train as a pilot?' he said.

'If that's what you want. But they won't take you without qualifications, darling. Half of England wants to join the RAF. They can pick and choose. If you're serious about pilot-training, you'll work like a horse.'

Rupert's face had lit up as she talked. Now it clouded over.

'It might all be ended before then.'

'Then you can be the best civil pilot in the world,' Diana said. 'New York to London every day.'

She had made him laugh. It was going to be all right. *I handled that rather well*, she thought as they ordered pudding. If the Allies could bring about a reversal in Hitler's fortunes, the war might be over before she had to contemplate the horror of Rupert's actually taking to the air. In one day this month, seventy British and forty French planes had been lost in a raid on the bridges over the Meuse. And he might change his mind. That's how they were at seventeen: planes one day, ships the next.

Diana wondered if she should tell Rupert about her own job as an ambulance driver, and decided against it. The less he thought about war-work and the more he concentrated on study, the better. All the same, it would have been nice to tell him about her first gas drill, going through a chamber with an official while vapour was given off. Afterwards her eyes had pricked – due, the official said, to gas in her hair. He had passed little bottles round: Lewisite, which smelled like geraniums; then another which smelled like decaying vegetables and was actually phosgene; and then mustard, which smelled strongly but not of mustard. It had been interesting, even a little frightening, and Diana had felt as though it was all beginning to happen at last.

They strolled back to school after lunch, past boys

walking purposefully in twos and threes, and others surrounded by doting parents and adoring younger sisters. Rupert was playing in a cricket match on the pitch behind the chapel, and Diana sat listening to the thwack of leather on wood and the cries of encouragement for a boundary or scorn for a dropped catch, until the calm of the scene swept over her. They had had cricket at Barthorpe in the summer when Derry was alive, and in winter the hunt had met in the courtyard with a yelping of hounds and the click of shod hoofs on cobblestones. Max had been there once, on a grey gelding, and she had passed him a stirrup cup and seen the admiration in his eyes. And then they had all grown up, and now these very English pursuits were under threat.

She thought of Churchill's speech, soon after he had become PM, a speech that had been pored over and read aloud in almost every home in the land. 'We have before us many, many long months of struggle and of suffering. You ask, "What is our policy?" It is to wage war, by sea, land and air, with all our might and with all the strength that God can give us. You ask, "What is our aim?" I can answer in one word: Victory: at all costs, in spite of all terror, however long and hard the road may be. For without victory there is no survival. Come, then: let us go forward together with our united strength.'

When Diana got home that night she wrote to Lee, something she did rarely because the telephone was so much more immediate. Tonight, however, she felt the need to put her thoughts on paper.

I felt strange, Lee, as I looked at Rupert. Proud, and fearful, but most of all amazed at the size and the strength of him. At the quick words and the fire in his eyes and his resolution. His bloody resolution! He is ready to take on the world, and it's only yesterday I had to kiss his knees better when he grazed them on the cinder path. It made me feel old, and somehow inadequate. He is a man, and I hadn't bargained for that; not yet, at least.

Still, enough of philosophizing. I hope Pamela et cie aren't driving you mad, and that rural ennui has not set in. I have enrolled with the ambulance service at last and am taking instruction in first aid. Try to save your seizure till I've had lesson three: at the moment all I can do is fractures and choking. Howard is quietly proud (I <u>think</u> – you know Howard) and Max is most impressed. He says if Hitler knew of my state of preparedness the invasion would never come...

When the letter was done she blotted it, and was searching for an envelope when she wondered if she should take out the reference to Max. On reflection she decided to leave it in because to delete it would be to suggest something improper – that something needed to be hidden. And that was completely untrue.

Anne made a final obeisance to the altar and came out into the sunshine. There was no getting away from it: this war was upsetting things. There had been a girl with lipstick on taking Mass, and the priest not batting an eye. She compressed her own unadorned lips and hurried towards Trenchard Street, passing the queue at the bread shop. She had stood there yesterday, for pasties, until the calves of her legs had ached. Now she needed to get home quick, before Mary arrived with the bairn.

She thought about Stella as she walked up the street. The girl was a law unto herself now, with a factory job and money in her pocket. Not yet seventeen and money to throw away – it couldn't be right. If only Stella had been like Catherine, her cousin, Mary's daughter, who was training to be a nurse and never putting a foot wrong.

There was no sign of Mary, and Anne let herself into the empty house. She put on the kettle and moved to the kitchen window to look out on the back yard. They had been in this house for years now, and she'd still not done half the things she wanted to do with it, like lime-washing the back-yard walls and having a rosebush in a tub.

Suddenly, she caught sight of herself in the piece of mirror that was propped on the window sill. The face that looked back at her was pasty and lined. *I'm thirty-seven*, she thought, *and I look like fifty*. She stared into the mirror, the kettle steaming on the fire behind her, remembering the girl she had been once: the best-looking girl in Belgate.

She walked to the range to scald the tea. Frank's paper was lying on his chair and she carried it back to the kitchen table, along with the teapot. There was a notice at the bottom of the page, giving instructions on how to spot paratroopers.

> *First, remember that while men in disguise may be dropped in ones or twos, the paratroops in uniform usually come down in a bunch. And this is what the uniformed paratroopers wear: high boots laced at the side, with heavy rubber soles, loose trousers like plus-fours, air-force grey colour. (Sometimes rations are carried in the bottoms of these trousers).*

Anne burst out laughing at this. They sounded proper clips: plus-fours filled with butter and bacon – a likely story. She read on, past zipped overalls and gauntlet gloves, to steel helmets. Here she began to know fear. 'Each man is armed with a revolver, and one in five has a machine pistol with a maximum range of 200 yards. Also, a paratrooper may have a couple of egg-shaped grenades.'

Anne put the paper aside and went back to the window, hoping for a sight of Mary and the baby: blessed normality. The Germans did terrible things to women, everyone knew that. But if they threatened her bairns, or Frank, come to that, it would be God help them, hand-grenades or no hand-grenades! The Germans might have walked through Holland and Belgium, but it would be different here.

According to Frank, the Germans would try invading any day now. They were almost on the other side of the Channel, and only a few British soldiers holding them back. The French had gone to pieces, just like everyone had said they would. What else could you expect of people who lived on frogs and snails? She looked through the kitchen window, seeing the patch of sky above the back-yard wall. Any moment now a German might come floating down with his trousers packed with rations. Anne opened the kitchen drawer and took out the gully-knife, with its razor-sharp blade and horn handle. It could slice a day-old loaf as though it were butter. If it came to it, she would stick it in the first German down with no more compunction than she would swat a fly.

Esther watched the countryside rattle by, pressed up against the window because the train was full of servicemen and every seat in her carriage taken. David Gilfillan's latest letter was in her handbag, and she closed her eyes, remembering some of the things he had said.

I wish I could find the words to tell you how much it means to know you are there, waiting for me. How happy we will be, Esther. I worried so much that I had wronged you on that last leave, but now I know we were meant to make that vow, to one another. War is terrible and no one knows what it's like until they are swept up in it. Death is sudden and definite, and could come at any time: to me, to the man next to me who was joking a moment before. If I am to keep my reason I must think of you.

Esther opened her eyes and looked at the Cleveland Hills, low and green in the distance. Those weeks after she had slept with David had been the longest of her life. If there had been a child, she could not have given it up: that was an agony to be endured only once. But how ironic it would have been if she had given up the child of the man she had loved with all her heart, and then kept the child of a man she had only taken pity on. For she did not love David Gilfillan, though she cared about him too much to write the truth to him now, when he was God-knew-where fighting a war. So she sent off her letters, wording them carefully so that they reassured him without making promises she could never keep.

'Got a light, love?'

Esther turned to the soldier beside her. 'I don't smoke, I'm afraid, but if you can get that basket down from the rack I have some matches in it.'

She was taking Sammy a host of useful items, along with gifts from his father and the girls. Between them they had knitted a pair of fingerless gloves, labouring over them with tongues poking from their lips as they reclaimed dropped stitches. Ruth's glove had tighter tension than Naomi's and was therefore smaller, but the thought was there. She rummaged in the basket and produced a box of matches. 'There, you can keep these. I have more.'

He said 'Ta', and lit up. There was fuzz on his chin and his nails were bitten. *He's only a boy*, Esther thought, and would have delved in the basket for chocolate if the carriage had not been full of other uniformed boys and girls, all laughing and chattering, sometimes looking wistful when conversation lagged.

She settled back and thought of Sammy. Her handbag bulged with facts and figures, projections and estimates. She must keep the business going, even improve it – but it was not going to be easy. Still, she was amazed at how quickly she managed to grasp details of those areas of their business that had been largely Sammy's concern up till now. And, almost to her horror, there was a terrible kind of excitement in it all, a feeling of mastery that carried her through even the most hitherto uncharted waters. There were new trading restrictions every day, and now a controller was in charge of the movement and allocation of supplies – a man called Gallagher, who had been the Brenton agent once. Anne had called him a bastard, but Esther meant to give him the benefit of the doubt – to start with, at least.

She dozed then, and woke with a start to find herself way up in the Pennines. There were huge mills there and streets of houses running up the hillsides at what looked like impossible angles. Sammy had promised to meet her at Stalybridge, the last stop before Manchester, if he could get away. If not, she was to take a cab to the Rose and Crown and wait for him there.

But he was waiting on the platform, the dark curls cut short now, his forage cap tucked into his epaulette. 'Esther! How's my girl? And a basket of cookies! I hardly dared to hope... How are the old man, and the *kinderlach*? Come' on, let's get you sitting down and a meal inside you.'

In vain for Esther to protest that she had been sitting down for hours and would be glad to stretch her legs; Sammy was already folding her into the seat of an ancient green motor-car with the shabbiest leather seats she had ever seen. Aware of her surprise, he held up a finger. 'Don't ask questions, Esther. You have to survive in this army; I'm surviving.'

A meal was laid out for them in the tap-room of the Rose and Crown, and a plump landlady fussed around them. 'Now you won't be disturbed here, son. Just shout if you or your lady-friend want anything.'

'See?' Sammy said when she'd gone, 'she knows you're my lady-friend. I know; the world knows. Only Esther won't admit it.' He sighed, but Esther merely produced her sheaf of notes and laid them before him.

'Get down to business, Sammy, and then I might decide you're worth marrying. I need advice right now, not a proposal. How long before you have to get back?'

For the next hour they ate and drank and pored over facts and figures. At last they were done with the fine details, and Sammy moved on to broader strategy.

'The way I see it, Esther, we'll have no difficulty in holding our own. We give value, so we'll get customers who'll register with us. But how to expand? We've got good stocks. You used to say I over-bought, but you'll be glad of it now. But the check-trading will suffer, what with coupons and shortages. And people won't feel the same need to compete with each other, for we'll all be shabby: look at me in this *drek*. So we'll have to find new lines, new ideas, and we'll have to attract as many rationed customers as we can; more than the rest of the trade.

'That's what I want you to tackle first. Bring in our own points scheme to make sure every Lanver customer gets a square deal. It means extra work, more staff, but it'll pay off in the end. And then I want you to get in your car and tour the district. Look for farmers with something to sell; look for little market gardeners. Offer them cash to expand, as long as they sell to us. I want our shops, our stalls, to be the places where there's always something to eat. So you've had your meat and butter ration – but at Lanver you'll find cucumbers, tomatoes, good bread. Find butchers to make us brawn, sausage, pies… You've got a heroine's job ahead of you, Esther: to keep the people fed and happy. The two go together. I only wish I could be with you instead of sweeping the parade ground here, but the Government is *meshuge* and there's nothing I can do about it.'

As they put away the papers, he asked about Ruth and Naomi, and his father. 'No news from Paris?'

'No, and he frets all the time. He would go to get them out if he could, but there's no way to get there now. He sends letters, but we don't know if they reach them. Still, the old folk are sensible, Sammy: they'll see what's happening, and they know you want them to come here. They'll come.'

'I should have forced them out, Esther, when I was there. I should've drugged them, if that was the only way. Yes, they're intelligent people, but they're not – you know, worldly wise. They'd walk right up to a storm trooper and hold out the hand of friendship. *Oy vey*!'

He sighed. 'Still, that's not your problem. You take care of the home and the business for me. I'll do the worrying.'

On the platform he took her in his arms. 'You're a pearl, Esther. And you're wearing well, for a business executive. When I get leave I'm going in to see whoever's taken Gilfillan's place, and arrange for the two of us to have an equal partnership in the business.'

'That's not fair,' Esther protested, but he covered her mouth with his hand.

'It's more than fair, Miss Gulliver. I'm a sleeping partner for the foreseeable future. If I didn't have you, where would my business be? Gone! Now, here's your train. Don't talk to any strange men and – ' His voice faltered. 'Kiss them all for me, Esther. I'll be seeing you.'

Esther waved until the train rounded a curve and the station was lost to sight, and then she sat back to consider the enormity of his suggestions. Market gardening. Butchers. New lines. She blew out her lips and theatrically tipped her hat back on her head – and then, suddenly aware of the other passengers, reached for her newspaper and hid her scarlet cheeks behind its folds.

Diana had been expecting Max to telephone, but he hadn't. And there was something terrible afoot: she had sensed it in Howard's voice when he had telephoned instead, from the House. He had not said anything specific, but the tension was there in his voice.

'Come home when you can,' she said, and went straight to the kitchen to make sure there would be food for him, whenever he arrived.

Once she was sure that Max would not ring, she went up to draw a bath, showering Chypre bath salts into the water and inhaling the fragrant steam in an effort to banish gloomy thoughts. It was useless. The fact that a mighty army was assembling across the narrow strip of water that separated England from France was inescapable. If Hitler chose... Diana tried to imagine him driving down the Mall, triumphant in an open car, forcing the King to appear with him on the Palace balcony, reaching in his odious way to pat the heads of children, as she had seen him do in countless newsreels. They might be her children: Ralph or Noel – even Pamela. They could all be drafted into the Hitler Youth. Rupert would make some terrible gesture of defiance, and be shot like a dog.

Diana stepped into the water and tried to relax. If Max could not get away, there must be activity at the War Office. Someone was doing something. If Hitler invaded Britain, Roosevelt would act – surely? Perhaps she should have sent the children to the States? They could have gone with Laura, and been safe.

In the end she got out of the bath and walked the floor for a while, smoking Sobranies, stubbing them out only to light another seconds later. Outside, the street seemed strangely silent. She would have welcomed noise, any noise, even an air raid. 'You're mad,' she told herself and lit another cigarette.

When Howard came home at dawn he found her curled at the foot of their bed, one arm beneath her head, the other curled protectively around a pillow. He was tiptoeing away when she woke, sitting bolt upright suddenly and pushing her hair back from her brow. 'What's up, Howard? Is it very bad?'

He came to sit beside her, pulling her towards him much as he might have cuddled and soothed a child.

'It's pretty bad. The British Expeditionary Force is in a pocket at a place called Dunkirk, and the Germans are roasting them. Winston has ordered the navy to assemble a flotilla, an armada, really, of small ships: anything that will float, and cross the Channel to the French coast. They may manage to get some of the soldiers off, but it will need a miracle.'

9

June 1940

Dawn was streaking the sky when Anne drew back the curtains. She had been awake for an hour or more, lying still so as not to wake Frank. He had a hard shift in front of him and it had been late when he had got to bed, first prancing about with his pals in the LDV, and then devouring his books and poring over union documents. She looked back at him now, sitting on the side of the bed pulling on his thick pit socks. She had a sudden longing to go to him, draw him back into bed, and tell him she was proud of him. A wry smile touched her lips. He would likely die of shock if she did; it wasn't her usual style.

Instead, she made her way carefully downstairs this time so as not to wake the bairns. She and Frank would have half an hour together before it was time to wake Joe and Stella for work, and then the younger ones for school. Gerard was away now, preparing for the priesthood. It had made more room in the house, but she missed him still.

She opened the range and riddled it, feeling the familiar leasure as a glow appeared. In the beginning, when her mother had died and tending the range fell to her, it had gone out nearly every night and her days had begun with picking out dead coal and starting from scratch. Esther had been a child then – a bonny little thing, fair like a flower – and now she was a businesswoman with a house and car.

'You're in a good mood,' Frank said, as Anne placed black pudding, eggs and fried bread before him.

'No more than usual.' Was he suggesting she was normally a shrew? Anne contemplated retaliation, and discarded it. Let him eat in peace. She sat opposite him, her hands clasped around a mug of tea, watching the clock to chart the passing of those precious minutes of peace.

There was no newspaper to read before this shift; it came after Frank had left for work. On other mornings he read it, tucked under his plate, folding and refolding it as the pages were scanned. This was the shift in which they talked, and she liked it.

'So we've got to take Musso on as well,' she said, to get things started. Mussolini had come out openly on Hitler's side, declaring war from the balcony of the Palazzo Venezia. 'We will conquer!' he had roared, but most people in Britain (everyone Anne knew, anyway) regarded him and his army as a joke.

Frank chewed on his breakfast for a moment. 'I'd rather face an Eyetie than a Hun.' He grinned. 'If they invade I won't need a gun, I'll just say "Buggera-offa" and they'll scram.' He was obviously delighted with his mock-Italian and said it again with gusto: 'Buggera-offa.'

But no amount of joking could disguise the facts. The rescue of the army at Dunkirk was spoken of as a miracle, but the men who had been taken off were still a defeated army. Frank and Anne had sat together, she twisting a handkerchief, he head propped on his hand, as the radio recounted Churchill's words: 'We shall defend our island, whatever the cost may be. We shall fight on the beaches, we shall fight on the landing grounds, we shall fight in the fields and in the streets, we shall fight in the hills. We shall never surrender.'

Anne had cried, then, but when Frank had gone to reassure her she had thrown off his hand. 'I'm not crying because I'm scared, man. I'm crying 'cos I once called him a bastard – and now he's all we've got!'

They had the LDV, too. Anthony Eden had come on the wireless late one night with his lovely, silky voice: 'We are going to ask you to help us in a manner which I know will be welcome to thousands of you. We want large numbers of men aged seventeen to sixty-five to come forward and offer their services. The name of the new force will be the Local Defence Volunteers.'

A quarter of a million men had rushed to their local police stations within the first twenty-four hours, Frank among them. Joe was walking the floor till his birthday came and he was eligible. There had been the promise of uniforms and arms, but all that had materialized up to now was an armband marked LDV. Still, it made the night-time patrols of Frank and his mates, with their broomshanks and pick-axes, seem more organized and effective. And with paratroopers coming down dressed as priests and clergymen, you needed something. Nuns and priests and dog-collars: the skies were more crowded than the churches, if you believed everything you heard.

Frank was picking up his snap tin and reaching for his cap when Anne spoke. 'I know what I meant to tell you. Our Esther came over, she was passing, and she called in. She says she had Gallagher round at her office, the other day.'

'Old man Gallagher? What was he doing?'

'Well, you might know what he was doing: throwing his weight around, like he always did. He's in charge of all the food in this area, like you said he was going to be.'

As Frank walked towards the pit he pondered the vagaries of fate. When Gallagher had been the Brenton agent, he had begrudged the men the wages to buy the food they put into their mouths. And now he was to be the overlord of everything they ate. Nothing changed.

*

'So it can only be a matter of time,' Howard said. He was standing at the window of the office above the pit yard, looking down on the comings and goings below. 'They've evacuated the Channel Islands, and I hear they're not to be defended against Hitler. After that –'

'And when the invasion comes, what then?' Stretton said from the desk.

Howard shrugged. We have about a million and a quarter men under arms, some of them still suffering the after-effects of Dunkirk. There are about half a million LDV, armed with everything from rolling-pins to blunderbusses. Add to that a handful of Dominion troops. Hitler has a massive army, coiled like a spring and armed to the teeth. We stand alone, Norman. Completely alone – and almost defenceless.'

'We have Churchill,' Stretton said, trying to make light of it.

'Yes,' Howard said. 'If oratory can hold the Germans off, we may just make it.' He turned back into the room. 'What do the men make of the strike ban? Are there any rumblings?' Ernest Bevin had announced emergency measures to ban strikes and lock-outs. Arms factories were to work seven days a week, but workers could have one day's rest in seven. Miners and farm-workers were to stay in their jobs, and it would henceforth be a criminal offence for workers in certain industries to be taken on without government permission.

'There's the odd grumble,' Stretton said. 'The men feel the right to withdraw their labour is inviolable. But they're a good bunch. Maguire is a steadying influence.'

'He was a firebrand once,' Howard said. 'I always liked him, but I wouldn't have called him a peacemaker.'

'He's well-read,' Stretton said. 'He knows the fascist beast, and he doesn't like it. He approves of this war, sees it as a crusade, and he won't do anything to interrupt production – not if we play fair with him. And the men will follow him or take the consequences. He – well, let's say he has a nice turn of phrase.'

Howard smiled. 'You mean he has a gob on him?'

'That's exactly what I mean,' Stretton said, grinning.

'Strange to think of a Socialist banning strikes,' Howard said. 'Although not so strange, if you believe all you hear. They say Halifax wanted Churchill to sue for peace when the news came of the Expeditionary Force's defeat. Chamberlain backed him, and if it hadn't been for Clem Attlee and Arthur Greenwood, Churchill would have lost and we'd be kowtowing to Hitler.'

'Good for them,' Stretton said.

'Yes,' Howard continued. 'I underestimated Mr Attlee a year or two ago. I'm wiser now.'

They got down to business then, for Howard had to return to London that night. Plans were approved and figures agreed, and then they drank whisky and ate sandwiches made of a peculiar meat-roll. 'Foul, isn't it?' Stretton said. 'Blame the war. By the way, do you remember a man called Fox?'

'Fox?' Howard said. 'There was a Fox who used to be my chauffeur. I had to get rid of him.'

Normally Howard was open with Stretton, but he didn't feel the need to tell his manager that Fox, his former chauffeur, had been sacked for trying to blackmail Diana.

'He came in here,' Stretton said, 'and mentioned that he'd worked for you – but not how he left your employ. He's a haulier now, and doing quite well. We might do business with him, if you've no objection? Not only here, in Belgate, but at the other pits?'

'No,' Howard said. 'No, I don't mind. But I should watch him, just the same.'

They walked together to the yard, where Howard's car

waited. As he made to get in, the cage rattled to the surface and he straightened up again.

'I'll just have a word,' he said to Stretton, and the manager walked beside him towards the group who had emerged from the cage.

'You'll be glad that's over,' Howard said, nodding towards the shaft. There was a murmur of agreement, but he could see the men were uneasy in his presence, shuffling their feet and transferring their snap tins from one arm to another. He wished he knew how to break the ice: Stretton could do it, but today he was holding back, leaving the field clear for Howard.

Howard tried again, directing his words to Frank Maguire, who was in the centre of the group.

'We hope to have the baths completed soon; that should make things easier. There are one or two problems over materials, I'm afraid – the war effort must have priority – but they should be overcome before too long.' The men nodded and shuffled, but no one glowed with gratitude. Not that that was what Howard wanted, but some response would have been nice.

He was about to turn away when Maguire came to his rescue. 'We'll know who to blame if the baths are held up then, Mr Brenton. That's something else we'll owe Adolf.'

There was a ripple of laughter and an easing of tension.

'True,' Howard said. 'We'll make him pay for any delay. How do you think the war is going?'

'Bloody badly,' a wag said from the edge of the group, but Maguire was more constructive.

'We only know what we read in the papers. You'll likely know more than us.'

'I don't know about that,' Howard said. We talk about little else in the House of Commons, but they don't tell even MPs everything. It wouldn't do. But I do know the coalition is working well, and that must be to the good.'

'You've got good men in Attlee and Greenwood,' Maguire said.

'And Ernie Bevin. He'll sort things out,' said another voice.

That's right,' Maguire said, 'he'll be good for the likes of us.'

Again the voice from the back: 'And when the war's over we'll own this lot.'

It was meant to be provocative, and the faces around Howard tensed, waiting to see his response. He smiled.

'Let's win the bloody thing first, then we'll decide who gets what.'

Where the words came from Howard didn't know, but they went down well. He could see that from Maguire's expression – a narrowing of the eyes in appreciation, a twitch of the lips.

'You're right there, Mr Brenton,' he said. 'You make the right decisions in London, and we'll take care of this place.'

It was a polite and patriotic remark, but there was a hidden meaning, too, and both men knew it.

He's staking his claim, Howard thought, and inclined his head in acknowledgement as the men filed away.

In May, the month before, Sammy had lain on his narrow bed, hands locked behind his head, imagining the chestnuts bursting into leaf on the Paris boulevards. He had read somewhere that the tune of the moment was the haunting *'J'attendrai'* – 'I will wait for you.' Were they waiting for him, his grandparents, in the house on Avenue Collaigne, with its *mezuzah* on every doorpost and his grandfather's study awash with works of scholarship? And then the papers were full of names forgotten since the last war: Sedan, Ypres, Verdun. The British were driven into the sea at Dunkirk, and still Sammy waited. When Marshal Pétain, the hero of Verdun, took over the government, Sammy hoped... and saw his hopes end in betrayal as Pétain threw in his lot with the Germans.

How had this happened? France had had the Maginot Line, a defensive wonder of the military world. It had had a superb army, or so it had thought. And now the Germans were almost at the gates of Paris. On the Left Bank the bookstalls would be trading; there would be artists painting on the quais, the theatres would be filled... or had everyone taken flight?

It was 14 June when Sammy heard a soft, melodious voice on the radio, a woman's voice speaking in French with an English accent. 'I, who have always loved France deeply, now share with you your suffering.'

'It's the Queen,' someone said. 'She's talking to the Frogs.'

'What's she saying?' someone asked. 'It's double-Dutch to me.'

'Shut up and I'll translate,' Sammy said, and began to echo her words.

'France is now defending with heroism and courage not only her own land but the lands and liberty of the whole world... a nation defended by such men, loved by such women, sooner or later is bound to conquer.'

'Don't you believe it,' a wag said, and was instantly hushed. The Queen was talking of her visits to wounded French soldiers: 'All of them, even the most gravely wounded, replied with one voice "*ça va*". I do believe with all my heart that when these dark days are gone, the time will come when our two nations will be able to say with one voice once more "*ça va*".'

'By gum, she's a good 'un,' a man said, but Sammy had turned away.

God save France, he thought.

The next day the letter came from Marc Luchaire in Paris. *They are gone, Samuel. I went to Avenue Collaigne today, to find it empty. I asked on the street, but no one knew how or when they went.*

The letter had come via Spain, so it was seven days old. Sammy went in search of a telephone.

In Sunderland Esther was scalding tea. 'Come and have breakfast,' she called to Lansky. 'The girls are already down.'

Light from the window fell across Emmanuel's face as he entered the room, and Esther shivered. Each day it seemed he aged a month; he was turning into an old man before her eyes. There had been no news of his parents-in-law, only tales of refugees running hither and thither, coupled with the horror stories of Dunkirk, of ambulance trains bombed, and the wounded being machine-gunned from the air.

In the hall the telephone rang. 'I'll get it,' Esther said. Sammy was on the other end of the line, and she knew at once that it was bad news.

'I've heard from a friend,' he said. 'Someone I know in Paris, a journalist. I asked him to keep an eye on the grandparents. He says they've left Paris: packed and gone.'

'Are they coming here?' Esther asked, mentally allocating rooms as she spoke.

'Don't be foolish, Esther. France is in turmoil. God knows where they'll wind up.'

'But they *might* get out?' She had to have some hope to offer Emmanuel.

'Tell him that,' Sammy said, reading her thoughts. 'Tell him anything that helps.'

As Esther went back into the dining-room her legs threatened to fail her.

'That was Sammy,' she said, and saw Emmanuel's head come up, ready for the blow. 'He's had news from Paris. His grandparents have left. They must be making for neutral territory: Spain, perhaps, or Switzerland.'

'Why aren't they coming here?' Lansky said, his

mouth above the greying beard beginning to tremble.

'They might be coming,' she said. 'All Sammy knows is that they've gone out of Paris, making for safety.' She tried to keep her voice cheerful because the two girls looked ready to cry. 'They can't come straight here; the ports are choked, and I'm not even sure you can get out there. The army is in control, and they may not allow civilian raffic. But if they get into Spain, they'll be safe, and we can arrange for them to come here. They've got money. Sammy will send more if that's what it takes…'

The old Jew threw up his hands. 'Money? What's money? They have money, I have money…'He shook his head. 'It's not a magic wand, Esther.'

'It helps,' she said stoutly. 'Don't tell me it doesn't. They'll be all right, they'll get out. All we have to do is be patient.'

Naomi was crying, now, and Esther went to hug her. 'It's going to be all right,' she said again. 'You'll see.'

But the girl lifted her tear-stained face and her eyes were scornful. 'It won't be all right,' she said. 'The Germans will come here, across the sea, and take people away like they did in Germany. No one can stop them. They'll kill us all.'

'No, they won't,' Esther said. 'Because Mr Churchill won't let them!'

Diana trailed a hand in the water, seeing the ripples spread and widen. 'It's heaven here, isn't it?' she said.

Beside her on the bank of the stream, Max grunted assent. He was stretched out on the grass, his uniform shirt pen at the neck, a straw hat borrowed from Pamela tipped over his face. Diana looked downstream, where willows trailed on the water and the children were pottering about, the girls with their dresses tucked into their knickers, the boys with the legs of their short trousers rolled higher.

In the distance the myriad chimneys of Valesworth

House showed above the treetops. Birds wheeled in the blue sky. On the surface of the water dragonflies dipped and zoomed. There was not a single sign of war: no balloons, no sandbags, no gas masks, no anxious faces such as she saw every day now in London. Elsewhere, open spaces were strewn with old cars, buses, scaffolding, even iron bedsteads: anything to stop gliders from landing. Signposts were gone and place-names painted out. Churchbells would only be rung to signal invasion. But here all was peace.

'What time do we have to leave?' Max tipped back the hat and looked at her.

Diana turned on her side, and then over on to her stomach, propping her chin on her arms.

'When I like. Howard won't be back from Durham before morning. He's dining with one or two constituency bigwigs tonight, after he's seen the Gorgon. He's catching an early train.'

'How is his mother?' Max said idly. 'Hasn't she died yet?'

'The Gorgon'll never die,' Diana said firmly. 'If there's any truth in the saying that the good die young, that woman is indestructible.'

'She is pretty awful, from what I remember,' Max said. 'At your wedding, dressed up like the old Q.M. What a hoot!'

Inside Diana unease stirred. Charlotte Brenton had been a cold and disapproving mother-in-law; and now she had shut herself away, never seeming to care about her son or her grandchildren. But she was Howard's mother. To make fun of her with Max would be disloyal.

'She's OK, I suppose. A bit stuffy, but that's not her fault. She's the Q.M.'s generation after all, and that must be a terrible millstone to have around one's neck. Anyway, don't let's talk about her; let's decide what we're going to do before tea. I think we should go back to London then.'

She stood up and began to discard her shoes and stockings. 'I'm going to play with the children now. Roll up your trousers and come along. You're getting lazy in your old age.'

A few moments later they were laughing and splashing in the water as though they hadn't ever to return to a London in the grip of fear.

The light was beginning to fade as their car came near to the capital, and with the approach of dusk Diana felt her spirits sink. *How long will this go on?* she thought. Not seeing the children except for snatched days. Glimpsing Howard as he came and went. Being with Max, who half the time was sunk in misery because he didn't know when, if ever, he would see his family again. She felt her eyes prick and reached for a handkerchief to blow her nose.

It wouldn't be so bad if she had a job to do, like Max and Howard. She had enrolled as an ambulance-driver and at first that had seemed the answer. But the long-awaited aerial onslaught on London had not materialized, except for odd uneventful air raids, and now her initial training was over she found the whole thing boring. She had wanted a holiday this summer with Howard and the children, but there was no foreseeable chance of that. A small sob escaped her, and she fished for her handkerchief gain.

'What's up?' Max said sympathetically, glancing sideways. 'Missing *les enfants*?'

'A bit,' Diana said, ashamed to admit how she had hated leaving her children when Max was never lucky enough to see his. 'Pamela was so sweet when we said goodbye.'

'Yes,' he said, 'she's a darling.' Suddenly he slowed the car and pulled onto the grass verge. 'Don't cry. Here, have a decent hanky. Blow your nose like a good girl, and tell me where you'd like to eat tonight; I can't let you go home like this. We could try the Embassy – not the Savoy, it's full of foreigners. Now, blow again. That's it. And we'll go to the theatre tomorrow: that'll cheer you up. Celia Johnson in *Rebecca*? Blow once more. Better?'

Afterwards Diana could not quite remember who had reached for whom. But she could remember how comforting it was to have a man's arms around her, holding her close in a very nice and gentle way, murmuring comforting things against her hair. Above all, making no demands. *He's changed*, she thought, remembering the young man whose only idea had once been to get her into bed. They had all changed, honed by life into the semblance of quite decent human beings.

10

September 1940

London had long awaited the promised onslaught from the air. There were some fierce raids, but they mostly targeted the southern suburban fringes where the airfields such as Biggin Hill and Kenley were situated. The city's heart remained virtually untouched. And then, as August drew to a close, the war of the capitals began.

German Heinkel 111s bombed the city on the night of 24 August. Churchill ordered immediate retaliation, and eighty-one British bombers attacked Berlin. Before the first week of September was out, Hitler had unleashed aerial terror on Britain's cities. On 7 September, 350 bombers pounded the London docks by day and 247 by night. Two thousand Londoners were dead or injured, and an invasion alert was sent out from GHQ Home Forces.

In her heart of hearts, Diana had longed to see action, but the carnage all around sickened her. She had never seen violent death before, never seen the hands of small children protruding from rubble, or pregnant women carried dead from their blasted homes. She drove her ambulance through streets where whole buildings had toppled, blocking the roads, and huge London buses had been thrown aside like toys.

She saw strain on other people's faces, not realizing it was mirrored in her own until Howard demanded she take a night off. 'You've been on duty for eight days,' he said. 'And besides, the tide has turned.' Spitfires and Hurricanes swarmed in the skies over London, the mere sight of the fighters they had been told did not exist demoralizing some German pilots, who jettisoned their bombs and turned for home.

They might not have been so over-awed if they had known the true state of the RAF. Casualty rates now showed that a pilot's expectation of life was fewer than ninety flying hours, and so many pilots were suffering battle-fatigue that few would have passed a stringent medical. Some of them landed their planes, taxied in, and slumped in their cockpits, fast asleep. Others could barely summon up the strength to complete their logbooks.

Howard sat behind Churchill in the House as he paid tribute to the RAF. The phrase 'Never in the field of human conflict was so much owed by so many to so few' was on everyone's lips for days afterwards, but it was another sentence from the speech that stayed with Howard. Churchill spoke of the war from the air involving everyone – not only soldiers, but the entire population: men, women and children. 'Our people are united and resolved, as they have never been before.' Churchill was speaking the truth. It showed every day in the faces of Londoners as they picked over the rubble of their homes or chalked messages on the ruins of their schools and churches: 'Hit the Hun and hit him hard' was one; 'Business as usual' another.

Howard went to the scene of one bomb blast, a street he had known well. Now there was no shape to it. The road, the gardens, the very foundations of the houses had disappeared in a heap of stone and wood and pathetic battered artefacts. A child's rag book fluttered from a pile of rubble; a doll stared up at him from sightless eyes. He walked along, trying to remember where the house with the blue door had been, or the one with the window-boxes trailing fern. They were all gone. And the survivors calmly went about the business of burying their dead and securing what remained of their possessions from looters.

He came upon a woman squatting in the gutter chipping old mortar from bricks with a kitchen knife. She saw him looking at her and grinned. 'Do for my old wash-house, won't it? Buggers blew a hole in it yesterday.'

Howard went straight home and found Diana, tired and worn, blue circles beneath her eyes after a night on duty, but with the same indomitable gleam in her eye. 'You're enjoying this,' he teased her, and would have taken her in his arms if he had not known where duty lay.

In June he had listened in the House as Churchill spoke of what was to come. 'The whole fury and might of the enemy must very soon be turned on us. Hitler knows he will have to break us in this island or lose the war. If we can stand up to him, all Europe may be free and the life of the world may move forward into broad, sunlit uplands...'

All in all, it hadn't been as bad as it might have been – at least not yet. A year ago official estimates had been for 600,000 civilian dead and one and a quarter million wounded in the first two months of war. That horror had not been realized, although thousands had died.

Howard followed Diana upstairs to tell her he would take a few days off soon, no matter what the situation, to take her to Valesworth to see the children. But first he must go north to check on Belgate and see to his mother. When he reached their bedroom he found Diana lying on the bed, still in her uniform and boots, fast asleep. He covered her gently with the coverlet and drew the curtains cautiously, so that the rings did not rattle along the curtain pole. He need not have bothered. She was too tired to be woken by anything, not even the kiss he planted upon her mouth.

While Howard went north Diana followed his advice: she slept for thirteen hours, and woke to run a bath, enjoying the scented water lapping against her limbs, letting the warmth seep into her bones. Outside the bathroom window she could hear the traffic, and somewhere, far off in the house, the muted laughter of the maid. They had lost the old servants, one by one, as the war made its demands. Soon the new girls would go, too, to join the services or to work in munitions factories.

Three letters were waiting on the breakfast table. The first, from Rupert, was full of aircraft news and pleas to be allowed to leave school and 'do something useful'. If Howard still cherished the dream of his son going on to Oxford, he would have to think again. The second letter was an invitation to a cocktail party in aid of the Free French, and the third was from Lee, a fat missive on blue paper, written over a period of days.

I have just heard from Elspeth Monroe, who was with me at the Academie. Like me, she can't get over Paris falling. Those pictures of the loathsome Schicklgruber in the Champs-Élysées stick in my mind and won't be dislodged. I think of the Avenue Octave Gérard and all the fun we had at the Academie. I learned about life there – or thought I did, and now some ghastly jack-booted SS man is probably sleeping in my bed. I really feel quite miserable about the whole thing, the air raids and being trapped here at Valesworth, and shortages, and everything. Henry says it won't go on for ever, but then I think of the last war and get the vapours. We've missed a whole Season, and nothing to look forward to the rest of the year. We can't even have a bonfire night because of their beastly regulations. I'm ashamed when I think how much worse it is for others, especially poor Max, who hasn't seen Laura or the children for months – how does he bear it? I'm so glad he has you and Howard...

Diana put down the letter, trying to remember the last

time Howard had been included in her meetings with Max. If only things weren't such a jumble. Howard had gone north, trying to persuade his mother to move to safety and Rupert to agree to the horses leaving the Scar. *We ought to be together more*, she thought. She drank another cup of tea, wishing she could have had an egg in spite of the shortage, and then went to the study to reply to Lee in the hope that she could cheer her up.

Of course it won't last forever [she wrote]. *Not now that I am part of the war effort. You should see me, Lee. I cut a martial figure in my navy-blue all-in-one. I also have a shoulder bag, brown leather and so useful. It takes my gas mask (you are court-martialled if you forget that), the last of my precious Chanel, a lipstick, a comb and mirror, and spare knickers in case I don't get home to change. What more could a girl want? If Herr Hitler knew how highly trained I am now, he'd probably capitulate.*

I hope you remember that if it weren't for you having the children, I couldn't do anything. The ancestral home is barred to me, so I'd be stuck in some country vicarage somewhere, living on seed cake and barley water. You've saved me from a fate worse than death, and deserve a medal, and I shall mention it to the King when I see him. Talking of which, the latest gossip about the Windsors is that the Nazis tried to pressure them into a coup against King George. Apparently von Ribbentrop persuaded the Portuguese to contact the Duke, who told them Churchill was a warmonger. And when you think how Winston defended the man! But when it came to it, the Windsors wouldn't come out against the King. They've gone off somewhere on a liner – the United States probably – and good riddance.

When it was done she put a stamp on it and left it on the hall table ready for the maid to take to the post.

Esther had wasted no time in putting Sammy's instructions into practice. She spent two fruitless days driving round in search of extra suppliers before she came across a market garden with several dilapidated glasshouses. By the end of the week she had arranged a loan for the proprietor in return for his promise to supply her with cucumbers, tomatoes and fresh fruits in season. She was well-pleased with the deal; cucumbers and lettuces would never be a substitute for red meat, but they would supplement the rations and show people that Lanver Products really cared for their customers. She managed to buy a large consignment of canned pineapple, too: 500 cases, from someone who needed ready money quickly. She divided them among the shops and stalls, with instructions to give regular customers priority. On her way back from her visit to Sammy she had been struck by another thought: if the war dragged on, people would try to produce their own food. She drove to a hardware wholesaler and bought up his stock of garden tools. Sammy wasn't the only one who could anticipate demand.

She was seated in her office one day, sipping tea from a mug and contemplating her stock lists, when a girl came up from the floor below to tell her that a Mr Gallagher had arrived.

'Show him up,' Esther said, and checked her hair and the set of her collar in the looking-glass. The man who entered the office was grey-haired and thin-faced, with an icy-cold handshake.

'This is just a courtesy visit,' Gallagher said, smiling. 'An opportunity for us to get to know one another, for me to acquaint myself with your business.'

His questions were searching, his eyes never still, flitting here, there and everywhere.

I don't like him, Esther thought at last, as she watched him go down the steps to the office floor. *And I don't think I ever will, not if the war lasts for twenty years.*

She couldn't take her troubles to Lansky, so it was a relief when Sammy came home on a forty-eight-hour pass. His first morning home they sat round the breakfast table, luxuriating in being together. Tales of Ruth and Naomi's progress were told for Sammy's approval, and he was suitably impressed.

'What will you do, Ruth, when you're finished with school?' he asked. 'You can do whatever you want to do. When this war is over they will need learning, from women as well as men.'

Ruth looked up at him. 'I want to be a doctor of medicine.'

'A doctor,' old Lansky said, pushing aside his plate to lean towards her. 'You will need to study for many years.'

Ruth nodded, and he moved nearer still. 'You can go to a university: the best.'

'Come on, Esther,' Sammy said. 'We are traders, you and I. Let's leave the scholars to their discussions.' He looked at Naomi. 'Are you a scholar or a trader, little one?'

She smiled at him, and went to link her arm in his.

'Can she come with us?' he asked Esther.

'Yes,' Esther said. 'We'll be back before lunch. Go and get ready.'

Naomi ran off, and Sammy got up from the table.

'Do you want to come with us, too, Ruth?' Esther asked, but seeing the girl's reluctance: 'Stay here, if you like. We're only going to the market garden.' They left Emmanuel and Ruth deep in conversation, and the three of them went out to the car.

Sammy handed Naomi into the back seat and sat down beside Esther, in the front. 'Right, then,' he said. 'Now, take me to see all these vegetables of yours that are going to save my business from ruin.' His voice changed suddenly and he sighed. 'It won't last, Esther. As things get tighter they'll bring in restrictions for everything, even cucumbers and tomatoes. Still, when that time comes, we'll think of something else. Mushroom-growing, for instance – in the warehouse cellar. You can sit on them like a broody hen when the air raids come. A pity to be wasting time.'

'Do you think there will be bad air raids soon?' Esther asked, lowering her voice from the girl in the back seat.

'Oh yes,' Sammy said, and now his tone was entirely serious. 'Bad raids will come.'

And I won't know whether or not my child survives them, Esther thought, but could not voice her fears aloud.

'I honestly think it's for the best, old chap.' In the sunlight the gelding's chestnut flanks gleamed. It pawed gently at the ground and snorted occasionally, as though to tell them to get the talking over and ride out. Rupert reached to pat the horse's neck.

'I'll miss Blaze, father, when I come here. I know it's not often now, but at least I know he's here, waiting.' It was odd, Howard thought, as he listened to Rupert – it was odd how your children grew up almost by stealth. He had always been 'papa'; now he was 'father', and his son was a man.

'I don't think it's safe here for any of the horses now, Rupert. The raids are intensifying; you can see that for yourself. One stock of bombs aimed at the pit might fall on the Scar. I've seen some terrible sights. Horses weren't made for aerial war.' He thought suddenly of France, all those years ago: horses screaming in terror as they raced through the battlefield, men dying, the bloated corpses of animals on rain-drenched fields.

'If you really care for these beasts, you'll let them go to

Swaledale. It's not forever; you can probably get over there quite often. And when all this is over and you're home again...' Rupert was nodding now, seeing the sense of it.

'You're right. Besides, I won't be home much, and the others are all at Valesworth for the duration. Their ponies are just going to seed up here.' He leaned his head against the horse's neck in a gesture of affection. 'I'll miss you, old thing' he said. 'Still, one last ride...'

Howard watched horse and rider canter off, and then went to look for his car. He had a lot to do before he returned to London.

He drove first to see his mother at the dark, forbidding house that had been his boyhood home. He had been happy there as a child – or he thought he had been happy. He remembered laughter and toys and romps with the servants. There had been one called Sally who had seemed to spend all day pushing him high in his swing: up and up into the air, till his stomach heaved and he cried out half in terror and half in pleasure. And another called Dobbs, who used to tickle him until he had no breath with which to beg for mercy.

He drew up at the door and got out of the car, noticing that the house needed painting, that the net curtains shrouding the windows were not the brilliant white of memory, that the whole place had a hang-dog air about it now that his mother lived there alone and was less and less willing to receive visitors.

He went through the hall, seeing motes of dust swimming in shafts of sunlight, smelling stale air and other, indefinable, unpleasant odours.

'Mother: how are you?'

Charlotte Brenton inclined her cheek, but seemed to recoil from Howard's kiss.

'Have you thought any more about leaving Sunderland, for a while at least?' Charlotte hardly seemed to hear him. He talked on and on, getting little or no response, telling her of the children, of Diana and her ambulance, of the doings of the House of Commons. And then his mother's face brightened as the door opened and Gallagher entered the room, without knocking as though it were his right.

'Brenton. Strange to see you here.' Gallagher spoke like the man of the house greeting a not particularly welcome visitor, and Howard noticed that he had dropped the courtesy of 'Mr'.

'Gallagher. Not so strange to see me, surely? This is my home.'

'*Was* your home, Howard.' His mother was suddenly animated. 'You left here a long time ago.'

It was a relief to be out of the gloomy house, away from his mother's icy disapproval and the agent's sneer. And to think he had almost suggested that Rupert accompany him. Well, he had tried to persuade his mother to evacuate; if she wouldn't move, she would have to accept the attendant risk. Howard tried to remember the time when there had been love between them, when he had been her ally, a buffer between her and his father. But it was too long ago. She seemed like a stranger now.

He went from house to house in Belgate, then, hearing of sons dead in the war or prisoners in Germany. But although there were tears sometimes, and anguish always, there was also pride and defiance and Churchill's words quoted again and again.

As Howard tipped his hat and closed each garden gate he wondered what they would make of the story current in London: that after his call to fight on the beaches, streets and hills, Churchill had turned to an aide and said: 'What with? Beer bottles, I suppose. They're all we've got.'

But Lord Beaverbrook was producing planes now, in an endless stream, armed as he was with carte blanche to commandeer whatever he needed. And everyone, from the highest to the lowest in the land, was puffing his or her weight, working twelve-hour shifts in some cases, with absenteeism a thing of the past. J. B. Priestley was broadcasting now on Sunday nights after the nine o'clock news, his gravelly, north-country voice oddly comforting even when his words were sombre. But Howard had particularly enjoyed a verse of A. P. Herbert's, printed in a popular newspaper and addressed to Hitler:

Napoleon tried. The Dutch were on the way. A Norman did it, and a Dane or two. Some sailor-king may follow one fine day. But not, I think, a low land-rat like you.

There was one last call he had to make. Stretton had obtained Mary Quinnell's address for him, and Howard had been surprised to find she lived in Sunderland now. When last they'd heard from her she'd been happily settled in Durham. He thought of her on her wedding day, serene in the Belgate church, Patrick at her side. He was a surgeon at the War Emergency Unit now, according to Stretton, and doing yeoman service there.

Howard drew up at the neat house, and got out of the car. He could see Mary in the doorway, her child in her arms, talking to another woman, who, though her back was turned to him, was familiar just the same.

'Mr Howard.' Mary's face lit up at the sight of him. Howard doffed his hat.

'Hello, Mary. And so this is Master Quinnell. What a splendid chap he is!'

The other woman was also smiling from him to the baby, as Howard turned to look at her. For a moment, he didn't recognize her. Then the blue eyes and the curve of her delighted smile reminded him: 'It's Esther, isn't it? Esther Gulliver?'

'Yes, Mr How – Mr Brenton.'

Esther had come to the Scar as a maid for Diana, ten – no, nearly twenty – years ago, a child with fair hair plaited round her head. And now she was a smart woman: chic, even, in her green swagger coat, and a little hat tilted forward over her eyes. At Mary's wedding he had thought her poised and pretty; now she looked almost glamorous.

'This is Esther's house, Mr Brenton,' Mary was saying, gesturing behind her. 'We're renting it, Pat and I, while the war's on. You are coming in, aren't you? Esther, you'll stay for another cup of tea, too?'

But Esther was drawing soft leather gloves over her still- ringless hands.

'Thank you, Mary, but I must get on. My business partner's on leave at the moment, and time's precious.'

She went off down the path, and Howard stood watching her as she opened the car door and waved goodbye. He had been fond of her as a girl, and so had Diana – until it all went wrong, through no fault of Esther's.

As Mary bustled round making tea, he played with the child, handing him toys and making appropriate noises; but all the while he was remembering Diana, the beautiful girl of nineteen he had brought to the Scar, and Mary's first husband lying dead in front of the half-built house, and little Esther Gulliver, Diana's accomplice in those early days when they had been allies as much as mistress and servant.

'It's a very nice house Esther has,' he said, when Mary sat down with the tea.

'Esther's done well for herself, Mr Brenton. She went into service in Sunderland when she left the Scar, and met her business partner there.'

Howard wondered, as Mary spoke, whether she knew the circumstances in which Esther had left his employ. The two were close friends, obviously; perhaps something had been said? But there was something about Esther, had always been, that suggested she would keep her own counsel. He gave his attention to Mary's words once more.

'They've got a good business now, and she's keeping it

going for him while he's away in the army. Lanver Products, they call it, the "Lan" from Lansky and the "ver" from Gulliver. She's moved in with Mr Lansky while Sammy's away, because there's two refugees there to be looked after, poor things. Young German girls – although you wouldn't think they were German citizens, the way the Nazis treated them.'

Howard had heard that Lansky had taken in two youngsters. So Esther was mothering them. He must remember to tell that to Diana.

'It's a terrible war, this,' Mary said, suddenly morose.

'It is. I hear Patrick is working at the Emergency Hospital. I hope he's well and happy?'

'It's brought back memories, Mr Brenton. He cried at first – to himself, at night, but I knew. Now, though, I think he's pleased they're able to help. The boys don't die, the most of them – not if he gets a chance at them, he says. In the last war it was just senseless killing: men lying dying in the mud. But this time they're getting the wounded out. He's got ever so many from Dunkirk, and he says they'll be all right in the long run.'

'That's good,' Howard said. 'Very good to hear. It's about the war that I came, really. I wanted to see you anyway, and this little chap –', he looked at the baby, 'so that I can tell Diana you're well. She's an ambulance driver now, and very taken up with it. But I did have another reason.' He paused, then said gently: 'The gate at the Scar.'

He saw Mary's face cloud at the memory. 'It's a beautiful artefact; your husband made a splendid job of it. But they're asking us to give railings and gates – anything made of iron.'

He waited, watching her face. Would she be stricken at the thought of her dead husband's handiwork reduced to molten metal? Or, like him, would she be relieved to be rid of the grim reminder of tragedy? For it was that gate that had fallen on her husband while the house was being built, and had crushed the life out of him. Howard had never driven through the gates with their monogrammed HB without remembering the day the blacksmith's body had lain on the ground, with the great iron grille on top of him, and blood oozing from the dead mouth.

Mary looked away for a moment, then she reached to draw her son to her knee, as though for comfort. 'I think it should go, Mr Brenton – if it's going to help. Stephen had a son and a daughter; he'd want this war over for their sakes.'

Howard nodded.

'I thought you'd say that, but I felt I must ask. Now, tell me about John and Catherine.'

'Catherine's well on in her nursing now… and John's a proper countryman; you'd think he'd been bred to it. I'll show you some photos of them by and by, when you've had your tea.'

Frank had put boards down in the shelter to make a floor, and Anne had covered them with an old clippy mat, but still there was the smell of oozing damp about the place, and when they lifted the children into the bunks and bedded them down for the night, the bedding felt damp to the touch. 'Pneumonia'll get us if the Germans don't,' Anne declared. They had taken to the shelter for three nights running, although there had been bombing on only one of those nights, emerging stiff and blinking into the garden to begin the business of the day. 'The bairns'll fall behind at school,' Anne said darkly, as though the raids were Frank's fault. 'And as for me, I could feel the cold striking through. And this is still summer.'

The first air raid had come almost as a relief. They had dreaded this thing for so long; now it had come, and they were still alive! They had laughed and joked when it was over, saying, in effect: 'Is that all it was? We can stand that!' But by the third night euphoria was dwindling. The children stopped being wide-eyed with wonder and became querulous; the next-door neighbours, who were sharing the shelter, began to make territorial demands, taking the best bunks, bringing their German shepherd dog into the shelter with them, and falling over themselves to get in first when the siren went.

'You'll have to put up with it,' Frank said, when Anne complained. But he was off to man his road-block as soon as the air raid started – unless he was down the pit – and Anne was quick to point this out. More than a million men were in the LDV now; most of them older, veterans of the last war, even a few generals among them. They still had no uniforms, no ranks, and precious few weapons, but they were learning to make Molotov cocktails: bottles of petrol that could be flung like fire-bombs. Churchill was now urging Eden to call them the Home Guard.

'Do you think we did right, keeping the bairns here in Sunderland with us?' Anne asked, for the hundredth time.

'I think so,' Frank said equably. One good thing had come out of the mounting crisis, he reflected: Anne had realized that she had other children besides Joe.

'It's a worry feeding them sometimes,' she said ruefully. And suddenly her eyes gleamed. 'What we need is hens,' she said. 'This year's pullets: six should do. Then if you put your back into the vegetables, we should be all right.'

'What about a pig or two?' Frank said. It was meant as sarcasm but Anne knitted her brow before dismissing the idea.

'No. Smelly things. Besides, they'd come along and commandeer them, like as not. But hens... if we do well with them, we can swop eggs for other things.' She looked at Frank darkly. 'I hope you're not going to be difficult?'

'Not me. But how will you fit in looking after hens with the bairns and the house and your sewing?'

Last night Anne had made thirty little chintz bags. Mary

had brought the material from the WVS, and asked Anne to turn it into 'hospital supplies'. 'They're for the wounded,' Mary had said. 'To hold the things out of their pockets till they're better again.' Frank had looked at Anne and seen she was thinking the same thing as he was, that for the ones who didn't 'get better' the bags and their pathetic contents could be sent to relatives. He had gone outside and dug the garden till his back threatened to break. Never mind the 'dig for victory' they were always on about; it was 'dig for sanity', more like.

Anne was pleased at the thought of having her own fresh eggs, so pleased that she gave Frank faggots in gravy with chips for his dinner, followed by a jam sponge drowned in custard. 'Make it last,' she said as he gobbled it down. 'There's half the week's rations in there.'

A singer on the radio was belting out the song that was on everyone's lips now: 'We'll meet again, don't know where, don't know when, but I know we'll meet again some sunny day.' Frank belched gently on the last of the custard. He didn't often get a meal like that nowadays, good manager though Anne was.

He watched her as she sat at the machine, pinning a piece of flannelette in the middle of a worn blanket and quilting it, fiddling with her machine, the dreamy look on her face showing she was still thinking of a garden full of hens, all laying like the clappers. It would be God help the bloody birds if they didn't. All the same, she was still a nice-looking woman. Frank smiled foolishly, remembering her in her father's shop with a waist he could get his hands round, and a head of hair like a raven's wing. It was funny but he loved her more now that she had 'gone off' a bit, worn down by hard times, and mothering a pack of bairns, and a war.

He went to the table and rested his hand lightly on the nape of her neck. For a wonder, she did not toss her head impatiently to throw it off. He bent to kiss the crown of her head, and still she stayed put. He cleared his throat and moved his hand to cover her breast. She had stopped sewing now, her hands still among the fabric. 'Come upstairs, pet,' he said, never dreaming she would, with the sun high in the heavens. But, wonder of wonders, she was getting to her feet, her eyes averted, and leading the way to the stairs.

She drew the curtains across the bedroom window and then began to shed her clothes slowly, laying them across the post at the foot of the bed. He was quicker, for he was less encumbered; and he stood there, waiting, shaking like a young lad while she went on unclothing herself. She was in a funny mood, he could see it in her face. Then she let the last garment fall and held out her arms to him.

It was twenty years since that first time. Now the tight, up-tilting breasts were full and sagging, her waist and hips almost merged, but Frank felt a welling-up of love in him that the boy he had once been could not even have imagined.

'I want you,' he said as they came together, and he felt her shake gently with laughter.

'I can tell that,' she said, and then her hands were on him, pleasuring him, and he could feel foolish and unexpected tears pricking his eyes. And all of this at one o'clock in the afternoon!

Rupert had ridden the length and breadth of Brenton land. Now he turned for home, half sorrowful that his horse was going away, half excited at the thought of adult life opening up in front of him. He was a man now, and must put away childish things. He was getting ready to spur the horse into a last gallop when he saw a flash of red in a corner of the field. It looked like a body lying on the ground. Rupert goaded his mount instead to speed in that direction.

But it was not a body he found in the shelter of a corn stook: at least, not a lifeless one. It was Stella Maguire, stretched out in the sun, her peasant blouse pulled down from her shoulders, her red dirndl skirt above her knees. She was taking a day off from her factory job which she now found unutterably boring. Her father would never allow her to stay at home, therefore she had left that morning as though to catch the bus and had made for open country to lie in the sun.

She would have preferred to go into Sunderland and window-shop, but the last time she had tried that she had turned the corner of an arcade and come face to face with her mother, and the resulting row had gone on for days.

So she had spent the day lazing in the sun, picking flowers from the hedgerows, eating the pie and cheese and bread she had been given for snap, and dreaming dreams, the latest of which concerned Laurence Olivier as Heathcliff to her Catherine. She opened her eyes to see young Brenton a full seven feet above her on his horse, and it gave her a shock.

'What the hell are you doing, sneaking up on me like that?'

It was an unfair remark and Rupert was stung. 'What are you doing lying about in a field?' he said haughtily, trying not to notice that one of her breasts was almost exposed and there were wilting ox-eye daisies in her hair.

'I hurt my leg,' Stella said, to enlist his sympathy. 'I hurt my leg on the stile, and so I sat down. That's allowed, I suppose?' She stood up and began to put her clothing to rights, making sure each movement showed her body.

Rupert hesitated and then dismounted and drew the reins forward over the horse's head.

'I'm sorry,' he said stiffly. 'I didn't mean to be rude. I just saw you lying there and thought the worst. You could have been injured...'

'Well, now you know I'm not,' Stella said, pulling up her skirt and running a hand up and down her shin and then over her smooth, dimpled knee. 'Ouch,' she said, pretending to find a sore spot.

'Look,' Rupert said, 'do you think you could mount my

horse if I help? Then I can walk you home. Or I can go and get someone to come and collect you, if that would be better?'

Stella made a rapid calculation. If he went for help, some-one else would come with a car and he would go off, duty done. She would be better off accepting the lift, although the horse, viewed from below, looked like a shivering, sweating mountain. 'I'll go on the horse,' she said, trying to sound nonchalant. 'You'll have to get me up there, though.'

He moved over to the fence and tethered the animal, then he came back to where Stella was standing, awkwardly, on one leg. 'Put your arms round my neck,' he said, blushing slightly when she swayed against him and twined thin arms around him. There was a strange smell about her, sweaty but not unpleasant: it made Rupert think of warm summer days and butter melting in the sun. She was light enough for him to lift her and carry her to the fence.

'Put your good foot in the stirrup and hold on to the saddle,' he said, 'and then I'll hoist you up.' She had black patent shoes on with pointed toes and a silver buckle. He knew instinctively that they were cheap, and the thought provoked a strange feeling within him: pity, and a desire to protect her. 'There now,' he said, 'up you go!'

Stella smiled when she was upright in the saddle, putting one hand to the pommel and rearranging her skirt with the other.

They started off, Stella sitting proudly like Lady Godiva, Rupert walking her mount down the field and through the gate. There was a pause while he closed it behind them, and then they went on along the road to Belgate.

Looking down on him, Stella admired the short hair with its tendency to curl, the set of his shoulders, and the gloved hands holding the reins. His shirt was a lovely thick linen, and had a pleat up the back the like of which she had never seen. There was a blue cravat tucked into the neck, and he wore riding breeches with leather pads on the inside leg. A special set of clothes for riding! So that was what it was like to be rich.

'All right?' he said anxiously, looking back at her.

'It hurts,' she said bravely, 'but I can bear it.' She sighed a little and rubbed her bare knee. 'I've seen you before,' she said. 'Down the road. You were on about aeroplanes.' She saw his face light up and knew she had found the key.

'Imagine you remembering that,' he said in wonder. 'I am rather interested in them. I intend to join the RAF as soon as –' He was about to say 'as soon as I'm old enough', but somehow it sounded demeaning. '–as soon as it can be arranged,' he said instead.

'Go on!' Stella said admiringly. 'Aren't you scared?'

Rupert flowered, then, as she had guessed he would, and they talked of the terrible air raids on the south coast. '"Hellfire Corner", they call it now,' Rupert said. 'But we're shooting down ever so many German planes. Hundreds.'

The conversation went on happily all the way to the outskirts of Belgate. Stella knew little or nothing of the Messerschmitt BF109E with its three 20mm cannon and two 7.0mm machine-guns, but she knew how to widen her eyes in wonder at someone else's expertise.

'Put me down here,' she said when they reached the village, her instinct telling her that keeping Anne out of the picture was the right thing to do. Rupert protested, but she was firm; and at last he held up his arms and she came down to him, leaning against him, her hands like feathers on his shoulders. 'Thank you,' she said, drawing back to look up into his face. He saw that her eyes were blue-green, flecked with amber, the lashes around them thick and fair, her skin patterned with faint freckles like a dusting of honey. He wondered if he should say something – anything – to keep her there, but Stella was already moving away, looking over her shoulder to smile at him, hobbling bravely towards the houses.

'Ta,' she called. 'I'll see you some time.'

Rupert swung into the saddle and stood for a moment, watching her, until the faint roar of an aircraft engine distracted him. Two Hurricanes were making for the coast. He watched, fascinated, until they were out of sight, and when he turned back the girl had gone. *I don't even know her name*, he thought, and was regretful.

Diana had looked forward all day to the moment when Howard would return from Durham. She had refused Max's offer to take her to the Café de Paris to see Ken 'Snakehips' Johnson and his grey-suited negro band: 'No, Max, not tonight. Howard has promised to come home.' But Howard did not come home. There was only a call from some man in Durham who tendered her husband's apologies, and said, 'He'll be back tomorrow.'

She was running a bath and preparing for another early night when the urge to go out overcame her. She had asked for soup and sandwiches in her room but when the maid knocked with the tray she sent her away. 'I'm going out,' she said. 'No one needs to wait up. I may not be back until late.'

Max responded to her call within minutes. 'I'm so glad, old girl. I had a letter from Laura today; one from Lee, too. They cast me down, I don't mind telling you.'

At the Embassy Club they had veal washed down with a Vouvray, and reminisced for a while, deliberately nostalgic as though to block out the painful present. Then he produced the letter from his wife.

'That's Laura's letter. What do you make of it?'

At first Diana was reluctant to read a private communication between husband and wife, but soon she realized that the letter was more formal than loving. Laura was well. The children were well. America was holding its own. No terms of endearment; no anguish of separation. *It reads like a business letter,* Diana thought, and was filled with pity for Max.

The energetic rhythm of the band changed as they played a request. 'South of the border...' It was a love song, evocative of the time before the war when everything had been simple. She felt herself drawn more closely into the circle of Max's arms, and then his cheek was on her hair and she gave herself up to the dreamy music.

'Let's get out of here,' Max said at last, and Diana knew what he meant to happen. She collected her coat, but even as he slipped it around her shoulders her resolution was strong. She could not be unfaithful to Howard: not twice in a lifetime.

They came out into the street and began to grope their way forward, all the while looking for a cab. 'I will simply give Mount Street to the driver,' she thought, 'and then Max will see it can't be.'

But before a cab materialized out of the blackness, the steady pump-pump of ack-ack guns began; and then the siren was sounding and a dozen silver fish were caught in the searchlight beams against the black sky.

'We'll go to Scotland Gate,' Max said, 'and drown our sorrows in some of the Old Medieval's booze.'

'No, thank you,' Diana said firmly. 'Not tonight. In case it escapes your notice, I have a job. War work. I can no longer stay in bed all day to recover from a late night out.'

She had on one of the new red snoods, and the weight of it on her neck was rather satisfying. She moved her head from side to side, teasing him. 'We can't all be War Office wallahs with nothing to do!'

There was a sudden terrible crumping sound, and the pavement seemed to shake beneath them.

'It looks like a big one,' Max said and began to hurry her towards the shelter. There was a screaming sound of something falling, and then the ground trembled again and there was the sound of tumbling masonry. 'Come on,' Max said urgently. 'This way!' And then they were squashing into a shelter full of bodies. Some were crying, one was giggling nervously, all of them were cursing Hitler and all his works.

When they came out into the street an hour later, a scene of devastation met them. There was an acrid smell. 'Cordite,' Max said tersely. Timber and lath and plaster lay everywhere, and the pavement gleamed with glittering powdered glass, for all the world like a hoar frost.

'Move along there,' a voice said out of the darkness. 'There's a gas main broken. Keep moving!' In the distance an ambulance charged past, and Diana had to feel her way over the rubble.

'Come on,' Max said, tugging at her arm. 'Scotland Gate is only round the corner. We need a drink.'

Diana stood still for a moment, weighing up the situation. If she went to his home she knew what would happen: they would be lovers again, this time for mutual comfort where once it had been for excitement and passion.

That's not what I want, she said to herself, and would have turned away but that she saw a dog, dead on the rubble, one paw out-flung as though to beg for mercy. It reminded her of Mephisto, the dog from her childhood – and suddenly she was sobbing in Max's arms and a caped warden was saying, 'Stand clear please, let the lady and gentleman through.'

'It's going to be all right, Di,' Max said against her cheek. 'Cling on to me and we'll go home.' He sounded so reassuring that it made her feel a child again, safe in someone's arms. And she realized suddenly why she felt safe: Max could not be amorous and protective at the same time. It was not possible. As long as they were under threat, it was safe to relax against him and think how nice it was to be held in someone's arms. She closed her eyes and tried to remember how long it was since she and Howard had made love.

And then they were at Scotland Gate, and Max was

loosing his hold on her to fumble with the key. And they were over the threshold, and she was no longer safe, and nothing at all was childlike.

They had decorated the table with candlesticks and flowers, and produced the best meal possible for Sammy's farewell supper. They said prayers of thanksgiving, and ate and drank and laughed and teased the girls, for all the world as though it was Rosh Hashanah and war was not even a speck on the horizon. But at last the time came for the final toast.

'*Lechayim*, Samuel.' Emmanuel raised his glass to his son, the last of the Lanskys.

'*Lechayim*, father.' Sammy drank and then turned to raise his glass to Esther and the two girls. 'To life – and to my *oytsers*, all three of you.' They raised their glasses and returned his toast, and then Esther slipped away to collect the parcel she had packed for him, honey-cake and cookies and a small bottle of his favourite Armagnac.

As she put on her coat and hat to take Sammy to the station she could hear Naomi weeping. She always took it hard when Sammy left. *They have lost so much*, Esther thought wearily, *and now they're afraid they'll lose what little they have left.* But when she got back to the hall, Sammy had worked his miracle once more. Naomi was smiling, the tears drying on her cheeks as he touched her face and called her *onna noz*, which Esther knew meant 'button-nose'.

'That girl adores you,' she said when they were in the car and the three figures in the doorway were retreating in the dusk.

'Look after them, Esther. And watch papa. He's desperate for news of the old people, and losing France has just about finished him. He courted my mother in Paris; he can tell you every street, every tree. I think *I* know the city, but he can outdo me. The thought of the Germans there... *Fe!*'

Esther went into the station with him, trying not to see other couples clinging, mothers weeping, fathers carrying kit-bags for soldier sons. Who was this Hitler, that he could turn the whole world upside-down?

'Why so serious, Esther?' Sammy said, as they waited on the crowded, chilly platform. He was trying to tease her back to cheerfulness, and she tried to smile, but it wasn't easy.

'I don't like you going away.'

'You mean you miss me?' He rolled his eyes heaven-wards. 'She has come to her senses: she loves me!'

No such thing,' Esther said, but the smile came readily now. 'I hate you going off and leaving me to cope with the points system and shortages and stock discrepancies and my friend Gallagher. Especially him.'

'Forget Gallagher. He is a little man, as I remember him: a leech, a parasite. He will feast on the war; there are always parasites in war. But in the end... in the end it's the Lanskys and the Gullivers who win wars. Who feed people; who grow very rich while doing it; and probably get medals into the bargain.'

'We both know it's the Gallaghers who wind up with the medals – and the money, too, given half the chance,' Esther said.

There was a hiss of steam as a train began to pull away from the far platform.

'Mine will be next,' Sammy said.

'When do you think you'll be home again?'

He shook his head. 'Who knows? When I can. But I think we took care of most things in these last few days. You're my partner: my full partner. If – well, if I'm posted and I don't get back – for a while – you'll manage.'

And then his train was steaming in, already crowded, and people were pushing and pulling, hauling the new passengers aboard, stowing their baggage, making room. A quick kiss, and Sammy had heaved himself on board with the others.

'They help one another, don't they?' a woman said to Esther. The train was moving now, a forest of hands waving from windows, a host of messages being shouted to and fro. Hands clutching each other desperately were parted as the train slowly gathered speed.

As she walked away, Esther was remembering something she had read... lines from *Mrs Miniver*. 'This is the people's war. It is our war. We are the fighters. Fight it, then. Fight it with all that is in us. And may God defend the right.'

BOOK THREE

11

June 1941

Frank straightened up and looked at the neat rows of peas. He had come out at sun-up, glad to get out of bed and away from the dark thoughts of the night. He put a hand to the small of his back, pressing the aching muscles. By God, gardening was more back-breaking than hewing, and that was saying something.

Around him Belgate still slept. A paper-boy moved sluggishly from door to door, pausing to rub sleep from his eyes; in the distance a milk cart rattled on an unmade road; birds cheeped from every ledge and wire in appreciation of a sunny day. You could almost imagine it was pre-war, and yet Britain was not five minutes away from defeat, if you believed the newspapers.

In Crete, the beaches were strewn with British dead, cut down by Stuka dive-bombers while they waited for the navy to rescue them. It was a year since Dunkirk, and still the Allies were in retreat and Churchill under fire in the Commons for failure.

They had a cheek to censure Churchill, Frank thought. '*We shall not fail or falter; we shall not weaken or tire...*' That had been a good speech, inspiring Anne to make a plate of black-pudding sandwiches that had melted in the mouth. It would probably turn out all right in the end; it would bloody well have to. At least the war was filling the churches... there were faces at Mass nowadays that hadn't been seen there since their baptism.

The stories coming out of the Belgian and Dutch coalfields were terrible, though: of fellow miners butchered like dogs. The Miners' Union Executive at Durham had passed a resolution that Frank had copied and put on the wall of the lamp-cabin for everyone to see. It said: 'We have made an unflinching resolve that these crimes shall be avenged.' It ended: 'In this conflict there will be no neutrals. All must play their part, be it large or small, and we appreciate the desire of the Labour movement to play its part in this struggle.'

So if Joe had to go to fight, so be it. If prayer could bring him safe back, he would survive. And then, after the war, when the people came into their own... A few months ago Frank had seen the gates come down from the house on the Scar, to be carted away with a load of other scrap. Stephen Hardman had lost his life for those gates, and all for Brenton vanity. There would be no more of that in the new Jersualem.

All the same, war was senseless. Last week he had seen a German plane caught in searchlights over Sunderland way, twisting and turning to escape the beam. They had got the bugger with the coastal ack-ack and sent it plummeting down to earth to a cheer from the onlookers. But Frank had remembered that the Nazi pilot would only be a bairn like Joe, and the thought had sickened him.

Anne came into the garden, a pan of mash in her arms. The hens burst into life at the smell of food, and she vanished inside the run, shouting at them to wait their turn. Her face looked care-worn. Frank held out his hand, but she brushed past him.

'Don't clart on, Frank. Our Stella'll miss her bus if I don't get her out of bed, and that's enough war work for anyone.'

In the kitchen she put the mash pan to soak in the sink, and set about breakfast. 'You can have a bacon sandwich. No butter, but it's streaky bacon so that'll moisten it up. I want to get down the shops to see if there's any tomatoes yet. One and four a pound, Frank: tomatoes! That'll work out about five pence each. Do you remember when there was gluts and they'd shovel them into your bag for coppers? Now tomatoes are the price of peaches, and if you throw mouldy bread out for the birds they can fine you. No wonder I'm looking old, Frank. It's a wonder I'm still sane.'

'Shall I call our Stella?' Frank said.

'Yes,' Anne said. 'And then she'll come down, done up to the eyes, and a mouth on her like a foghorn.'

But when Stella appeared she was still in her nightdress. 'I've got a day off,' she said, yawning and rubbing her eyes.

'You never mentioned it last night,' Anne said, bristling.

'I forgot. Anyway, I'm going back to bed.' For a moment Anne wondered whether or not to make a fight of it. In the end she gave way.

'Well,' she said, 'I suppose I'll have to take your word for it. You can make yourself useful when you do get up. I've got two ham shanks – two! I'm going to the pictures this afternoon, and I'll put them on boiling, and you can watch them. Keep the pan topped up, and you might get a sandwich off them when I get back.'

Stella groaned and turned for the stairs. 'Well, will you watch them?' Anne said.

'If I must,' Stella said and exited with a swing of her hips.

Esther was the first to rise, going to the bathroom to wash from head to foot, then waking the girls and Lansky as she passed by their rooms.

In the kitchen she riddled the range and put on the kettle and then set about making porridge and toast, to be eaten with the last jar of Rachael's preserves. As she worked she remembered the old Jewess with her lame leg and her kindly face. It was a blessing she was not alive to see what was happening now, for she had brought up Sammy, loving him with a rare intensity. *She couldn't have borne his going away*, Esther thought, *much less his being in danger*. For Sammy *would* be in danger if he was posted overseas.

Ruth came into the kitchen then, fastening her braids around her head as she walked, the letters she had collected from the doormat clenched between her teeth.

'Post,' she said and laid them on the table. 'But no letter from Sammy.' It was Ruth's turn for a letter, and Esther could see she was disappointed.

'There'll probably be one by the second post,' she said. 'Maybe even with news of his next leave. Now sit down and eat. We're all late this morning.'

There was one letter for her, and her heart sank when she recognized David Gilfillan's handwriting. He had survived Dunkirk but had spent a long time in a military hospital. Now he was back in camp, and awaiting another move.

She dreaded his letters, which grew steadily more loving as the weeks went by. And yet each one was a reassurance that he was still alive and well. Esther didn't love him, but she didn't want anything to happen to him, either. It was the same when he got a forty-eight-hour leave: a mixture of emotions that left her weary.

My dearest Esther, it began. That was new: it had been 'Dear Esther', then 'My dear Esther'. Now she was 'dearest'. She read on:

> *They say I will get leave before I go off again, and for that I am thankful, but the thought of going back to that hell horrifies me. I know it is my duty, and I won't shirk it, but I can't forget the utter desolation of that time on the beaches, wondering if we would get away or be captured or slaughtered. Ninety men of the Norfolks were slaughtered by the SS at Le Paradis – did you know that? Marched to a barn and gunned down. We were lucky to get off. I'll never forget that little cockleshell armada, boats of every shape and*

*size, even a London Fire Brigade boat... and the icy
water, and the hands reaching out to grab you and
haul you aboard. But I'd literally rather die than go
through that again. Does that make me a coward? I
hope not.*

*I most close now, my darling, in the hope that you will
keep safe. I need you, Esther. I have wanted you since
that first time I saw you in the Lanver office, so proper
with your lovely hair and that determined mouth that
can smile like no other. But now it is more than
wanting, more than love. It's the need of you in my
life, something to come home to, someone to fight for.
That's what keeps us all going: the thought of loved
ones who need protecting. I kiss you now on paper as
soon, God willing, I shall kiss your lips. I have forty-
eight hours' leave, Esther. Forty-eight precious hours
to be with you. I keep thinking something will happen,
invasion or earthquake, to stop me from travelling north.
However, if the gods are kind, I will be with you on
Thursday, arriving in Sunderland on the 8.15 p.m. train.*

Esther would never have thought the upright young
solicitor she had met in Sammy's office could have been so
sentimental, but then the war was changing people. There
was no time any longer for niceties; everywhere people
were throwing themselves into living and loving, while
they still had the chance.

As she drove the girls to school she chatted about everything and nothing, as she did each morning, but when she
was by herself she gave way to tears. It wasn't fair, this game
life played. She had thought it the end of the world when
Philip died; and then her life had picked up again, thanks to
Sammy. Now she had the weight of Gilfillan's love on her
conscience, and Sammy might be lost to her forever before
the war was over. And the memory of Emmanuel's sad face

lingered in her mind. It was months since he had had word of his parents-in-law. Were they in Vichy France, unable to communicate, or were they incarcerated in Sachsenhausen or Dachau or Gross-Rosen? Every Sunday night, when the anthems of the occupied countries were played on the wireless, she saw a tear form in his eye for the 'Marseillaise'.

Howard moved cautiously towards the window, anxious to leave Diana sleeping. Her face had been white with exhaustion the night before, and the bruise on her forehead stood out like a wound. It was two nights since she had been hit by falling debris when the ambulance station was caught in the blast from a nearby explosion.

Since last September, when the great fires of docklands had reddened the sky, Hitler's bombers had hammered unmercifully at the heart of London. Howard had seen the face of the city changed forever, ancient buildings wiped out in seconds, whole streets gone, landmarks like the dome of St Paul's and the spire of St Bride's standing out starkly against the burning city's skyline. On bleak, grey mornings people picked their way to work through the rubble of what had once been houses or shops full of smiling animated people, but was now only bricks and tortured wood or steel girders, with pathetic mementoes of the former occupants fluttering amid the chaos, and the smell of burnt and damped-down wooden beams hanging over all. It was a rank, raw smell which came from the dust of dissolved brickwork and masonry, mixed with domestic gas from broken pipes and the acrid overtone of the high-explosive itself. Once you had encountered it, you couldn't forget it, for it was the smell of death.

And, in the midst of it, people tunnelled through the debris, removing it by a chain of baskets, stopping every few minutes to listen for signs of life. Rescue workers were paid £3 10s a week, but they never knocked off if there was the prospect of pulling a pathetic but living bundle from the wreckage.

There had been a lull in the bombardment between January and March, the air raids continuing but less intense, and then in April there were two terrible 'vengeance' raids, retaliation for RAF strikes against Berlin. But the worst raid had come on the night of 10 May, when for six-and-a-half hours Göring's Heinkels and Junkers had pulverized London. When it was over, there was carnage in the streets: over 1,400 dead and 1,800 injured. Westminster Abbey, the Tower of London, the British Museum and other landmarks had suffered damage, and transport was completely disrupted.

The debating chamber of the House of Commons had been razed, only the outer walls left standing, but mercifully the Chamber had been empty, night-sitting having been suspended because of the air raids. Members now moved to the House of Lords, which the Lords vacated for the Robing Room. If small shops could do 'business as usual', so could the Mother of Parliaments.

Through all this, Diana had toiled without complaint, the only visible sign of strain the shadows beneath her eyes.

The night before they had dined at home, the first evening in an age that they had been alone together. But Diana had been strangely withdrawn, and when they had climbed into bed and Howard had reached for her, she had kissed him gently on the mouth and whispered, 'I must sleep, darling. Do you mind?'

But she had not slept. Howard had woken once to find her gone from the bed, and at other times had been aware that she was lying tense and wakeful beside him.

Now he moved the curtain aside and looked out on the waking street. Postmen, milkmen, paper-boys: a familiar London scene... except for the sandbags and the painted windows and the brutal scars where the railings had been taken away for scrap. Someone, somewhere, was whistling the ubiquitous 'White Cliffs of Dover'. Everything looked and sounded tranquil.

There were rumours of German troop movements on the Russian border. If Hitler was mad enough to anger the Russian bear, what would happen then? What was it Churchill had once called the Russians? 'A riddle wrapped in a mystery inside an enigma.' Churchill had gone on to say: 'Perhaps there is a key. That key is Russian national interest.' They had defeated Finland but the Finnish defence had been brilliant. The Soviets had lost perhaps a million dead, before sheer weight of numbers had over-whelmed the smaller nation. One thing was certain: the weakness of the Russian army had been exposed for every-one to see, including Hitler.

Howard turned as Diana stirred on the bed.

'Tea?' he said, and went over to the spirit kettle on the tray, an innovation since most of the servants had gone off to war.

'Please,' Diana said, moving up on to her pillows and run-ning fingers through her hair. 'God, I was tired last night,' she yawned, reaching for the robe that lay at the foot of the bed.

Howard watched in the mirror as she padded across to the bathroom. He heard the cistern flush, and then running water. When Diana came back, her hair had been combed and she was running her tongue over her teeth. 'That's better. I can't bear a sleepy mouth.'

She climbed back into bed and pulled up the covers as he carried her tea across to her. She sipped appreciatively. 'Lovely. Do you have to leave early?' There was such a note of entreaty in her voice that he shelved his plans to go early to the House.

'No,' he said. Not before luncheon. Let's walk in the park, and then I'll take you somewhere very nice where they've never heard of food shortages. How would that do?'

'That would do nicely, sir,' she said, and suddenly laid a hand on his arm. 'Don't ever get fed-up with me, Howard.'

And then she was turning away and the moment of intimacy was gone.

They walked in Green Park, and then ate at the Ritz. When they parted, each to a separate cab, Howard could see that there was colour in Diana's cheeks, and the slight frown had vanished from her brow.

'I may not see you tonight,' she said in farewell, 'but let's go and see the children soon? Loelia is calling this afternoon.'

'Good,' Howard said, 'we'll go soon.' And then she was slamming the door and her cab was moving away, and he was climbing into his cab and turning his attention to the afternoon ahead.

Loelia came at 4 o'clock and the charlady carried in a tray. The tea was lukewarm, and the biscuits surrounded by crumbs.

'Sorry,' Diana said apologetically but Loelia lifted a peremptory hand.

'Don't apologize, darling. You're lucky to have someone, even a dreadful Mrs Mop. Think what it's like at Valesworth: old men and halfwits – that's what we're left with. I can't honestly believe it makes sense to take all the manpower – and woman-power. I haven't even got a tweeny; how am I expected to keep the place going? As soon as there's a lull in the air raids, I'm coming back to London. The children can stay in the country but I must come back.'

She bit into her biscuit, licked in a crumb and continued. 'And now clothes-rationing. Sixty-six coupons for a whole year: that won't cover the underpinnings, let alone changing styles. A suit is eighteen coupons – one suit! Even a blouse is seven, and handkerchiefs are a coupon each. Five and a half dozen hankies, and that's my year's allowance.'

Loelia's voice went on, but Diana's attention wandered. If Howard was correct, there would be a German offensive against Russia soon. What would that mean? Rupert was fretting, desperate to get into uniform.

'I'm trusting Norman Hartnell,' Loelia was saying, and Diana tried to pay attention. 'I can't believe he'll see me go without. And of course we can have things made over for the children, so there'll be their allowance to use, too. And Henry has clothes enough to last for years, so there's his coupons, and hats are coupon-free. I expect I'll manage, but it's too unutterably unfair. "Keep up morale," they say, and then they do this. Even cosmetics are unreliable – full of the most unsuitable ingredients.'

Has Loelia changed, or have I? Diana wondered, and could find no answer. Somewhere, in the dim recesses of her memory, she could remember being passionate about *robes de style*, or coloured stockings, or the height of hemlines. And now... the night before last she had seen them bring out a pregnant woman from the rubble. She was almost near her time, from the size of her belly, and she was dead. They had covered her face and folded the thin fingers across the womb that had become her baby's tomb.

'How are the children?' Diana quickly said aloud, afraid of what else she might say if she pursued her line of thought.

'Stoic,' Loelia said proudly. 'Terribly good about everything: the shortages, and black-outs, and no one to take them riding. Pamela is such a helpful child in the holidays. And the twins adore her. I dread her going back to school.'

There was, thought Diana, an almost proprietorial note in Loelia's voice. *Did* she know that Pamela was her brother's child? *I've got to stop seeing Max,* Diana told herself. *I can't let it happen again.*

But as they went on talking about the minutiae of war-time life, she knew she could not stop seeing Max, could not stop having sex with him. Not now – not when everything was so uncertain, even whether you'd be alive when the all clear came. *At least I know it isn't love*, she thought. *At least, this time, I know that.*

She came out of her reverie at the mention of Rupert. 'Is he still seeing that girl, what was her name? Caroline? Catherine? The cook's daughter? The cook who married the war-hero...'

'You mean Catherine Hardman,' Diana said. 'They're still friends, but Rupert's away most of the time and Catherine is nurse-training somewhere, some northern hospital. It never was a grand passion. They were simply childhood friends.'

She felt a sense of relief that the words she spoke were the truth. It would never have done for anything to come of Rupert and Catherine; not just for reasons of class, but because he must spread his wings before he picked a wife. Her choice of words reminded her that Rupert was hell-bent on spreading his wings – but not in the way she had meant.

'Oh, let's go out somewhere, Lee,' she said, jumping up and ringing the bell for the tray to be cleared. 'Let's go somewhere and be madly extravagant and think about nothing at all to do with war.'

'You'll have to do something about that bruise,' Loelia said, as they went downstairs. 'No one will ever think you got it in the Blitz. It looks completely disreputable.'

A welcome letter from Sammy was waiting for Esther at the warehouse, enclosed in some papers he had returned to the book-keeper. It began on a low note:

If I was doing something useful I wouldn't mind, but all I do is sit around or march up and down, up and down. I keep thinking of all of you crouching in the shelter when I should be there to protect you. And I think of the profits I could be making. Oy vey, I think of the profits! I dream of expanding, of taking the

*shops to the people, and all I can do is go to seed
here. It's punishment on me for all my naarishkeit.
Still, God is good. Soon I will have served my
penance; he will drown the Axis in the Red Sea; and
I will come home to you, Esther. You'll have seen
sense by then – even if it took a war to do it – and will
snap me up. Together we'll be even bigger than the
Maypole Dairies.*

Esther always laughed at his letters; sometimes she cried,
too, thinking of him far away from home, not knowing when,
if ever, he would return. But at least he would have something
to come back to, a business and a home and people who
loved him.

Esther's work at Lanver Products was classed as 'essential', and since almost everyone else who worked there had
been whisked away, she certainly *was* essential, especially
with foodstuffs so hard to come by, and so much red tape to
deal with. She worked long hours, and often at weekends,
too, except when David Gilfillan had a weekend pass.

It's the war, she thought now, as she hung up her coat.
We're all so afraid of dying that we're living too hard.
Sooner or later she would have to tell him that there was no
future in the relationship. When the tide turned, perhaps;
when there was at least the prospect of peace, and return to
normality. She sat down at her desk and began to sort the
buff official envelopes that littered it. And then she found
another letter in familiar handwriting.

She had lost her right-hand helper, Mary Webster, who
had gone off to join the WAAF, and this letter came from her.

*Sometimes I wish I was back at Lanver, having a laugh
with you all, and I worry about my lovely stock records
and whether someone's keeping them straight. But
mostly I'm glad I did it. We're all determined to do our*

*best to back up the air crew. That's our main job,
according to our sergeant: keeping the men happy.
Some of the girls giggle about it, but I take it seriously.
A lot of these young lads are going to die before this
is over, so if I can help them in any way, I'm going to.
I remember the way you backed up Mr Sammy in the
old days, and I'm going to try to be like that. Give him
my best regards when you hear from him. He's probably running the War Ministry by now, knowing him.
And take care of yourself.*

Love, Mary

'Who *is* looking after the stock records?' Esther asked
herself as she tried to negotiate her way through ever-
mounting piles of paper. She got a letter from Gallagher by
what seemed like every post, with reprimands, threats, and
sheets of instructions, each one seeming to contradict the
one before. When even big shops like Swan and Edgar
could be fined for accepting loose coupons, Esther didn't
dare to slip up.

She was still reading the letters and sorting the forms that
accompanied them when Gallagher himself was announced.
Esther had come to dread the controller's visits.

He took a seat opposite her and began to unbutton the
jacket of his three-piece suit. His hat was balanced on his
knee, and Esther knew she ought to ask him if he wanted to
be relieved of it but some devilish impulse refused to let
her utter the words. She didn't want him to be comfortable;
she wanted him out of her office.

'Well, Mr Gallagher, what can I do for you?' Wonder of
wonders, he was smiling, a thin smile that made his lips
look stretched over his large, uneven teeth.

'It's more a case of what I can do for you, Miss Gulliver.'
He picked up his hat and looked around for somewhere to

put it. All of a sudden, Esther remembered Sammy's words: 'Keep the bureaucrats sweet, Esther. Oil the wheels.' What would Sammy want her to do now?

'Well, Mr Gallagher,' she said at last, clearing her throat to gain time, 'I'm sure I'll be grateful for any help you can give. But let me take your hat – and shall I ask the girls to bring us some tea?'

An hour later she knew just what Gallagher was willing to do for her. It had all been couched in the vaguest terms, nothing she could take to a higher authority, but in fact what Gallagher was talking of was a trick, a fraud. He would send her extra goods as and when he had them available; goods over and above her legitimate allocation. She, in turn, would meekly sign for whatever the forms which came with her regular allocation said was there. The discrepancy would never be great; 'enough to cover short-fall', Gallagher called it. But if he was doing this with every wholesaler, it meant he was going to accumulate a huge pool of food and dry goods, for which he would have to account to no one.

When Esther got home she was greeted by the smell of food from the kitchen, so she knew Lansky had made an effort to prepare the meal.

'That smells nice?' she said, looking into his study. 'What is it?'

Lansky did not answer, but he levered himself from his chair, and went to the dining-room, to take out the cloth and the heavy cutlery from the sideboard. 'How did your day go, Esther?' he said, as she followed him.

'Do you remember Gallagher? Gallagher the agent?' Lansky nodded. 'Well, I had another visit from him. "To facilitate matters," he said, but if I'm any judge, all he wants to facilitate is Gallagher.'

'I believe it,' Lansky said, placing knives and forks with mathematical correctness. 'Not a good man.'

'The trouble is,' Esther said, 'I have to do business with him. He controls everything, so I can't afford to cross him, for Sammy's sake.'

'It's not for Sammy's sake you should do business with a *ganef*.'

'That's not what Sammy would say,' Esther said ruefully, but Lansky shook his head.

'My son has his standards, Esther. Perhaps not my standards, but standards just the same. He would not ask you to mix in the gutter with *drek*. Not even for his business.'

They ate at the wide table, the girls on either side of them, talking about the doings of the day. *They belong here*, Esther thought, seeing how their faces were relaxed, their voices and gestures those of young women, and not frightened as they had been when they came. They no longer had the pallor of too little sleep and too much anxiety, but had shining hair and rosy cheeks. Naomi had stopped plucking at her cuffs or the edges of her garments, but there was still a faint sadness in the eyes, a wistful down-turn to the lips. *They miss their parents*, Esther thought, and remembered how it had felt when she, too, was alone.

'Naomi had a letter from Sammy by the second post,' Ruth said, with a smirk.

'I said she would,' Esther answered. 'What did he have to say?'

'He's coming home next month,' Naomi said shyly, but Ruth leaned to Lansky and put up a hand to hide a stage whisper: 'She can hardly wait!'

Esther was about to laugh until she saw Naomi's imploring eyes. *The child's love-struck*, she thought, remembering all the pain of being sixteen and thinking that Howard Brenton had descended from Olympus.

'Neither can I,' she said aloud, and saw Naomi's eyes flash gratitude. 'Now, who's for pudding?'

12

June 1941

If it hadn't been for the worry of Joe, she might have enjoyed this war, Anne thought, as the lights went up before the B-picture. She had money, now; enough and a little bit over for the first time in her life. Moreover, she found a lot of satisfaction feeding everybody in spite of shortages. Doing her stint of fire-watching at the church. Being the acknowledged queen of make-do-and-mend. There was even fun to be had, if you looked for it. She and Frank had tried on their gas masks the other night, and he had shown her how to make farting noises out of the sides before the straps were tightened. She had laughed till she cried, nearly as much as she had when Nella Wynaham had stood up to sing at the social evening and had broken wind on the high note of 'When I'm calling you'.

As she watched the news and heard details of the London air raids – the Blitz, they were calling it – she gave thanks that they lived in an ordinary place, one that didn't seem to attract much attention. She thought with satisfaction of the two ham shanks, bubbling away on the stove, along with taties and carrots and a nice Spanish onion grown in Frank's allotment. Stella had been charged with tending the pot, and not even she could make a mess of that. There would be soup for everyone tomorrow, and she would get some chips on the way home tonight to eat with the fatty bits. And no mucky bath to clear out, because Frank got bathed at the pit now. All in all, things were looking up.

*

Howard signed the last letter and recapped his pen. The woman beside him began to gather up the letters and tap them into line in the manilla folder. He looked at her, seeing the pallor of the too-thin cheeks, the shadowed eyes, the tremor of the long, thin fingers. Her husband had gone down with the *Hood* a few weeks before and the trauma showed. He had engaged her as his secretary on the recommendation of a fellow MP, and she was struggling to come to terms with her grief and the need to make a living after a lapse of years. Her naval pension was not enough for a woman and child to exist on, in London. Suddenly and sharply, Howard remembered Michael Trenchard, another casualty of another war. Surely this time the country could do better by its heroes?

'How's your son?' he asked, and saw a smile touch her lips.

'He's doing well, now – at least, he's better. He's staying with my mother at the moment, and she's very good with him.'

Howard smiled and nodded his approval, and stood up to coiled his hat and briefcase from the stand.

Barbara Traske went to the door. 'Will you need me again tonight?' Framed in the huge doorway of his office she looked almost unbelievably frail.

'No. Go home – and don't hurry in tomorrow.' She was turning away when he had a sudden thought. 'If your son is away, does that mean you're alone this evening? I'm about to ring my wife; would you care to join us for dinner? I know Diana is looking forward to meeting you.'

Barbara's face had flushed at the invitation. 'That's very kind, but, I don't want to impose…'

Howard held up a hand.

'Please. I'll ring Diana. Get your things, and I'll be with you in a moment.'

He dialled Mount Street and waited for a reply, but the ringing tone went on and on, and eventually he put down the receiver. 'My wife must be at her ambulance station,' he said when he reached Barbara's office. 'I believe I told you she drives an ambulance? But we can still eat, if you could bear my company. I promise not to mention the House or the constituency. Now come: take pity on me. I don't want to eat alone.'

They walked on to Westminster Bridge before they saw a cruising cab. 'Quaglino's,' he said and handed Barbara into the cab's interior. Her gloved hand was like a child's in his, and there was a faint smell of flowers as she passed him. Carnation, perhaps? Or violet? She was a good-looking woman; beautiful, even, in a restrained way. Please God there would be another man some day to chase the sadness from her eyes. He would make sure she met Diana soon, and then they could bring her out of her shell.

Howard smiled at her as he settled back in his seat, and then looked out at the London scene as the last rays of daylight died away.

Esther dressed carefully to meet David Gilfillan. Her black linen suit with its velvet collar was smart, and set off her peacock-blue velvet hat. Why had she started this affair? Perhaps she had believed he would never come back, but if so, she had been wrong. Any minute now his train would chug into the station and disgorge a host of other homecoming servicemen, all of them longing to be clasped in loving arms.

And then she saw him, coming towards her through the crowds, shouldering people aside in his desire to be with her. He looked older, thinner, and tired. And in the instant that she took in the change in him, a wave of pity overtook her, casting out her former doubts. 'David,' she said, lifting her face for his kiss. 'David. How lovely to see you again.'

*

'He's a wonder,' Patrick Quinnell said, looking down on the sleeping child, whose lips were formed into a pout of satisfaction, his fair hair moist on his brow.

'Takes after his father,' Mary said. 'His mother's a nice woman, though.'

They went downstairs and settled by the fireplace, he in one chair, she watching him from the other. There was no need yet of a fire in the grate, but they still sat round it.

'There now,' Mary said. 'Let's hear about it.'

'It's nothing, really,' Patrick answered wearily. We lost two lads today, but that's bound to happen sometimes. It's just that the news is so bad, and I worry about you and Ben.'

'What news?' Mary said cheerfully.

'Well, the German invasion plans: it seems to be all they talk about in the wards. They make it sound almost a *fait accompli*.'

'Is that all?' Mary said. 'It'll never happen, so let it drop. We're just depressing ourselves by brooding on it. I had a visitor today, our Frank's Estelle. Said she was just passing by, but she's never felt the need to visit me before.'

'Why now, then?' Patrick said, tamping tobacco into his pipe.

'You might well ask. She beat around the bush a bit, but then she started on about the Brentons. "You used to work for them, Auntie Mary. What were they like?" I told her about Mrs Howard and Mr Howard and Miss Pamela for a bit, and then she got fed up. She can never possess herself when she wants something "What about the boy?" she said. "The oldest one, Rupert."

'Hah!' Patrick threw back his head and let a stream of smoke escape his lips. 'Eros has struck, has it?'

'I don't know about Eros,' Mary said, 'but something'll have struck, because halfway through she remembered her mam'd left a pan of broth on and she was supposed to be

– 183 –

watching it. She let out a wail like a banshee and took off. Her feet didn't touch the ground. And if she's ruined Anne's precious ham shanks, she'll rue the day she ever heard of Rupert Brenton.'

In the end Vivien Leigh took the noble way out in *Waterloo Bridge* and Anne stumbled, weeping, from the cinema. 'It was lovely,' she told Frank when she got home, with two lots of chips wrapped up in vinegar-soaked newspaper held in her gloved hands. 'She went wrong – more by accident than anything else. And she wouldn't give him damaged goods.'

'What did she do?' Frank asked, delaying the moment when the chips were unwrapped and Anne asked about the ham shanks.

'She killed herself.'

'That was clever.'

'It was the right thing to do. It was noble, Frank. I've never cried so much in me life.'

'Well, get your hanky out again, Annie; I've got bad news.'

Esther lay on her back watching the ceiling. It was dark in the room now, although the curtains were still open. The road outside the hotel was busy, just off Gateshead's main street, but the passing cars had shaded lights and the street lamps were dark. Beside her David slept at last, sated. He had made love to her with a vigour she had not anticipated: he knew more now, he spoke more, he wanted to experiment. He had produced French letters and knew how to use them. He was no longer the shy young man she had known.

After all possible passion had been spent, David talked of war.

'I prayed to die on that beach, Esther. We knew we couldn't all get off; there was an army there, queues of men winding like huge snakes from the sandhills out into the water. Waiting, hoping... like human piers, the men at the front up to their necks in water, some of them just slipping under when the boats didn't come.'

He had told her some of this before, but Esther knew he needed to talk and she let him go on. 'They dropped leaflets: "Your generals have gone home," that's what they said. And we were so hungry. I picked a dead man's pockets, Esther, just to find chocolate. But someone else had been there before me. The Stukas kept coming in. They had whistles fitted, and they screamed as they swooped down. Some men cracked then; the man next to me kept saying "Lord have mercy, Christ have mercy." One man, a major I think, went mad and thrashed into the water to get on board a boat – and the navy man aboard it shot him between the eyes. He fell into the water and floated past me, and he was smiling.'

It was dawn before he slept, and Esther eventually drifted off, to dream uneasily of being David's wife and waiting, babe in arms, for his return. But there would be no baby, she thought to herself when she woke with a start. She had not left the precautions to David Gilfillan, or relied on her old-fashioned device. She had walked boldly into a chemist and asked for advice. He had recommended Volpar Gels, and handed them over without a flicker of embarrassment. How times had changed since the time, twelve years ago, when she had crept into the seedy little shop near the docks and craved the protection that would allow Philip and her to love freely. She had paid dearly for it, in more ways than one. Her son would be nearly eleven now; living somewhere happily and, please God, safely away from bombs.

She tried to visualize him but couldn't. Whom would he resemble? She thought of the features he might possess, derived from one parent or another. If only he had Philip's mind, it didn't really matter who he took after. She cried, then, remembering love, but she did it silently so as not to wake the man beside her who must soon return to war.

13

July 1941

They had frames to black out the windows now, wooden affairs covered in thick black cotton, which could be fitted into the windows and clipped into place. Each morning Lansky and Esther made their rounds, releasing the catches and lifting the frames down to let in daylight. Until now they had managed with heavy curtains or black lacquered glass. The frames were somehow a symbol that war and black-out were here to stay, and required their own special accoutrements. Esther was growing used to planes in the sky now, to the boom of ack-ack batteries on the coast, and to the feel of her gas mask banging against her hip as she walked; but the permanency of the black-out was hard to bear.

David Gilfillan's letters were even more frequent and increasingly passionate. *All that keeps me sane here is thinking of the future when we can be together and build a decent life.* He was impatient for leave now, coming up on forty-eight-hour passes, sometimes standing the whole way to Sunderland in overcrowded trains, all to snatch a few hours of passion with her. They would check into the same seedy hotel in Gateshead, signing in as Mr and Mrs Gilfillan, and then go upstairs to the sparsely furnished room which smelled of dust and disinfectant. There he would take her face between his hands and kiss her vehemently, as though to imprint himself upon her memory. After that he would begin to unbutton her blouse or slip the jacket from her shoulders, all the while planting little kisses on her cheeks and forehead. He was not a skilful lover, although he tried; but Esther knew the fault was partly in her, in her own protesting body which did not want to accept him but could not say 'no' because his need of her was so great. *I will never love again*, she thought, remembering Philip and how they had been together. *He has spoiled me for all the rest.*

So when she woke on Sunday at the end of June to hear of Russia's entry into the war, it came almost as a relief. The might of Russia would now be turned against Hitler too, and the course of the war shortened. *You will soon be home again to remake your life*, she wrote to Gilfillan, careful not to say 'we or 'our'. But by return of post came news that he was coming to Sunderland again and wanted to spend time with her.

On the morning of the first day of his leave Esther told Lansky that she would not be coming home for a few days. 'Can you manage, you and the girls? I've promised my sister...' Lansky looked at her shrewdly, and she felt her cheeks flush. But then he was holding up a hand.

'Of course we'll manage. But we'll miss you, Esther. Hurry back.'

As she drove to the warehouse, Naomi in the seat beside her, she wondered if she dared tell Lansky about Gilfillan and her dilemma. He was a man of strong principles, but he had understood about Philip, and the reasons why they could never marry.

In the end she decided not to confide in him, just yet. Every day the course of the war was changing direction. Gilfillan might be sent to the other side of the world before long, and her situation relieved – for the time being at least. When he came back – she would not permit herself use of the word 'if' – when he came back, the war might well be over. She could be honest with David then, and Lansky would never need to know.

*

Every day Anne combed the Belgate shops for cigarettes. The de Reszke Minors Frank usually smoked were popular, at only sixpence for ten; but they were soon snapped up and Anne had to fork out for more expensive brands like Capstan. 'It's a bloody scandal,' she told Frank. 'All the conchies've gone into the wholesale trade: there's only them left for jobs nowadays. They're stockpiling fags, you can depend on that. Forcing up the price.' She was beginning to see conspiracy everywhere nowadays.

'She's whipping herself up,' Frank told Esther when she visited Belgate. 'She's letting out the anger on anyone and everyone, but it's really the loss of our Joc that's biting her.' For Joseph had gone off to Aldershot two weeks before.

'Watch what you're doing,' Anne had said roughly when she kissed him goodbye. She had vowed not to cry and upset him, and her eyes were dry. 'You've had a good upbringing; don't spoil it now. Remember our Gerard's a priest, or near enough will be. Don't let him down.'

They had gone with Joe to the station, and Anne had put a good face on it until he was gone, in a hiss of steam. She had cried then, tears of rage and fear and anguish that her first-born son had been wrested from her by war.

Today, though, she was going to meet Mary in town – and, who knew? They might find something worth buying.

'Do you like it?' Anne put up a complacent hand to stroke her freshly permed hair. 'I rued it while they were doing it, mind; wired up like that to an electric machine. And the smell! Enough to curdle milk. I said last time I'd never do it again. But in the end it was worth it. Frank likes it, and it's difficult enough to get him to make a remark, never mind notice.'

Opposite her, across the café table, Mary shook her head at this criticism of her brother, but Anne was not to be stayed. 'If I put a brown-paper carrier-bag over my head,

Mary, it'd be a week before your brother noticed. Still, he does like me hair, and it's a lot easier to manage like this. Now, what I fancy is a nice fish. What about you?

They checked their shopping-lists while waiting for their waitress. Anne had piled her aluminium pans on the 'Scrap for Spitfires' cart, and was in search of some enamel replacements. Mary needed baby clothes, and a shirt for Patrick. Both of them hoped to find in some shop, somewhere, something edible that could be bought without precious coupons.

'It's nice here in Meng's, isn't it?' Anne said, looking round. Once she had only dreamed of tea in Meng's; now she could afford it. There was a British restaurant down the road with meals for a shilling, but the decor was Spartan and the food humdrum. 'That's good,' she said, squeezing her lemon wedge over batter as crisp as celery. 'Eat up, Mary. You can't afford to waste food nowadays.'

'How's your Esther?' Mary asked. 'I hope she's still happy at Lansky's, because I'm very happy in her house. I don't know how Patrick would've managed without it, the little time he gets off.'

'Are they still busy at the Emergency Unit?' Anne asked. 'I thought the wounded had got fewer after Dunkirk.'

'No,' Mary said. 'They don't come in droves now, but the beds are still full.'

'Well, he's doing a good job,' Anne said firmly. After years of calling Patrick Quinnell a drunkard and a quack, she had graciously decided to forgive him the pain of her first confinement and accept him into the family. But remembering that first painful labour brought Joe to mind again. Mary saw her sister-in-law's eyes cloud and hurried to divert her.

'Does Esther still see that Gilfillan? The solicitor? He was sweet on her, but I was never sure what she felt. She's thick with young Lansky, isn't she?'

'She'd never marry a Jew-boy,' Anne said, scandalized. 'Oh, he runs after her, but it's all one-sided. And now he's in the army she runs that business: the lot. I never thought she had it in her, I'll be honest. Our Esther, a business- woman! She couldn't add up when we had the shop. Many a time I've stepped in when she was giving stuff away – four reels of cotton at twopence three-farthings; that was ninepence, according to her. Now she's a human dynamo. She'll take our Joe into the business after the war, if he sees sense.'

Before Mary could reply, her daughter appeared in the doorway, looking about her.

'It's your Catherine,' Anne said, surprised. 'I thought she'd be on duty.'

'So did I,' Mary said. There was something in her daughter's face that alarmed her, but she waited until Catherine had joined them at the table and ordered toasted teacakes before she said: 'What's up?'

'I've joined up, mam,' Catherine said simply. 'I've joined the Wrens as a nursing orderly, and it's no use making a fuss because it's settled.'

Howard came to the Scar at the end of July. The house was quiet, with Diana still in London, the children at school or at Valesworth, and most of the servants gone to war.

'Shut down some of the rooms,' he told the harassed daily woman who was doing her best to keep up standards. 'Sheet the furniture, and leave the black-outs in place. Keep the minimum rooms available; we'll only be paying flying visits until all this is over. As for the grounds: forget flowers, and see if there's anyone in the village who wants to cultivate the land for themselves. It's good soil, I believe.'

When he had put his own house in order, Howard steeled himself to visit his mother, for the first time in months.

He was shocked by the change in Charlotte. Her eyes looked unfocused and her words, when they came, were hesitant and slurred. She did not ask after his wife or his

children, and Howard felt irritation rise in him, until he saw
the tremor of her blue-veined hands and realized suddenly
that his mother was old. He tried to remember her age: she
had been thirty-three when he was born, so she must now
be seventy-seven. He leaned towards her, his face softened.

'Are you all right here alone?' he urged. 'Perhaps you –'
He was about to say, 'Perhaps you could come to London,
to us,' but he remembered the nightly air raids and Diana's
exhaustion. It simply wouldn't work. He changed his
words accordingly: 'Perhaps we could find someone – a
nice woman – to be a companion?'

Charlotte's eyes were on him, and Howard shrank from
the hostility in them.

'If I needed someone, Howard, I'm perfectly capable of
arranging it for myself.' Her words were definitely slurred.
Was it possible that she had suffered a stroke?

They talked for a little while longer, about war and
shortages, and then, perfunctorily about Rupert and the
other children. He stood up to go and leaned forward to
kiss her cheek. It was then that he smelled the spirit: gin,
probably. Their eyes met and he saw defiance there.

'Do you ever see Gallagher?' he said, surprising even
himself with the question. Why had the former agent come
into his mind? But even as he pondered, he saw alarm flare
in the old eyes opposite. *Yes*, he thought, *you do see
Gallagher still.*

'He calls,' Charlotte said, plucking at the heavy cameo
that closed the neck of her dress. 'In fact,' her confidence
was returning now, 'in fact, he is a great help to me.' She
paused. 'Some people are faithful.'

Howard smiled. 'I'm glad to hear it.'

He kissed her again at the door, regretting that she had
chosen to throw in her lot with Gallagher, but resigned to
it. He took her hand and held it, dry and fragile, between
his own. 'I love you, mother, and I want to look after you.

Please, if you think of something I can do, let me know. And I'll bring the children to you when I can. Perhaps there'll be a breakthrough in the war soon, a turn for the better.'

Charlotte shook her head. 'I never think about the war. It's all beyond me now.'

It was July, but as Howard walked across the gravel to his car he saw only dark laurel and darker ivy. Had there been flowers in this garden once, and a child's laughter in the house?

Esther crossed the hall and pushed open the door of the living-room. Lansky sat by the unlit fire, the evening paper fallen from his hand, his eyes closed. She hesitated, wondering whether or not to wake him. It was still an hour or two to nightfall and the start of the Sabbath, and she had left everything prepared. Even as she pondered, the great head came up and his eyes opened.

'Esther? Are you going now?'

She hated lying to him, but she couldn't tell him about Gilfillan. Not yet. She moved further into the room. 'Yes. Everything is ready for Shabbos. The girls are upstairs. Naomi had dropped some loops on Sammy's balaclava, but Ruth is retrieving them. We may win the war, after all.' She was trying to make him smile and the corners of his mouth did twitch. 'I'll be back on Sunday night, at the latest.' On the phone, David had said he had forty-eight hours: forty-eight hours during which to pretend to something she didn't feel. If only Sammy was here to confide in. But Sammy was dying of frustration in a Nissen hut: she couldn't burden him further.

She saw Emmanuel was making an effort, and smiled cheerfully at him. 'Not bad for wartime?' she said, twirling round in her newly shortened dress. He smiled approval and she leaned forward impulsively and planted a kiss on

his cheek. 'Bye-bye. Look after the girls, and yourself. I'll
be back as soon as I can.'

She called another goodbye to the stairs and saw
Naomi's head appear above the banisters. 'It'll be finished
by the time you come back, Esther.' The accent was so faint
now that only the precision of her speech betrayed her
foreign origin.

'Good,' Esther said. 'I know he's looking forward to it.
He says it's cold on guard duty, even in summer.'

She let herself out of the front door and opened her
weekend bag. They were there, the Volpar Gels and her
douching equipment. *Please God, let me make him happy,*
she thought. *And let there be no consequences. Please God,
that above all.*

The station was heaving with service men, kit-bags on their
shoulders, free arms around girls or grey-haired mothers. She
saw Gilfillan through the crowd and began to work her way
toward him, but as she neared him she saw from his face
that something was wrong.

'David?' He was clutching her, threatening to overbal-
ance them both. 'David, be careful. What's the matter?'
she asked.

'I've been posted – overseas. This is embarkation leave.'

She reached up to kiss him on the mouth. 'Hush,' she
said. 'We've got two whole days. Take my arm and let's get
out of here. We're going to have a wonderful weekend.'

Sammy folded Esther's letter and put it back in the envelope. She was doing well, no doubt about it. He smiled
wryly; at this rate he would have to watch himself.
Certainly little skill was needed to run shops stocked with
goods supplied by the Ministry of Food on allocation, but
Esther was diversifying cleverly; the latest idea being a
market stall for second-hand clothes on an exchange basis.

Customers brought in clothes they no longer wanted, and if they were in good condition they could trade them off against other goods. It was more of a public service than a profit-maker, but the stalls on either side were Lanver Products stalls, so customers came to exchange clothes and did their trade with those. *We make a pair, Esther and I*, Sammy thought, feeling warm at the thought of her there now, with his father and the two little girls, getting ready for Shabbos in the family home.

How much longer could he go on like this, twiddling his thumbs while everything he cared for was under threat? He had thought the flight of his grandparents and the fall of Paris would be the nadir; that from then on things could only get better. He had listened to Churchill as, at the height of the London blitz, he broadcast to the French people. His accent was execrable, his words incomparable: '*Français!*' he had cried. '*C'est moi, Churchill, qui parle!*'

Sammy had listened to a crackling set, feeling the tears gather on his lashes as the old man continued: 'For more than thirty years, in peace and war, I have marched with you...' He had exhorted and then amused: 'We are waiting for the long-promised invasion; so are the fishes.' And then had come the words of comfort, words that had inspired Sammy. 'Goodnight, then: sleep to gather strength for the morning. For the morning will come. *Vive la France!*'

But even inspiration could expire. Sammy looked round the hut, seeing the bareness of it, paint rusting on metal, brown smears where condensation had run down the walls, the comfortless beds with their army-issue blankets, the pictures of Jane, the pin-up girl from the *Daily Mirror*, on almost every locker.

The door at the other end opened and a boy appeared, fresh-faced and looking distinctly uneasy. 'Is this Hut B?' he asked.

'I'm afraid so,' Sammy replied. 'I keep telling myself

it's the Ritz or the Dorchester, but I'm forced to admit it's Hut B.'

The boy was looking round, lowering his kit-bag to the floor. 'They said there was a spare bed here?'

'Yeah,' Sammy said. 'Two down. Here, I'll give you a hand.' He swung his legs to the floor and moved across the space between the rows of beds. 'You sound like a northerner?'

'I'm from Durham – well, a place called Belgate. You won't have heard of it.'

'*Heard* of it?' Sammy said. 'My name's Samuel Lansky, and you're Jim – no, Joe – Maguire. The day of the pit accident, when your mam sat in my van... ?'

The boy's face beamed. 'You're my Auntie's friend – well, her boss.'

'Friend,' Sammy said firmly. 'Your Aunt Esther is my partner and my salvation. Let's get your stuff stowed and we'll go to the Naafi for a *simcha*: a knees-up to you. I could do with some support around here. You're welcome.'

Frank moved the folded blanket behind him and wriggled into a more comfortable position. The sun was almost down now. He watched the glow fading in the west, seeing birds float like black specks homeward across the sky, seeing the bulk of the pit heap soften and grow less solid as the sky darkened behind it and stars came out here and there. The last bird cheeped and was silent and Frank reached for his snap tin. It was his turn to fire-watch the spoil heap in case of combustion.

Anne had given him cheese in new-baked bread, a saveloy and a crumbling saucer pie with a filling that smelled like rhubarb. He bit into the bread and cheese and wished he had a glass of beer. Not that beer was worth it nowadays. Hops begrudged and water bewitched. Someone somewhere must be making profits out of this war.

The sky was streaked navy and red with lakes of pearl grey. He had looked at it when he was a child and thought that God was up there; now he was more likely to think of paratroopers. If only he had a cigarette – but they were scarcer than hen's teeth, nowadays, and under the counter when they did exist.

He felt pins and needles attack his buttocks and moved to shift his weight. It was a bugger, this fire-watching. The AFS got £3 10s, according to informed opinion in the Half Moon: a fortune!

Belgate was almost shrouded in night now, the black-out perfect. There were some sad houses in the village, with lads dead, or gone away like Joe. Brenton was paying out of his own pocket for every death, funeral expenses and something over. There would be nationalization after the war, no doubt about it, but he wouldn't rejoice to see the back of Howard Brenton.

By God, he thought, wiping his mouth, *if Anne heard me say that she'd shit herself.* He was wondering why his wife's hatred of the coal-owner was so much more savage than his own when he heard a distant rumble. It was the smoke-screen lorries trundling to or away from Sunderland. They lined the roads there, throwing up smoke, though what they were blocking out with a black-out in force he didn't know. He heard rather than saw them go past and then looked back at the tip. Was that a glow? By God it was! He put aside his bait and reached for the klaxon: that would summon aid.

'Enjoy it?' Max asked, as they settled back in the cab.

'It was bliss,' Diana said. 'Not a single mention of the war. Incredible.' They had been to the Piccadilly Theatre to see Noël Coward's latest play, *Blithe Spirit*, a witty and wonderful story of a man trying to cope with two wives, one alive and one dead. Margaret Rutherford had played the dotty medium Madame Arcati, who evoked the ghost, and the laughter had been unbounded.

'Want to eat?' Max had asked as they left their seats but Diana had shaken her head. She had told Howard she was fire-watching tonight. He was dining his secretary, the poor little war widow with a look of Greta Garbo. It would be quite disastrous if she and Max came face to face with him in a restaurant. It was a pity, because she would've liked to go somewhere nice tonight, to drink Champagne and circle a tiny, packed dance floor. She began to hum under her breath, the song that had transcended the Blitz and made everyone remember better times: 'I don't know why, I don't know when, but I'm perfectly willing to swear, there were angels dining at the Ritz, and a nightingale sang in Berkeley Square.'

'Happy?' Max asked, reaching for her hand.

'Blissfully! Love me?'

'Madly. Well, as madly as you can love a body-snatcher.'

'Beast,' she said, reacting to the nickname all ambulance workers had to bear. 'Are *you* happy?'

'I will be as soon as we hit the bedroom,' Max said. In front the cabbie's ears were tuned, the glass partition opened.

'Hush, darling.'

'What shall I talk about then?' Max said loudly. 'Fornication? Nibbling? Yum-yum?'

'Shut up,' she said, striking his thigh. But this was what she loved about him. *He's mischievous,* she thought. *That's what it is I like: he stirs things up.*

Max paid off the cab and followed her up the steps of the Eaton Square house. 'There's no one here tonight,' he said. 'No need to be discreet.'

'I must be home by eight in the morning,' she said, as they crossed the hail. 'By the way, did you know Bunty Adlard's parents are being booted out of Vichy France? She heard about it this morning. The British are all being deported even though some of them have been there for simply yonks.'

'It's just as well,' Max said, crossing the bedroom to check the black-out. 'Most of them have been cut off from their money since the French collapse. I pity the Jews there, though: they won't get out. They say the Côte d'Azur is crawling with them. Do you want some Moët, or some whisky?'

'Whisky, please – with a splash. Is there any hot water?'

'Should be, if we have coal. God, the way we took baths for granted. I used to steep, up to my chin. Now it's five inches or you're a traitor.

They say the King has a ruler painted on all the palace baths, so no one can cheat.'

'Apocryphal,' Max said.

'I don't know; he's terribly worthy. It might be true.'

Diana bathed in five or six inches of lukewarm water, and ran naked and shivering to Max's bed. He was moving around the room, casting off his clothes, laying change on one chest, cufflinks on another.

He's just like Howard, Diana thought, suddenly. *He has a routine. They're all the same.*

But he was not the same as Howard when it came to loving her. He pleasured her more now than he had done in the old days, exciting her with his fingers until she almost screamed with desire. 'Quickly, quickly or it'll be too late.' He was on her and in her, then, and they were riding together to the crest. 'Oh God,' she breathed, 'I do love you so.'

They were lying apart, breathing like stranded whales, when the siren wailed. 'Hell,' Max said. 'Of all the bloody moments.' She rose onto her knees and moved to straddle him.

'Stay here,' she said. 'I want more.'

'God,' he groaned, 'the woman's insatiable.' His face brightened suddenly. 'You mean I'm worth the risk of being blown up?'

'No,' Diana answered demurely. 'But I can't be bothered to get dressed.'

14

November 1941

As the summer of 1941 turned to autumn and then to winter, the war news was unrelievedly gloomy. Malta and Tobruk were under siege, and constant accounts of German atrocities came from Russia and Europe. U-boats menaced shipping everywhere, and England seemed a grey and hungry place filled with anxious people. In Russia, the German tanks pressed onwards relentlessly: Kiev, Odessa, Kharkov... now they were at the gates of Moscow. And still America stayed aloof.

The US had signed the Atlantic Charter in August, but it was simply a declaration of common principles. Roosevelt helped wherever he could, but many Americans were isolationist. The British Ambassador, Lord Halifax, was pelted with eggs and tomatoes by women protesters in Detroit to underline their resistance to America's entry into the war. On the other hand, individual Americans had sent arms for the Home Guard, everything from sporting guns to gangster's tommy-guns.

Cheerful posters everywhere in Britain showed Churchill resolute and half-smiling, and on the wireless or in the House of Commons his words were as inspirational as ever: 'We shall not fail or falter; we shall not weaken or tire,' he said – but people were visibly tiring. He rallied Londoners: 'The people of London with one voice would say to Hitler: we will have no truce or parley with you, or the grisly gang who work your wicked will. You do your worst – and we will do our best.' Still the bombs rained down. 'These are not dark days: these are great days,' he told the boys of Harrow School in October; but Howard thought he could detect more determination than conviction in the words.

The *Daily Express* headline was 'Only 40 miles from Moscow'. If Stalin's scorched-earth policy could not stop the Germans, what would? Both Howard and Diana were becoming reconciled to Rupert's resolve to fly. What was the point of preserving your children if there would be no future for them? The boy would have to go, as other sons – and daughters – were going.

'Trust in God,' they said from pulpits, but some of the stories circulating in the House, stories coming out of Russia and Poland, made Howard wonder if there was a God at all, let alone one in whom you could place your trust. He had it on good authority that an *Einsatzgruppe* in Russia had murdered more than 30,000 Jews at a place called Babi Yar, a ravine on the outskirts of Kiev. They had done it by the simple expedient of forcing them over the cliff, shooting some of them, allowing the dead and half-dead to pile up in the ravine, throwing the children into the moving, struggling heap. He thought of the old Jew, Lansky, driving his trap into Belgate before the war, sometimes with his curly-haired son beside him. What would become of British Jewry if Hitler prevailed? For the first time since the onset of the war Howard felt despair.

He would have carried his anxiety to Diana, but she was never at home. All her time was taken up with her ambulance work or fire-watching, and on the odd occasions when they did meet, he was reluctant to spoil things by talking of such grave matters.

At the beginning of December he tried to remember when he had last made love to his wife. It shocked him to realize that it was six months ago, or more. It shocked him even more that he had not felt the lack of it. He spent more time with Barbara Traske now, but he missed the intimacy, the shared love and laughter, he had known with Diana, and he wondered what would happen at Christmas. His wife was in London, unable to leave her war work; his children were at Valesworth, except for Rupert who for some bizarre reason wanted to go to the Scar. His mother was in Sunderland, growing more and more withdrawn. To whom did he owe his allegiance?

The Friday night that he came in early, hoping to find Diana at home, she was in fact on duty. He found a note by the tantalus in his study: *Home for breakfast. Sleep well. There are real pork sausages for your breakfast. Don't waste a crumb: I got them by bribery and corruption. Love, Diana.*

For Diana it was a night of false alarms. The sirens went twice, closely followed by the all-clear. An emergency call to take a pregnant woman to hospital freed Diana from tossing and turning on a narrow bunk-bed covered by a smelly grey blanket, her head on a pillow that rustled and contrived to form lumps which had to be dispersed every five minutes with a blow from her fist.

It was a relief when morning came, and with it the shift change-over. She got a lift as far as Victoria and walked the last few blocks to Eaton Square, collecting the milk and papers from the step while she waited for Max, or the ancient Valesworth butler who now looked after him, to answer the door. It was Max who came, bleary-eyed and unshaven, a maroon silk dressing-gown belted over grey silk pyjamas.

'Good morning,' she said, reaching to kiss his bristled cheek.

'God, don't be cheerful,' he said, leading the way to the basement kitchen. 'My head feels like a drum. Too much port at Reggie's last night – or too much cheese. I don't think Stilton agrees with me. Take a pew. We've got some eggs.'

Diana sank into a seat at the scrubbed pine table and stretched, turning her head this way and that to ease the tension. Far off she heard the rattle of the letter-box. Letters meant so much nowadays, with everyone separated. If only Rupert knew how to put pen to paper. 'I'll get the post for you,' she said. 'I think that's it I just heard.'

She left him scooping fat onto the spitting eggs, and went to collect the pile of mail from the front door: numerous buff envelopes, a thick white one which felt like an invitation, and an airmail letter with a US stamp.

'Anything exciting?' he asked as she put them beside his place.

'One from Laura, I think – someone in the States, anyway.' If he had rushed to open it she would have been hurt, but he made no move. He was ladling eggs onto a plate and putting it under the warm grill before dropping bread into the spitting fat. 'My God, you're domesticated,' she said in wonder. The old Max couldn't have brewed tea, let alone cooked.

'Needs must,' he said but a grin had crept round his mouth. 'Actually, it's quite good fun. I made cheese on toast yesterday. Scrumptious!'

They sat down at the table, each with an egg and a cup of tea. He ate for a moment, and then reached for the American letter. 'It is from Laura.' He was opening the envelope and straightening out the single sheet of paper it contained, and Diana felt a sudden stab of pity for him. The least Laura could do was give him a bulletin on his children's progress. But then she remembered the years when she had been in Mount Street and Howard far away in Durham: how often had she written to him then? *I was a selfish bitch,* she thought and was ashamed, not only for the past but for the present betrayal.

'I must go,' she said but Max's brow had lowered and he threw the letter contemptuously aside.

'Isolationist rubbish,' he said. 'She thinks the best thing

I can do is scuttle over there, too. England is finished, she thinks: Joe Kennedy says so.'

'So what?' Diana said. 'He's only a bootlegger.'

'The trouble with Laura,' Max said firmly, 'is that she has forgotten my heritage. And my children's heritage. If I did go to America, it would be to remind her of it. As it is, there's a war to win – and then we shall see.'

Diana had wanted to talk to Max, to draw comfort from him, but he was too taken up with his own troubles. 'Take care,' she said instead, kissing him lightly on the forehead. 'Ring me when you can.'

Outside the air was cold and dear: it would be Christmas soon. Poor Max! To be alone at Christmas, and nothing she could do for him because her duty lay elsewhere.

'Are you warm enough?' Rupert looked anxiously at Stella, snuggling against him in the front seat of the car. Her blonde hair was swept up in front and turned under behind in a page-boy bob that fell to her shoulders. Her blue coat looked skimpy, but above it her pale face seemed to glow. He repeated his question.

'Yes,' Stella said. 'Just get us away from here: somewhere nice.'

'Where?' he said grandly. We can go anywhere. Anywhere you'd like.'

He expected and wanted her eyes to widen at his largesse, but she did not seem over-impressed. Instead, she yawned, putting up red fingertips to cover her mouth.

'Don't ask me. You're the one who knows everything.'

It was the way Stella spoke to him, almost contemptuously, that had intrigued him at first. He had thought everyone in Belgate would defer to him, but she had not, right from that first day they had met. He had wanted to bring her to heel; that was why he had sought her out, lurking near the village until he saw her again. And then she had begun to get to him. Now all he wanted was to be alone with her, here in the car. In the dark.

He thought now of the first time they had had sex. Everything had exploded. He had sobbed, and she had held him in her thin arms and called him a cry-baby, and then she had reached down and touched him and it had all begun again.

'What time do you have to be home tonight?' he asked, hoping against hope it would be late.

'Any time,' she said carelessly.

'I thought your mother was strict?'

'She is, but that doesn't change nothing.'

Rupert winced at her grammar, but an idea had come into his head.

'Won't they worry? I mean, where will they think you are?'

'Don't fuss. They think I'm at work now, but I'm not, am I? They can think what they like tonight. I'll only get a clip when I get in, and I can stand that.'

'We could stay somewhere for the night, if you'd like?'

He hardly dared to hope she'd say yes, but Stella was nodding.

'OK. Let's get some dinner first, though. I'm famished.'

Rupert turned the car towards the Cleveland Hills. There were inns there, country places, where they could register as Mr and Mrs and no one would argue. And be in bed together all night. At it all night! 'Oh God, I love you, Stella,' he said and felt his throat tighten with the excitement of it all.

There would be time enough then to tell her what he had done, to explain why he had to get into the war now. Perhaps she could come with him? Anything was possible with the world turned upside down. He began to whistle 'Run Rabbit, Run', the tune that everyone was whistling. It was good to be alive, he thought. Bloody, bloody good! He would have a night with Stella, and then he would report for training. The papers were in his pocket, duly signed. No one could stop him now.

*

Lansky and the girls had been up early to go to *shul*, and Esther had completed the Sabbath tasks before she went to get out the car and drive to the warehouse. She had had two letters that morning: one from Sammy and the other from David Gilfillan. Sammy's letter was despondent. *When I think that this could go on for years, Esther, I wonder if I can stick it. I joined up to fight, but all I do is play at soldiers. I'd be better off at home, although I don't see that I could do a better job than you're doing.*

Esther tried to keep business worries from him, especially the Gallagher story, being fearful of his reaction. If only Sammy could get home for Christmas. But perhaps Christians got preference for a Christian festival? If so, she and the girls would have to send him a parcel full of good things. She could mention it tonight; that might cheer everybody up.

But it wouldn't do anything for David, whose letter lay now in her handbag, five pages of trivia, of reminiscence and talk of the future, all of it reeking of fear. He was 'overseas' now, and she guessed he was in the Western Desert. *We don't get much sleep. I think about you in the waking hours. Do you remember the day we walked in the field of cornflowers? I remember that day. It all comes back so clearly. Dear Esther, if only the world had stayed sane.*

Esther turned her thoughts away to happier things, to Anne and her children, and the gifts she must buy for Christmas. And then she was in the warehouse, and people were bombarding her with questions and forms and letters and discrepancies, and she could forget her worries in the comfortable world of work.

When she listened to Tommy Handley's wireless programme, ITMA, with its talk of the Minister of Aggravation and Office of Twerps, she wondered if he drew his details from the workings of the Ministry of Food.

Everything was in short supply, so some regulations were needed, but some of the rules were inoperable and some of the food inedible. Dried eggs, imported from the United States, tasted of chalk and when made into omelettes looked like lino tiles. National dried milk was no better. And yet women bought it and some, like Anne, swore by it. The National wheatmeal loaf was a dirty beige concoction, hated by everyone; the British were a nation of white-bread eaters. Now they were being wooed to become potato-eaters like the Irish: a poster on the warehouse wall proclaimed it.

Those who have the will to win,
Cook potatoes in their skin,
Knowing that the sight of peelings
Deeply hurts Lord Woolton's feelings.

Woolton pie, named after the popular Minister of Food, was a concoction of potato, swede and carrot under potato pastry. Women were exhorted to add an Oxo cube to vegetable water to make 'delicious soup', and Potato Pete even suggested mashed potato as a sandwich filling. And if by any chance you wasted food, the Squander Bug would get you.

From time to time Esther got hold of luxuries and allotted them to Lanver customers on a fair-shares basis. But under-the-counter luxuries did not come cheap. She worried about passing on the high prices, until Sammy issued a rule: 'Feed the people, Esther, as cheaply as you can – but keep us in business. Make just enough profit for that. And keep track of what friend Gallagher does. Every piece of paper.'

Everyone had to register to get milk now, and was exhorted to leave what milk there was for babies and nursing mothers. Herds had been slaughtered for lack of feedstuff. So Esther filled in her forms and racked her brains, and kept her jam factory going night and day; and when she was able to slip a war widow a tin or a pound of fruit, or give an old-age pensioner a piece of cheese with a wave of the hand that meant 'free', she felt a kinship with the pilot above or the miner below. She was doing her bit, and it was good. The fact that she was also becoming rich was a new and uneasy addition.

'Any chance of a cuppa?' Frank asked.

Anne raised floured hands from her scone mixture. 'With these? Make one yourself, and give me one. And get a shave, Frank – you look like a tramp. I told you your Mary might look in, and I'll say one thing for her man: he always looks clean.'

'So I don't?' Frank had come up behind her and was circling her waist. 'So I'm dirty, am I? Women have died for less than that.'

'Give over, Frank. Just do as I say, and pass me that basin while you're on. It's a struggle, feeding a family now, so I could do without you carrying on like a honeymooner. Make that tea ... and while you're on put some of that bromide in, what they say they give the army.'

She was making a lovely casserole with scrag-end of mutton, frying it first, and then adding onion and carrot and turnip. When it was nearly ready she would add the potatoes and thicken the gravy. Stirring it made her mouth water. To top it all, there was a big suet pudding boiling in a cloth on the back of the fire. They would have half of it with the mutton, and the rest with jam and custard. She made the custard now with half-milk, half-water, which was a scandal but that was war. All her older children had good limbs on them, thanks to milk, but now the youngest two were threatened with rickets because of Hitler. It was enough to make you spit. She rapped the spoon on the side of the casserole to dislodge the last bits of stew, and put back the lid.

They always ate late on a Saturday now. Sometimes she got heartburn when she went to bed, but it made a nice night. First the big meal, the best she could manage, and then the bairns up to bed with a lick and a promise, or out with their mates. She shuddered briefly at the thought of what Stella got up to, but then, as she cut out the scones, returned to happy contemplation of the evening ahead. She and Frank would sit listening to the wireless, which was lovely on Saturdays, moving closer together as the night went on. Moving closer until they touched, her hand on his knee, his arm around her. And then up to bed, and no need to leap up the next morning. There was some as said it was a sin not to go to first Mass, but keeping your husband happy was part of God's plan, too. And it was a bit of a wild night outside, so that would keep the Jerries away, God willing.

She glanced at the clock. 'Our Stella should be in by now.'

But Frank was deep in his paper and only grunted.

'Interesting?' she said sarcastically, but he was too deep in to get her point.

'Depressing! The Aussies are preparing for invasion. It says here the Japs are on the move, so something's up. And Rommel's still on top in the desert. It says here, an' all, that unmarried women are going to be called up! That's your Esther.'

'They'll never take her,' Anne said confidently. 'She's too important – although I wouldn't say that to her face, so don't say I said it. If the Germans invade Australia, what happens then?'

'Search me,' Frank said. 'It says Japan's told Roosevelt that it's all just defence, all this build-up.'

'I wouldn't trust the Japs an inch.'

'They'd never take on America, Anne: no one would. Any road, the Russian winter's playing havoc with the Jerries round Moscow, so there's something to cheer you up.'

'The British winter's playing havoc with me, Frank,

that's all I know. And when I think it's December the 7th, and Christmas two weeks off... I'll never be ready in time.'

He levered himself from his seat and crossed to kiss her. 'You've been saying that every Christmas since we wed, and every year we have the best Christmas of anyone – round here, anyway. So I don't expect 1941'll be any different.'

'Get off,' Anne said, but Frank could tell she was pleased. Her face darkened again: 'And don't say this'll be a good Christmas, Frank. It's the first without our Joe, and I'm dreading it.' She looked at the clock. 'Where's that imp of Satan? She should've been home by now.'

Stella was the first to wake, knowing instinctively that it was morning in spite of the pitch-blackness of the room. She lay for a moment, regret coming sharp upon her. It had seemed like a good idea yesterday, a night in an hotel with Rupert. And it had been posh: a meal in a restaurant, with wine and an ancient, hovering waiter, and then coffee and brandy in the lounge, in big deep chairs. He knew how to do things, for all he was only a bairn. He hadn't been a bairn last night though: more like a ravening wolfhound. She'd be stiff for a week. And her mother would kill her when she got back; she had a chance to have the pollis out by now.

Stella thought of how her ears would ring from one of her mother's clouts, or the sting of a damp tea-towel flicked at her legs as she ran up the stairs. Oh God! She turned over and looked at Rupert, asleep like a baby, both arms thrown up behind his head. All right for him; no one would be waiting to clout him.

She sat up and thumped him on the arm. 'Wake up, you. I've got to get back home.'

They dressed in silence, taking turns at the ice-cold jug and bowl, shivering as they towelled dry, turning away from one another to pull on their clothes.

'We'll start straight after breakfast,' he said as he knotted his tie.

'Breakfast!' Stella said. She had never felt less like food in her life.

'Calm down,' Rupert said, suddenly taking pity on the last night's woman-of-the-world who was this morning's waif. He moved to take her face in his hands. 'We'll have a quick breakfast, and then I'll break the speed limit home.'

There was a moment's hesitation, and then Stella slumped against him. 'OK. But I just want toast…'

'And bacon? And eggs? They do you well in the country.'

Rupert felt suddenly protective towards her. She had been heaven last night, more than anyone could ask for. He drew her arm through his and led her proudly down to the dining room, making sure her ringless left hand was covered by his own. A vision of his mother rose before him, one day she would have to know about Stella, but she would understand. Everyone would have to understand.

It was cold. As Sammy and Joe marched towards the pub, hands deep in their pockets, their breath came out in crisp white clouds and their steps rang on the frozen track.

'The door's shut,' Joe said as the Haycock came into view.

'They're never shut to me,' Sammy said. 'Round the back and knock twice. Leave it to Sammy.'

But they had to knock three times before the landlord appeared, and there was no smile of welcome on his face.

'There's something up,' he said, turning away even as he opened the door. They followed him into the bar where the regulars were clustered around the wireless set that occupied pride of place among the bottles. The announcer's voice was sombre.

'Several battleships are believed hit, but there are no official estimates of casualties.'

'What's happened?' Sammy said, looking around at the gloomy faces. 'What's he talking about?'

Beside him, Joe took off his cap and threaded it slowly through his epaulette.

'It's the Japs,' the landlord said. 'They've gone and bombed Pearl Harbour.'

Joe tugged at Sammy's sleeve. 'Pearl Harbour?' He couldn't understand why a slow grin was spreading over his companion's face. 'Where's Pearl Harbour?'

Sammy was pushing coins over the counter and taking delivery of two brimming tankards. 'Drink up,' he said, raising his glass. 'Pearl Harbour, my son, is the favourite resting-place of the American Pacific fleet. If the Japs have bombed it, it means the Yanks are now in the war – and we are as good as on our way back home.'

Diana bumped into some sandbags, and Max had to steady her, and then they were going through a back entrance of the Café Royal, pushing aside heavy velvet curtains and moving into dazzling light from crystal chandeliers, with Napoleon's arms above them and everywhere red plush and gilt and chatter, the people in the balcony looking down curiously at the newcomers.

'So, what will it mean?' Diana said, sipping her wine and lighting a cigarette.

'It means isolationism is dead, darling,' said Max. 'That's number one. It means, two, that the whole economy of the United States will be turned over to waging war, and we're bound to benefit from that. And it means Roosevelt will now be able to help us overtly, as he's been doing covertly all along.'

'So it's good news – in spite of the landing in Malaya?'

'It's good news in the long term. In the short term there may be difficulties: what weaponry we're getting from the

States will probably dry up for a while. Until they gear up – then there'll be plenty for everyone.'

'What about planes? Rupert –'

'It won't affect him, Di, except in so far as it makes victory certain and probably shortens the war.' Max reached out to cover her hand with his own. 'Don't worry, Rupert's training will take ages. It may all be over before he's operational.'

They danced, cheek to cheek, not caring who saw them.

'What about us?' he said against her ear as the band began to play 'Perfidia'.

'What *about* us?' Diana countered, unable to ignore the words that went with the song: 'And now, I see my love is not for you and so I take it back with a sigh; perfidious one, goodbye.' Had Max been lying to her these past months when he told her she meant everything to him? That they must find a way to be together because he could not live without her?

'I love you, Di. You know that.'

'What about Laura?' There was a pause. 'She's a long, long way away,' Max said at last, and tightened his arms around her.

BOOK FOUR

15

May 1942

This is good,' Sammy said, leaning back from the table and stretching his arms above his head.

'You have a nice rest,' Esther said soothingly, beginning to clear the dishes. Sammy leaned forward again, smiling and shaking his head.

'No, Esther, I didn't mean it was nice to relax. It is, and the food – oh boy! But what is better is that I've got a million things to do today. Most days in camp I do nothing. Today, I want to see my business empire, inspect the books, sack my manager if they don't come up to expectations, treat my manager to Champagne if they do. But first, come upstairs a moment. I need a helping hand.'

It was nine-thirty. The girls had gone off to school, reluctantly today because they wanted to be with Sammy.

He had placated them with the promise of a night out at a restaurant. 'Dress up,' he said, 'all three of you. I want to be proud of my girls.' Now he and Esther went upstairs, he two at a time and determined, she wondering why he wanted her help.

Sammy's bedroom was a cluttered place, but there was order of a kind there. He took down some photograph albums and passed them to Esther. 'Go through these. You're looking for any photographs of me as a boy in France. They'll be with Grandpère and Grandmère usually, though some will be of me on my own. I'll do the boxes.'

Esther frowned. 'I thought we were going to the warehouse. It's quite important –'

'Not as important as this!' Sammy said firmly. 'Start looking and I'll explain. If you don't know whether or not the photo is of France, ask.'

He took the lid from the first box and began rapidly leafing through the contents. 'A few days ago, not long after the Bruneval raid, I heard something on the BBC. A naval commander was talking about the planning of the raid, and he said it was successful because the men who were dropped there "knew" the terrain. They knew it because they'd been taught it: every bank, every ditch, every building. They learned it from a model and the model was made up by people who either knew the place or had quite explicit photographs of it. He said they already had thousands of photographs, but they needed more, so if anyone had holiday snaps of occupied Europe…'

He broke off, scrutinized a photograph and put it on one side. 'Well, I thought, "Sammy, you had a box-Brownie and you took photographs." Then I thought: "No, they'll have hundreds already." And then I thought, "That's what a *shlemiel* would say." So, first time home, I'm looking: and so are you. Search!'

An hour later they had a pile of photographs, all annotated on the reverse with precise details of the location.

'These ought to be sent to the Admiralty,' Sammy said thoughtfully, 'but I'm a loyal soldier: I'll send mine to the War Office, I think. I'll write the covering letter now and get a stamp from papa. You get your bonnet, and we'll be off. And while we drive I'll tell you about your nephew, the gallant Joseph, who's currently in line for a stripe and is my best mate.'

Esther had a letter to post, too, containing a cheque for £5 9s 11d, the rates on her house. The rent she received from Mary and Patrick was mounting up nicely in the bank, and Lansky stoutly refused to accept any payment for her lodging. He allowed her to bring in food, and she knew it pleased him when she bought things for the girls, but rationing limited what she could do there, and Lansky would not relent about rent. 'You bring a blessing to my house, Esther; you care for the *kinderlach*. How would I manage without you? And you should pay for doing this favour?'

As Esther went to join Sammy in the car she thought of Lansky's face tonight when he saw Ruth and Naomi in the dresses Anne had made for them from two of Esther's own.

These days, most of her pleasure came from watching the others in the household enjoy: Lansky with Ruth, poring over her textbooks, encouraging her blazing intelligence; Naomi, concentrating on her knitting for Sammy, intent on making him the warmest soldier in the British army, squealing with delight when there was a letter for her, putting her hair in rags when he was coming home. And Sammy, seeing him smile at his family or glow with pleasure when business went well. *They're all I've got,* she thought. She had not heard from Gilfillan for two weeks now, but his last letter had been even more emotional and sad than before. Still, today was Sammy's day and not a time for brooding.

'Now,' he said when they were in the car, 'this nephew of yours: a *mentsh*. For me it was a desert until he came, but now – a soul-mate, no less. He does your sister credit. And a good soldier; already I see him a sergeant-major. Unlike yours truly, his worth is about to be recognized.'

'Do you think you'll all be sent overseas?' Esther had felt afraid to discuss this with Sammy before, but now that Joe was involved, it seemed easier.

There was a pause before he replied.

'Eventually. This war isn't going to fizzle out, Es. Sooner or later we'll have to go and finish it off. In the meantime we have charmers and bottled sunshine, we get into our swanks occasionally and we get yum-yum from the postman.' He was laughing now, knowing he had her foxed.

'Talk English,' she said.

'Yes, sprog,' he said. 'Well, sprog means mate. Charmers are girls, swanks mean civvies. What else did I say? Bottled sunshine, otherwise known as brown food, is beer. Essential!'

'And yum-yum?' Esther asked weakly.

'That's love by post. The kind of letter I'm always hoping to get from you.'

'Hush,' she said. 'And watch what you're doing with my car.' It was only afterwards that she realized how skilfully he had diverted her from the prospect of their going off to war, and by then they were deep into the problems of the business. Erratic food convoys; demand for the fresh produce from the market garden far outstripping supply; the difficulty of retaining customer goodwill when supplies were scarce; rationing, which took away the excitement of trying to attract custom… these were some of Esther's problems, but the biggest was Gallagher.

'The crook,' Sammy said when she told him of the former agent's latest exploits. 'He's got us where he wants us – or thinks he has.'

'They say he's got all his cronies working in the Food Office now, but then rumours are rife all the time. The latest is that he's up to no good with Mrs Brenton, the old lady: Mr Howard's mother.'

'She must be a hundred!' Sammy said, aghast.

'Not *that* kind of "no good". And she's only in her seventies. No, they say he's got her in his pocket. She does what he says, lets him run her affairs, that sort of thing. And they also say she's taken to the bottle, and he eggs her on.'

'What does her son, the MP, do about it?' Sammy's eyebrows were raised.

'I don't suppose he knows,' Esther said. 'He's in London most of the time.'

'He should know,' Sammy said firmly. 'It's his business

to know about his mother. Still, we have troubles enough: let's look at those stock-projections again.'

Diana relaxed into the back seat of the cab and looked out on London, flashing past. Everyone looked so preoccupied nowadays, and the sandbags around windows and doors were unkempt. Still, it was nice to be out of uniform or slacks, and dressed up, quite like the old days. She looked down at her gloved hands and well-shod feet. She had bought the suit from Molyneux in 1938, when everyone had believed there would be peace. And now it was the third year of war. In the old days she would have discarded the suit after the first season; now it was a prized possession, since coupons seemed to vanish on essentials like nightwear and shirts for the men. She felt good today. It was ages since she and Lee had had a lovely, uncomplicated lunch together, and yesterday her period had started, which was always a relief.

Suddenly her spirits dropped, as she thought of the web of lies in which she was now enmeshed. That was another incredible thing: if anyone had told her in 1939 that she would be back with Max, she would have called for a psychiatrist to have them committed. *It can't go on,* she thought, but she had been saying that to herself for months.

The colonnade of the Ritz came into view, and Diana opened her bag for the fare. 'Darling!' Loelia was alighting, too, and they swept into the Ritz foyer together and on to the glittering dining-room with its ornate and beautiful ceiling.

'Now,' Lee said, when they had settled themselves with an aperitif, 'tell me your news. And where did you get the divine suit? Is it Lanvin?'

'Molyneux,' Diana said. 'And three years old.'

Loelia's face wrinkled with anguish. 'What if this goes on and on, Di? Soap's rationed now, and I'm down to my last box of sandalwood. What do I do then? Use some terrible green carbolic, I suppose. And Max says turn-ups on trousers will go, and double-breasted coats; we'll have to raise skirts, whether or not it's *à la mode*; and there'll be this dreadful Utility stuff: hardly any choice of style, and only two or three colours. No more embroidery; no appliqué or lace; buttons and pleats having to be counted; and no pockets on men's pyjamas. It's terrible! But I refuse to put gravy browning on my legs instead of stockings. That's where I draw the line!'

Diana was no more approving of all the petty Board of Trade restrictions than Loelia, but her friend's endless litany of complaint was jarring. This morning a letter from Rupert, who was halfway through his air force training, had told her excitedly of his hopes for the future. *I mean to do my best, ma, and make you proud of me. God help Schicklgruber when I get up there.* Someone had told Diana once that the life of a young fighter-pilot could be measured in months, if not weeks. And Loelia was short of silk stockings!

'Let's order,' she said shortly. 'You have wardrobes of clothes, Lee. I expect you'll survive.'

Anne scalded a spoonful of tea, and sat down with her cup. Her back ached and her head ached, too. Three of the children had scabies, and the ritual bathing and anointing with lotion was an extra burden. It was rife in the local school, but there was still a bit of a stigma about it, and she was trying to stop it spreading to the rest of the family and keep it quiet at the same time.

On top of that there was the extra worry of Stella, eighteen now and a law unto herself. Anne's eyes strayed constantly to her daughter's waistline, convinced there would be signs of thickening there. It was almost inevitable, with her in and out of the house at all hours, always 'going to work' but done up like a dog's dinner – which was a funny way of going to any job Anne had ever heard of, let alone one in a factory. If it was Americans, Anne would flay her alive! The 'doughboys' had now been in Britain for three months, and already the tales about them were scandalous.

She supped her tea and thought about her family. Little Philomena had been dead for twelve years now, and yet it seemed like yesterday she had been stood on a chair in liberty bodice and knickers, to get topped and tailed for bed. She went down the ranks of her remaining children, seeing each in her mind's eye. Joe coming up to nineteen, never giving a moment's trouble except in his determination to join up. Gerard, a born monsignor; then Angela, Theresa, David, and Bernard. 'My God,' she said aloud. 'I could wind up with thirty-odd grandbairns!'

She was not at all sure about the friendship that was growing between Joe and young Lansky, who'd always been a wide boy. Not to mention being a sheeny – they did nowt for nowt. A guilty recollection of the day Frank broke his legs and they had been so kind arose, and was quickly dismissed. Most people behave well in a crisis, so you couldn't count that.

Suddenly Anne remembered what she had intended to do that morning, with Stella out of the way. She had seen a Ministry of Information film about being alert: a woman had searched her lodger's bedroom and discovered him to be a spy. Stella was no spy, but a quick look through her drawers might reveal what she was up to.

Anne went upstairs, reminding herself that she was mistress of her own home and could go where she pleased. All the same, as she eased open the first drawer the hair on the back of her neck prickled. You were supposed to trust your children, the priest had said so only the other week. On the other hand, no seminary in the land could prepare a man to deal with the likes of Stella.

Fight fire with fire; that was the only way with that one.

The top drawer yielded nothing except an empty envelope addressed to Miss Stella Maguire: nice-quality paper and classy handwriting. She turned it over, hoping to find a sender's name on the flap, but there were only two crosses and the letters B.O.L.T.O.P., which obviously meant something – but what? Anne rifled on, and then went down to the bottom drawer. Underclothes, and a Valentine card with a lace edge but no signature. And a tin box which was heavy and rattled. Anne opened it with a sense of foreboding, knowing instinctively that what it contained was a devil's device: with its rubber bulb and long tube it looked like what the district nurse used to give enemas, but that was not what Stella used it for. She used it to flush out any chance of a pregnancy. Anne sank onto the bed and contemplated her daughter's duplicity, acknowledging as she did so that she had really known it all along.

She was still sitting there ten minutes later when a knock came at the door. She crammed the tin back into the drawer and fled downstairs, her heart hammering against her ribs as though she had been caught out in a crime.

The woman on the step was rattling a tin. 'Comforts for soldiers?' she said sweetly, and like one in a daze Anne went for her purse and handed over a shilling she could ill afford.

Howard closed *The Times* to shut out the tales of the Japanese advance, and reached for his coffee cup. Since Singapore had fallen in February, he had felt a great weight of depression about the course of the war. Sometimes he felt as though Churchill's rhetoric and the opening bars of Beethoven's *Fifth Symphony* were all that stood between Britain and extinction. The Beethoven theme was used by the BBC on its broadcasts to occupied Europe because it sounded like the Morse-code rhythm for V for victory: three dots and a dash.

Even the young Princess Elizabeth had been drawn into the war now, registering for call-up dressed in her Girl Guide uniform, looking younger than her sixteen years. So far, local panels had been reluctant to call up such young girls, but the fact that they had to register at all was chilling.

There was a knock at the door, and Howard lifted his napkin to dab his lips before he called, 'Come in.'

Barbara Traske crossed to the desk and put a folder on the blotter. 'All ready for signature,' she said.

Howard smiled acknowledgement and reached for a folded document. 'That house in Maida Vale, the one you couldn't afford: I've taken a lease on it. It's for you and Richard, for as long as you remain in my employ, which I hope will be a very long time.'

Howard had grown very fond of the young widow, watching the shadows depart from her face as she began to enjoy her job and emerge a little into the world again. One night, after a late sitting and an urgent letter to despatch, they had had a drink together and she had talked for the first time of the sinking of the *Hood* and her husband's death. Her eyes had grown dark, but she had not wept, and he admired her for it. But as she talked of her son and the future, he had realized the dreadful insecurity of her position and the meagreness of her naval pension. She was pinching and scraping to keep her son at his father's old school and renting a down-at-heel upstairs flat in Tottenham.

He had taken her to see the Maida Vale house on the pretext of looking at it for a friend. Her eyes had grown wide with appreciation of the four spacious rooms, the wide hall and staircase, the well-fitted bathroom. 'You should rent it,' he'd said, and seen her pleasure fade. It had been a temptation to tell her then that the friend was a pretext and he meant the house for her, but he had restrained himself until it was a *fait accompli*. When he signed the lease he thought of Michael Trenchard. It was nearly twenty years since Trenchard's death but the guilt remained. They had served together in France and celebrated the Armistice together. But when Trenchard had been out of work and desperate, Howard had failed him, and Trenchard had taken his own life. Now, by helping the wife of a dead serviceman, he felt he was making a partial atonement.

He let her stammer out her thanks and then held up his hand.

'Go and enjoy it. I mean to come and see that for myself – and that will be my reward. Now, my beautiful twelve-year-old daughter is coming to London today to get her teeth attended to, and has demanded lunch at the Savoy as a sweetener. I will be late if I'm not careful. Can you call me a cab?'

There was no rest for Anne once she had made her discovery. She had to talk to someone, and it couldn't be Frank. Nor Esther, who, being barren, couldn't understand a mother's pain. There was only Mary Quinnell, her sister-in-law. Half an hour after she had handed over her shilling for the soldiers she was on the bus to Sunderland, praying that Mary would be at home.

She found her seated at her kitchen table making wax flowers. 'Sit down,' she said, pushing aside the pile of twigs and setting the pan of wax back on the stove.

'What are they for?' Anne said, looking at the decorated fronds already standing in a jar. A tiny petal of wax had been shaped around the ends and protuberances of each twig so that they appeared to be flowers, yellow in this case, so that the winter twigs looked for all the world like forsythia in full bloom.

'They're to cheer up the house in the first place,' Mary

said. 'And what I don't need'll go to the bazaar. They always sell.'

Anne drank her tea carefully, and wondered how to broach the subject. She decided to settle in with a bit of gossip first. 'Have you heard about old Mrs Brenton? Taken to the bottle, apparently. It's all round the pit. Annie Swanson's niece went in service there, and she says the old lady's pickled – and Gallagher never away from the house!'

Mary's face twisted at the mention of the agent. 'No wonder she drinks if she has much to do with that one. What about Mrs Howard? I never hear news of her nowadays.'

'Nor see her,' Anne said. 'She's gallivanting round London, very likely, dressed to kill. Which brings me to a problem, Mary.' And she poured out her tale of Stella's mystery outings, her cheek, her high-handedness and – at last and with difficulty – her fall from grace, all the while telling herself that if Mary sympathized or referred to her own saintly Catherine, working like Florence Nightingale in Portsmouth, or to John in his reserved occupation in Yorkshire, she would give her a piece of her mind.

But Mary did none of this. 'Have you spoken to Stella? she asked quietly.

'Spoken to her? Ordinary talking's double-Dutch to that one, Mary. I've been speaking to her since she was five, and she hasn't paid attention yet. I've leathered her; I've begged her; I've threatened to put her out; I've had the priest round; I went to her schoolteachers. Who do I see next? Churchill?'

Mary picked up the teapot. 'Have another cuppa and calm down. Girls will be girls, Anne: you should know that. How old were you when you went with our Frank?'

Anne was about to say, 'But I only did that to get out of going into service,' when she remembered and held her tongue. Instead she said: 'It's your Frank I worry about, Mary. He's got a future when this war's over. He can go to the top in the Labour Party. But not if he's the father of the Whore of Babylon.'

Before Mary could reply, there came a whimper from the adjoining room, and almost at the same moment the sound of a key in the front door.

'That'll be Patrick,' Mary said, her face lighting up. Anne had come to like and respect Patrick Quinnell, but her heart sank. They could not discuss Stella's shortcomings in front of a man, doctor or no doctor, so she would not now get the comfort she had come for.

'I'll get him,' Patrick called from the hail, and the next moment he came into the room carrying his son, flushed still with sleep and rubbing his eyes. *He's a lovely bairn,* Anne thought, *but they dote on him too much. What would they do if they lost him, and him an only one?*

'Anne,' Patrick said, bending to kiss her cheek, 'we don't see you often enough. This is nice.'

Anne smiled thinly, but at heart she was pleased. He sounded as though he meant what he said.

'How's the hospital?' she asked. 'Full of wounded?' She had seen some of the wounded, in their blue uniforms, walking about the streets of Sunderland.

'The hospital is doing well,' Patrick said, threading the baby's legs into a high chair. We are making men better...' He smiled wryly. 'And then sending them back to war. But tell me about Frank and the family – and especially Joe. How does the army suit him?'

'He likes it,' Anne said grimly. 'Don't ask me why, but he does. He's with that Lansky's lad: not who I'd've chosen for a mate for him, but according to Joe, he's a genius. And a saint!' This last was accompanied by a gargantuan sniff.

'Joe won't go far wrong with Sammy Lansky for a mentor,' Patrick said. 'He's a bright man, and he has a heart. You know I take a special interest in Joe, so I wouldn't say this lightly. Sammy will be good for him.'

'Oh well,' Anne said, 'I'm not going to argue. You know him, I don't. I only hope you're right. But it's a crazy world now, Pat. I don't know if I'm on me head or me heels.'

'It's good to have you here again,' Lansky said. He was sitting with Sammy in his study, the boy who was now a man seated on a stool and looking handsomer than ever in his evening clothes, a white silk scarf draped round his neck. They were waiting for Esther and the girls to come downstairs, but judging from the giggling and scurrying about upstairs that might not be for some time.

More brandy?' Sammy said and then, as he refilled their glasses, 'I wanted to be home for Passover, but it couldn't be.'

Did you keep the Passover?' Emmanuel asked.

'I did,' Sammy said seriously. 'I went by the rules.'

'And they let you?' Lansky sounded surprised.

'There are two things the army respects, papa: religion and rules. I am down on their books as a Jew, therefore I am allowed to be a good Jew. And I try.' He smiled ruefully. 'I'm not your scholar, papa, but striving to be a *mentsh*. And you have your scholar.'

'Ruth will be a doctor,' Lansky said, trying not to smile with satisfaction. 'Such grasp of facts, such thirst to know things. Wonderful!'

'And the little one?' Sammy hoped his voice was non-chalant, and then asked himself why he wanted to disguise a perfectly normal interest.

'Naomi will break somebody's heart one day – and mend it again. She is a good girl.'

There was a sudden flurry of activity on the stairs, and then Esther and the girls were in the room. Ruth wore blue with white collar and cuffs and a red belt. Naomi was in a yellow dress, which set off her dark eyes and hair, and her pretty figure. Both of them had had their hair cut and waved, and each wore tiny pearl earrings, the gift of Emmanuel Lansky.

Sammy went to Naomi admiringly and held up a crooked arm. '*Mademoiselle*,' he said, '*voulez-vous promenader avec moi?*'

Naomi took his arm, her cheeks flushing as their eyes met and held. *He's fond of her*, Esther thought – and felt a pang of jealousy. Sammy had always been *hers*, right from the start, whatever either of them might have done or said. 'Shall we go?' she said, to cover her discomfiture, and went out into the hail.

She was pulling on her gloves when Lansky called out.

'Did you see that letter for you, Esther, that came by the second post?'

It was unfamiliar writing, and Esther opened it and smoothed out the single page.

Dear Miss Gulliver, I believe you were a close friend of my nephew, David Gilfillan, during his time in Sunderland. His mother has asked me to inform you that she has received notification that he is missing, believed killed...

The rest of the words faded as Esther crumpled the letter and held it to her mouth.

'What is it, Esther?' Ruth said, and there was terror in her tone.

Esther swayed, and would have fallen but suddenly Sammy's arms were around her. 'Whatever it is, Esther, I'll make it right, you'll see,' he said urgently.

She looked up at him and shook her head. Not even Sammy Lansky could raise the dead.

<u>16</u>

July 1942

Howard gave up looking for a cab and began to walk, seeing on all sides the wounds of war inflicted on London. Some of the bombsites were mellowed now, with rose-bay willowherb pushing up to cloak the scars. And everywhere there was the scrawled 'V' for victory. Germany was getting a taste of its own medicine; one air raid on Cologne had been the largest raid in the history of aerial warfare, employing a thousand bombers. Was that the way to wage war? The city's chemical works had been wrecked, but so had the cathedral. Difficult to say simply, *C'est la guerre*, when a thousand years of history could be eliminated in a single night.

There had been other massive air raids, and Germany was devastated, but Churchill still was under constant pressure. He had beaten off a formal vote of censure, but opinion polls showed that less than half the public were satisfied with the conduct of the war. A woman in Belgate had put it plainly to Howard: 'We can't see light at the end of the tunnel, that's the trouble.' She had turned to her fire then, and put on the kettle for tea, but when she turned back she was smiling.

If one thing had come out of this war it was that the idea of women as the weaker sex had been ruled out forever. Diana had been magnificent, running about with her ambulance all night, and up and about the next day as though nothing had happened. She had been good about Rupert, too, seeing him off to begin his air force training dry-eyed and smiling. It was afterwards that she had cried, more tears than he had ever seen her shed before. But the boy's letters had helped, for he was euphoric about taking to the air at last. Howard looked up, seeing the barrage balloons in the sky, as familiar now as nimbus or cumulus. How odd to think of his son up there!

'You'd better watch it, dearie.' Howard looked down at the cheery Cockney tones, and saw that he had almost walked into a pile of sandbags. 'Wot yer looking for up there?' the woman said. Her blouse strained over a flowing bosom, and there were beads of sweat on her brow, but she was smiling.

'I was thinking,' Howard said, taking off his hat and smiling back.

The woman pursed her lips. 'Oooh,' she said, shaking her head. 'It don't pay to do that, ducks, not nowadays.' She was moving away, her fat arms wobbling as she walked. 'Live a day at a time: that's the ticket.' Her bosom began to heave with laughter. 'You might be up there tomorrow, mate, where you was staring. Sitting on one of them balloons, playing yer harp.'

Esther found Emmanuel standing in the hall, the open letter in his hand, the discarded envelope fallen to the floor. His face was sunk in grief but his eyes were dry. 'They're gone,' he said. 'Both of them. In Dachau.

'Are you sure?' Esther asked, and Lansky inclined his head. She guided him into the dining-room and sat him in his carver chair at the head of the table. A former neighbour of his parents-in-law, who was now safe in Switzerland, had sent him the news of their capture and death. The information was detailed, and impossible to dismiss.

'Try to bear up until I get the girls off to school,' Esther urged. 'Then we'll talk. Do you want me to send for Sammy?'

Lansky shook his head. 'What can he do? They are gone now, Esther, and we could not even say *kaddish* for them.'

She knew then what she should do, but first she must see to Ruth and Naomi. She had not intended to tell them of the death of people they had never known, but one look at their faces when she met them on the stairs told her that it was too late to keep it from them. Naomi was weeping quietly and Ruth's eyes were angry. 'It's the grandparents, isn't it?' she said.

'Yes.' Esther put out a hand and touched Naomi's arm. 'Stop crying, Naomi, and go to Mr Lansky and comfort him.'

They went to stand on either side of the old Jew's chair. Naomi put her cheek to his and kissed him, but it was to Ruth that he turned.

'Cry if you want to,' she told him, 'but I am glad they are safe. No one can hurt them now.'

Esther put on her coat and let herself quietly out of the house. She hurried to the house of Eli Cohen, Lansky's friend, and knocked at his door. He came, hastily buttoning his waistcoat, and his face paled when he saw her.

'Esther,' he said. 'Not Sammy?'

'No,' Esther said, 'but you're needed. Emmanuel has had bad news of his parents-in-law, and he needs friends to mourn with him now.'

When she left Lansky's house an hour later the *minyan*, the requisite group of mourners, was present, and the sad tones of the *kaddish* could be heard. And the *shiva*, the seven days of mourning, had begun. Knowing the strict rules that must be followed after a death, Esther had questioned Eli Cohen. 'He doesn't know when they died, Mr Cohen, not exactly. How will he manage?'

Eli Cohen smiled and patted her arm.

'Don't worry, Esther. God is good, and even when the world goes mad He understands. All will be done correctly, we will see to it. But you, too, must pray for your friend and his sorrow.' He shook his head. 'For the girls, this may be too much.'

'Leave them to me, Mr Cohen,' Esther said. 'You leave them to me.'

'I must go,' Max said. 'There's a bit of a flap on over our friends the Russkies.'

'Oh,' Diana said, being careful not to sound enquiring. Max was quite sensitive about his work at the War Office, immediately withdrawing if he thought anyone was probing. Sometimes, though, if she was careful, he would drop a tit-bit. Now he warmed to his theme.

'Churchill may love the Russians but most of us still think of them as bloody Bolsheviks. Now they're going over to the Germans in droves. Keep it quiet – morale and all that – but the commander of their Second Assault Army has defected. Vlasov, they call the chap, Andrei Vlasov. One of the saviours of Moscow, according to Stalin, but he's thrown in his lot with Hitler. And one of the Cossack regiments has gone over to them, lock, stock and barrel.'

'My God,' Diana said in genuine horror.

'It won't make that much difference.' Max sounded smug. 'We knew there was an element that might change sides. Stalin's liquidated thousands of senior Red Army officers over the years, so there was bound to be disaffection. But by the same token, there can't be many men left now that aren't Stalin's men. So one or two here or there...' He drained his glass and set it down.

Around them the Café Royal hummed with lunch-time conversation. Somewhere a woman's laugh tinkled and a deeper voice brayed laughter. Diana shivered. 'All the same, a commander...'

Max patted her hand and then signalled to the waiter. 'I

must go.' He was standing up now, impatient as ever. 'See you tonight?'

'I don't know,' Diana said. 'I'm not sure what Howard's doing, and it's ages since we spent an evening at home.'

'I'll ring you,' Max said, eyeing the bill briefly and laying down notes. 'We'll take in a tea-dance as soon as I get the chance: they say they're all the rage: no black-out, no risk of bombs. Must dash. Love you.' He threaded his way through the tables, accepting his hat and cane from the hovering *maître d'hôtel* and turned for a final wave. Diana lifted a hand, and then looked quickly and guiltily around.

We can't go on like this, she thought and then bit her lip at her own weakness. She said that all the time now, and still did nothing about it. But what could she do? Tell Howard she wanted her freedom, at a time when he was burdened down with his dual role as MP and coal-owner? Or tell Max that she would not sleep with him until the war was over and she was free again? She was not capable of such self-denial, especially at a time when each night might be their last on earth. But sooner or later this juggling of relationships would end, and probably in disaster. She gathered up her bag and gloves, settled her hat more firmly on her head and made a stately exit, glancing neither to right nor left for fear of who might be watching her.

'Right,' Sammy said, as they moved aside the black-out curtains and entered the pub. There was already a fug of smoke, although it was only just seven o'clock. 'I'll get them,' Joe said, and began to shoulder his way to the bar.

Sammy let him go, knowing that the boy's pride demanded he pay his share now and again. *He has nothing,* Sammy thought, *and still I envy him.* There was something about the boy, a kind of optimistic innocence, that marked him out. And yet his mother was a shrew, according to most reports. Of course, he had Esther for an aunt, which couldn't be bad.

Sammy spotted two seats in a corner and made haste to grab them. By God, he would make things hum when the war was over and he got back to his proper job. Sometimes the ideas for expansion so crowded his head that it pained him, but all he did here was hang around. If he stopped larking about they might promote him – but what to? Any rank above that of corporal would cut him off from his friends, and friends were the only things here that made life bearable.

'There,' Joe said, putting two half-pint glasses down. 'Only halves, but it doesn't look too bad.'

Sammy held his glass up to the light and squinted. 'Watered,' he pronounced, 'but not drowned. Thank heaven for small mercies. Now, young Joe, what's the news from Belgate? I saw you got two letters this morning.'

'One was from me mam. Everyone's all right. They're all knitting and saving and scrimping. Our Stella's still causing trouble, but that's about normal. Otherwise, no news – oh, me dad won a pie in a raffle. Big excitement.'

From the corner of his eye Sammy had seen two girls enter the pub and go to the bar. Nice legs and fashionably dressed, but bold. The men at the bar were eyeing them askance. The war had changed a lot of things, but not the attitude to unaccompanied women in public houses.

Joe took a drink of beer, and wiped the froth from his lip. 'The other letter was from Auntie Esther. She sends her love to you.'

'Good,' Sammy said, turning his attention from the girls. 'She's a gem, your Auntie. A jewel. I'd marry her tomorrow if she'd have me.'

'Auntie Esther?' Joe said, astounded.

'Yes, Auntie Esther,' Sammy mimicked. 'Have you *looked* at your Auntie Esther? Any man would have her.'

'Me mam always says we should be sorry for her,' Joe

said. 'On account of her being a spinster, and having no children.'

'Esther a spinster?' Sammy said. '*Oy vey*!' He wondered what Joe, let alone his mother, would think if he told them Esther did have a child: a child she had been brave enough to part with. But that was a secret and would remain so. He fished in his pocket. 'Look at this.'

It was a photograph of Esther between Ruth and Naomi, all of them smiling at the camera.

'Very nice,' Joe said. 'That's a pretty girl – well, they're all pretty but she's lovely.'

'Yes,' Sammy said. That's Naomi – Naomi Guttman. She lives with us – well, I've told you about her before, but that's what she looks like.

'Have you had any news about their family?' Joe asked.

'No,' Sammy said. 'No word. Still, no news is good news.'

'It'll be nice when the war's over and everyone can get together again,' Joe said, suddenly looking a little forlorn.

'You miss home, don't you?' Sammy said. Well, we all do. What will you do when it's over?'

'Get married,' Joe said, taking Sammy by surprise with his vehemence. 'Find a nice girl, a Belgate girl, properly brought up – a Catholic if possible, but not definitely – and have a happy home, like we had.'

'Well,' Sammy said, nonplussed, 'I like that. You being definite, I mean. All I ever think about is making money. When you find this girl, you can come and work for me. You'll have your Auntie Esther on your back, but you can manage her – she's always doted on you. Same again?'

As he went to the bar he thought over Joe's words. The boy had his priorities right: a happy home, that was the main thing. What did money or business success amount to if you had no one to pass it on to when you went? The thought made him uncomfortable. He leaned forward and looked along the bar to where the two girls were now perched on stools. They were painted and dressed up like film stars, but their faces were still the faces of country girls. 'Can I buy you a drink?' he mouthed, and grinned when the blonde mouthed back, 'Two gin and limes.'

'This is a wonderful surprise,' Howard said, as he came through the door. Rupert was standing in the hall in his blazingly new uniform.

'I don't know where mother is,' the boy said. 'I rang several times on my way here, but there was no answer. And then I thought of ringing the House in case she was with you.'

'No,' Howard said, 'but I expect she'll be in before long. Are you hungry? There's probably something in the kitchen, and we can go out later, when your mother arrives. Somewhere special, to celebrate.'

They went down to the kitchen and foraged for bread and cheese and pickle. 'Are you sure it's OK to eat it?' Rupert said. 'I've brought my ration card, and a tin of peaches I got from a Yank. I gave him my squadron scarf for it.'

'Eat away,' Howard said. The piece of cheese, a week's ration, was hardly enough for a decent sandwich. 'And tell me what's been happening to you.'

It all came tumbling out, in between mouthfuls of bread and cheese. 'I went solo after eight hours, father! That's good – well, pretty good. I'm doing meteorology now, and navigation and instrument-flying, but – God! The exhilaration of being airborne.' He paused for breath and more bread. 'I worried, you know, that it wouldn't be how I imagined it – not as good. You know what I mean: an anti-climax. But when I got up there, it was glorious! I didn't mind the drill and all the bull; it was just a bit like school, actually, but worth it. I did my "air familiarity" flight in a biplane. It looked awfully flimsy but it flew. After that it was take-offs, landings, circuits and bumps, spins and stalls…'

'I think I know what you mean,' Howard said drily, 'but I wouldn't make too much of it to your mama.'

'No,' Rupert said carefully, 'I must watch what I say: no need to scare the old girl. I move to intermediate training when I go back, and after that advanced training, exams, then my wings. I want to join a fighter squadron, so I'll go to an Operational Training unit to convert to Hurricanes or Spits. That bread and cheese was awfully good... I don't suppose there's anything else, is there? Or are we going to eat somewhere soon? If so, I'll wait.'

Howard looked at his watch. 'I can't imagine where your mother is. You go and get ready and I'll ring one or two people. She must be somewhere.'

He rang the ambulance station, and then the friend who was her fire-watching partner, Celia Clavelle. They did not know where Diana was. 'I haven't seen her for ages,' Celia said.

Howard was about to say, 'But you were on duty last night?' when he thought better of it. He made his goodbyes and then put down the receiver. The next moment he found Max Dunane's name in the pad beside the telephone, and dialled his number.

'Max? Howard Brenton.'

There was a moment's silence and then a sound of Max drawing breath. 'Howard. Good to hear you.'

'I'm trying to locate Diana. You haven't seen her, have you? Rupert's come home unexpectedly, and she'll want to know.'

'Of course. I wish I could help but I haven't seen her for ages. Except of course with Lee at Valesworth...'

The voice at the other end trailed off and Howard suddenly realized that his knuckles had whitened where he was gripping the telephone receiver.

'Oh, well, sorry to have bothered you. We must get together some time...'

When he had put down the phone he looked at the clock.

Ten minutes to nine. It was twenty minutes from Eaton Square to Mount Street, and if his suspicions were correct Diana would be here in that time. He went upstairs and washed his hands and face before telephoning for a table at the Ritz.

Diana arrived at a quarter past nine, coming into the hall in a too-nonchalant fashion.

'Howard, darling! How lovely you're home. I've been at Celia's, sorting out the details for the Red Cross Benefit Lunch. Have you been in long?

Should he tell her he had already spoken to Celia? Not with the boy in the house. Howard descended the final stair, and moved to help her out of her coat.

'I've a surprise for you – a very nice one. Rupert is upstairs, settling into his room. I've booked us all a table at the Ritz. Do you want to change?

The next moment she was running upstairs, whooping with delight at the prospect of seeing her son, leaving him to go in search of a brandy and wondering what sort of a woman could be so duplicitous and still draw breath.

17

August 1942

By the time Rupert's leave was up and he had returned to his station, Howard had lost the urge to confront Diana. Lying beside her as she slept, he tried to analyse his own emotions. His wife had betrayed him; worse, she had betrayed him for the second time with the same man. He remembered her anguish in the early days of her pregnancy with Pamela, when she had hated Max Dunane with a bitterness that had been almost frightening. And yet she had been drawn back to him as remorselessly as moth to flame. It was not easy to understand – and nor were his own reactions.

He would have been entitled to a scene, an angry, emotional showdown. In law, he could have turned her out of doors. And yet he did nothing. Was it because he was afraid of her reaction; afraid of pushing her to a decision? Would she leave him for Max if he forced her to choose between them? Yet if he was a man, would he not do exactly that? Each night Howard turned on his side and tried to dismiss the whole sorry mess from his mind, trying to accept the fact that his relationship with his wife had never followed the conventional pattern.

But then Rupert was turning on the step to call a last goodbye, and he and Diana were suddenly united in worried parenthood, turning back into the hall full of unspoken fear that they might have seen their son for the last time.

The war in the desert raged on. Churchill had appointed a new commander to the Eighth Army, Lieutenant-General

Bill 'Strafer' Gort. He had been a popular officer under Auchinleck, but his reign at the Eighth Army was brief: twenty-four hours after his appointment he was dead, his RAF transport aircraft shot out of the sky over the desert by a swarm of German fighters. His replacement was a little-known general named Bernard Law Montgomery. Howard had met him once at a Colville party. Henry had introduced them, and then, when Montgomery moved away, given a brief résumé of his career. At school he had been good at games, but only if he was captain of the side. He had won a DSO and been seriously wounded in the First War, and had commanded the Third Division before the retreat from Dunkirk. 'He believes in God,' Henry had concluded gloomily. 'In fact, he thinks the Almighty is under his command.' This diminutive figure with the bird-like features was now in command of an army and facing his greatest challenge: defeating Rommel, the Desert Fox.

On 12 August, Churchill arrived in Moscow for a conference with Stalin. In private he had confided to fellow Conservatives that he considered the Russian leader a peasant: 'I can handle him,' he had boasted. Howard was less sure.

Three days later the battered tanker *Ohio* limped into Malta, followed by four other ships. The island had been on the point of surrender, for the islanders were starving. On its way to Malta the convoy had been escorted by aircraft-carriers and a host of cruisers and destroyers. By the time the convoy reached Valetta, *Eagle* was gone, *Indomitable* was out of action, the cruisers *Nigeria*, *Cairo* and *Manchester* had been torpedoed, and the *Ohio* reduced to a speed of two knots. But though attack from air and sea had decimated the convoy, it could not obliterate it. Malta was saved, and somehow the relief of the tiny island brought hope to millions of Britons, some of whom might never even have heard of it without the war.

The US Air Force was hammering European cities now:

first the marshalling yards at Rouen, then Amiens. The nation rejoiced – until it heard of the abortive commando raid on Dieppe, Operation Jubilee. Of the 6,100-strong force of Canadian, British, American and French there, more than 4,000 were reported killed, wounded or missing. The mood in the House was sombre again. 'It will be two years at least before we can mount a second front,' Howard told Diana and saw fear in her eyes for her son. *I can't tackle her now*, he thought. Instead, he proposed that he should move into another room – 'as a temporary measure, while we are both under so much stress'.

'If you think so, darling,' Diana answered carefully, and turned away. But not before he had seen the relief in her eyes.

Until Joe's enlistment Anne had not paid particular attention to the conduct of the war. Now she monitored every move. At first she was sceptical about Montgomery, but news of his God-fearing ways soon percolated as far as Belgate. Monty, as he had become known, was not a Catholic, as far as she knew, but at least he knew the meaning of the Word, which was more than could be said for some of them. She gave thanks for his appointment at Mass, and prayed fervently that Stella might be protected from the Yanks, who by all accounts were raping and pillaging their way across Britain.

Privately she and Frank agreed that Monty was infinitely superior to the American commander 'Ike' Eisenhower, who had never heard a shot fired in anger before the war, according to the papers. 'Paper soldiers,' Frank said scornfully.

'Like the Eye-ties,' Anne replied but Frank shook a cautious head.

'Not as bad as that,' he said. Allies were allies, after all, and not to be too much derided.

Anne's worries about Joe increased on two fronts: the

possibility of his being sent to a war zone, and his growing friendship with the Jew-boy. Sammy Lansky's exploits with girls had been legion in Belgate before the war, and that at a time when the world had been comparatively sane. Now that it had gone mad, what evils might he not introduce Joe? And why had she not had a frank conversation with her son before he left home?

'You should have talked to him,' she told Frank.

'What about?' he asked, wide-eyed.

'You know.'

'How do I know? I don't know what you're talking about.'

'That's right, act glakey, Frank. But we both know what I mean. And if you've fathered eight bairns and you still don't know…

'Oh – that,' Frank said sheepishly.

'Yes, that. There's our boy, out there in all that wickedness, with a devil's apprentice at his elbow, and knowing nothing, because his own father let him down.'

'Hold on,' Frank said, firm now that further evasion was pointless. 'First, if Joe doesn't know what's what at his age, he's lacking. And if someone should've told him, you should – it's woman's work, that lot.'

Anne would have fired back at him, but Frank was too fly to hang around once he had scored. 'Any road, I'm off. I should've been at the pit-head by now.'

She let him go, and sat down at her machine, vowing as she did so to bone Esther about Sammy Lansky the very next time she saw her. In the meantime, she would ask the priest to intercede with Our Lady on Joe's behalf. If anything could keep the boy safe, that would.

August was nearly at an end when Diana announced over breakfast her intention of going to Valesworth for a week at the beginning of September. 'Come if you can,' she told

Howard, but he could sense she was holding her breath against his acceptance.

'I'd like to,' he said, 'but this is an awkward time, and I need to go up to Belgate first. Tell the children I'll come in a week or two – and tell them I miss them.'

He walked to the House of Commons holding his hat, lifting his face to the sun. What a mess his life had become. He would have liked to visit his children, to have been together as a family for a little while. But Valesworth was Dunane territory, and at the moment he couldn't bear the thought of being a guest of Max Dunane's family.

Barbara Traske was waiting when Howard arrived at his office, a kettle on the boil on the tiny spirit-stove. 'I expect you'd like a cup of tea,' she said and her tone was so kind that he felt his throat constrict.

'Yes,' he said. 'That would be very nice.' She was wearing a blue dress today, with cap sleeves and a small Chinese stand-up collar. Her neck and arms were slender, thin almost, and her hand, when she handed him cup and saucer, was unbelievably fragile.

'Do you eat properly?' he asked abruptly and saw colour flood Barbara's throat. 'Forgive me for being so forthright, but I do care about you.'

Her eyes were fixed on his, pale-blue eyes, with a terrible resignation in them. Howard gestured towards the desk. 'Let's see off this lot as quickly as we can, and then I'll take you to lunch. Name the place: wherever they've meat, I suppose?'

As Barbara dithered, first about accepting and then about the venue, Howard felt his spirits lift. It would be nice to face a woman across a table again without a mountain of resentment between them. They were still discussing where to go when the door opened, and a fellow-member put his head in, his eyes starting from his face.

'Have you heard the news? The Duke of Kent has bought

it: crashed in the north of Scotland. He was on his way to Iceland, apparently.'

'Is that definite?' Howard asked. The King's youngest brother, who had served in the Royal Navy, had left it for medical reasons and had taken to flying as a hobby. Now he was an air commodore, a serving member of the RAF. Or he had been.

'Positive,' the caller said sombrely. 'They're bringing down his body now. It was a Sunderland flying boat, so he won't be the only one killed. Damned bad luck for the King...'

'And for Princess Marina,' Barbara said suddenly, putting down her cup with an unsteady hand. 'Their latest child is only a few weeks old.'

Esther sucked the end of her pen and re-read the last few lines of her letter to Sammy. *I know how bored you must be in barracks all the time, but this waiting is inevitable.* She turned the full stop into an exclamation mark and wrote on: *Naomi's bread-making is improving. Almost professional, according to your father – but he is biased.* She sucked her pen again, at a loss to know what to say to Sammy to cheer him up. Useless to tell him of the Duke of Kent's death; he'd know that already from the wireless. And difficult to tell him all was well at home, with his father so low about the news that Swiss border-guards were refusing entry to Jews who were escaping from the brutal mass round-ups in Vichy France. She tapped her teeth with the pen – until inspiration struck.

Wait till you hear about Gallagher. Apparently he bought a load of bacon from a spiv – on the black market, naturally. He was going to make a killing, but when he examined his haul it was lifting with maggots. Under-cured and of course he couldn't do a thing about it. Not that he'll lose in the long run, because he'll simply take it out of the rest of us. Still, it's nice to think of him being out-crooked, isn't it? Once this war is over I shall denounce him and demand he be shot. All around me l see spivs and profiteers, and, as the Government seems determined to put them in positions of authority, they're growing fat on this war. Still, so are we: profits up and turnover doubling. I almost feel ashamed. As you suggested, I'm seeing to the people who are most in need, and their numbers grow by the day. Two of our women have lost sons in the last month, one fighting in the desert and the other a merchant seaman. The seamen don't get the limelight the other services get, but if they didn't keep chugging across the oceans we'd all starve. I went to Belgate yesterday, on my way back from Wingate. Anne is sewing with one hand, stirring the pot with the other. She used to scorn cooking in the old days; now she's like a demented chef.

Did I tell you there's a new magazine out? Woman, *it's called. Anne lent me a copy. It had a woman factory worker on the front with her hair tied up in a turban, which was all right – but her fingernails were ten long perfect ovals wrapped round the machine she was operating. Our Stella's nails get chipped and broken from her factory work, and her wails about it can be heard night and day! Still, what was inside was all right so I'll probably buy it again.*

That's about all, I think.

Love from us all. Shalom.

Esther

'Stella!' In spite of herself, Estelle had to smile at the sight of Rupert, his face lit up like a beacon at the sight of her.

'All right!' she said, putting up a hand to protect her hair-style. 'Don't go mad.' He was kissing her – warm, quick kisses like a puppy – and it was nice to know how much he wanted her. *I've got him in the palm of my hand*, she thought, and it made her inclined to indulge him. They were standing in the street, outside the Odeon, with people staring at them. Not that she minded that, but all the same she pulled him into the alley at the side of the cinema and leaned against the wall. 'Come here,' she said and drew him against her, feeling the smooth cloth of his officer's uniform under her fingers. He was nice-looking – classy. No one could deny that. She lifted her face to his and kissed him as his hands moved gently inside her blouse.

Afterwards, in the cinema, with Greer Garson above her on the screen, Stella thought about the future. She would probably wind up married to Rupert, living at the Scar, driving around with a chauffeur like his mother. It would be all right. On the other hand, if she ended up with a Yank instead, it would be more colourful. Everything over there was brighter; you could pick peaches off trees in your own garden; and they had lovely white shoes with ankle-straps, and motorcars the size of chara-bancs with no tops on because the sun never stopped shining.

'Happy?' Rupert whispered in her ear.

'Yes,' Stella said against his cheek. 'Did you manage any chocolate?'

'Happy?' Max rolled off her with a grunt, and Diana heard him reaching for his lighter and cigarettes. 'Want one?'

She opened her eyes and raised herself on her elbow. 'Yes, please.'

They smoked companionably, propped up on pillows, talking desultorily.

'Pity about the Duke of Kent,' Max said. 'They say it was pretty horrific. Only one survivor, badly burned and shocked.'

'Don't talk about it,' Diana said. 'You know how I worry about Rupert. Do they think it was sabotage?'

'Mist,' Max said, blowing a perfect smoke ring. 'Mist

and a Scottish hillside. No one about but sheep. It was shepherds who sounded the alarm.' There was a pause. 'Is Howard all right?'

'Yes. Preoccupied, as usual, but all right.' To herself she was less emphatic: there was something wrong with Howard, an indefinable withdrawal, a coldness. Not that he had ever been given to passion. She stubbed out her cigarette and would have turned to Max again, but he was moving, swinging his legs to the floor and shuffling his feet into slippers.

'Must get going, old girl. Duty calls. I'll ring you in the morning. Daphne Ledering wants us to spend the weekend with her, if you're free? It might be a bit of fun –' Suddenly the familiar wail of the siren filled the room. 'Damn,' Max said. 'I'll have the devil's own job to get a cab now.'

When he had gone, Diana put out the light and went to the window to draw back the curtains. Eaton Square was cold in the moonlight, and above the roofs of the opposite houses she could see searchlights stabbing the sky, and once the tiny black fleck of a plane caught in their web. Would it be like that for Rupert over Germany, caught by those remorseless, searching fingers, and then the shells slicing the sky and the plane burning, cutting through leather and rubber, searing and scorching flesh, melting his beloved face? 'Oh God,' she said aloud, 'don't punish Rupert for my sins.'

Anne shifted her knees on the lino and reclasped her hands. She had prayed for Queen Mary with one son dead, now, and another a bad 'un sunning himself somewhere while England burned. Please God, make sure everyone gets punished when this lot's over, and succour the widows and orphans.' At least Princess Marina wouldn't go short, that was one thing; there was plenty had lost their man in Belgate and having to scrat. She would go through her pieces box tomorrow, and see what she could make for the Collyer baby, not a week old and without a dad. 'God bless all bairns,' she said, squeezing eye-lids and fingers together to intensify her plea. 'And send the forces of hell to Hitler and all his works.' Tonight she had finished making over a coat of Esther's for the younger Jewish girl, who looked more like Louise Rainer with every day that passed. In the old days it was Stella who had come in for Esther's cast-offs; now they all went to the Jews. Still, Stella had a father and mother to see to her – not that she couldn't look after. herself. 'Please God, keep an eye on our Stella…' Anne paused, lost for words at the enormity of what she was asking, even for Our Lord.

Above her, the bed stirred. 'Come to bed, Annie.' Frank's tones were weary. 'If you haven't saved the world by now, you never will.'

18

November 1942

Howard paused on the bridge and gazed down the Thames. It looked much as it had always looked, except for the gun-emplacement and the sandbags everywhere. When he started walking again he saw a flower-seller at the kerb; they were a rare sight nowadays, and she reminded him of those heady early days between the wars when he had bought Parma violets for pretty girls. And of the happy days after Pamela's birth, when he had carried freesias home to Mount Street for Diana. He paused to buy a bunch of chrysanthemums for Barbara. He would be lost without her, now, and it was nice to show appreciation.

Barbara's pale face flushed when Howard presented her with the flowers. In the days since he had discovered his wife's deception he had come closer to his secretary. He ate with her at her house, sometimes, or called there to pick her up. She carried out the small tasks that once Diana would have performed: gifts, and birthday cards, new socks or shirts. She knew him almost as well as his wife – better perhaps, for she understood constituency matters now and the work of the House of Commons.

'It's a lovely morning,' she said. Howard's office looked out over the river, and today the sky outside was blue. Howard had a sudden impulse.

'How would you like to walk in the park?'

Barbara put a hand to her startled mouth. 'The park? When?'

'Now,' he said. 'This moment, before we get involved in work or some brouhaha. Get your coat.'

Twenty minutes later they were in St James's Park, bleak now in winter, and leaf-strewn. Barbara's step was as long as his own, so they kept pace easily; Howard had not realized how tall she was. It seemed the most natural thing in the world to take her hand and draw her arm through his. There was only a momentary resistance, and then it came willingly enough. They walked on, their feet ringing on the frosty paths, their breath coming out in white puffs that hung in the air for a second and then vanished. He looked down at her, noticing suddenly that the lashes that covered her eyes were dark and thick. She looked up at him and smiled.

'Happy?' he asked and was glad when she nodded her head.

'There now,' Esther said, plumping the books down on the eiderdown. 'I still say you ought to rest, but if you're determined...' Ruth lay back on her pillows, her eyes heavy with the cold that had laid her low but her expression determined. She was almost eighteen, now, and studying for her Highers. To Lansky's delight she had definitely decided to try for a place at medical school. Short of being a rabbi, he considered this the best choice she could have made.

'A doctor, Esther: a healer. Truly, I have been blessed with these girls.' Two days ago, when Ruth had had a temperature of 100, Lansky had walked the floor, for all the world as if she had cholera.

'Aspirin, Mr Lansky, that's all she needs: leave it to me.' He had often suggested Esther call him by his first name, but much as she loved him she couldn't bring herself to do it. So he was still Mr Lansky, but she was the boss, now; the one he deferred to on all but the most vital details. She had come home today at noon, ostensibly to see to

Ruth but really to make sure Lansky was not fretting.

He was downstairs now, eating his lunch, because she had assured him that Ruth had had nourishing soup and was going to sleep the afternoon away. But Ruth had other ideas, so the books now littered the bed and she was reaching for her spectacles.

'Don't read for too long,' Esther said firmly. 'Naomi will be home at four, and I'll be home this evening in time to see to supper.'

Ruth nodded, and then patted the bed. 'Can you sit down for a moment? Just a short moment?' When she was agitated her accent deepened.

Esther sat down. 'When is Sammy coming home?' Ruth said. 'It's for Naomi I ask. She… I think she has a lot of daydreams. She thinks she loves him.'

'She'll grow out of it,' Esther said soothingly, feeling agitation grow. She wasn't up to this: not schoolgirl crushes. But who else was there for Ruth to talk to? 'Everyone goes through first love. It's normal,' she said, helplessly.

'Did you?'

The question threw Esther. 'No. Yes – well, I suppose so.' Ruth's eyes were on her face, earnest and enquiring. 'There was someone once. I loved him a lot.'

'And?'

'He died,' Esther said, remembering Philip, and saw Ruth's eyes fill with tears. She shook her head. 'It wasn't terrible, Ruth. We were very happy for a while, and then he died, quite quickly and peacefully.'

She couldn't bear to see how the mention of loss had affected Ruth, and held out her arms. 'Give me a hug. I have you and Naomi, and Mr Lansky, and that terrible Sammy – there's nothing to cry about. Dry your eyes and read your books. I'll need you to be my doctor when I'm old and grey.'

Which might be sooner than I reckon, she thought, as she went downstairs. Gallagher was making his monthly visit this afternoon, and that was enough to turn anyone's hair white. The sooner the war was over and Sammy was back in charge, the better.

As she drove to her office, she thought about Naomi. So she was in love with Sammy, was she? And how did Sammy feel? That was the question. And how would she, Esther Gulliver, feel if he did fall in love: with Naomi, or with anyone else? His frequent proposals had been jokes, or she had treated them that way, but they had been comforting, a kind of security that she was loved. It was strange to think that they might never come again.

Rain had started a while ago and now was lashing the windows. Anne stopped treadling and went to make up the fire. It was nice to be here, in her own home, cosy and warm and with plenty of work for her sewing-machine. She could make a fortune if she had the time, now that everyone had to make do and mend. It was only a month to Christmas, or little more, and she had her presents to make: a pinafore dress for Stella, dirndls for the younger girls, and an astrakhan cap for Esther. She had got the, pattern for that from a magazine, and the material was off-cuts from a full-length coat she had made into a three-quarter one for the wife of the Half Moon landlord.

She was cutting the threads on the garment she was sewing when a knock came at the door. It was her next-door neighbour, a mine of information at any time.

'Have you heard, Anne? Wilfie Potts is dead. You remember Wilfie – his mother gave us those chrysanths for the raffle.'

'Was he out in the Middle East?' Anne asked. She had come to dread those words, for all Frank said things were going well out there.

The woman was nodding. 'Yes. That's him gone, and

two seriously wounded. And all for a place most of us never knew existed before all this.'

'I'll put the kettle on,' Anne said, heaving a sigh. 'A cup of tea always helps.' But as she scalded the tea she thought about how her neighbour would spread the news if it was Joe who was dead. As it might be, one day.

When the woman had gone she set about making a meal. She tipped pilchards out of a tin and put aside two; later those would go onto toast glistening with margarine. The pilchards had cost 5½ pence though she had bought them not for their cheapness but out of desperation. Food was short now, even if you had money and coupons; today there had only been pilchards in the shop, and only two tins of them. She had put one aside for Frank, and now was mashing the other with tatie to make fish-cakes for everyone else.

'By God, if I ever get my hands on a Jerry I'll have his guts for garters,' she said to no one in particular. She mentally apportioned the fish-cakes as she shaped and floured them: one for Bernard, one for David, two each for Theresa, Angela, and Estelle, and one for herself. Tears nearly came when she thought of the two absentees from the table: Gerard training for the priesthood; Joe somewhere in the Midlands learning to shoot, or be shot. She put the frying pan on the new-raked coal, and dropped a lump of lard into it, to spit away and grease the pan. While it heated she took out her prize purchase: six small Jaffa oranges for a shilling, each one sweet and heavy with juice. When she gave her family something nutritious, now, she had a strange feeling of excitement, of beating the system, of doing her bit for the war-effort. There was one for everyone except her, and she didn't need one. She'd had her satisfaction already in easing her way up the queue before the precious fruit ran out.

Everything was now rationed, even coal. They were sitting on top of the stuff, and still it was rationed: one ton a month per household, and production falling because there were no young men left to work the pit. Ernie Bevin was ordering men who had left the pit to go back; it was coming to something, if men were to be forced down the hole. Anne thought of young Brenton, still at his fancy school probably – it would be nice to see him get dirty for a change. Nice, but unlikely. Mary swore she had seen him in Sunderland, driving a big car; and if anyone should recognize him it would be Mary, who had practically brought him up.

Anne began to put the fish-cakes one by one into the fat, wishing all the time she was putting in thick slices of bacon, or ham for preference. Someone was getting it, that was for sure. Ever since Anne had heard from Esther that Gallagher had his hands on the reins, she had smelled a rat. As for Esther – fancy having a sister with a food business and still having to scrat for your bairns! But Esther was a stickler for the rules, that was the trouble. Too straight by half.

It was all a power struggle, the food business, thought Anne. Yesterday she had queued for pies and got nearly to the front, only to see the shutter brought down in her face. She was sure it was spite! Nella Lamb had always had a knife in her because she was better-bred.

Her thoughts turned to Stella. She was sure there was a man in the background somewhere; a man with a car and money. But the little bitch wouldn't be pinned down on his identity. She felt uncomfortable about Stella now. It didn't seem right to have a daughter who was a woman and who could do as she pleased.

'They've got tripe down the pork shop,' her neighbour said, poking her head in at the back door.

'Tripe?' Anne reached for her coat, feverishly working out coppers as she went in the hope that she had enough.

*

'Oh, tea: lovely,' Loelia said. She patted the sofa she was sitting on. 'This is nice. New? Or is it just that I'm so used to seeing Scotland Gate under dust-sheets that I've forgotten what real furniture looks like?'

Loelia had been in London for four days, shopping and visiting friends. Tonight she and Henry were going to the Mansion House with Diana and Howard, to hear Winston Churchill speak.

'I hope he's cheerful,' Diana said as they drank their tea. She wanted to keep the conversation on the war and off the subject of Howard, if she could. If Loelia knew how bad things were between them, she might guess Max was to blame, and Diana was not in the mood for more censure. She had quite enough to put up with from Howard, whose displeasure now was almost tangible. He must know. *Oh God, it's a mess*, she thought, and offered Loelia a slice of fatless sponge which tasted strongly of liquid paraffin.

'Even sweets rationed now, Di,' said Loelia, nibbling at the cake with reluctance. 'Not that you could get anything really nice anyway: no more of those divine Continental chocolates. They'll never come back, Henry says. He's always so cheerful. According to him, the war is a stalemate.'

'Max says the campaign in North Africa's going well,' Diana said, realizing too late that she was trying not to mention Max.

'Oh,' Lee said brusquely. 'Well, of course, he would be sure of that, the insufferable know-all.' Diana would have liked to argue but didn't dare.

'Henry says North Africa was almost a disaster,' Loelia continued. 'Men and ships lost, the whole thing hardly worth it. But don't let's talk about the war. What are you wearing tonight?'

'The first thing that comes to hand,' Diana said airily. 'Like most other people, nowadays. I don't have time to worry about fashion, now, Lee; I'm too busy staying alive.'

'The world's dreadfully changed,' Loelia said, dolefully. 'I mean, what's happening to standards? Look at Laura, deserting her husband. Because it *is* desertion: her place is at his side. She's his wife.'

This is for my benefit, Diana thought, but managed to look nonchalant and keep the talk going, until Loelia departed in a welter of admonitions not to be late tonight and not to come in some splendid new garment – 'when all I have is rags!'

Mary drew the curtains over the windows and went to let out the damper on the fire. Patrick should be home soon. Benjamin was playing contentedly on the floor, ready for his bath when his father arrived, and she had a good, rich pannacalty in the oven. Patrick looked tired, sometimes, when he came back from the hospital; but Mary knew he enjoyed his work: healing limbs, mending torn flesh, giving young men a chance to live complete lives again.

Tonight, when he arrived, she could see he was troubled, but she didn't mention it. Instead she encouraged him to carry his son up to the bath, and soon the familiar sounds of splashing and laughter rang out. The baby was safely in bed and their food on the table when he told her what was troubling him.

'They want me to set up a special clinic for venereal diseases. It's becoming a real threat to the war effort. Syphilis is up by 70 percent: as bad now as it was in the bad old days after the last war. There are probably 150,000 cases in Britain, and if each of those infects another, and they in turn infect another – work it out. It's in the factories and on the ships, not just in the army. They mean to bring in compulsory registration and treatment; I know it sounds awful, but what else are they to do? Anyway, they want me to set up a clinic in Sunderland. There aren't many people with relevant experience, and I have some, which is better than nothing.'

Will you do it?' Mary asked.

He paused. 'I haven't much choice,' he said at last. 'We'll call it my contribution to the war effort.'

'Well, have some more of this. There's a kidney in there, so don't waste it.'

Patrick threw back his head and laughed. 'My darling wife, no wonder I love you so much. You have the best set of priorities in the world. And I couldn't live without you.'

The club throbbed with noise and smelled of sweat mingled with perfume. Stella nestled close to Rupert, her arms twined around his neck, her eyes exulting at his lovely uniform. They made no pretence of dancing properly, and nor did the other couples on the floor. All they wanted was an excuse to be close together, breast to breast, thigh to thigh. Occasionally a pair would peel apart and vanish, hand in hand, to somewhere more private. One couple decided to jazz things up and began to dance in a more lively fashion, but all round disapproval soon drove them back into one another's arms.

'Love me?' Rupert whispered.

'Of course,' Stella said, mimicking his posh tone in the way that always made him laugh. She snuggled closer. 'I'll prove it to you later on.'

He put his cheek on the top of her head, and held her closer until she felt his body start to harden against her and he put her hastily away.

'Shall we go?' he said.

'Not yet.' Stella liked to see him suffer a little. 'I never get out, when you're away. Now I want to enjoy myself a bit.'

'Don't you enjoy yourself being with me?'

'You know I do. But let's stop on here for a bit longer. And I'd love another drink: one of those big ones with the stick in it. No, I've changed my mind: a rum and blackcurrant.'

Rupert led her back to their table, and went in search of the drinks while Stella looked around her. Everyone was laughing a lot, or else looking glakey because they were in love. And some of the girls had glittering eyes which everyone said meant they were taking benzedrine. Someone had offered her some once, but she hadn't dared.

Rupert came back and set the drinks on the table, moving his chair closer to hers. 'I wish you could come down to the base,' he said. 'We could get a flat there, lots of the chaps do that. Or you could stay in a hotel.'

'I couldn't,' Stella said. 'I'm on vital war work; they wouldn't let me shift. Anyway, what would I do there on me own, while you were off somewhere? I'd die of boredom.'

Out of the corner of her eye she saw a group of men enter the club. Their uniforms were strange: khaki, but smarter than British uniforms. They were laughing loudly, and she saw the gleam of gold on their wrists. She caught her breath. 'My God: they're Yanks,' she said and almost spilt her drink.

It had been a carnival evening: the men were buoyant in their evening wear; here and there was the smoke from a precious cigar; the air was thick with talk of victory at El Alamein, the North Africa landings, and the relief of Malta

'I'm so glad we came,' Loelia whispered to Howard. 'I wasn't looking forward to it at all, but it's quite like old times, really. Except that I haven't a new gown.'

'You look splendid,' Howard told her gravely. He was still fond of Loelia, and besides, he mustn't betray that anything was wrong. He wasn't sure of the future, but he recognized the need to be discreet – for the time being at least.

Across the table, Diana sat with Henry, her head inclined as though intent on his every word. She looked particularly beautiful tonight, in a low-cut dress of green panne velvet which was one he liked to see her in.

The tables fell silent as the speeches began, and by the time Churchill rose to speak the air was tense with expectation. He spoke of effort and of achievement, and suddenly Diana felt full of hope.

'A bright gleam has caught the helmets of our soldiers, and warmed and cheered all our hearts. Now this is not the end.' The sonorous voice paused. 'It is not even the beginning of the end.' A longer pause. 'But it is, perhaps, the end of the beginning.'

19

February 1943

Max's eyes were shining as he spoke of Churchill. 'So he gets off the train, fresh as a daisy, and announces that tonight he wants to see Ingrid Bergman in *Casablanca*.'

'Not bad for sixty-eight – or is he sixty-nine?' Diana said. Churchill had just returned from a 10,000-mile journey to meet with Roosevelt in Casablanca and to visit the victorious Eighth Army in Tripoli. Max had been among the official reception at Paddington, and had arrived at the restaurant half an hour late for his lunch with Diana.

'He's sixty-nine, I think – anyway, nudging his three-score years and ten. Do you think they'll have any salmon? One gets so fed up with game.'

There was no salmon, but freshwater trout was available. They ordered, and sat back to look around at the other tables.

'This room is full of Americans,' Max said gloomily. 'You'd think they'd have a conscience about eating our food when their damned PXs are bursting with goodies.'

'Americans don't have consciences,' Diana said, remembering too late that Laura was of that ilk.

He saw her moue of discomfort, and pressed her hand. 'Don't mind me, Di; it's only my upbringing that prevents me giving forth on that subject. When I think of my sons growing up to play baseball... God!'

'They'll forget it as soon as they get back here,' Diana said comfortingly. 'A few months at school, and you'll never know they've been away.'

'Your brood are thriving,' Max said. 'Lee telephoned last night. She always enthuses about them, especially –'

'Especially Pamela,' Diana said drily. 'I wonder why.'

'Not now, Di,' Max said. 'I feel badly enough about what we're doing to Howard without dragging Pammy in.'

For some reason his use of his daughter's pet-name filled Diana with rage, but she was relieved of the need to reply by the appearance of the waiter with the first course. She had not told Max of her suspicion that Howard knew of their affair; now, not for the first time, she asked herself why. Was she afraid of his reaction? Afraid he might demand a decision once he knew the secret was out? 'Howard or me': was that what he would say? Or would he shy away from his responsibility once again, and suggest they cool things down?

I love him, she thought, watching him sip his wine. *God help me, I really do love him, but I can't trust him an inch.* As she raised her own glass, she thought of Howard, who did not excite her at all but whose word was his bond. *Life isn't fair, she thought. At least, it never has been fair to me.*

But even as she thought it, she dismissed the idea. She had always been the author of her own misfortunes; it was too late now to blame anyone else.

Anne looked at the clock. Half-past three: the bairns would be home before long. Since a daylight air raid had wiped out more than forty children and teachers in a London school the month before, she had been glad when her children were safe at home. The Germans were getting desperate now, bombing anything and everything. If they had to die, she would rather they were wiped out as a family – except that Frank would probably be left, safe in the pit. Would he marry again? My God, she would haunt him if he did.

Anne looked around her kitchen. It wasn't much, but it had taken a lot of getting together. The thought of another woman lording it over her pots and pans was too much to bear.

She went to the range and lifted the lid from a pan. Meat for Frank: a good, thick gravy for the bairns. All in all, they were getting through the war nicely. Joe got fed in the army - not home cooking, but still a proper diet. And Gerard fed well with the brothers in the seminary.

She paused, the pan lid aloft, contemplating the wonder of her, Anne Maguire, being mother to a priest. And once she had not even believed in Our Lord. She put the pan lid back, crossed herself hastily to beg forgiveness, and would have reached for her rosary if she had not heard the familiar sound of Esther's motorcar out in the street. What was bringing her to Belgate in the middle of the week?

Esther had been visiting a farmer who just might have had some winter greens to sell, but the visit had been unprofitable and the prospect of a cup of tea had lured her to Anne's – that, and a desire to see if the things Anne was altering for Ruth and Naomi were ready. She liked to see their faces light up at the sight of pretty things. *I suppose I feel maternal towards them*, she thought and suddenly felt old.

The sight of her sister did nothing to cheer her. Anne was looking every day of her thirty-nine years: her skin sallow, her dark hair speckled pepper and salt. *I could do more for her,* Esther thought, as she hugged her sister. But no one had ever been able to move Anne to anything unless she had a mind to be moved.

'Sit down,' Anne said now, swinging the kettle on to the glowing coals, 'and tell me what you've heard from that Lansky lad about my poor little Joe.'

'Your poor little Joe is a very good soldier, according to my Sammy,' Esther said firmly.

'"My Sammy",' Anne said, winking at no one in particular. '"My Sammy"! Well, well.'

'You know what I mean,' Esther said, loosening her coat. She was about to say, 'Cut out the *plaplen*,' but stopped her-

self just in time. Instead she said, 'Any news?' knowing
that the chance to gossip could divert Anne from anything.

'Not much you'll be interested in,' Anne said, wrinkling
her brow. 'Potts's lad's dead, in the Middle East – but I
told you that last time. Oh, and her ladyship's up to her
tricks again.'

'Mrs Brenton?' Esther was surprised. Diana had not
been north for months; a year even. 'How do you know?'

'Ha, ha!' Anne smiled knowingly. 'Be sure your sins
will find you out, sooner or later.'

I hope not, Esther thought, and clamped an expectant
smile on her face.

'Remember Mary Scott?' Anne said. 'Went down
London before the war. Her with the gammy leg?'

'She went into service,' Esther said, remembering the little girl with the limp who had still been nimble on her feet.

'Well, she wound up with the Londonderrys at Wynyard,
in the kitchen, then. Didn't get called up on account of her leg
– so of course she's like gold now. "Mary" this and "Mary"
that, and nothing too much trouble. Lady Londonderry treats
her like one of the family, according to her mother. Any road,
she heard them talking about the Brentons and saying as how
it was a shame he was being shown up, and her up to no good
with some lord or other. I always told you she was wicked.'

'It was him you once had marked down as wicked,'
Esther said reprovingly. 'And if this lot's as true as that lot
was, then it's a load of lies. She has her faults, Diana
Brenton, but she wouldn't be unfaithful.' Ignoring the
pained roll of her sister's eyes, she advanced on the kettle.
'Where's this tea, then? I haven't got all day.'

It was not until she was on her way home in the car that
Esther reflected that sticking up for a former employer was
fair enough, but that in her heart of hearts she could not be
certain that Diana would be true to her marriage amid all
the temptations of war.

The morals of all of us are affected by it, she thought, remembering David Gilfillan. *No one knows how much time is left, so it's foolish to waste it.* She thought of Sammy then: dear, funny, clever Sammy. *Would it have worked with us?* she wondered, and was saved from an answer by the angry tooting of the car behind her.

She put up a hand and tugged down the brim of her felt hat. 'Keep your mind on the road, Esther Gulliver,' she said aloud, and smiled sweetly as the offended driver drew level enough to glare.

Sammy boarded the train and sat down uncomfortably in the middle of two sleeping sailors, moving gratefully to a window seat when a pretty ATS corporal got out at Runcorn. He leaned his head against the glass and looked out at the countryside. He was trying to make sense of the last few days and it wasn't easy.

It had been Wednesday when he was summoned to the CO's office. That in itself was abnormal for a humble private. 'What for?' he had asked the sergeant.

'How the hell do I know?' was the answer.

The CO was not alone when Sammy reached the office. An older, grey-haired man was with him, the three pips of a captain on his shoulders.

'At ease,' the CO said, when Sammy had saluted. 'This is Captain Gray. He wants to have a few words with you.'

The other man smiled. 'Don't look so anxious. I'm hoping you can help me, that's all.'

Instinctively, Sammy liked the man. His words were comforting but his manner wasn't patronizing.

'I'll help if I can, sir.'

'Good. Could you look at this: it's a map of Paris. I drew it myself, so forgive the draughtsmanship.' He pushed a piece of paper towards Sammy. On it was a crudely drawn maze of streets, none of them named except for the avenue Victor Hugo. The Captain's finger jabbed at one of the unnamed streets. 'Can you tell me what that is?'

'Er... the avenue Foch, sir.'

'And that?'

'That would be the avenue de Grande-Armée.'

'And this little street here: hardly a street, a lane?'

Sammy frowned. 'It runs between Foch and Victor Hugo, but I can't remember its ever having a name. Halfway along there's a window-box of wrought iron... and the house at the end had an iron boot-scraper, I remember...'

'Lansky!' The CO's voice was sharp, but Captain Gray held up a hand.

'No, please, it's details I'm after. Now, Lansky, you said in your letter...'

Suddenly Sammy understood. This visit was as a result of the photographs he had sent to London. 'You said you went regularly to the avenue Collaigne from 1924 to 1939?'

'I went from 1910, sir, the year I was born – in the beginning with my mother. It was her girlhood home. She took me there until she died, and after that my father took me at yearly intervals until I was considered old enough to go by myself. The first time I was put in the charge of someone who was making the journey, but after that I went alone, at least once a year and sometimes twice.'

'How long did you spend there usually? A week? More?'

'More, usually: two weeks or three. Sometimes in the school holidays it was a month. Towards the end my visits were shorter, because I had a business here to see to.'

'But you know the area around Victor Hugo well?'

'Yes, sir.'

'Would you be willing to help us by providing us with some detailed information – all that you can remember?' Behind the adjutant's head there was a group photograph, some kind of army sports team. A fire was crackling in the

grate to the right. Somewhere outside, someone was boom-
ing out orders and then there was the sound of marching
feet. Sammy licked his lips.

'I'd like that, sir,' he said.

Now, five days later, he was on a London-bound train, a
signed pass in his pocket giving him indefinite leave. He was
to report to Captain Gray at the Hotel Victoria, Whitehall.

'And keep your mouth shut, Lansky,' the sergeant-major
had said on parting, with the irritated air of someone who
isn't quite sure what is going on but knows he wouldn't
approve of it if he did know. Sammy had nodded obediently
and then, when the NCO turned away, had held up two
fingers in reply.

He took a cab to Whitehall, giving the driver a tip that
made his eyes shine. He had expected a small private hotel
but this was a large building in Northumberland Avenue, its
corridors swarming with uniformed men. He filled in a
form, and then a bespectacled messenger took him up to
the third floor and tapped on a door. 'Wait here,' he said to
Sammy and vanished inside.

When Sammy was admitted he found a bare room that had
once been a hotel bedroom. The wallpaper was faded, the curtains threadbare; the hand-basin at the side had a dripping tap.

'Sit down, Private Lansky.' Today, the captain wore a dark
suit and his tie was loosely knotted. 'Now,' he said, reaching
for a telephone, 'let's get some help and make a start.'

An ATS sergeant appeared and took a seat by the desk,
opening a notebook and raising a pencil. Sammy realized
she had done this before.

'Your grandparents' house was No. 4, avenue Collaigne.
Can you describe it to me, beginning with the front step?'

It seemed a little strange but the captain clearly knew
what he was doing. Sammy half-closed his eyes and began.

'There were three steps up to the door. Well-worn, usually kept stoned. Three locks on the door: one lock and two

bolts actually.' And suddenly he was seeing it again, smelling the new-baked *lochsen kugl*, seeing Grandmère holding out her arms when he appeared. And now she was dead, and only God knew exactly how she had died. His voice faltered for a moment and then went on, stronger than ever.

'The lobby inside the front door is square, with a horse-hair mat sunk in a well in the floor. One step from the lobby to the hall. It has a brass shield over it. The inner door is half wood, half stained-glass. Inside the inner door...'

Stella Maguire crossed her fingers inside her knitted mitts and gazed out of the bus window. The gutters were filled with dirty slush and it had been dark since mid-afternoon. Still, if she was OK, the skies could rain blood and she wouldn't care. She had felt a sticky wetness between her legs as she sat down on the bus. It could be a false alarm – there'd been plenty of them already – but if it was the real thing...! She let out her breath in a low whistle and settled in her seat. No good fretting; there was a half-hour journey before she got home and nothing she could do in the meantime except dream, or read the paperback romance in her shoulder-bag. She elected to daydream and leaned her head against the window.

If it was a baby, Rupert would stand by her. He would have to. They would have a nice wedding, with a guard of honour, and confetti, and everyone around the doors would give her a clothing coupon. They always did that for a trousseau – not that there was anything decent to be got, coupons or no. Still, the Brentons had connections; he was always on about Aunt this and Aunt that. They would have to divvy up, if it came to it, and knit for the baby, an' all. For a few miles Stella thought about being Rupert Brenton's wife. He was going to university after he left the RAF. Once it had been aeroplanes and more aeroplanes; now it was all bachelor of something or other. She couldn't see the sense of getting letters after your name when you already had money.

'Ticket?' Stella looked up as the conductor swung over her.

'All right!' she said irritably, fishing in her bag for her twelve-journey. By the time it had been punched and returned, she had tired of the Brentons. If she was all right – and she had an increasingly uncomfortable idea that she was – she would be more careful in future. It didn't do to be forced into marriage, or anything else, for that matter.

She thought of the GI she had met at the weekend dance – Ricky was his name. He came from California, and had a gold bracelet and hair like a lavvy-brush. He had promised her some nylons next time. *Nylons!* She'd only had one pair in the whole of her life, and they had felt like silk – no, better than silk. She put out a hand to her lisle-clad knee: good enough for work, but death to glamour. That was what Ricky had called her: glamour girl. If she married a Yank, she'd get some white wedges like Betty Grable. They looked ripping with leg tan.

'Ripping' – that was one of Rupert's words. If she was having Rupert's baby it would put an end to nylons.

When the bus pulled up at her stop, Stella flung herself to the pavement and began to run, anxious to confirm that all was well and the option of a life in California still open to her.

Emmanuel Lansky looked around the table, seeing the animated faces of the three girls: he could not think of Esther as a woman, although he had known her for twenty years. At least they were happy: that was something. There had been no letter or phone-call from Sammy for three days now, and the young ones had been down until Esther provoked them to laughter. Not for the first time, he gave thanks far the advent of Esther Gulliver into his life.

'More macaroni cheese?' she asked now.

Lansky put up a hand in protest. 'I'm full. But it was delicious,' he added, knowing that Naomi had hurried home from school to prepare it.

The truth was that he seldom felt like eating nowadays, not with Sammy away from home and the papers full of misery. Two weeks ago he had read of the tragic plea from the Warsaw ghetto-dwellers; read and re-read it until the words were imprinted on his mind. *We notify you of the greatest crime of all times, about the murder of millions of Jews in Poland... brothers... the remaining Jews... live with the awareness that in the most terrible days of our history you did not come to our aid. Respond, at least, in the last days of our life.*

He looked up to find Esther's eyes on him, full of compassion but also wary. 'Don't upset the *kinder*,' they seemed to be saying.

Lansky drew in a deep breath. 'Now,' he said, cheerfully, 'shall it be chess tonight, or Ludo?' and pushed back his chair to set out the chosen board.

Esther cleared the table and put the dishes to steep, listening to the babble of voices and the click of dice in the next room. If only they could hear from Sammy: that would cheer everyone up.

She ran upstairs when the chores were done and laid out her nightclothes. She would have a bath tonight if the water held out and probably use a Yeast-pac on her face. In the mirror her eyes looked drawn and there were the faint beginnings of lines around her mouth: not much different to Anne, really. She sat down on the dressing-stool and leaned forward. Esther Gulliver, thirty-six years old: spinster, unattached, businesswoman, sister and aunt; and foster-mother to two refugees. It was a full life. It was. It must be.

A sudden picture of Howard Brenton came into her mind. He had always looked care-worn, even when he was young, with that little scar on his cheek and the limp when he was tired. And now, if Anne was to be believed, he was also a cuckold. 'This bloody war,' she swore aloud – but softly, for fear of being overheard.

Howard opened the door of the Maida Vale house and stood back to let Barbara precede him inside. They had been to see Terence Rattigan's *Flare Path*, a play about the anguish of RAF wives. It had been a tense, dramatic production, arousing uncomfortable thoughts about Rupert, and Howard was glad to be home. He was suddenly surprised by his thinking of this house as home.

'Tea, or a night-cap?' Barbara asked, bending to stir the few coals in the grate.

'Whisky, I think. To get rid of the chill.'

'Yes, it's not very warm in here,' she said anxiously.

No – I didn't mean that – it's comfortable enough. I meant the night air – and the play.'

'Yes. I thought of Rupert, too. Water or soda?'

'A splash. Then come and sit beside me. What are you having?'

'Whisky, too, I think: a small one with lots of soda. They say the PM's back?'

'Yes,' Howard said. 'But for how long, who knows? I think he's got a taste for these jaunts now.'

'It'll be a heavy week next week.' Barbara seated herself beside him on the sofa and he put out an arm to draw her closer.

'Yes. I finished the Beveridge report last night. A Welfare State: I like the sound of it. Protection against sickness and unemployment, support for the aged, family allowances… it's a grand concept.'

'Will the Bill pass?'

'I think so. There's agreement in principle. Both sides

want a land fit for heroes; it's the pace of change they can't agree upon. The Tories want it next week, and Labour wants it yesterday.'

There was silence for a moment and then Howard spoke: 'Shall I stay tonight?' They had been lovers for seven weeks, and he still could not believe it.

'If you want to, of course.' Her voice was pleasant – no, accommodating was the word. She would never say 'No' to him, and that was the drawback. He would never ever be able to be sure she wanted him. She was an Englishwoman in every sense of the word: elegant, genteel, accommodating... that bloody word again. In a moment they would damp down the fire and go in single file up the oak-panelled stair. She would change in the bathroom and be between the sheets by the time he, too, was ready. He would climb in beside her and say, 'Ready for the light?' She would say 'Yes,' and he would turn out the bedside lamp. They would lie silently for a moment, he trying to decide whether or not he wanted to make love, she no doubt thinking of England.

Howard had a sudden crazy desire to laugh and had to turn it into a strangled cough. 'Another drink?' he asked; and, as he rose to take her glass, he thought suddenly of Diana, abandoned and wanton in Max Dunane's bed. God damn this war! There were more victims of its ravages than ever made the casualty lists.

20

May 1943

Diana had come home at eight a.m., weary from a hard night on duty, to find Howard in the hall on the telephone, still wearing the dinner jacket he had worn the night before. She might have wondered where he had spent the night if he had not replaced the receiver and moved towards the stairs. 'My mother is dying,' he said. 'I'm going north.'

'I'm coming with you,' Diana said. Six hours later they were in Sunderland, but they were too late. Charlotte Brenton had died an hour before.

'I'm so sorry, darling,' Diana said, the old endearment, missing during the last few months, slipping out unawares.

Howard sighed. 'I'm not sorry she's dead, Diana; she wasn't happy. But I regret the breach between us. And the worst of it is, I can't work out how or why it came about.'

They had arrived at the Brenton house to find Gallagher in charge. 'I'm your mother's executor, I'm afraid,' he said with an attempt at an apologetic air.

'I never doubted that you would be,' Howard replied. 'I neither know nor care about the disposition of my mother's estate. I would like to arrange her funeral. I imagine you have no objection?'

Their eyes met and for a moment held. In the old days Gallagher would have backed down, but now he was no longer a Brenton employee. Howard held his breath until the other man glanced away.

'Of course,' he said. 'As her son you should do whatever is necessary.'

So Howard had arranged a simple ceremony and chosen hymns he knew his mother liked. Tomorrow they would follow her coffin to the church where she had married his father, and then to go Bishopwearmouth Cemetery. Today he sat with his wife in the house on the Scar, wondering what on earth to say to her.

'It seems a lifetime since we were last here,' Diana said. She was standing by the window of the drawing-room, looking out on the hillside that so conveniently hid the pit and its surrounding houses. 'I never realized how badly they'd suffered in air raids up here until last night.' They had watched from the window as searchlights criss-crossed the sky, and seen flashes of light and heard the distant rumble of explosions as bombs landed.

'Yes, they've taken their share.' Howard's tone was flat, and Diana turned, sympathetic to his mood, remembering how she had felt when her own parents died. Yesterday he had toured Belgate, visiting the war-bereaved, congratulating the people who were working hard for war charities, and praising Norman Stretton for the efficient running of all the Brenton interests. Today Howard wanted to have one last silent communion with his mother, trying to remember what had once been: that vague, unreal world of childhood which must have been happy because childhood was supposed to be so. Diana could sympathize with that.

'I'll come with you when you go into town,' she said, wanting to help him, sensing his inner conflict; and thinking all the while that Rupert might not survive to mourn her, that she might have to mourn him.

When they reached the Brenton house again, the odour of death greeted them, a mingling of intense cleanliness and corruption and floral perfume.

'Please don't have flowers if I die,' Diana said as they

mounted the stairs to the room where Charlotte Brenton's body lay. Howard did not answer, and she saw that his face was etched with pain. But nothing in his expression prepared her for his words as they stood beside the coffin.

'I want you to get a divorce, Diana.'

Diana had been thinking of little else for months. Now she could only stand, open-mouthed, as Howard continued.

'I know about Max, I've known for a while – but that's not the reason I'm speaking now. I watched my parents devour one another, year after year, blotting out any small prospect of happiness in one another's lives. And in the end there was that terrible spectacle of her revenge: he lay there, mute and unable to move for months, while she repaid him for all the slights, the rejections. It mustn't happen to us.'

'It wouldn't,' Diana said, suddenly horrified. 'We're not like that. I do love you, Howard – in a way. In quite a big way. I owe you a great deal: for what you've been to Pamela, if for nothing else. You knew she was Max's child and you couldn't have treated her better if she had been your own. How can I forget that?'

'But you love Max?'

It took her a moment to reply. 'Yes, I think I do. I don't always admire him; I certainly don't respect him as I respect you. But I think I love what's in him because it's in me, too. Does that make sense?'

Howard's only response was a weary shake of the head.

She left him after a while, pleading the need to go shopping for things she had left behind in her haste to leave London, but really anxious to get away from the presence of death and think over what he had said.

She drove into Sunderland, her mind racing. What had made him do this? Was it what she wanted? What would Max say? What would become of Howard, and the children? How would they tell the children?

Diana was almost in the town centre when she remembered his evening dress on the morning he had learned of his mother's collapse. Where had he spent that night? Perhaps there was another woman in his life, and that was why he wanted his freedom? As she parked in the town centre, she was trying to work out why she found the thought of her husband with another woman quite so intolerable.

While Diana pondered, Howard kissed his mother's icy brow one last time and then walked out into the sunshine, thinking of Barbara Traske, the woman who now gave him antiseptic sex and mostly sterile conversation, but who also gave him peace. Perhaps they should marry after a while? At least, he could then do something for her boy.

Frank emerged first from the shelter into the early morning light, half expecting to see Trenchard Street razed. It was still there, however, and he popped his head back inside to reassure Anne. 'I'll put the kettle on and come back for the bairns. You take your time.' The younger children slept on in their bunk beds; even the canary was quiet in his cage under the cover of an old cot sheet. Stella was asleep in the corner, a curler come loose from her hair and dangling on her forehead.

'Did you see anything?' Anne asked when Frank came back. All night there had been thumps and bumps, the crumping sound of bombs exploding, the roar of vehicles on the road and planes in the sky above.

'There's smoke over Sunderland way – a lot of it. That's all, though.' He gathered his youngest child in his arms, blanket and all, ducked out of the shelter and began to pick his way up the garden, between the rows of potatoes and broccoli. The child in his arms slept on, even when he tripped over the step and banged his shoulder on the door jamb. It never ceased to amaze Frank, the capacity of children to come through, unscathed and untroubled.

While he restored the little ones to their beds, Anne was making breakfast, heating the porridge she had made the night before, scalding tea, spreading bread with marge.

'Somebody'll've caught it last night,' she said, when at last they were seated. 'Judging by the noise.'

'You can't tell.' Frank was always the optimist. 'The bombers were probably going for the docks, and there's acres there with nothing on. No houses, anyway.'

'They fly in by the papermill chimneys,' Anne said. 'That's why they've never bombed them, because they need them – straight past and on to Sunderland.' She looked towards the stairs. 'I hope our Stelia hasn't gone back to bed.'

'Our lot's got all sorts of tricks, though,' Frank said, ignoring her last remark. 'Any more bread and scrape? I heard there's a field somewhere they light up to look like Sunderland, so it gets the bombs.'

'Where is it?' Anne said, cutting another slice.

'Near here. I don't know exactly where, but near here somewhere.'

'What bloody impudence,' Anne said; 'attracting them to us. That's nice –' She broke off as her youngest son appeared in the doorway, rubbing sleep from his eyes. 'Come here, pet. Let's see you: ooh, there's a sleepy boy. That's it, on your chair. Now, where's your plate?'

'What's on today, then?' Frank asked, looking at the clock. He was due at the council offices at ten.

'I'm meeting your Mary in Sunderland,' Anne said. 'If the town's still there.'

The Lansky house had escaped with nothing worse than some tiles off and a cracked kitchen window.

'*Oy vey*,' Lansky said, when the four of them emerged from the cellar. 'That was the worst yet.'

'Well, we'll have some breakfast now,' Esther said

soothingly. Both the girls were tense, and she had felt them flinch once or twice when a blast had shuddered through the cellar. She went through to the step, wondering whether or not there would be any milk delivered. It was there, and she stood with it in her arms, grateful for the normality of the familiar bottle and the cardboard top with the 'V-for-Victory' sign on it, looking up and down the street. Last week the house five doors down had had its roof burned through with incendiaries, but today everything looked peaceful.

A man came out of the house opposite and waved to her as he shut his gate. 'Nice night last night?' he called. 'Jerry left a few calling cards. None here, though.'

'No,' Esther called back. 'Thank goodness.' The postman was coming up the street, delivering at a door here and a door there. 'Anything for us?' she said, smiling. There was a bill in a brown envelope, and another letter in a sprawling hand. Nothing from Sammy.

'Everything's all right in the street,' she reported when she was back in the kitchen. There was porridge for breakfast and slices from a Hovis loaf. Esther tried to make small talk while they all ate, but it was difficult.

'Well,' she said at last, 'if anyone wants a lift to school they'd better get ready now. I expect it'll be a quiet night tonight, but watch what you're doing if you go into town after school; there could be trouble there after last night.'

'What kind of trouble?' Naomi asked apprehensively.

'Well, traffic holdups... if buildings've come down. Or unexploded bombs. But they'll be well-signed, and the wardens will be there. I'll be back here about half-past five, and I'll try and bring something nice for tea. Now, let's get in the car and get off.'

As she climbed behind the wheel, Esther remembered that she had seen the notice of old Mrs Brenton's death in the paper last night. No doubt Gallagher would come in for a packet in her will! Well, if it kept him off her back for a while she wouldn't begrudge a penny of it.

'Now stand still,' Mary Quinnell said. Benjamin stood on a chair, his Chilprufe vest slipping from his shoulder, his plump legs covered in striped socks. She bent to kiss his bare arms, aiming for the dimpled elbows.

'No,' he said, pulling away. The next minute he had slipped from the chair and was crawling under the table.

'Ben, come out of there, you little monkey,' Mary said, dropping to her knees to reach for him. He had just had his fourth birthday, and he was getting to be a handful. 'Come here,' she said again, but could not bring herself to threaten him. She loved him so much, this child of her late years; and his father was even more besotted.

'All right,' she said to him now, 'I'll just go to meet Auntie Anne without you. And when we go to the toy shop...'

He was out from under the table, holding his arms docilely for his little Viyella shirt.

'I'm a good boy,' he told her confidentially. 'You know I am really. So will I get something nice?'

'We'll see,' she said gravely and then, giving way, she hugged him until he had to squirm his protest.

Anne bought a pound of tripe in Jacky White's market, and two big Portugal onions. She would stew it tonight with milk and Oxo, and serve it with mashed potato. 'Potato Pete' leered down at her from the fruiterer's stall: where would they all be without potatoes? Starved to death, no doubt.

She waited for Mary on the Ritz corner, stretching out her hand for Ben to take when he came along, holding his mother's hand. He walked between them, swinging on their arms, while they caught up on each other's news.

'Everything all right your way?' Mary said.

'Yes. And you?'

'A few tiles off, some windows gone. The woman next door says a bit of an aeroplane came down. in Shaw Street, but you know what rumour's like. Did you hear about old Mrs Brenton? She's buried tomorrow.'

Ahead of them they saw the clutter of vehicles and uniforms that meant bomb damage to a building.

'We'd better go round and down Holmeside,' Mary said, and they were turning away when someone called out behind them.

'Mary? It is Mary Hardman, isn't it? I'm sorry, Mary Quinnell.' They turned to see Diana Brenton smiling at them.

She looks tired but she's still smart, Anne thought as she hung back while they chatted, not at ease with Diana as Mary seemed to be. She felt Ben's hand twist in hers, wanting to be free. Since his mother had his other hand, it seemed safe to let go; she didn't notice that Mary, intent on commiserating with Diana Brenton about her mother- in-law's death, had made the same assumption and also released her grip.

Benjamin looked around him, fascinated by the clutter of hoses that snaked across the pavement, the one remaining wall of a house papered with flowers, the cast-iron fireplace still in place and a picture crooked on the wall. He saw the pile of rubble beyond the ropes, and sticking out from it something bright and desirable. What could it be? He moved towards it, ducking easily under a rope meant to deter adults, oblivious of the ripple that had begun in the bricks of the gable-end.

'I don't know how long we'll stay up here after the funeral,' Diana was saying, 'but if there's time it would be so nice to see you and Dr Quinnell at the Scar.' Anne preened inwardly. Wait till Frank heard his sister was invited to the Brentons'! She heard someone shouting, and then a rumbling noise, and turned to look at the cordoned-off area.

What she saw there stopped the breath in her throat so that she could not cry out however hard she tried.

Benjamin Quinnell was walking confidently across the expanse of brick and scorched timbers towards the red and white ball, half buried in rubble. And above him the wall of the adjoining house had suddenly started to sway gently, as though in a breeze.

The other women had seen, too. A thin moan escaped Mary's lips as her hands came up to cover her mouth. It was Diana who leaped the rope and ran towards the child. There was shouting and confusion, and men were moving but the wall was moving faster. As Diana came up to the child and grabbed him, the wall crashed down, engulfing them both. And suddenly the noise had ceased, and only a thin pall of dust shimmered above the silent site.

Esther was at her desk when there was a tap at her office door. It was Molly, the receptionist. 'There's someone to see you, Miss Gulliver. His name's Fox. This is his card.'

Esther glanced at the card: *E. Fox. Motor Haulage. 3 Nile Street, Sunderland.* She looked through the glass partition to the office floor below, and saw a tall, dark man standing dressed in a dark suit, holding a grey Homburg in his hand. There was something familiar about him and she looked at the card again. Fox ... E. Fox. Of course: Edward Fox, once the Brentons' chauffeur. The one who had left under a bit of a cloud. 'What does he want?' she asked Molly.

'He wouldn't say,' the girl said. 'He asked for you, and said Mr Gallagher had sent him.'

Gallagher! Inwardly Esther groaned. Still, better not be awkward. 'Show him up,' she said and closed the books she had been poring over before the interruption.

'Esther?' The man was holding out his hand, and reluctantly she offered her own. 'Remember me, Esther? When you were just a little girl up at the Scar, running after the Brentons?' He looked around, smiling. 'You've come a long way.'

There was something odious about him, Esther decided, and it made her voice brusque. 'What can I do for you, Mr Fox?'

'It's more what I can do for you, Esther. I'm in business now. I have quite a thriving company, everything from light haulage to heavy freight. I was talking to Jack Gallagher, and he suggested you and I would be useful to one another.'

'I'm not sure how,' Esther said. 'We have our own wagons.'

'But should you?' Fox said. 'That's the point. Could I do it better and cheaper on contract?'

Esther was saved from having to answer by another knock at her door. She had always ruled out interruptions when she was in discussion, but this time she welcomed it, though it was unusual for her orders to be disobeyed.

'I'm sorry,' Molly looked apologetic but determined. 'But it's the hospital. There's been an accident in the town the remains of last night's bombing. Your sister Anne's at the Infirmary and she wants to know if you can come and fetch her in the car?'

'It's all right,' Howard said, stroking Diana's hand where it lay on the coverlet. It looked white and the veins stood out like blue cord. There was dried blood around her fingernails and her knuckles were skinned. But it was her head that had taken the full onslaught of the flying debris, and was swathed now in bandages. Diana had been unconscious for five hours, while Howard had sat by her bedside, wondering if he was to bury his wife as well as his mother. Her eyes were covered by the bandages and he did not know she had recovered consciousness until he saw her hand move on the cover. Her other arm was splinted and attached to a saline drip.

The doctors had come and examined Diana and told Howard he could talk to her for a moment. Then she must rest. 'Will she remember what happened?' he had asked, and had received a shrug in reply.

But she did remember.

'What about the child, Howard?'

'He has a fractured femur, just a greenstick fracture. And some bumps and bruises. But he's fine, thanks to you.' They had found the child underneath her, shielded by her body. 'You were incredibly brave,' Howard said. 'I'm so proud of you, and his parents are so grateful.'

He heard Diana sigh and then she spoke, so softly that he had to bend to hear.

'I gave something back, didn't I, for what we took at the Scar?'

Across the desk the officer settled into his chair. 'Right, Lansky. I hope you slept well last night? Now, to work.' They were in the library of the magnificent country house Sammy had come to last night. He had slept in a high-ceilinged bedroom with William Morris wallpaper and ivy at the window. Or rather, he had tried to sleep. It was all too bizarre – too strange to permit easy slumber. His eyes burned, but he tried now to look alert and interested as the man went on.

'The reason why you're of value to us is your detailed knowledge of your grandparents' house in the avenue Collaigne. It's occupied now by a German officer, a man named Rascher. He lives there with his wife and children, and he loves his home, so he returns there promptly at five each day, usually carrying documents to work on after his evening meal. His job is in the transport section of the headquarters building, so the time may come when we would like sight of what he has there. He is in charge of movements to and from the coastal sector. His wife will not allow any Frenchwomen into the house; it is staffed by German orderlies, so we have no means of knowing what goes on in there except what we can see from outside. We've made those observations, but they're incomplete – and the houses in the avenue Collaigne are not all alike. The friends we have there know little or nothing of No. 4. Your grandparents kept themselves to themselves... and so does Rascher. But we think you can help us get someone into the house. You mentioned an unorthodox way of entering known to you and to Jean-Paul Lefèvre.'

In the long debriefings Sammy had told them of his clandestine visits to his friend, Jean-Paul Lefèvre, three doors away, creeping along the coping of the roof and getting in at the dormer window. The boards used to give if you pressed in the right way. You could put in a hand and unlatch the window. 'I used to go out after dark and along to Jean-Paul, or he'd come to me – while my grandmother thought I was fast asleep.'

'We're looking for Lefèvre,' the officer said, 'but in the meantime I want to press you for any detail we might have missed...'

21

June 1943

Anne turned the herring over with a scornful finger. Herrings! More like pilchards. Still, she'd got twelve to the pound, which meant one each for the bairns, so it wasn't all bad. She had gutted them, salted and peppered and rolled them and put them in the dish to bake, when she saw the letter on the mantelpiece. Joe's handwriting! Frank must've picked it up when he went out early on. She rinsed her hands under the tap to rid them of the fishy smell, and then dried them hastily on her pinny before she tore the letter open with shaking hands.

Dear mam, it said. Anne subsided into a chair at the table and counted the sheets: one, two, three – good! Plenty to read. A tear formed, and she drew her arm across her eyes and blinked to dear them. She wasn't going to start crying. She had cried so much when Leslie Howard's plane was shot down that her eyes had ached for a week. All those lovely films, *Pimpernel Smith* and *Intermezzo*, not to mention *Gone with the Wind* – though Leslie Howard had been a bit too weak in that. Anne shook out the sheets and firmed her lips; she had nothing to cry about compared with some, like Diana Brenton lying blind in the Infirmary. No one would have wished that on their worst enemy. And her mother-in-law leaving everything to a stranger – Gallagher, into the bargain. The Brentons were getting their come-uppance now, all right.

Dear mam [she read], *Hope this finds all of you as it leaves me. I had a letter from you, mam, this morning, which was nice and gave all the news. Hope the air raids aren't too bad your way. We get off lightly here by all accounts. Don't know about Xmas leave yet; Sammy says I can have his if necessary. He is a real good mate and I couldn't wish for better. Is our Stella OK? Tell her I think she never learned to write because she never remembers her brother to drop him a line. The grub here is OK, but not like yours, mam. Wouldn't mind some bread-and-butter pudding right now, or a nice fresh stotty. Roll on peacetime. Seriously, mam and dad, keep your peckers up. No one here thinks it will be much longer, and I will be glad to be home. Yes, mam, I've decided the army's not for me, not when this lot's over. I can stick it till then and enjoy it, but once we've licked the Jerries I'm coming home for good.*

Anne folded the letter and put it back in the envelope. She would put the herrings in the oven and do the veg, and then she would make a cup of Camp coffee – a proper treat – and have a digestive biscuit and read the letter again. The boy had seen sense about his future, and who said Our Lady couldn't work miracles when asked?

'That's it, then,' Sammy said, shoving the last item into his kit-bag and pulling it shut. Joe sat morosely on the next bed, looking downcast.

'Come on,' Sammy teased, 'what's that face for? This is my last night, and we should be having a *simcha*. You look like a wet weekend.'

'I thought we were mates,' Joe said.

'We are.'

'Mates don't go off without telling where.'

'Not again,' Sammy said, pleadingly. 'I'm being posted. I didn't ask for it; it came. And I'm under orders not to speak about it, to anyone.'

'I'm not anyone,' Joe said. His chin was trembling, and suddenly Sammy remembered that his friend was still a boy.

'No,' he said, sitting down on the bed beside Joe. 'No, you are not anyone. Next to Esther, you're the best friend I've ever had. So I'll tell you what I can. Will that do?'

Joe nodded, and Sammy put his hands palm down on his knees. 'Remember that course I went on last month? I have some knowledge – knowledge I got as a boy about France. They need it, so I'm going off to one of their places to have my head turned inside-out. Then I'll brief people who need to go there, so that they know the territory. But for their sakes it has to be done quietly: so, not a word to anyone else.'

Joe nodded, satisfied now. 'Not a word. And you'll write when you can? I've got your home address. I'll keep in touch.'

'I'll write,' Sammy said, getting to his feet. Now, what about the *simcha*?'

Esther switched off the engine and steered the car into the kerb behind another, larger car. She always did this now in the hope that it would save petrol. A business call had brought her into the neighbourhood and she had suddenly felt the urge to see her own house. She was happy at the Lanskys', and probably safer there, while there was a war on, but sometimes a longing for her own home overtook her. She gathered up bag and gloves, checked her hat in the driving-mirror, and got out. She was halfway up the path when the door opened, and she saw the tall figure of Howard Brenton come onto the step. She checked momentarily, but it was too late to back out now. He was transferring his hat to his other hand and holding the free hand out to her.

'Miss Gulliver – Esther! How are you?' She gave him her hand and he shook it warmly.

'I'm very well, thank you. How is Mrs Brenton?'

Howard was smiling as he looked at her, but his eyes were sad. 'She's well in herself, much better. But I'm afraid she is… she had…' He was finding it difficult to choose the words, and behind him, in the doorway, Mary's face flinched. Esther stepped in.

'I heard about her sight – I'm very sorry. Is there anything I can do? I'd be very happy if there was.'

Howard had recovered himself now. 'Could you spare some time to visit her? I have to go back to London, and my son Rupert is in the RAF now. The other children are too young to help much, although they write and telephone. But I'm sure she'd appreciate a visit. Mary has been in several times, and it's helped Diana a great deal.'

'Of course I'll go,' Esther said. She stood at the door with Mary as Howard put on his hat and walked to the gate and the long black car. He turned and tipped his hat to the two women, and a moment later the car was gliding away.

Esther followed Mary into the house. 'Poor man,' she said. In the corner Ben was playing with a toy car, his leg encased in a plaster cast.

'I never had much room for Diana Brenton,' Mary said quietly. 'But I owe her everything now. It would've killed Patrick if we'd lost the boy. And she's paid a terrible price: I wake up in the night, and I remember that she's in the dark all the time. It doesn't bear thinking about.'

'How's she taking it?' Esther said, unpinning her hat and sinking into an easy chair.

'Very well, on the face of it,' Mary said. 'Bright, chatty, making jokes about it. "I can put lipstick on," she said, last time I was in. "Watch me." She put lipstick on, quick as a flash, round her lips. But it went a little too far, and I didn't like to say so…'

'She was always so proud of her appearance,' Esther said. A gloom had settled on the two women. Esther closed her eyes for a moment and tried to imagine permanent darkness. Diana Brenton had hated darkness; had commanded a night-light in the nursery and a guarded fire.

'I'll make some tea,' Mary said, getting to her feet. 'For God's sake think of something to cheer me up. Patrick has a new job now, at the Infirmary: a special clinic, they call it. It's treating VD. Can you remember a time when we didn't even know what VD was?'

'I still don't know much about it,' Esther said.

'Nor me,' Mary said. 'Except that, according to Patrick, no one deserves it, and those that have it go through hell. Did you know he treats little children, too, Esther? I called for him the other day, and I heard children laughing. "What's that?" I said, and a nurse said, "Oh, it's children's day today." My blood ran cold.'

They drank their tea in silence, each lost in contemplation of traumas quite beyond their comprehension. When they spoke again it was of tiny things: how much they missed lemons, and Leslie Howard, and the foolishness of cups being made without handles. And then it was time for Esther to say goodbye and drive home.

She had hardly got rid of her hat and greeted the girls, when there was the sound of the outer door closing. 'We're in here,' she called and Lansky came into the room. Today he was smiling and there was a twinkle in his eye.

'Tea's almost ready,' Esther said. 'Go through and we'll be with you in a moment.' But Lansky stayed where he was and delved into his pocket, producing a letter.

'Aha,' he said.

'It's from Sammy.' Ruth's eyes were shining, but Esther looked at Naomi. The colour had left her face and her eyes seemed dark caverns in her head.

'What does it say? Put us out of our misery.' Esther put

an arm around Naomi's waist. The girl was trembling, but she suddenly spoke.

'He's coming home,' she said. 'I know it! He's coming home.'

Howard sat back in his seat and watched the countryside glide past. It would take hours to get back to London by train, hours in which to get his thoughts into some sort of order.

A few weeks ago he had known – or almost known – where he was going. For the past few months he had had a tranquil sexual relationship with Barbara, without great heights or abysmal depths. Sometimes he had had an uneasy thought that she was sleeping with him because he had provided a roof for herself and Richard. In the end, though, he had decided that she was probably grateful for their physical relationship in the same way that he himself was grateful. It was intimacy of a kind, it was warmth to a degree, and it was a release.

He had watched Diana, seen the intensity of her affair with Max Dunane, and realized that he could never equal that kind of passion. He believed himself to be a loving man; he certainly loved his children; but no woman had ever truly unlocked his heart – perhaps because he had nothing there to give to that kind of relationship. It was then he had decided to give Diana her freedom. If she could make a life with Max, she should. The world was changing with the war, and lots of things would be more acceptable after it. Perhaps they could all find some kind of peace.

That was what he had decided. Now, everything had been turned on its head. As the Cleveland Hills came into view, Howard acknowledged that his liaison with Barbara must end. Diana was his wife and she needed him; he would never, ever let her down. As he made the decision a sense of relief came over him; he knew what must be done, and he would do it.

*

The great vaulted entrance of the hospital was forbidding. Esther gripped the flowers she was carrying and looked around for a sign. At last she saw it: 'P.P.3', standing for 'Private Patients Ward 3'. She followed the signs until she came to a ward of small rooms, chintz-curtained and cosy. A sister in navy blue, with a bow at her chin and a lace-trimmed cap, looked at her enquiringly. 'Mrs Brenton?' Esther asked and was directed to Room 14.

In the first moment she thought Diana Brenton was looking at her, but then she saw that the blue eyes were unfocused. 'It's Esther Gulliver, Mrs Brenton. I worked for you at the Scar... quite a few years ago.'

'Esther! How kind of you to come.' Diana was holding out a hand.

Esther put the flowers down on the bedside table and took the outstretched hand in her own. There were heavy scars above one eye, and at the other temple, but Diana's face was still beautiful.

'Sit down. Ah, I can smell carnations. I love carnations.' Esther picked up the flowers and held them while Diana inhaled their fragrance. 'Lovely! Thank you. Now, don't waste time commiserating with me – I did something which was probably quite foolish, and this is the result. It can't be helped, and you mustn't mind. Tell me about you: where do you live now?

As Esther began to describe her present circumstances, Diana lay back on the pillow, smiling and nodding, apparently serene except for the fingers that plucked ceaselessly at the linen counterpane. Esther talked on, but her eyes had fallen on a writing-pad that lay on the bed, an uncapped fountain pen beside it. Writing was scrawled on the pad, spidery writing that slanted upwards across the page, looking as though it had been written by a drunkard. For the first time since she had entered the room, Esther felt tears prick her eyes.

She kept on talking, but the writing pad fascinated her. Was it the outpourings of a distracted woman, or a list of things to be done? When she at last deciphered the first line it was neither of these. It read: *My darling, darling Max, I am so lost without you...*

The papers were full of the successful Sicily landings, the first on an Axis homeland, but Howard merely skimmed the headlines, his thoughts on the ordeal ahead and on Rupert's letter, lying beside his plate. *I can't believe there's nothing to be done for her, father. Ma couldn't bear to be shut up in darkness for the rest of time. Remember the nightlights she gave me? She hated darkness.*

Howard put the papers aside and went out into the street to summon a cab. 'Maida Vale,' he said to the cabbie and settled back in the seat.

Barbara came to him when he let himself into the hall, sliding her arms around his neck. He did not put her away; that would have been cruel. Instead he returned her kiss, gently, and then led the way into the living-room.

'How is Diana?' Barbara asked as she poured him a whisky and soda. He sat down in a chair by the unlit fire And accepted the drink.

'Thank you. She's better: very brave, as I told you on the telephone. But her sight is irreparably damaged, the surgeon told me this morning. The optic nerve is gone in both eyes, and there's nothing they can do.'

'When is she coming home? Will she come here, to Mount Street?'

'Yes,' Howard said. 'She loves London, and I think she will be happiest here. She may go to Valesworth for a while, to her friend, Loelia Colville. After that it will be

Mount Street. I'll have to find someone to take care of her, and…' He hesitated.

Barbara sat down opposite him, putting up a hand to draw the edges of her silk housecoat together at neck and knees, and he saw that she was apprehensive. There was no other way but to tell her quickly. He moved to crouch beside her chair.

'My dear, I'm grateful to you for these last few months, but it has to end here. Diana needs me now, and needs my undivided attention.'

He could see that Barbara had been expecting this – so why was she so tense? Howard had never considered the possibility that she might love him.

'Will I have to give up my job?' she said suddenly, and then he understood.

'Don't worry,' he said. 'You're not going to suffer because of this. I think it would be difficult for us to go on working together in the long term, but until you find another MP who needs a secretary – and I think I may know of one now – you will stay as you are. I intend to set up a trust for Richard, too.'

Barbara put up a hand and touched his cheek. 'You are a good man, Howard. I hope you will be happy one day.'

Howard was out in the street before he thought to wonder how she knew he had not been happy in the past.

22

September 1943

Anne was peering from her kitchen window, clutching at a cardigan she had put on over her nightdress. 'It looks as though it's going to rain.' Frank was standing at the range, frying bread in beef dripping.

'There,' he said, slapping two slices onto a plate and adding a fried egg. 'Get that down, and never say I don't do anything for you.'

Anne pulled her cardigan together across her chest and eyed the plate. 'I ought to get dressed.'

'Sit down,' Frank said agreeably. 'I've made the tea. Pour it out and eat up. The horde'll be down in a moment.' He crossed to the door and shouted up the stairs.

'Stella!'

There was no sound.

'Stella' Have you left work?'

This time there was a moan and then: 'I'm saying my prayers.'

Before he could answer her, Anne intervened. 'Let her say her prayers, Frank.'

He turned in exasperation. 'Prayers, Anne? The last time that one said her prayers the midwife was washing her down. Any road, I've called her. It's up to her now.'

He collected his breakfast and sat down opposite his wife. 'It was a rough shift last night – two men short. Ernie Bevin can say what he likes, but the men get fed up. No wonder they want to strike.'

'They shouldn't strike while the war's on,' Anne said firmly, her mouth full of fried bread. 'It's illegal, anyway – and after the war you'll be the masters. You can't strike then, against yourselves.'

'We'll have a Welfare State, then,' Frank said. 'Sick pay, unemployment pay, a health service. It'll be bloody Jerusalem.'

'Call our Stella again.' Frank ignored her and went on cleaning his plate with the blade of his knife, licking off what he managed to pick up.

'I thought I might pop in to the British Restaurant this week,' Anne said. 'They say their fish and chips are lovely, and dirt cheap.'

Frank nodded. 'They're having a football tournament for Warship Week,' he said. 'Bearpark v. Brandon, us v. Stanley, Langley Moor v. Seaham Harbour, and Shotton v. Murton. We'll win.'

'Ha!' Anne said. 'That'll call for the church bells. Now, will you call our Stella?'

But Stella had appeared in the doorway, barefooted, shrugging into a blouse with one hand, wiping sleep from her eyes with the other.

By, she's a bonny lass, Anne thought proudly, *even when she's just up.* Aloud she said: 'Button yourself up in front of your father. You should be ashamed.'

Stella went to the window, buttoning her blouse as she went. 'Oh God,' she said. 'Another bloody working day.'

'Stella!' The voices of her parents reproved her in unison but she was oblivious. She switched on the wireless, gyrating to the Glenn Miller music that poured forth.

Anne looked at Frank. 'She's not plumb, Frank – I've said it all along. And it doesn't come from my side.'

*

'Are you comfortable there?' Rupert asked anxiously. He had settled his mother in a chair with her back to the window, because somehow it was easier to bear her sightless eyes if they were not staring vaguely into the light.

'I'm fine, darling. Sit down beside me. It's so nice to have you home. Tell me about Martlesham Heath.'

'Oh, it's like any other station. Quite boring most of the time. The CO's a good sort.'

Diana put out a hand, and to his horror Rupert realized she was feeling for him. He was about to twist away when he saw her face. There was a tenderness there that he had never seen before, but the beautiful, brilliant, amusing, chal-lenging woman he had known seemed to have gone. He steeled himself to stay still while her hand searched then found his face and tenderly traced his features, one by one.

'You've changed,' she said, feeling the line of his jaw, the faint stubble, the resolution of his chin.

'I've grown up,' Rupert said, trying to sound light-hearted, desperately afraid that the lump in his throat would take away his words. He was trying to smile when she suddenly withdrew her hand.

'I know, darling,' she said. 'I know.'

'What do you mean?' he said, but this time his voice did quaver and he hated himself for it. *I can't face this,* he thought. *Not down all the years. Not seeing her like this.* He tried to remind himself that he was a flyer, a fighting man, but this was different.

Diana was feeling for her braille watch. 'I forgot I promised to call Aunt Lee. Do run along now, darling, but put the telephone by me before you go.'

But when he had gone she sat on, the receiver still in place at her side. *He's like me,* she thought. *He can't face things that aren't...* She sought for the right word but it eluded her. Instead, she remembered the Scar, and the blacksmith's body lying on the ground, and her own flight to London to escape the horridness of it all. *He won't be able to face it, not forever. He'll mean to; he'll try, but in the end he'll run away from me. And he'll hate himself for it for the rest of his life.*

If only Rupert were like Pamela, who had simply clasped her mother in her arms and hugged her until her bones creaked – and had then gone on to exchange news of tiny, everyday things as though everything was as it should be. *But he is not like Pamela,* she thought. *He is my son in every single part of him.*

'You're sure you still want to go through with this?' The major's eyes were kind in an otherwise stern face.

'Yes, sir.' Sammy's voice was firm. Opposite him the man picked up a ruler, examined it and put it down again.

'I have to be blunt. Our people run unbelievable risks. If they're caught – well, their chances of getting away with it are slim. You are a Jew, so normally I wouldn't even consider you, but your knowing the house is unbelievable good luck. If the chap you told us of had been available – but as I told you, he died in the fall of France.'

'Yes,' Sammy said. 'He was a good friend.'

'I have to say it once more,' the officer said. 'Another agent would have a one-in-five chance of survival if he was caught; your chances would be nil.'

'I know,' Sammy said.

'You look Jewish,' the other man said. 'If you'll forgive my saying so.'

'Don't apologize,' Sammy said. 'I look what I am. However, I take your point. I'll lie low as much as possible, but, let's face it, inside that house, if I'm caught I'm lost anyway, Jew or not.'

'True, but if – *when* you get out of the house, you lie low in our safe place – no heroics – until we get you back here?'

Sammy smiled grimly. If they were expecting heroics they'd be disappointed. His mouth was already dry at the prospect of what was to come.

'Well,' the major said at last. 'There'll be weeks of training, months probably, then we'll wait for the opportune moment. Mustn't blow the chance too soon.'

'How long?' Sammy asked weakly.

The man shrugged. 'A few months. We want you in there during the lead-up to invasion, but the decision about timing will be made on high.'

'What if Rascher moves out before then?' Sammy said, his heart sinking at the thought of waiting months with his courage ebbing all the time.

'He may move, but the house is assigned to the post, so if he goes, his successor will move in. Though of course he may prefer to stay at his office and work there. Still, we'll cross that bridge when we come to it. But you'll be leaving here tonight.'

Esther laid down her pen as one of the office girls came in carrying her morning coffee and the arrowroot biscuit she usually had with it.

'Thank you,' Esther said gratefully. 'I'm ready for that. After the war I never want to see a form again as long as I live.'

'The troops are doing well in Italy, aren't they?' the girl said, clearing a space on the desk for the tray.

'Yes. Your brother's somewhere out there, isn't he?'

The girl nodded. 'And my boyfriend – well, friend. I met him when he came up with me brother. It's not really serious.'

'Is he nice?' Esther said teasingly.

The girl flushed and grinned. 'I see,' Esther said. 'Well, I'm sure they'll both be all right – and we could do with a nice wedding in this place. Cheer us all up.'

When the girl had gone she opened her handbag and took out the letters she hadn't had time to open before she left the house. One was from Patrick Quinnell, a brief friendly note accompanying the rent cheque. The other was in a hand she didn't recognize, and it bore a London postmark.

'Dear Esther,' she read. 'I can't bring myself to call you Miss Gulliver, remembering as I do the splendid little girl who came to the Scar all those years ago. It has given my wife and me very real pleasure to see how well you have done and to become reacquainted with the grown woman. I am immensely grateful to you for your visits to Diana in the Infirmary, and I know she found them helpful. She is getting on well here in London and asks me to tell you that she looks forward to meeting you again when next we come north to the Scar.'

The letter went on to talk about the war and his son in the air force. Esther raised her cup to her lips, suddenly remembering the day Rupert Brenton was born, when Diana's eyes had positively glowed with rage. 'I'll never go through this again, Esther, you'll see. Never again.' But she had given Howard Brenton three more children...

She was roused from her reverie by the same girl. 'That man's here: that Fox. The one who's been ringing you.'

'Show him in,' Esther said wearily. 'And let's hear what he's after this time.'

Howard found his wife sitting by the window as though she was looking out, and the sight disconcerted him. 'Diana,' he said. He felt an immense tenderness for her tow, a depth of emotion she had never ever aroused in him before.

'You're home,' she said, turning towards him. 'This is unexpected.'

'The war is going well,' Howard said with mock self-importance, trying for a light tone. 'I thought it could get along without me for a while.' In his office in Westminster, letters from constituents were piled high, and white papers and green papers demanded attention, but he wanted to be with his wife.

She was smiling and feeling the table beside her. Howard resisted the temptation to say, 'What is it? I'll get it for you.' He knew she must learn to fend for herself if she was be happy. Instead he said, 'Seriously, things are going better now. I think I can dimly see light at the end of the tunnel.' The words were not out before he was cursing himself for their inappropriateness.

Diana's fingers had found what they were looking for. 'Look what Pamela sent me. It arrived this morning.' It was a chintz bag, painstakingly sewn, with several pockets on either side so that precious things could be kept in them and be easily located.

'It's splendid,' Howard said. 'She really is a nice child, isn't she?' Diana felt for the table with one hand and then placed the bag with the other.

'Let's go to Valesworth soon and see them all. She can come over from school for the weekend. I'd like that. Oh, by the way…' Her voice had suddenly become nonchalant. 'Are you going to be free tonight? Max Dunane wondered if we'd like to dine out?'

For once Howard was glad that Diana could not see the mingled emotions on his face.

'I'd like to come, and it's good of Max to ask us, but could you possibly bear to go alone? With Max, I mean? I have an awful lot of things to do still.'

Was there relief on her face? Did Max still mean so much to her? Since she came back to London they had shared a bed again – it had seemed the natural thing, because she needed help at bedtime. But they had not made love. Howard tried to sort out the tangled feelings in his mind, while Diana assured him that she would be quite all right on her own and he wasn't to worry about her at all.

'Come and sit down,' she said at last, 'and tell me all about Il Duce. I heard it on the wireless...

'You have to raise your hat to Germans,' Howard said drily. 'We had Mussolini trapped in what we thought was the perfect place, only accessible by a cable-car. So the Germans drop from the skies, overpower the guards, and fly off with him from his mountain-top.'

'I remember the Apennines in 1933: you and I and Rupert. Do you?'

'Yes, I remember.' Howard pictured her in the hot Italian sunshine with the child holding her hand, shading her eyes and calling to him to come and see the view. And she would never see another mountain. 'Mussolini made a speech, apparently, tearing the House of Savoy to pieces.' To his own ears, his voice was shaky, but she seemed not to notice. Instead she laughed.

'Once we have Adolf boxed in, perhaps Tojo will come and rescue them both? Could you ring for some tea, darling? I'm simply parched.'

Emmanuel Lansky laid aside the paper and took off his spectacles. His eyes ached often nowadays. *I'm getting old,* he thought and could not find it in him to regret that his life was drawing to a close. He had just read a report from the Polish interior ministry in exile, according to which German doctors were using healthy prisoners in Ravensbruck as human guinea-pigs for gruesome, often futile, medical experiments: unnecessary abdominal surgery, the removal of bone and muscle from limbs, deliberate infection with tetanus or tuberculosis. And in Dachau, Czech surgeons had become expert in stripping skin from corpses and tanning it to make into artefacts. *I want to see these people brought to justice before I die*, Emmanuel thought.

But most of all he wanted to see his son settled in life. They hardly ever heard from Sammy, now. His letters, when they came, were as loving as ever, but they were not open. Lansky knew his son: there was something, something indefinable, that was not in the letters.

There was a tap at the door and Naomi entered. He smiled at her as she put down the tray she was carrying.

'What have we here?' he said. The tray was laid with an embroidered cloth and the best china. He smiled at the blush that mantled this girl's cheek at every opportunity. *I do love her*, he thought, *but the other one, my Ruth...* It was two weeks since she had gone to begin her medical studies and he missed her.

He bit into a biscuit, and then looked quizzically at it. 'What went into this? Sometimes, when Esther tells me what we are eating nowadays, I wonder if I will survive this war!' He reached out and took Naomi's hand in his. 'They are wonderful. Make some for Sammy when he comes home.'

They dined at Max's club in a small private room. Diana would have preferred somewhere more lively, but she did not say so. Afterwards they sat for a while over coffee and Armagnac, and then made their way out to the street, Max's hand on Diana's arm to guide her. 'Cab, sir?' The commissionaire sounded ancient, she thought, feeling for the edge of the step with her foot, and he probably was, with younger men at war.

'Now,' Max said, as the cab drew away from the kerb, 'where shall I tell him to go?'

'Eaton Square,' Diana said firmly.

Will Howard be...?' Max sounded tentative.

'He won't be home – not yet. And he knows I'm with you, so he won't worry.'

Max reached forward and gave the cabbie the Eaton Square address, then sat back and pulled her hand through the crook of his arm.

'It's lovely to be alone with you again,' he said. 'It's been such a long time.' She felt his lips brush her cheek, but by the time she turned he had sat back again, and Diana's pursed lips met nothing but air. She faced forwards again, telling herself not to worry: once they were in bed it would be all right. You did not need eyes to make love, only mouth and hands and body – and thank God she had all those.

She ached to make love, to enjoy the physical intimacy and abandon of sex. But she was confused. Often, at night, with Howard sleeping beside her, she had put out a hand, running it over his ribs, his shoulders, his thighs – never knowing what she would do if he should wake and turn to her. Now, though, with Max, there would be no doubt, only the familiar ritual of lovemaking, crying out at the pleasure and the pain of it. She was trembling, as Max handed her out of the cab, and turned to pay the fare, before helping her up the steps to the door.

'Make love to me, Max,' she said without preamble when the door to the street was closed.

'Are you sure?' Max sounded doubtful, and she put out a hand, feeling for his arm.

'It's the one thing I want, darling, after all this time. Surely you can understand that?'

They mounted the stairs together, but she broke away on the landing, anxious to demonstrate that she could manage on her own. 'There,' she said triumphantly, when she was in his room, her hand on the bed post. 'Oh, Max, I want you so very, very much.'

She was first into bed, shivering although it was not cold. He came to her, sliding under the sheets, putting his arms around her, kissing her fervently and for too long, until she became impatient and twisted her head away.

'Come on, darling, come on.'

There was a moment's silence and then he moved away to lie back on his pillow.

'I can't, my love. I want to, but – I simply can't.'

23

December 1943

There was still frost on the pavements when Howard looked from the Mount Street windows, and his breath made a damp orb on the window pane. He turned back into the room and looked at the bed where Diana lay on her pillows, eyes closed, hands folded across her breast as though she were a corpse.

'It's cold this morning,' he said, and she smiled agreement without opening her eyes. Howard had never imagined a day would come when he would be cold in his own home, but fuel was in short supply and bedroom fires a thing of the past. He moved back to the bed and sat down. 'Penny for them?' he said and then, when there was no response but another faint smile, 'I've been thinking, Diana: why don't we see another surgeon? The man Loelia told me about – he's working with air crews but he sees some civilians.'

Her eyelids flickered but did not lift. 'There's not a great deal of point. We've seen three already. There's nothing there, my love; I'm out like the proverbial light.'

Howard would have persisted, but she put a finger to her lips. 'Hush. I want to talk to you about Christmas. Do you think Rupert will get leave? Even a forty-eight would be something. Loelia has promised us a bird.'

'I think it will depend on whether or not there's been some sort of second front,' Howard said.

'Second front, second front – that's all we hear nowadays.'

'Bomber Harris wants to step up the air assault on

Germany. He means to have forty squadrons of Lancasters operational in the next few months.'

We're losing so many planes over Berlin. I can't see the sense of it.'

'It's a question of morale. We make the Germans cower with the intensity of the onslaught; they give up. I think that's the theory.'

'The Germans couldn't do it to us,' Diana pointed out tartly, and he was relieved to see he had roused her.

'Ah, but we are a special case! Now, stop talking about matters neither of us truly understands, and tell me if you'd like to go to a concert. Pablo Casals is playing the Elgar, I believe – or we could have Mahler at the Albert Hall.'

'I'd rather have Tommy Dorsey,' Diana said. 'You know me and my low, low taste in music. In everything, come to that.'

We could go dancing then,' he offered. 'I'm not Fred Astaire, but I can still get round a floor. Let's go somewhere nice tonight.'

'We can't, we're dining with Loelia and all the ghastly Colvilles. Had you forgotten?'

'I had,' Howard said, rising from the bed and tightening the belt of his dressing-gown. 'I had erased it from my memory. Will the kleptomaniac aunt be there?'

'And the nymphomaniac niece, and Ma-in-law Colville who thinks she's descended from George IV. How does Henry manage to be so dull when he belongs to such a crazy family?' Diana was smiling and animated now, and Howard congratulated himself as he went into his dressing room.

Tonight they would have to bear the Colville dinner-party, but tomorrow he would take her somewhere – the 400, perhaps – and have some decent food and dance. He should have thought of that before; she had always loved dancing and, safe in his arms on a crowded floor, she would be no more disadvantaged than anyone else.

*

'It's lovely,' Mary said, stepping back to look at the Christmas tree they had just set up in the hall.

'Lovely,' Ben said. 'Is it for Santa Claus?'

'Yes, pet. Now, get out of the way while daddy makes it safe.' She held the tip while Patrick packed the bucket with wet newspaper, cramming it down until the trunk was jammed in and the tree stood safely upright. They decked it with pre-war trimmings, and joked about Santa Claus and Christmas Day, but the image in both their minds was the same: that of a home without a child at Christmas, and how easily it might have been their home if it had not been for Diana Brenton.

'I want to do something for her, Pat,' Mary said, when at last they were seated with mugs of Bovril either side of a struggling fire, Ben playing with his toys nearby. 'But what can you give someone who has everything?'

'I've thought about it myself,' Patrick answered. 'In fact, I've thought of little else. The price she's paid…'

'I blame myself. She wouldn't've needed to do it if I hadn't let go of his hand.'

'Stop it, Mary: that's idle speculation. If you'd held him, if Anne had held him – it was fate: nemesis. She's never reproached you, and I don't suppose it's crossed her mind.'

'No,' Mary said wonderingly, 'no, she never has. "I did what had to be done," that's all she said. She even looked glad to have done it. I never gave twopence for her, before, you know. And now Christmas is coming…'

'Well,' Patrick said, 'I think I may just have the answer to your problem.' He stood up and disappeared to the hall. When he returned he had a brown paper bag in his hand. 'I got this from a grateful patient. I refused it, but she was adamant. It's not new, but it's rather nice.'

It was a small carved box with a circle of ivory set in the

lid. He opened it and the sound of music came into the room.

'It's lovely, Pat, What is the tune? I know it .

'"O Tannenbaum",' Patrick said. 'An old German song, stolen by the Yanks. I believe they call it something else. It's pretty, isn't it? Do you think she'll like it?'

'I would,' Mary said. 'But then with her, you never know. Still, I doubt we'd find anything better. How will we get it to her?'

'Leave that to me,' Patrick said. 'Let's have another cup of this excellent Oxo…'

'Marmite,' Mary said.

'Hot brown liquid,' he compromised. 'And then if I can find my fiddle, I'll play "Tannenbaum" for you both.'

It was two weeks since Ernest Bevin, the Minister of Labour, had announced that 30,000 men were to be conscripted to work in the mines. They would be aged twenty-five or under, and chosen from the call-up intake by ballot, one recruit in every ten. Now, in the pit, the men were discussing the prospective newcomers.

'I want one for meself,' a wag said. 'I'll sit in-bye and tell him how to cut coal. By lad, it'll be champion.'

'Four weeks' training, they're going to get,' Frank said. '*Four weeks!* I've been at this game all my life and I still don't know it all, but they'll be deputies in a month.'

'I don't think it's right,' someone said, from the depths of the refuge. 'I don't fancy working alongside pressed men. It's bad enough working with you buggers.' There was laughter, but he went on, 'No, laugh away, but we depend on each other down here. Your marrer's your lifeline half the time. So I have to depend on some nancy-boy drafted in by ballot, have I? Thanks!'

'It's Ernie Bevin,' someone said. 'He's drunk with power, that one. Did you read what he said in the papers when someone asked if he had a right to do it; "Oh, yes," he says, "I'm entitled to direct anybody anywhere".'

Frank decided the conversation had gone far enough. Ernest Bevin was one of his idols and not to be criticized. 'Listen, thou,' he said to the man. 'When thou gets up there, look on the wall by the gate. There's a poster there of a soldier and a hewer with a windy pick, and it says the soldier depends on the miner. Now thou has a lad in the army, Bart, and so do I; and coal production's down this year. If Ernie Bevin's got a way to put production up and shorten the war so my lad can come home, I'm all in favour.'

'By lad: thou's a gobby bugger,' the man said good-humouredly, but the argument had been defused. Frank was almost ready to pick up his tools again when someone else spoke up.

'Never mind a lad in the army, Frank, thou's almost got a lad in the air force. A gold-braid job, at that.'

Frank turned. 'What d'you mean?'

'Young Brenton, the eldest lad, the pilot. He's walking out with your Stella. Our lass's seen them more than once in Durham – closer than new pound notes, according to her.'

'Did you know, Frank?' someone asked.

"Course I did,' Frank said. 'I know everything. I tell you lot that, but you never listen. Happen the Bevin boys'll give me a bit more respect.'

He sounded confident, almost cocky, but inside he was quaking. Would he have to tell Anne what had been said? Because if he did, the balloon would go up and that was a fact!

Emmanuel Lansky pursued the fortunes of the Allies through the newspapers, missing not a column inch. Bomber Command continued to shatter German cities and the Russians had launched a major offensive in Byelorussia. Already the Russians were bringing German war criminals to book; the first tribunal had taken place in Krasnodar in July, when eight Germans had been shot, and other trials had followed.

In London, Lord Vansittart, former head of the Foreign Office, had warned: 'We shall not establish sanity in Germany without a considerable measure of sanitation. War criminals must be followed to the uttermost ends of the earth.' And yet the House of Commons had recently endorsed the Home Secretary's decision to free Oswald Mosley from prison. Herbert Morrison had defended the release on health grounds, but Lansky could not understand how the man who had struck such terror into the hearts of Jews throughout Britain could be freed at this juncture. The war was not over yet, and Churchill, the man on whom Lansky had pinned his faith, was old and ill, struck down by pneumonia before he left the Middle East at the end of the summit conference there. His condition was said to be 'as satisfactory as can be expected' – what did that mean? And even if he recovered, would he be fit to take on once more the conduct of the war?

Still, Sammy was home on leave, and they were all together again. Lansky went to his room and donned the apparel of prayer; and while he prayed, his son was teasing Esther Gulliver.

'Go on, then,' he said. 'After you'd all cried yourselves sick at Bette Davis, you went and had another go at *Jane Eyre*. You're gluttons for punishment.'

'*Jane Eyre* was lovely,' Esther said fervently. 'But *Now Voyager*: when he lit those two cigarettes! And then she said, "Why ask for the moon, we already have the stars".'

'Ooooh,' Sammy said, as though in pain, 'I can't bear it but don't stop! Honestly, Esther Gulliver: how old are you?'

'Old enough to box your ears, Sammy Lansky, so stop scoffing. I suppose you never go to the pictures?'

'I do! Betty Grable, Veronica Lake, Alice Faye – *oy vey*

Alice Faye! And war films: I've seen more war on the screen than in real life, and that's a fact.'

'I liked *The Gentle Sex*,' Esther said. 'Leslie Howard. Our Anne cried for a week when he was shot down. There was a mystery about that, you know; it wasn't straightforward.'

'You love your little mystery,' Sammy said. They were sitting in the office above the warehouse, sifting through invoices and checking stock records. 'There'll be no turkeys around this Christmas,' he said dolefully. 'Remember '38? We made a packet on turkeys that year.'

'Never mind turkeys,' Esther said, tilting back in her chair. 'You were saying I like a mystery – I don't. But I know one when I see one, Sammy, and I see one now. What are you up to? You say you're being posted, but you don't say where or why.'

Sammy smiled, shook his head, and went on sorting.

'You haven't deserted, have you?' Esther asked tentatively.

He threw back his head and roared with laughter. 'No, Esther, I can say, hand on heart, that I have not deserted.'

'Well, what *are* you doing?' Esther persisted.

He tapped his nose. 'See this, Esther? It's a *noz*. I've got one, you've got one: a nice, little one. Keep it out of what doesn't concern you. What does concern you is what I'm going to give the girls for Christmas.'

'They don't keep Christmas. And you won't be here.'

'No, but you do, and you will be here,' Sammy said. 'And this year you live under our roof, so for you we celebrate. Not Christmas, but Esther's Day: what could be fairer than that? And what better excuse to give gifts?'

'Whatever you give the girls, they'll be pleased, feeling as they do about you: especially Naomi.'

The *girl t'shikl*,' Sammy said thoughtfully. 'Yes, she has a loving heart, that one. But it won't do, Esther. Don't encourage her. It simply won't do.'

Esther was taken aback by his sudden vehemence.

'It's just a crush,' she said defensively. 'That's all.'

'As long as that's all it is,' he said. 'You know there's only one woman for me. And still you refuse me: me, the hero of the cookhouse.'

'All right, Sammy,' Esther said. 'I can see you're not going to tell me what you're up to, so let's get on with this, lot. And then we can get out to the shops and see what's to be had for Christmas.'

Anne lifted the lid of the pan and checked that it had not boiled dry. It was only bread-crust-and-bit-of-kidney pudding, but it was the best she could do till next week's ration. She had discovered that bread soaked in kidney gravy made quite an acceptable meal inside a suet crust, especially with grated carrot and plenty of onion in it. Life was a constant struggle, now: no coal, no sugar, meat for only two days a week, bread scarce, jam non-existent, and everything to be queued for even when it was available. At least there were plenty of taties; Frank had planted them everywhere, in every inch of soil, and it had paid off. If only Joe could be home for Christmas; she would make a feast then, even if she had to kill to get it. Stuff was to be had on the black market, if you had the money.

Anne closed her eyes, thinking of the times when Joe came home on leave: always smiling, always apologetic about bringing clothes for her to wash, as if she didn't revel in it. How she would cosset him if he came home now. At least she had managed to make a bit of sweet mince, which was maturing nicely in the larder. They would have mince pies and pudding, and she had picked out an old hen to kill. It hurt her to think of the lost eggs, but Christmas wouldn't be Christmas without a bird. There wasn't even rabbit in the shops.

She heard Frank at the door and called out, 'Take your boots off. I've just used the sweeper.' She reached for the kettle, checked there was water in it, and planted it firmly on the heart of the fire. 'Tea in a minute.' Frank did not reply, and she turned as he pulled a chair out from the table and sat down. 'What's the matter? Your face is like a fiddle.'

'I don't know whether I should tell you this,' he said.

'What?'

He didn't answer and she flicked the tea-towel she was holding towards his face. 'What, Frank? Don't tantalize, you'll drive me mad.'

'You won't like it.'

Something in his voice made Anne put down the tea-towel and slide into a chair. 'What is it? It's not our Joe?' Frank's face cleared. 'No, it's not Joe. It's nothing like as bad as that.' Anne's irritation returned now that fear had been lifted. 'For God's sake, tell me, then. I'll have a stroke in a minute.'

'Well, will you keep calm...?'

He would keep this going all night if she wasn't careful.

'I *am* calm, Frank. I am calm, calm, *calm*.' She spoke softly, banging her hand on the table and smiling to reinforce her words.

'All right, then,' he said. 'If you must know, it's our Stella: she's going about with young Brenton. The air force one... Rupert.'

'How do you know?' Anne's voice was still controlled.

'From one of the lads at the pit. His missus's seen them in Durham, more than once.'

'Oh, my God...' Her voice escalated as the truth struck home. 'Oh, my God: he'll use her, Frank. He'll get her into trouble, and then he'll drop her like a toe-rag. My God, Frank! My God, what have I done to deserve this?'

'Keep calm, Anne. They're only bairns – it won't last.'

'It'll last long enough to ruin her life, Frank. I should know: it happened to me.' She had lived the lie of a forced marriage for so long that she had come to believe it. Now she glanced at the clock. 'If I live to see her come home tonight, it'll be a miracle. And when she does come home, Frank, I will flay her alive!'

The guests were all drinking sherry in the drawing-room when the phone rang. A moment later the footman Loelia had brought out of retirement came in to whisper discreetly in his mistress's ear.

'Oh dear,' Loelia said. 'Max has been badly detained. He says we should go ahead without him; he's not sure if he can get here at all.'

Howard glanced at Diana but she was sitting serenely in a wing chair, glass in hand. He wondered how long it had been since she had seen Max: quite a while, if he was any judge. He felt a spasm of hatred for the man who had been so keen to take his wife from him until she fell upon hard times, and now was letting her down just as he'd done before. He went to her side.

'All right?' he said. Her smile was brilliant. 'I'm fine, Howard. Looking forward to some Valesworth venison.'

'Will you take Amanda in, Howard?' Loelia said. 'Henry will see to Diana.'

It was a small, thoughtless slip, but Howard could see the ill-chosen words had hurt. Small patches of colour burned high on Diana's pale cheeks; her, unseeing eyes glittered. The next moment Henry appeared and folded her hand over his arm.

'All right, old girl?' he said and drew her towards the dining-room.

There were twelve of them at a table glittering with silver and crystal, and loaded with Valesworth food, for all the world as though it were peacetime.

They had finished the entrée and were waiting for the plates to be cleared when Howard saw the shred of meat that was clinging to Diana's upper lip. It hung there, quivering slightly, while she talked animatedly to the man in air force uniform who was sitting on her right. Howard could hear enough to know she was talking about Rupert.

The fragment of food still clung. He wondered if he should draw her attention to it – but how could he do it from across the table without alerting everyone else? He saw the wing commander had noticed it, too, and was losing the thread of his discourse as he stared, fascinated. Somehow the whole thing was made more bizarre by the perfection of Diana's features. She was reed-thin now, gaunt almost, her face fined down to the bone. And the irritating fragment clung to the perfect lips, moving with every word she spoke.

Howard saw that Loelia had noticed what was going on, and had also ceased to talk to her neighbour. One by one people fell silent; all eyes were on Diana, who still chattered on unawares. The tension built, until at last even Diana sensed it. There was one terrible moment of complete silence, and then Amanda, Henry's foolish cousin, gave a tinkling, nervous laugh. Loelia leaned forward, then, and with her napkin wiped Diana's mouth.

Conversation broke out, furious, unnatural conversation, everyone trying to assuage their own embarrassment. But Howard was dumb, watching the red tide that slowly engulfed his wife's neck and face.

It seemed hours before they had made their farewells and were safe in the car going home. 'Tired?' Howard said.

Suddenly Diana laid her head on his shoulder, something she had not done for a very long time. 'A little,' she said. 'But could we have a nightcap before we go up? Whisky, I think: whisky and water. And let's talk about the children. I've missed them so much. This damn war!'

'It's my turn to fire-watch, remember,' Howard said. 'But I can stay for a while.'

They sat by a fire stirred to life with a poker, and talked about their children. Diana slipped from her chair at last, feeling her way, and came to sit at Howard's feet. He put a hand on her hair, wondering if he should mention the ghastly incident at dinner. But something held him back, and at last she lifted her face to him.

'Would you help me up, darling, and kiss me, and then let me go up alone? I'd like to take my time getting ready for bed tonight.'

Howard walked with his arm round her to the foot of the stairs, and then she put him away. 'I'm fine now. I know this house so well.' She climbed a few stairs and then looked down at him.

We have been happy, haven't we, Howard? Some of the time?'

'Most of the time,' he answered. 'But it will be better in the future, you'll see.' Suddenly he mounted the stairs and took her in his arms again. 'Sleep well. I'll see you in the morning.' They kissed, and she clung for a moment before pulling away.

He watched until she was safely on the landing, and then he went back to the fire. It was sinking now, and he dared not use more coal. He shivered. He'd finish his drink, and then he would go. He sat and watched the flames flicker and die, one by one. He would give Diana a wonderful Christmas, and Pamela would help him – thank God for Pamela. And Rupert... but the boy was under immense pressure, and it couldn't be easy for him. He tried to remember what he had been like at Rupert's age, but it eluded him. It was such a long time ago.

He stood up at last, put a guard to the fire, and replaced his glass on the tray. As he walked through the hall the clock struck the quarter hour. Twelve-fifteen: he would have to hurry.

Upstairs, Diana sat in her room, smoking a precious cigarette, fingering the pearls at her throat, thinking of her husband. She had been married to him for twenty-one years, and it had taken all that time for them to come close to one another. She felt a tear form in her eye for all the wasted time, and then she put out her cigarette, got to her feet and felt her way to the dressing table. There were pills there, in the centre drawer, hoarded against the need of sleep. But first the letter. She held the paper down with finger and thumb, and tried to write as evenly as she could.

My darling, this is best. I really did love you, you know. I wish I had always known that. Take care of the children, as I know they will care for you; and, when it seems appropriate, tell them I loved them. But not too often. You know how I hate a fuss.

Bless you,
Diana

24

December 1943

The inquest on the death of Diana Brenton took place on 23rd December. Rupert sat next to Howard, his face white and looking unbelievably young above the collar of his uniform. The verdict was predictable: she had died by her own hand while the balance of her mind was disturbed, as a result of injuries sustained in an enemy attack. The Germans had many atrocities to answer for; this tragedy was another, the coroner said, and he expressed profound sympathy for the deceased's husband and family.

Loelia and Henry were waiting when Howard and Rupert returned to Mount Street. The funeral was to take place the following Wednesday, after Christmas, on 29th December. 'Come to Valesworth until then,' Loelia pleaded, but Howard was adamant. He must stay in London, near to where Diana lay, her face surrounded wimple-like by pleated satin, the sightless eyes closed above a mouth that seemed to wear a faint smile, as if she was dismissing all the panoply of death. 'Isn't it a hoot?' Howard could hear her saying. At first he had been angry with her; furiously angry at what she had done. But it had been no more than an instinctive reaction to tragedy.

'Take Rupert,' he said to Loelia; and, to his son: 'The others need you – Pamela and the boys. Give them the best Christmas you can, and bring them up to town on Tuesday.'

He saw relief in Rupert's eyes, followed by concern. 'It's the way you can most help me,' Howard said, and it was settled.

Howard had not bargained for the agony of being alone in a large house, while outside London was preparing to celebrate. He looked from an upstairs window at a young couple lugging home a tree, scarcer than gold this wartime Christmas. He saw a father bearing his son on his shoulders, his arms full of parcels; he saw visitors arrive opposite, to be welcomed over the step; and somewhere, far off, he heard carols.

It was late on Christmas Eve when the doorbell rang. The only servant remaining had long since left, in a flurry of goodbyes and injunctions to eat up what was in the larder. Howard opened the door to see fine snow falling from the night sky, and Norman Stretton, the Belgate pit manager, standing on the step with an overnight case in his hand. 'I thought you might want company,' Stretton said, 'but I can just as easily go to my club...'

They sat on either side of the fire, made up of logs chopped from war-damaged timber, and drank the malt whisky Rupert had left for Christmas Day. 'The men send their regards,' Stretton said. 'They feel for you. Especially Maguire – remember him?'

'Yes,' Howard said. 'I know Maguire well. What did he say?'

There was a pause, and then Stretton spoke. '"Tell the gaffer to hold on," that's what he said.'

'Thank you,' Howard said, and leaned forward to refill their glasses.

Sammy went straight from his leave to the manor house deep in the countryside. There they lived well, but worked hard: map-reading, signalling, weaponry, and the art of the rolling fall as a preliminary to parachute training. There was strenuous drill, and physical jerks, and games to train the eye and the reflexes. He spent Christmas Day with his fellow-trainees, playing board-games, listening to the radio, eating and drinking; all of them pretending that they were sure of dozens of Christmases to come, each of them knowing this might be his last. On Boxing Day, Sammy wrote a separate letter to everyone in the Lansky household, hinting vaguely at being tied to cookhouse duties or polishing the barrack square with a toothbrush as punishment for various trivial misdemeanours. *Never mind,* he added. *At least I am helping to shorten the war.*

Christmas day in the Lansky household was subdued. They all tried to be cheerful, for Esther's sake, but the day had little significance for them. They exchanged gifts, and Esther handed over the carefully wrapped parcels Sammy had left for all of them: for his father a complete edition of the plays of Shakespeare, handsomely bound in green leather with gold tooling; for Ruth an aquamarine pendant, blue drops hanging from a fine chain; for Naomi a bracelet of pearls and garnets that hung on the slender wrist like a garland.

His gift to Esther was a pearl necklace with a diamond clasp. *For my oytser* the card read, and it reduced her to tears. It was Emmanuel who placed the gifts one by one around each recipient's throat or wrist. Then Esther handed over her gifts: a warm cashmere muffler for Lansky, and blouses made by Anne for each of the girls, delicate confections of fine lawn with inserts of satin embroidered with the butterfly motif that was all the rage. Their eyes shone, until they realized the full implications of the gifts.

'Coupons, Esther,' Ruth said, her eyes widening. 'These things are new!'

'You will go short now,' Naomi said ruefully, her enchantment at the gift fading.

'I have enough clothes to see me to Armageddon,'

Esther said firmly, and began to gather up wrapping paper and string.

There was one more gift to be given.

'It is from the three of us,' Ruth said.

'With love,' Naomi added, and then Emmanuel was handing over the bulky parcel. It contained a painting in oils of the mouth of the Wear, with Sunderland stretching behind under a grey northern sky.

'It was specially painted for you,' Ruth said.

'By an ARA,' said Lansky.

'And I knew for weeks, and never gave it away,' said Naomi.

'*Oy vey*, a miracle!' Lansky said, and held out his arms to embrace them all.

The day after Boxing Day, Esther went over to Belgate. Her gifts to Anne and her family had been left under the tree before Christmas, but she took with her a box of sweets, saved from her ration, and a few precious oranges. After tea she and Anne went to the pictures to see Greer Garson again, glowing as *Mrs Miniver*. They cried and felt proud by turns, and walked home together through the black-out, arm in arm.

'They were all too posh in that picture,' Anne said. 'Real life's not like that. All the same, it was good.' They rounded the Half Moon corner as snow began to fall. 'What did you think about the Brentons?' Anne continued. 'They're doomed, that family; I'm only glad I put a stop to our Stella and the boy. She was always wild, that Diana. Stands to reason it would end in tears.'

It was sad,' Esther said, 'and not her fault. She saved Mary's son.'

'She took Mary's husband,' Anne countered. 'Well, the first one. You remember that day at the Scar, and him carried down on a shutter? Still, she's dead now and has to make her peace.'

'It's him I'm sorry for.' Esther did not say she had written to Howard Brenton to express her condolences. Better by far to keep Anne sweet. 'Losing his mother and his wife and his son in the forces.'

'He'll be a back-seat soldier, that boy,' Anne sniffed. 'They never put toffs in the firing line. Trust them to look after their own.'

'Rupert's in the air force,' Esther said mildly, 'and there's not much room for class distinction in a Spitfire, Anne.'

That's as may be,' Anne said, pushing open her yard door. 'But if he doesn't stay away from our Stella, he'll be airborne without a Spitfire, Brenton or no Brenton.'

Esther Gulliver's letter had arrived at Mount Street that day, and its contents touched Howard deeply. *I will always remember how happy she was when first she came to the Scar,* Esther concluded. *Please believe that you and your family are in my thoughts.*

As Howard drove to the church behind Diana's coffin, he remembered the Scar in those early days: Diana that first Christmas in the red velvet dress with lace at the neck, the boy who now sat beside him in uniform already quickened within her. Twenty years ago – a lifetime. *I am growing old,* he thought, and was comforted when Pamela's hand crept into his.

They sang Diana's favourite hymn, 'The King of Love my Shepherd is, whose goodness faileth never'. But goodness *had* failed. Diana was dead, and Howard could not be sure that she had ever been happy, even when she was alive. Worst of all, Max Dunane, the man she had risked so much for, was not even at her funeral. Howard tried in vain to convince himself that Max's absence was due to uncontrollable grief, but in his heart he knew it was funk. Dunane was a shirker, a man who ran away whenever it was the easier option. And when his eyes met those of Max's sister, he saw his own conclusion mirrored there.

At Mount Street afterwards Loelia devoted herself to Diana's children, the two young boys clinging to the woman who had mothered them for the last three years. But when they repaired to the drawing-room at the end of lunch, something had to be said.

'Max is devastated by Diana's death,' Loelia began. 'We were childhood friends, all three of us.' Indeed, her eyes were red with weeping, but Howard was not inclined to compassion today of all days. 'He'd have been with us all today if he could,' Loelia continued, 'but you know the War Office…'

'It's of no account,' Howard said. 'The people who mattered were there. Our children…' He looked quite deliberately towards Pamela, who was standing thoughtfully by the window looking out on the winter street, and he emphasized the word 'our'. Pamela was a Brenton, and God help the Dunanes if they dared try to lay claim to her now.

The music box with its tinkling 'Oh Tannenbaum' was never sent, for Diana Brenton's suicide made front-page news before the Quinnells could post it. *Society beauty's tragic death*, the headline read, and though the Diana pictured in the text bore little relationship to the woman Mary Quinnell had known at the Scar, she devoured every word of it.

She had not realized until now how much her life had been bound up with the Brentons, and with Diana in particular. The other woman's desire for a house set high on a hill had taken the life of Mary's first husband; the pampered birth of her first child, attracting as it did every doctor in the place, had led to Patrick's attendance at Joe's birth, and thus to his meeting with Mary. *Without Diana Brenton we would never have come together,* Mary thought. *She took one man from me, and gave me another.* And now she had saved the life of Mary's child at the expense of her own – for the papers were in little doubt that Diana's suicide was the direct result of the bomb-site tragedy.

When Patrick came home that day, he and Mary sat either side of the table with the newspaper between them, the sound of children's laughter percolating through the house as their son played with his friends; and they thought about Howard Brenton. Patrick had not been to church in thirty years, except for his marriage and the christening of his son, but on the day of Diana Brenton's funeral he sat with his wife in St Mary's church in the centre of Sunderland, and prayed that Diana Brenton had at last found peace.

Outside in the Christmas crowded streets Stella Maguire moved from shop to shop, pressing her nose against jewellers' windows, trying to decide how big a ring she would get when she got engaged. The giver of the ring changed from time to time. Sometimes, gazing at solitaires, she thought of Rupert, her favourite mental image being of the two of them running through a guard of fellow officers and a storm of confetti. At other times, seeing rubies and emeralds in clusters, she pictured herself on a liner entering New York Harbour, the Statue of Liberty smiling benignly as Ricky showered her with the riches of the New World.

Once or twice Stella wondered how Rupert was bearing up at his mother's funeral. He had cried in her arms on a swift dash to Belgate before he went to London, and she had told him he would get over it with time. Which he would. She, Stella, would lose her own mother one day and – an uneasy feeling that life might then be a lot easier overtook her, and provoked an unaccustomed twinge of conscience. Things had not been too bad at home since she had convinced her mother that Rupert Brenton was a thing of the past. As for Ricky, her mother knew nothing of him at all, which was fair enough as he wasn't really a boyfriend, more a passing acquaintance. It paid to keep Americans at arms' length. *She* wasn't getting caught.

At least if she took risks with Rupert, she knew he would stand by her. Yanks were good for nylons and peanut butter, which Stella could eat by the jar, but their trousers, like their cigarettes, were too loosely packed. She went into the milk bar, and sat in a booth drinking coffee and listening to Glenn Miller on the radio, wondering how long it would be before Rupert pulled himself together again and they could have some fun.

BOOK FIVE

25

May 1944

When his initial training was complete, Sammy went to the parachute-training school at Ringway. He made interminable practice jumps, first suspended from a cable, and then, with a 'chute, from a tower. It was not as bad as he had expected, except for the first heart-stopping moment when he felt himself falling like a stone and there was an eternity before he felt the sudden jerk of the harness as the 'chute opened and his descent was checked.

He learned to land with both legs together and roll to the side, gathering in the strings of the 'chute even as he hit the ground. His first real jump was from a platform attached to a balloon 900 feet in the air. 'Well-done,' the instructor said. 'You'll be doing it for real soon.'

Sammy wrote constantly to his father, to Esther and the girls, trying to keep his letters light and jokey, as they had always been. But there was a constraint upon him now; he had to consider every word he wrote, for he knew that his father's mind, to say nothing of Esther's, was acute. The slightest thing might betray not that he was embarking on a dangerous pursuit, but that something unusual was happening. And he was aware, too, with each passing day, of his own mortality and the depth of his fear.

If he died now, what had his life been? He had never done anyone a bad turn, not knowingly; and he had tried to be a dutiful son and a good friend. Or had he? Had not his whole life been spent in the pursuit of what Sammy Lansky wanted? Sometimes he went to bed feeling that things could have been worse; at other times he scourged himself mentally for all the years he had spent in *naarishkeit*. And he prayed, the familiar litanies of childhood coming now to grateful lips. A voice in his head accused him of finding faith only because he had need of it: 'You're a user, Sammy Lansky; if you get out of this you'll be the same *shlubber* you always were.' But when the time came for him to leave for France, he felt a greater sense of his Jewishness than he had known since his barmitzvah.

He was given a pack of postcards: rude ones with jokey captions and sepia-tinted scenes of town and country. 'Fill them as naturally as you can,' his mentor said. 'It's not easy, but you must omit anything topical. "I'm fine, hope you are, too": that's the tone. We'll post them at regular intervals while you're away, to keep the folks at home happy.'

Sammy made a list of the people he cared for: his father, Esther, Ruth and Naomi, Joe Maguire... Five friends; it wasn't much to show for a lifetime. He wrote two cards to Joe, four each to the three girls, and six for his father. He yearned to say something profound: 'I love you. Thank you. May God let us meet again.' But it wouldn't do.

And then he was in a car, speeding to a deserted airfield, and the moment had come. He huddled in his seat, trying to slow down his heartbeat, breathing slowly and deeply. They were aboard a 'Lizzie': the smallest of the planes in use. The moment he saw the Lysander on the tarmac he knew they were going to land and all his parachute training had been for nothing.

'OK?' The navigator was looking at him curiously. 'First time?'

Sammy nodded. The airman looked about seventeen. *I'm getting old,* he thought. *Too old for this game.*

'Cheer up,' the navigator said. 'Piece of cake.'

The plane droned on, as Sammy tried to work out what

had brought him to this. The photographs: that had been the beginning. If he had never bothered with the photographs... It had been a matter of pride since then to do well, to survive the course when others were weeded out, but at times the relentless routine at the manor had irked him. 'Is all this necessary for me?' he had asked once. 'I'm just going in and out. I won't need half of this.'

'What if we can't get you out straightaway?' the instructor had said. 'You might be glad of it then.'

And now he was in a Lysander crossing the French coast, wearing a flying suit over well-worn clothes of French make, with a set of papers that gave him an Italian mother and a French father, and with an L-pill, the 'L' standing for 'lethal', to be used at his own discretion. Could he do it, if it came to it? End his own life with one bite? And if he had to stay in France for any length of time what chance would he have of *not* using it?

'Not much longer now,' the navigator said, and Sammy smiled acknowledgement. The plane was moving slowly and losing height.

'We're picking up landmarks now,' the airman said. There's a good moon, and we'll get a signal soon. There's an ultra-shortwave set upfront. After that, it's lights from your reception committee.'

'You make it sound easy,' Sammy said.

'It is, usually. Last time we were spotted by a Messerschmitt and had to run for it, but it's going well tonight.'

'*Baruch hashem*,' Sammy said then louder, 'Thank God.' Suddenly the engine cut out and it seemed they were gliding silently down. Sammy braced himself, but there was only a series of gentle bumps; and then someone was urging him to the hatch and onto a steel ladder to the ground.

'Welcome to France,' a voice said in lightly accented English, and a hand on his arm was urging him away from the plane.

Thank you,' Sammy said, gasping as he raced for cover on legs that threatened to give way. Panting, they stopped among some sheltering trees. 'What happens now?'

'You can't travel tonight because of the curfew. We have supper and a bed for you near here. You go on to Paris tomorrow.'

Esther paused on Binn's corner and waited for a break in the traffic. Around her people swarmed, laughing and chattering. There was a new mood of optimism now that the threat of invasion was over and the air war had diminished to little more than a bad memory. Hardly anyone carried a gas mask now, and there were cheerful Americans on every corner.

'Esther?' She turned at the sound of her name and saw Howard Brenton behind her. He doffed his hat and smiled at her. 'How nice to see you.'

'We don't often see you up here, Mr Brenton.'

'No, I don't come north often enough. I'm here on business today – and to visit the constituency.' He replaced his hat and looked left and right. 'We can cross now, I think.' She felt his hand on her elbow as they negotiated the traffic, and then they were safe on the other side. 'Which way are you going?' he said.

'I'm going to cut through the park. Our warehouse is down Borough Road.'

'I'll walk with you, if I may. I haven't seen the park for a while, not since the Winter Gardens were bombed.'

Around them trees were newly in leaf and sunlight glinted from the lake. Howard felt a sudden sense of satisfaction and a desire to prolong this moment if he could.

'Have you had lunch, Esther?' She shook her head. 'I wonder, would you join me? I hate eating alone. We could go to the Grand Hotel – or anywhere else, if you prefer'

Esther hesitated, looking at her watch. 'I'm not sure.'

But Howard's eyes were tired when she looked into them, and there was a button missing from his jacket. *He is forlorn,* she thought, and made up her mind. 'Well, if we're not too long...'

As they walked along John Street, she tried to work out how many years had elapsed since she had run to see his car pass, carrying his new bride. She had been fifteen, and now she was thirty-seven and Diana Brenton was dead She had been Howard's upstairs maid, and now she was well-dressed and was walking beside him to dine in the town's leading hotel. It was a strange world.

They sat in a panelled dining-room while an elderly waiter served them the best that shortages allowed. 'It must be terribly interesting to be in Parliament now,' Esther said, and saw Howard's lips twitch.

'Sometimes it is,' he said. 'At others it's pure Gilbert and Sullivan. A few weeks ago, for instance, we debated crooners.'

'Crooners? You mean –'

'Yes,' he said. 'Miss Anne Sheridan, Miss Vera Lynn, and others. According to Lord Winterton, they reminded him "of the caterwauling of an inebriated cockatoo". Furthermore, he considered that their constant wailing about lost love and baby, baby might have a bad effect on the second front.'

'I don't believe you,' Esther said, in amazement.

'It's true. Check in Hansard.'

'What was his point?' Esther was laughing now, and Howard grinned in return.

'He wanted the BBC to ban them, of course. But the Parliamentary Secretary to the Minister of Information said the government could not interfere with the BBC. Even God dare not do that.'

'Didn't you all laugh?' Esther asked. '*I* would have laughed.'

'I believe you would, Esther. I remember what a merry

child you were...' Howard looked sad, and she hurried to change the subject.

'How are your children?' she asked. 'It's four you have, isn't it? I only knew Rupert, but I heard when the others were born – my sister told me.'

'Now, your sister is married to Frank Maguire, am I right?'

'Yes,' Esther said. 'And she's always a mine of information on Belgate affairs. How are the children?'

'They're well. Rupert is a pilot officer now, stationed in East Anglia. And Pamela is at school. She's fourteen. My other sons are thirteen and eleven, and they're in Berkshire with Loelia Colville. You'll remember her as Loelia Dunane: she was Diana's greatest friend. I owe her a great deal.'

'It was such a tragedy,' Esther said. 'I really meant what I said in my letter, Mr Brenton..

'Please, call me Howard. I call you Esther, because, well, I've known you from being a child. I hope you don't think it impertinent of me. So please make it Howard from now on. And tell me about you. Your business is thriving, so my manager tells me. Do you know Norman Stretton?'

'We've met once or twice. He's a very pleasant man.'

'I couldn't have managed without him. But he tells me that you have been an enormous success, running a quite sizeable business single-handed. How is young Lansky?'

'I don't know where he is at the moment – on some sort of special assignment, I think.'

'He always was a bright young man. He must be in his thirties now.'

Esther grinned. 'He's thirty-four, Mr B – Howard. Three years younger than me.'

'You *can't* be thirty-seven?' The frank amazement in Howard's face brought a blush to Esther's cheek, and, looking at her, Howard saw that he had been right years ago when he had thought she would be a good-looking woman one day. Her features were strong, but there was a softness about her mouth and eyes. She had a fine, fair skin and colour in her cheeks. She wore lipstick but no other noticeable cosmetic, and her hair waved prettily about her face. Her clothes were sensible but smart. Yes: all in all, she looked – he sought for a word – 'chic'. That had been Diana's word, and she would have used it today.

They talked about the influenza epidemic over coffee, and their own good fortune in keeping well. 'What do you do in your spare time?' Howard asked. 'If tycoons have any spare time?'

'I like the countryside. I don't see enough of it, except when I go out to visit my growers. I keep them very warm, I can tell you. That's Sammy's idea: "Make them feel cherished," he said and I have. And I love my home – well, I live at the Lanskys' for the moment, as you know, to help with things there. And I like listening to the wireless.'

'What programmes do you enjoy?' he asked. 'I like the *Brains Trust*…'

'So do I,' Esther said enthusiastically. 'Professor Joad and Malcolm Sargent: they're my favourites. And I like *Any Questions*. Did you hear the Transatlantic one with Dr Summerskill? She's a dragon.'

'What about *Itma*,' he asked, 'with Mona Lot? "Can I do you now, sir?", and *Funf*?' They were both laughing talking easily, forgetting their worries for a moment, until she looked at her wrist-watch and saw it was time to go.

They parted on the pavement, he to go back to Belgate, she to her office. 'I hope there'll be peace in the coalfield with the new four-year agreement,' Howard said. 'The government may have sponsored it, but it was owners and unions that hammered it out. I hope it will keep the peace.'

'I hope so too,' Esther said. 'I hated it when there was trouble in Belgate.'

He smiled and shook her hand. 'I mustn't fall out with

Maguire – not when I have renewed my friendship with his sister-in-law.'

Long after he was gone, Esther felt the warmth of his grip and the pressure of his fingers on hers.

The hotel was huge and impressive, and far enough away from Belgate for Stella to forget the wrath that would be sure to come. For months now she had sworn to her mother that her affair with Rupert Brenton was over, when in fact it was flourishing: by letter, by calls to the box outside the Half Moon, and in snatched meetings whenever Rupert could get away. Now, though, they had driven to Yorkshire for two days together: Rupert had begged and pleaded, and promised Stella ultimate luxury, and in the end she had thought, *Why not?* The most her mother could do was box her ears, and that only stung for a moment or so. The difficult thing had been fobbing off Ricky; in the end he had gone away in a huff, and good riddance.

Now, as Stella mounted the wide stairs behind the porter carrying their bags, she glanced down into the huge lobby and lifted her chin. She looked as good as any of the women down there, and better than most. There was a group of Yanks at the reception desk, hats pushed to the back of their heads, gold identity bracelets gleaming, smart in their uniforms, and laughing. You could always tell Yanks by their laughter – and their lovely, smooth uniforms which made the British ones look shoddy.

'What do you think of this?' Rupert said proudly as the porter flung open the door. The room was as big as a ballroom, with a four-poster bed, the first Stella had ever seen except in pictures, and a French window looking on to the sea and the promenade. So this was Scarborough.

Rupert was tipping the porter, and the man was withdrawing. 'Come here,' Rupert said as the door closed, and she went into his arms, feeling his wings against her breast. He was so proud of those wings – cocky about them, even.

'Love me?' he asked.

'I must do,' she said, 'or else I wouldn't be here, would I?' They sat on the bed, kissing and fondling, until Stella grew tired of it. 'Come on: we can't stay here all day. You men can only think of one thing. We've got two days and nights, and I want to enjoy myself.'

'Don't you enjoy it when we make love?' Rupert was talking about sex again, the one topic of conversation where men were concerned.

'Of course,' Stella said. 'But where's that surprise you said you had?'

He had bought her a ring, a pretty little thing with a blue stone surrounded by diamonds.

'Is it real?' she asked dubiously.

He laughed at her, then, and slipped it on her finger. It sparkled and made her hand look nice, but what she had really wanted was some nylons. Everyone was talking about nylons nowadays, and you could only get them from Yanks.

Anne settled into her seat and let the bliss of Hollywood flood over her. It was *Stage Door Canteen*, and nearly every star was in there somewhere: Joan Crawford was dancing with a GI, Bette Davis jitter-bugging, Joan Leslie and a soldier so in love that Anne couldn't decide whether or not that bit was real.

She felt good tonight. Stelia was toeing the line for once, and that Brenton carry-on was a thing of the past. Once or twice Anne had thought of all the Brenton money, but that sort didn't offer marriage, they wanted everything for nothing and then threw the girl on the scrap-heap. It wasn't going to happen to her Stella – not if she could help it. Any road, if the thing ever reared its head again she would get Esther to speak to her niece. Esther knew all about the Brentons. Like father, like son, that was the Brentons for you.

Several Ministry of Information films were shown before the B-picture. Frank said they were propaganda but they were good, some of them. Anne had brought some toffee with her, and she relished it, wiping her mouth with a hanky when it was done. As she returned the hanky to her bag she felt the comfortable prickle of Joe's letters. She carried them wherever she went, and treasured every one.

His latest had been full of the Jew-boy Lansky, and how much Joe was looking forward to him coming back. That wouldn't last once the war was over and Lansky had money again. Except that he might well do something for Joe – you never could tell what came out of a friendship.

On the way home Anne called at the fish-and-chip shop for patties and chips for four: one lot for Frank and the rest between her and the bairns. She was feeling really happy until she let herself in at the back door and saw Frank's face.

'It's our Stella,' he said. 'She's left a note to say she's gone off for a day or two. Not to worry, she says, she'll be back by the weekend.'

Anne sank wearily into a chair. 'I knew that bit of peace was too good to be true,' she said.

As the train thundered south, Howard found himself thinking again of Esther Gulliver. Thirty-seven years old! It didn't seem possible. The evening of Rupert's birth he had poured Champagne for the servants, and she had eyed her glass as though it was poison. 'Drink up, Esther,' he had said. 'The bubbles won't bite you.' And now she could sit across a restaurant table and talk with him about anything under the sun. She had completely grasped the Italian situation, the way the workers were beginning to revolt against German domination and the deportation of Italian labour to Germany. It was not prominent in the popular newspapers, so she must read them widely. He glanced out at the darkening landscape. Two hours or more before King's Cross. He closed his eyes, remembering.

Diana had been able to skim a newspaper in two minutes. 'Society columns, and hatches, matches and despatches, darling: that's all I need to peruse. If the sky has fallen in elsewhere you'll be sure to tell me, so why should I read it myself and be depressed twice?' Howard found he was smiling at the memory and was glad the first-class compartment was empty. How gay Diana had been, and brave. And foolish in her choice of men. He had let her down in so many ways, and Max Dunane had betrayed her.

He had come face to face with Max the week before, in the foyer of the Savoy hotel. 'I hope you got my letter, Howard? I was devastated by Diana's death.' There had been real distress in Dunane's look, but Howard had wanted to smash his fist into the fellow's face. In the end, though, he had simply inclined his head in acknowledgement and passed on, leaving Max babbling foolishly about how bad he felt about being unable to get to the funeral.

Had he himself behaved as badly to Barbara? Howard wondered. He had seen her once or twice in the lobby of the House, had smiled discreetly and passed on. Had he damaged her life? Please God, he had not. He closed his eyes again and thought of Esther Gulliver. She had dignity. She would not allow a man to hurt her unless she chose. And the man she chose would be a lucky man indeed.

26

May 1944

They had watched the house in the avenue Collaigne many times now from their vantage-point in the house of a resistance sympathizer. When Sammy had first looked at the familiar building he was gripped with fear; had he really traversed that guttering, clung to those tiles and pushed at the timbered side of the dormer window? It looked unbelievably flimsy, and a mile from the ground. But with each observation his confidence increased. When the time came, they could get him into No 6, the house where Jean-Paul had lived. The Lefèvres still occupied it, and would help him, but only once. And if he was caught, he must never tell how he had gained access to No 4. No need to feel the pill in his pocket; it burned against his consciousness.

There were several imponderables. Did he still have a head for heights? He had done some climbing as part of his training, but not on a sloping roof four floors above a French street with German patrols below. Would the guttering take his adult weight? It looked substantial enough, but they had no way of checking. And most important of all, would the cladding still give and allow the window to open? There was no way of knowing that until he had traversed the roof and was clinging there like a fly on a wall.

Sammy was hidden in several houses: first in the rue Des Alpes, then above a boulangerie in Montmartre, and finally in the rue de Sts-Pères. His hosts were mostly taciturn men and women who fed him and gave him a roof, but did not often enter into conversation. Roger, the courier who conducted him back and forth, was more forthcoming, and told of members of the *maquis* who had fallen foul of the Germans. Some were in various prisons in northern France, others in Germany, but still resistance continued.

'We can smell the end now,' Roger said. 'There is much more activity. The coastal batteries are being constantly strengthened, and even the sea is mined for miles.'

'Why don't we move, then?' Sammy asked. He was trying to keep fit, but in his confined quarters it wasn't easy. And he would need all his strength up there, forty feet from the pavement. He listened to the BBC broadcasts which went out nightly at seven-thirty and quarter past midnight, waiting for the agreed code words which would mean action. And then they came: 'Grandmother is better.' They were repeated: 'Grandmother is better.' Two hours later, Sammy and Roger were entering No 6, avenue Collaigne, and ascending to the fourth floor.

The plan was that Sammy would get into No 4 if he could, and would secure or copy any documents that came to hand. He carried a camera and a torch; if photography were not possible he would take the documents. But if he could find time to copy them, and then remove all traces of his presence, the Germans would never know anyone had seen their plans. If he could find a hiding place in the house he was to stay there for one day at least, fielding any fresh documents Rascher brought with him the second night, if he did not find what he was looking for, he would either have to wait another day and try again, or make his escape and return later. The thought of making a second trip was unbearable.

'Ready?' Roger said. The temptation to say 'No' was almost overwhelming.

'As ready as I'll ever be,' Sammy said, and stepped on to the sill.

The night had been chosen for its moonlessness, but

once he was out, lowering his feet to the gutter, moving crab-like towards the next house, he felt unbelievably exposed. There seemed to be wind whistling about his head, and he knew if he looked down he was lost. When at last he felt the flashing that marked the roof of No 5, he paused for a moment.

He was stuck now: afraid to go forward, afraid to go back, and no friendly hands to haul him to safety. *God help me,* he thought. *Don't let it end here, not in a* naarishkeit *like this.* He moved a leg cautiously and then he was away, up and over the window of No 5, past the roof division, and then at the window of No 4. He put out a hand and felt for give, as he had done a dozen times before. Had it been repaired? Would he have to turn and go back empty-handed? What would happen then?

He pushed again, to no avail. Had it been nailed from inside? He pressed once more, and harder; there was a crack that sounded like a gunshot. He froze, but there was no shout from a guard below. Sammy waited for a long moment, then he pressed again – and felt the wood give. A moment later, he lifted the sash window, moved cautiously onto the front of the window-frame, and put first one leg and then the other over the sill.

Once he was in the room he sat for a long moment getting his breath back, and resting his strained muscles. He could hear planes droning above but the house was quiet. After fifteen minutes he got to his feet cautiously, crept down one flight of stairs and began to pad from room to room; remembering the feel of the house, working out who slept where from the list of occupants Roger had given him.

The Raschers, husband and wife, were not sleeping in the master bedroom, as he had expected. They were in the back bedroom, both snoring. Sammy stood in the doorway until his eyes grew accustomed to the gloom, and all the familiar furniture and objects sprang to view. This had always been his room on his visits, and now these German bastards were defiling it with their presence. If Sammy had had a weapon, he might have done for them there and then, but all he did was back silently on to the landing, and tip-toe down the next flight, in search of Rascher's workspace.

As he had suspected, it was the room where his grand-father had worked. The same desk, the same chair – only the filing cabinet was new, and the leather briefcase with its ghastly insignia. Sammy shut the door carefully, checked the shutters and curtains were closed, by torch-light, and spread the contents of the briefcase out on the desk, seeing the sector numbers, the details, the dates. Verily, corn in Egypt! He began assembling his camera.

An hour later, the room was as he had found it, and he was back in the attic, signalling to the house across the way that he was staying put, squeezing himself into the space behind the huge chintz-covered ottoman, taking chocolate and cheese from his pocket, his mouth fresh with water from the tap in the bathroom which had a trickle on it that had filled his hand in seconds, so he had not needed to turn on a tap and risk disturbing the household. He had emptied his bladder into the sink, too, delighting in this small return for the defilement of his grandparents' home.

Now he closed his eyes and prepared to try to sleep. Tonight he would go downstairs again, but till then he must try to refresh himself. First, though, he prayed for his father, for Naomi and Ruth and Esther, and especially for the people he had known in this house in the days before madness was let loose upon the world.

When he had prayed, he closed his eyes but sleep would not come. He was afraid: so full of fear that his very innards felt liquid within him. How could he survive such a crazy venture? But equally, how could he run away? Suddenly, he remembered the day when Churchill had spoken to a conquered France in execrable French but with splendid words: '*Français! C'est moi, Churchill, qui parle!*' He had exhorted them to courage and patience, and then had bidden them goodnight. 'Sleep... to gather strength for the morning. For the morning will come.' Those words might have been meant for Sammy now. He needed strength for the morning.

He closed his eyes once more, and suddenly an image of Naomi was there. Little Naomi: a child no longer, but a woman, a woman who baked and swept and smiled – and laughed a lot. *I love her*, he thought. *I don't know how or why, but I do*. He turned on his side then, suddenly unafraid, and in a little while he slept.

Esther Gulliver was awake too, lying in her bed and trying to make sense of what was happening to her life. If only Sammy were here, or would telephone. She had written to him suggesting he should call her, but as yet he had not responded.

But even if he arrived on the doorstep this very moment, would she confide in him? What could she say? That she felt something growing between her and Howard Brenton? What presumption! He was the richest man she knew – the richest she was ever likely to know, unless Sammy kept his word to make them millionaires.

Was he writing to her regularly because he liked her company, or because she reminded him of happier times? And if he was interested in her as a woman, did she find that interest welcome? As a child she had thought him handsomer even than Douglas Fairbanks. Now she both respected and pitied him; life had not been fair to him, leaving him with four motherless children. Anyway, Brenton ways were not her ways; she could never adapt to them, not even for the occasional outing.

As she said that to herself she heard Sammy chiding her:

'You are the equal of anyone, Esther Gulliver. You are a pearl.'

Oh, Sammy, she thought as dawn appeared. *Oh, Sammy, if only you were here now.*

Anne tipped out the mash and stood back as the hens gathered. A bird was singing somewhere, and the air was heavy with the scents of summer. You could kid yourself there was no war on if you weren't wondering how to feed ten people on thin air. The women of Britain were performing the miracle of the loaves and fishes every day of the week, but there'd be no medals for them. Still, juggling food was a little enough price to pay for freedom; there were homes in Belgate that would never see their men again, and that was sacrifice.

Anne dashed the hens out of her way and went back to the house and her sewing-machine. As she treadled, she thought about the day, not too far off, when Gerard would be Father Maguire. If the war was still on, the army might take him for a padre, but perhaps it would all be over by then.

Her shoulders began to ache, and she got to her feet and crossed to the fire to put on the kettle. While she waited for it to boil, she looked at the picture of Joe in uniform which held pride of place on the mantelshelf. God would bring him home, and she would see him thrive, and please God she would keep him home for a year or two; but then there would be a girl and a wedding and bairns of his own. What sewing she would do for grandbairns! There'd be no coupons then, and plenty of everything to make them the best-dressed children in Durham.

Anne carried her tea back to the machine and began to treadle again, thinking how awful it must be for Esther with no children of her own. She had finished a French seam and begun another when the old saying came into her mind:

'If you have none to make you laugh, you'll have none to make you cry.'

Howard had dozed in a chair after the sitting at the House of Commons broke up. Now he came out into a half-sleeping London, and bade the policeman on the gate good morning. There was a breeze on Westminster Bridge, and he took off his hat, the sun caressing his head like a benediction. He felt a sense of elation at the way the war was going. Monte Cassino had finally fallen, and the road to Rome was now open. It could only be a matter of time before Italy sued for peace. Targets in Europe essential to invasion plans were being hammered day and night: the Seine bridges, the German railway yards, the oil refinery at Ploesti, the beach defences anywhere that might be a likely bridgehead.

Howard paused and leaned on the parapet, hearing the sounds of the river drifting up, looking at the mighty river below. Cars were moving on the embankment, and above him a plane, like a bird, appeared and reappeared from behind clouds. Rupert would be involved in fighting when the assault on France began. His latest letter was in Howard's breast pocket. Howard took it out and read it again, the corners of the pages rustling in the breeze.

You can feel it coming, and not before time. I drew my escape kit today, which included three silk maps, one of northern France, one of Belgium, and one of part of Germany. Also some steel trouser-buttons which can be used to form a compass of sorts. And a wad of French francs for which I had to sign in triplicate. Red tape, even on the brink of victory.
I mean to make the Germans pay for what they did to mother; then, when war is over, I'm going to try to make things up to you. There is something I haven't

*told you, something which has made me very happy,
and of which I hope you will approve – but more of
that when I get leave. Kiss Pammy for me, and tell the
boys I have some wizard souvenirs for them, mostly
German, which are quite hard to come by. And do a
good job of caring for this old country, papa. It's the
best one we have.*

*My love, always,
Rupert*

*PS: I mean to get to know Belgate after the war. After
all, I was born there, and I'm abysmally ignorant
about the place, I now discover.*

*Yours, to a cinder,
Rupert*

And care for this old country, papa. It was a long time
since he had been 'papa' to Rupert. Howard moved on, feeling tiredness overtake him but gratified by Rupert's letter.
After the war they would have time to spend together, but till
then he must 'care for this old country'. He turned to look
back at the Palace of Westminster. Was it and what it represented worth dying for? Please God he would not have to
surrender his son, not when he had already given his wife.

Miners' strikes were responsible for almost half the working
days lost now. Frank had some sympathy with the men, for
miners' wages were low in the wage table, and many of them
were seeing wives and daughters earning more, sometimes
twice or three times as much, in war factories. 'Why should
I go down the pit for a pittance?' was the cry. The Miners
Federation had asked for £6 a week minimum underground,

but it had come to nothing, and an 'unofficial' strike was joined by colliery after colliery until a better offer was forthcoming.

Coal output was dropping. There was no new recruitment, and absenteeism, through sickness or exhaustion, grew higher as the productivity per worker declined. Bevin directed anyone with mining experience back to the pit, but this was not enough, and his 'Bevin boy' scheme was a desperate attempt to raise manpower and production. For the most part, the newcomers were unwilling recruits. 'I wanted to wear my country's uniform,' one public-school boy told Frank, 'and they send me down a bloody hole in the ground.' Few of them had been used to physical effort, and their puny attempts to compete with men hardened by years of graft ended sometimes in laughter and sometimes in tears.

But Ernie Bevin had become Frank Maguire's idol, even replacing his revered Peter Lee. For Bevin conceived of a cooperation between workers and government, of fair negotiation, arbitration, welfare provision.

'It's the way of the future,' Frank told Anne. 'We can get some things by fighting the bosses. We can get everything if we box clever.' So he kept the Belgate pit running sweetly, and shielded the Bevin boys from the worst of the teasing, and as the liberation of Europe became more than a pious hope he listened to Churchill: 'Britain has never flinched or failed. And when the signal is given, the whole circle of avenging nations will hurl themselves upon the foe and batter out the life of the cruellest tyranny which has ever sought to bar the progress of mankind.'

As Frank hewed away at a solid wall of glistening coal, he imagined it to be the Axis powers. As the seam splintered and fell to his pick, he felt like a conqueror, like Joe would feel when he rode, victorious, into some freed European capital. And, regretfully, he 'stood down' from the Home Guard, for the dread of invasion was now over.

Anne watched him preparing his Home Guard equipment to be handed in. 'You never struck a bat,' she said scornfully. 'All that palaver, and not a shot fired.'

Frank did not argue. Anything to keep her sweet – and keep her mind off the day when Joe would be hurled into real war. For this would not be over without blood being spilt somewhere.

He watched the smart little Poles, the Czechs and the Free French whenever he made a trip to Sunderland or Durham. They looked as though they would give a good account of themselves when the time came, but the Yanks, camped outside Belgate now, looked more like pantomime fairies than fighting men. He saw girls who were little more than children hanging around the camp gates, and he thanked God that Stella was staying close to home since the row over the missing two days. Perhaps Anne had got the better of her, in the end.

Lansky drew the curtains, wondering as he did so when it would be safe to leave down the black-outs. Esther said it would be soon. Far off, in the kitchen, he could hear the rumble of the wireless. Naomi listened to it all the time now, as though she expected the announcer any minute to say: 'Now, news of Private Sammy Lansky.' Esther said no news was good news, but that sounded like so much *plaplen* to Lansky.

When he sat down at his desk, he took up his pen and continued his letter to Ruth.

So your sister put barley in with the meat, as Esther had said. Several handfuls of barley, which swelled and overflowed the pan. Oy vey, how can such little grains spread so far? But the little one is learning.

She misses you, Ruth, but she exults in your success. When she reads aloud from your letters she sounds like a proud mama. So do not fret about her, she is fine. As for Sammy, still no news except for the post-cards, which are full of words but say nothing. Esther is working very hard; these years of war are hard for traders and she feels a great responsibility to Samuel. One innovation is the making of jam for sale. She has a workforce of women, and they are making rhubarb and ginger jam, and will use what fruit comes to hand through the summer. They have taken a factory which used to make boot-laces. Where will this Esther/ Samuel empire end, I ask myself? And, a piece of gossip I am ashamed to write but can't resist: Esther has had two letters from Mr Howard Brenton, the coal-owner and MP. Not surprising, I hear you say, but the hoo-hah when they come, and the blush when she opens them should be seen. He is a sad man since the death of his wife, and Esther was not meant for an altemoyd.

So come home soon, my Ruth, and restore calm to this establishment and joy to the heart of your friend,

Emmanuel Lansky

PS: Do not write to say thank you for the enclosed small sum. Ni to far vus. *E. L.*

27

June 1944

Now that it had come, Joe felt cheerful about it. It was an adventure, after all: the first time he had ever set foot on foreign soil. Would he feel strange, stepping ashore in France? For it would be France, everyone said so. They went to the embarkation point in lorries, huddled amid equipment. 'It's Shoreham,' someone hissed when they got out. 'My auntie lives here. I know.'

'Step along, here.'

Joe shuffled obediently forward, suddenly aware that whatever this was, it was big. Around him men and vehicles milled, and the silver sea, in the distance, was black with craft.

They'll never go in this,' someone said. It was raining, and a driving wind was whipping the tarpaulins on the lorries into a frenzy.

'We're going, all right, mate.' This was a Welsh voice. 'We're too far in now to pull out for a show-ah!'

There was a laugh and someone else mimicked him: 'Show-ah! You tell them, Taffy. No going back.'

And then they were moving, hampered by their equipment, stumbling forward into the bowels of the landing craft. Someone was whistling Frank Sinatra's hit, 'I didn't sleep a wink last night'.

Joe's stomach heaved as they crossed the Channel, but whether with seasickness or fright he could not be sure. His mouth was dry until someone passed him a fruit drop. As he sucked, he ticked off in his mind the things he had wanted to do before leaving – just in case. He had done them all, including filling in the will form in his pay-book. He gripped his weapon and tried to work out how much longer it would be before they landed.

'I wish I had a bacon sandwich,' someone said plaintively. 'With tomato,' someone else added. There was a chorus of disapproval. 'Black pudding,' a firm voice said. 'That's what you want with bacon.'

Joe listened to the banter, marvelling that they could talk about such little things in the middle of an invasion. Perhaps the French would be waiting with open arms and plates of food for their liberators? But the only thing he knew about the French was that they ate frogs and snails. His stomach heaved again, and he quelled it by thinking of his mother getting up with daylight to do the family breakfast. He smiled to himself, thinking of her grumbles about wartime food. On his first leave he would take her something nice from France: cheese, or silk stockings. Even a hat, a real posh hat. He had never seen her dressed up, not in a fancy way. And he would take Sammy home, and let them see what a good bloke he was. Where *was* Sammy? It would be nice to hear from him soon.

'Steady on there…' It was the sergeant's voice. 'Not much longer now.'

As they neared the shore, Joe craned his neck. His landing craft was one of an unending line flowing towards a dark, forbidding shore. Naval guns were blazing from somewhere behind them, smashing shells into the fortifications guarding the beach. As the ramp of his craft began to rattle down into the shallows of the shore, he saw a concrete wall ahead, about 300 yards away. He could see movement along the top of it – Jerries – and hear the rat-tat-tat of machine guns. If he ran like hell, he could get to the lee of that wall, catch his breath and then take them on.

There was a shout, and sounds of splashing, and then the

men in front of him were falling away, and he, too, was stumbling downwards and splashing forward, water sucking at his legs. *Plodging,* he thought, *just like the beach at home.* He was halfway to the wall when he felt a dull thud against his chest. It was nothing, because he kept on moving forward... except that the shouting was getting fainter, and the light was fading, until he could no longer see the wall at all.

Lansky came into the kitchen with news of the Normandy landings. Naomi was finishing her breakfast at the table, and Esther was stacking dishes in the sink. 'They say paratroopers are landing in the Seine estuary, Esther, and there are barges full of our troops in the Channel.' Esther could hear the far-off sound of the wireless in the living-room, but somehow she couldn't take in what the old Jew was saying.

'I'm going to be late,' she said mechanically, looking at the clock.

'Late?' Lansky's voice boomed, filling the kitchen. 'We have a second front, and she talks of "late"? I'm talking of invasion, Esther, of liberation. Don't give me this "late".'

Esther came to her senses then, and followed him to the living-room, Naomi hurrying behind, wiping crumbs from her mouth.

There was only patchy comment at first, but now there was no question of moving away from the source of news. They huddled around the polished wooden box with its fretted panels as though in front of some delphic oracle, all thought of work or school dismissed.

And then they heard it, the reassuring, official voice: 'D-Day has come. Early this morning the Allies began the assault on the northwest face of Hitler's European fortress. The first official news came just after half-past nine, when Supreme Headquarters of the Allied Expeditionary Force issued Communique No 1. That said: Under the command of General Eisenhower, Allied naval forces began landing Allied forces on the northern coast of France.'

'Do you think that's where Sammy is?' Lansky asked her.

It was not a time for telling lies. 'I don't know where Sammy is,' Esther said. 'But I think he's doing something we can't know about – which means it's important. And I'll tell you something: I'd back Sammy in any sort of crisis. He'll be all right, you'll see. Now, I'm going to make some tea. You two listen, and shout if I miss anything important. And then I'm going to work, and so are you two. No, don't shake your head: the least we can do for Sammy now is behave sensibly. We owe him that.'

'But we don't know where he is,' Naomi said desperately. 'That's what hurts, Esther. Not knowing if it's him they're talking about now. There, in all that fighting –'

'There are lots of troops there,' Esther said, 'but that doesn't mean he's one of them. This is the push that's going to end the war, so I have to go and see to Sammy's business. I may have to work late tonight.'

Naomi nodded, suddenly resolute. 'I'll take care of Papa Lansky, and I'll clean out the kitchen cupboard when I get home. You said it needed doing. And I'll have cocoa and *kichl* ready for you when you get back. Then we can all listen to the wireless, and hear whether we've won the war.'

If only it were that easy, Esther thought as she made the tea. The second front might have started, but its success was far from assured. She thought of young men throwing themselves up a beach against a barrage of guns, or dropping from the sky on to bayonets below. How could it possibly work? And what about Joe? He was, surely, out there, too.

Anne came in from the hens and put the mash pan to steep in the sink. She felt out of sorts this morning, properly fed-up: it would be heaven help the first one to cross her, so they'd all better watch it. Life was such a struggle now, that was the trouble. She was sick of the hens, if the truth were told, feeling they begrudged her every egg they laid. She ran her hands under the tap, wishing she had a decent bar of soap. Even in her poorest days before the war she'd never had to scrat for soap, but now it was like gold, and when you did get a bar it couldn't lather for toffee. She was sick of cutting up newspaper to hang in the lavatory, and re-using brown paper, and drinking from chipped cups because there was a crockery famine. They'd all wind up with a disease shortly, if they didn't die of exhaustion trekking round looking for the necessities of life: pencils, kirby grips, matches. The girl up the street couldn't even find a teat for her baby's bottle until her sister's GI boyfriend got one posted.

Anne was fulminating about queues when Frank came in, just off shift. 'Put the wireless on,' he said. 'Stretton says it's started: they've landed in France.'

But Anne did not want to hear the wireless. Stricken by conscience that she had been bellyaching while lads were dying, she snatched up a scarf and hurried to St Benedict's, there to promise to queue without complaining if God would only bring every mother's son safely home.

Rupert Brenton was high above Omaha Beach. The Yanks had invaded from the six ports from Torbay to Poole; he could see them now, marching in to die as though they were going to the State fair. There was no cover, except for craters, but the sky was black with aircraft, harrying the Germans, towing gliders, dropping paratroopers. Rupert's role was to wait for the Luftwaffe to appear, but the Luftwaffe was limping, now, with most of its planes out of action. Spitfires and Typhoons and Thunderbolts and

Mustangs were the masters: Rupert had one of the Mark V Spits with the new gyroscopic gunsight, which was a big improvement on the fixed reflector sight. God help any Jerry he saw today!

Suddenly he saw something out of the corner of his eye: an M1109 coming at him out of the sun. He let out a little yelp of delight as he rotated the twist grip on the throttle to target the enemy. The diamond-shaped lights in the reflector contracted... he pressed the gun button, and saw the large plane apparently explode. And then he was whirling away and banking, coming in again just to make sure. He'd got it: a kill, the thing that made all the practice scrambles and fake interceptions worthwhile!

Down below him there was smoke and confusion and death, but he was here in the high, clean stratosphere, and glad to be alive and part of such a day as this.

The House was quiet as Churchill spoke. 'Many dangers and difficulties which this time last night appeared extremely formidable are behind us.' There was cheering, and one or two MPs were wiping their noses or staring fixedly ahead. The man next to Howard bent to whisper, 'Good show, isn't it?' Howard nodded. The man wore a black armband for a son lost at Monte Cassino. 'You've got a boy in the service, haven't you?' the man asked.

'Yes,' Howard answered. 'In the RAF.'

'Ah yes,' the man said.

Howard's euphoria subsided as the business of the House continued. Would Rupert be safe? *I have to believe he will be,* Howard told himself, *for that's the only way I can cope.*

Usually the girl looked worried, but today she looked no more than sixteen, Sammy thought. She put down the tray and smiled shyly. 'It has started.' Her English was halting, but her face glowed.

Sammy sat up on his bed. 'The invasion?'

'*Oui*. In Normandy. We create confusion, to stop the Boche getting there. It has been arranged for a long time.' She looked at the tray. 'Coffee,' she screwed up her face, 'terrible coffee, but hot. And bread. I'll bring you more news tonight.'

'What's your name?' Sammy asked. 'Surely you can tell me now?'

She hesitated, but only for a moment. 'It's Martine: Martine Desbeau. And you're Samuel Lansky. You told me. And now we're introduced.'

When Martine had gone, Sammy went to the narrow window, but all he could see were the slanting roofs of Montmartre, not even a strip of pavement or a moving human being. *I might as well be in prison as here,* he thought. And then he remembered the roll of film he had brought out of the house in the avenue Collaigne: troop movements in the Pas de Calais and Normandy, and a dozen other places. Perhaps he had helped, after all. He reached for the coffee cup. '*Lechayim,*' he said to no one in particular, and sat down again – to think of home, and of Naomi, and to wait.

'Yes, it's been quite a week,' Esther said smoothly. 'First Rome liberated, and now the second front.' On the other end of the line the oily tones of Gallagher droned on, but Esther thought she could detect a subtle difference today. For four years he had been a king – no, not a king: a dictator. And a thief. *How I despise you,* she thought and wondered if she dared say so. Perhaps not yet; they were not out of the wood yet. But she couldn't resist a little dig.

'There are big changes ahead, Mr Gallagher. A big day

of reckoning...' She paused as long as she dared. 'For the Germans, I mean, and for anyone who's profited from their nasty ways. Still, I mustn't waste your valuable time. What can I do for you?'

She wrote down his queries and promised an answer before the end of the day, but when she put down the phone she pushed the paper aside. In the bottom drawer of the desk she had a bottle of Moët et Chandon, a parting gift from Sammy. She had kept it for a special occasion, and what else was today? She gritted her teeth and shut her eyes till the cork was popped, and then she carried the foaming bottle down to the office.

'Pass those cups, Molly; I want you to drink a toast. To the second front – and to Sammy Lansky, wherever he may be. *Lechayim!*'

Mary and Patrick came down from Ben's bedroom and into their living-room. 'Esther will want the house back when it's over,' Mary said. 'It'll seem strange to leave here now, but I expect we'll cope.'

'I expect so,' Patrick said. 'Now, port or sherry? It's the last of the port, and I don't suppose we'll get any more for the duration, but, hell's teeth, this is not a day to quibble.'

They listened at nine o'clock as the King spoke to the nation, haltingly but with conviction, bringing in the Queen and telling his people to pray. 'Do you think they love one another?' Mary asked.

'Who?'

The King and Queen. I mean, *really* love, like we do?'

'Nobody loves like we do, silly,' Patrick said. 'But I expect they quite like each other – enough to rub along.'

'Idiot,' Mary said. 'How you can be so clever with your patients and such a fool at home?

'I practise,' Patrick said seriously. 'That's what does it:

practice.' And suddenly they were both silent, remembering the man he had been once, who couldn't have made a joke to save his life.

'Do you know how grateful I am?' he asked at last, but Mary put down her glass and crossed to silence him with a kiss. 'Now for some supper,' she said when she straightened up. 'Bread and scrape'll be about the limit – it's not much for a second front.'

'Ha!' Patrick said, throwing up his hands. 'I completely forgot.' He was out into the hail, rummaging in his coat. 'Another gift of a grateful patient,' he said, triumphantly. It was a jar of fish paste.

'I don't believe it,' Mary said. 'Salmon and Shrimp! I hope this day will never end.'

In his bedroom Emmanuel Lansky had prayed for his son. Now he let familiar words flow through his mind, giving him peace. It was the twenty-third psalm of David.

The Lord is my shepherd, I shall not want. He makes me he down in green pastures. He leads me beside the still waters. He revives my spirit. He guides me in the paths of righteousness for his name's sake. Though I walk through the valley of the shadow of death, I fear no harm, for you are with me...

'...Thy rod and thy staff, they comfort me.' Anne let the Bible fall from her hand for she knew the words. 'Thou preparest a table before me in the presence of my foes. Thou annointest my head with oil; my cup runneth over. Surely goodness and mercy shall follow me all the days of my life, and I shall dwell in the House of the Lord forever.' She kneeled then, the lino cold and hard against her knees which she always thought made prayer more effective.

'Take care of Joe, God. And everyone else.' She would have gone on but there was a tap at the bedroom door.

'Mam?' It was Stella, edging into the room, pale but determined. 'I'll come straight out with it, 'cos there's no easy way. I've fallen wrong. And don't say drink gin, because I've done that for three weeks.'

28

August 1944

Frank lay watching the light strengthen and dapple the bedroom ceiling. Beside him Anne slept deeply, and he was afraid to move and disturb her. In the days after the news of Joe's death, he had feared her grief would kill her or, more likely, drive her mad. Patrick Quinnell had given her something to dope her, but in her brief moments of animation, when the drug was wearing off, her anger had frightened him. He had felt only a great sadness: a sense of loss that somehow had cleansed him of other emotions. His son had died not only for his country but for a just world. Other men, men he worked with, had borne the same pain, and born it stoically. He would do no less.

But Anne was different. When Norman Stretton, the pit manager, came to see them she wanted to know only what the Brenton compensation scheme would do for them. And when Howard Brenton visited, on his first trip to Belgate after Joe's death, she was barely civil to him and Frank had been relieved to see the MP take his leave. 'There was no need to treat him like that,' he had said and Anne flashed back at him: 'No need? He's still got his lad, hasn't he? It's all right for him.'

But at least news of Joe's death had taken the sting out of Stella's news. Not even disgrace compared with death.

Now Frank listened to Anne's heavy breathing, and felt a great pity for his tempestuous wife. She took things hard and she loved her bairns – whatever else you could say about her you couldn't deny that. He began to slide a leg cautiously towards the floor. So far so good. When he was upright he reached for his trousers and slipped them over his bare legs, then he gathered up the rest of his clothes and tiptoed from the room.

He checked the kitchen cupboard, afraid to use anything Anne might be saving for later. In the end he decided on bread and marge and tea, and sat down at the table to enjoy it, spreading the morning paper out before him. According to the headlines, American forces were now only forty miles from Paris. Creampuff soldiers, that's what Yanks were called, and yet they had Jerry on the run. He turned the pages with one hand, eating and drinking with the other. There were terrible pictures of London, devastated now by flying bombs. Trust Hitler to come up with an evil trick like that, just when the Allies were winning for a change. Frank refilled his cup and read on.

The announcement was in the Deaths Column: *Brenton, Charles Rupert Neville, killed in action, 31 July 1944. Beloved son of Howard and the late Diana Brenton.*

Frank felt tears prick his eyes. One more lad gone, one more father bereft. Mary and Esther had told him of Diana Brenton when she was sightless and pathetic in the Infirmary, and in their telling they had cured him of any lingering bitterness he had felt about Stephen Hardman's death at the Scar. And now her son was gone. He wanted to believe they were reunited, mother and son. The priest said it was so, but sometimes... Frank filled a mug with tea and mounted the stairs to Anne, and this time he could not control his tongue.

'Young Brenton's dead,' he said, as he set down the mug. 'Killed in action. You'll be satisfied now.'

But Anne did not react as he'd expected. She sat up in the bed, looking suddenly stricken.

'Are you sure?'

'It's in the paper,' Frank said. 'There's no mistake.'

Anne was out of bed and scrabbling for her clothes. 'Hide that paper till I get down,' she said. 'We'll have to break it to our Stella.'

And then, when he looked at her stupidly, 'Whose bairn is it she's having, Frank? Young Brenton's, that's who.'

Frank felt his legs tremble and sat down on the side of the bed.

'What d'you mean? You told me...' They had told him it was a soldier, a Birmingham lad, someone she'd met at a dance and couldn't trace now. They'd told him it was only the once... 'You lied to me,' he said.

'For your own good.' Anne's voice was tart.

'But why?' he said. 'Why lie about it?'

'Because the Brentons are not having my grandbairn, Frank, that's why. They've had the best of you; they've kept me tied to a kitchen range; but they're not making a skivvy of our Stella – which is all she'd be, if she took up with him. Now, get out of my way and let me work out how I'm going to break the news to her.'

Stella didn't get out of bed before noon nowadays, but Anne had given up remonstrating with her about the value of exercise and fresh air. Instead she concentrated on giving her good food, the best she could manage, and making sure Stella took the vitamins and cod-liver oil she was getting from the Welfare.

Today, though, there was no time for niceties.

'It's no use taking on,' she said, eyeing her sleepy daughter as she came into the kitchen. 'But young Brenton's been shot down. It's not a rumour; your dad read it in the paper. I've seen it, too.'

Stella's reaction to the news was exactly what Anne had expected. There was a genuine howl of anguish, and then an immediate examination of how the altered situation would affect her.

'Well, the Brentons'll have to pay,' Stella said at

last. 'It's their grandbairn – they'll have to pay.'

'I knew you'd say that,' Anne shot back, 'and the answer's "No". Oh they'd pay, all right – or *he* would: Howard Brenton. But they'd take your bairn from you. Don't think they'd take you along with it – not them. I know them, Stella. I've watched them over the years, ever since they killed your Uncle Stephen. The bairn'll be taken over and packed off somewhere to school: a cold, awful place where he'd go through God knows what. But he'll learn one thing there: he'll learn to despise his mother.' Seeing that Stella was unconvinced Anne added the clincher: 'And there'll be no money in it, not for you.'

'What else can I do?' Stella was weeping now.

'There's plenty you can do,' Anne said firmly. 'Drink your tea and listen to me.'

She outlined her scheme for looking round for a likely local lad and snapping him up. He would not be told of the pregnancy, and by the time he found out it would be too late. 'You're only twelve weeks gone,' Anne said. 'You can say the baby's premature.'

'It'd never work,' Stella said. 'By the time I'd got them to the getting-wed stage, I'd be too far on. You can't bring a lad round to proposing overnight.'

'Can't you?' Anne said grimly, folding her arms. 'It's time you knew the facts of life, my girl: the *real* facts of life. Let me tell you how I got your dad.' She licked her lips for a moment, and then launched into her tale.

'He'd always had a soft spot for me, and I knew it, but I didn't fancy him; I wanted something better. And then my dad died, and we were out on the street, your Aunt Esther and me. "Go into service," my uncle said. "Work for the Brentons." Well, I don't need to tell you what I thought of that. It's bad enough having to scrub your own floors, so I got your dad on his own one night, and I did it with him. Oh, you can smirk – I didn't do it for lust, miss, like some

I could mention. I did it for necessity. And then I told him I'd fallen wrong and he, being the man he is, did the right thing. And we've been happy, Stella, you know that. We've had our ups and downs, but it's worked. And your poor Auntie Esther, who had to do as our uncle told her, is an old maid now, with nothing!'

Privately, Stella thought Aunt Esther's lot, with a house and car and a business, was infinitely preferable to a houseful of bairns and a coal-range, but she didn't argue. She had other things on her mind.

In the weeks following D-Day, Sammy had been moved to a different safe-house four times. Every day he begged for news of his return to Britain, but the people who came to him were preoccupied with other things. Since the invasion, a stream of coded messages had been beamed to the French Resistance, urging them to come out fighting, according to pre-arranged plans. They had rushed to obey.

Gradually the rail network had been paralysed and German traffic, driven onto the roads, had met with countless roadblocks. The military phone-system was constantly disrupted, and individual Germans were being harried whenever possible.

'We'll get you out when we can,' Roger said, towards the end of June. 'But you are safe at present so be content.' Sammy would have argued, but Roger held up a hand. 'Please. We French have much to bear. Two weeks ago the SS wiped out the village of Oradour. A village, *mon ami*; all 642 people – men, women and children.'

'What do you mean, "wiped them out"?' Sammy asked.

'They shot the men, and herded the women and children into the church. They they fired the church.' There was silence in the room for a moment and then Roger let out a sigh. 'But this is not your fault. The other news is good: the

Americans are in Cherbourg, and the Resistance is taking over in many places. When we can we will get you out of Paris, or the Allies will come and get you. Either way, you are going home.'

It was August before that promise was kept. On 10 August, the railway workers of Paris, the *cheminots*, went on strike, paralysing the capital. The following day Roger brought news. 'You are moving tonight. We have orders to ship you to Chartres, and Chartres will move you on. Things are hotting up here, and we want rid of you.' He grinned. 'No disrespect, my friend...'

'Just get me moving,' Sammy said fervently, 'and you can be as disrespectful as you like.'

Esther had taken the Hillman to be serviced, but it was a lovely day and she welcomed the walk into town. Events were moving fast now, but she was managing to keep on top of things at work. If only Sammy were here – or any-where where she could talk things over with him. All they got were silly little postcards with meaningless sentences on the back. It was Sammy's handwriting, and sometimes his *chutzpah* showed through, but there was no backbone to what he said. He was fine. He hoped they were fine. Wasn't the weather good. He hoped they were getting enough to eat. There was nothing relevant to the changing times; it was as though he was writing them in a vacuum.

When Sammy did re-appear – and Esther wouldn't even consider the other option – they would have to talk about the business and clothing. It was expensive and scarce: at least good-quality clothing was. An ordinary ladies' suit cost eleven guineas, and hats, coupon-free and the only way you could change your appearance, were a scandalous three or four guineas. Esther had paid £2 10s for her Tengal blouse, and eight guineas for her new handmade brogues.

Eight guineas! It was enough to make you weep. All the same, a Lanver range of good-quality clothing at affordable prices would be something to surprise Sammy with. She might talk to Anne about it when she had time. What Anne didn't know about materials and making do wasn't worth knowing. And they would have to make do for a long time yet, there was no doubt about it.

Poor Anne, thought Esther, she was still grief-stricken over Joe – and now this business of Stella. Esther's own pain at the boy's death was dreadful; what must it be like for his mother?

She was halfway down Holmside and about to cross the road when a grey car drew up beside her. 'Esther!'

It was Fox and Esther bridled at his use of her Christian name.

'Mr Fox,' she replied, with emphasis.

'Hop in,' he said, leaning to open the passenger door.

'Thank you, but I'm enjoying the walk and I haven't much further to go.'

He was grinning. 'You're not scared, are you, Esther? A competent young lady like you?'

Esther had heard about Fox, about the money he was making from his dealings with Gallagher, about the wife he kept pregnant and at home in a big house near Tunstall Hill that had been built for better men than he, who had fallen on hard times.

'I'm never scared, Mr Fox,' she said sweetly. And then, bending down to the open door: 'Do give my regards to your wife!'

A week after D-Day, the first V1 flying bomb had landed on London. Since then they had fallen thick and fast, more deadly even than ordinary bombs for they were completely unheralded and indiscriminate in their choice of target. At first Herbert Morrison had claimed the damage was relatively small, but as the death-toll mounted it had to be admitted that V1s were a disaster for Britain. They were, in essence, low-flying bombs launched from the Pas-de-Calais, fitted with wings and a primitive pulse-jet engine which was programmed to cut out over London. The V1 would then nose-dive silently down to detonate its ton of explosive wherever it happened to land. No one wanted to dine at the Savoy any longer, because it was said to be right in the flying bombs' flight-path.

Howard watched brave men go white as they heard the sound of the engine cease, and fling themselves to the ground to await the explosion. Someone had christened them 'buzz bombs', for the drone of their engines, but 'doodlebugs' had become the popular sobriquet. People were now coming to terms with them, a case of familiarity breeding a tremulous contempt. The craters they caused could not be compared in size with bomb craters, but their blast was still massive and deadly. In the Guards Chapel, only yards from Buckingham Palace, 119 worshippers were killed. Another 102 were seriously injured. The Royal family stayed put, to keep up morale, even when the King's tennis court was devastated.

'We have to keep the scale of the damage quiet,' one of the Whips told Howard. 'If people knew the truth, there'd be wholesale panic.'

'You can't keep it quiet forever,' Howard said stonily. 'There's a steady stream of doodlebugs, night and day. That speaks for itself.'

'Well, we can't make it official,' the man said irritably. 'We'll have to evacuate mothers and children again if it goes on, but the barrage on the North Downs is now gearing up to repel them. However, they're a blow, especially now when we're making a breakthrough.' The following day 198 Londoners were killed in the Aldwych, as they were on their way to lunch.

Howard watched fear return to people's faces, and rubble and desolation to the streets.

And then a simple telegram came and told him his son was dead: *Killed in action.* A letter followed from the squadron leader, extolling Rupert's virtues. Howard assumed the mantle of grief, but he felt strangely unmoved by the whole affair; remote, as though it were all happening to someone else. Loelia wept, but he felt her tears were as much for her own elder son, who was soon to be out of his training, as for her dead friend's son, lost in action.

Rupert had been dead for ten days when a messenger came to tell Howard that a visitor was waiting for him in the lobby of the House of Commons. It was a boy in uniform, with wings on his chest and his face the face of a child, except for the wary eyes. 'David Sterling, sir. I was a friend of Rupert's. We trained together.'

'Oh, yes,' Howard said. 'I've heard him speak of you. Let's get out of here, somewhere we can talk.'

'I wanted to tell you how it happened,' the boy said, when they were safe in a side room, plunging in as though words would fail him if he hesitated. 'We were patrolling the Channel, about twenty miles out, gunning doodlebugs. Sometimes you can just catch their wing-tips and tip them over, so they fall into the sea. We're getting quite good at that. I could hear Rupert whooping because he'd got one. And then three of the Huns came out of the sun, above and behind him. He was shot up, and I saw oil blow over his cockpit cowl. "How bad is it?" I asked him on the radio, but he didn't answer. There was a lot of static. And then I heard him say, "They're not supposed to leave me in the dark." Well, I think that's what he said. I was half-rolling to get out of trouble, and when I looked back, his plane had ditched.'

'Could he have got out of it?' The boy shook his head. 'When you ditch, the scoops under your wings ram into the water and the kite up-ends and dives nose first. So you can't get out of the cockpit. Besides...' He hesitated. 'I think Rupert bought it before he hit the water. The hood – he'd have slid back the hood when the oil was thrown, if he'd been able to. Well, that's what I think...' He looked desolate suddenly, now that his tale was told.

'And you managed to get back to base?'

'Yes, sir.' The boy looked apologetic, as though it were a sin to live when others died. Howard well-remembered that feeling, in 1918.

'I'm glad,' he said firmly, 'I'm glad you survived. It makes me feel so much better. You may not understand that, but it's true. So never, *ever* feel guilty for being alive. And thank you for telling me all this. It's been a great help. Now, it's almost noon; can I take you somewhere to eat?'

He would dine the boy, and try to lift his spirits –and then, when he was alone, he would cry. And Howard was looking forward to that moment, the moment when he could at last cry for his son, who had always hated the dark.

'They're beastly things, these doodlebugs, aren't they?' the boy said, as they left the House and the familiar coughing noise was heard in the sky. 'But I expect we shall lick them in the end.'

Esther went home early to help Ruth to prepare her clothes for the return to university, and to cheer up Lansky and Naomi, who moped incessantly as day after day passed without news of Sammy. As she offered Ruth items from her own wardrobe, Esther thought of the havoc the war had created for people like Howard Brenton and Emmanuel Lansky. They were good men who deserved better, and now they were mourning their sons – for Lansky seemed to have lost hope of ever seeing Sammy again, and Howard had written to tell her how much he was grieving for Rupert.

'If we think you haven't enough clothes when we've finished, we'll see what Anne can come up with,' Esther told Ruth. 'You've never had a chance to get a real wardrobe together, what with coupons and everything. But our Anne can knock something up out of nothing and she knows about styles. She chooses not to look it herself, but that's just her being contrary.'

She was ruminating on why stylish Anne of the old days had become couldn't-care-less Anne of today, when the phone rang in the hall. 'I'll get it,' she said and ran down the stairs.

On the crackling line the female voice was faint and abrupt. 'Is that the Lansky residence?'

'Yes,' Esther said, fear prickling at her skin. Was this bad news? The next moment she heard another voice.

'Hallo – who's there?'

'It's me, Esther. Is that *you*? Oh, Sammy!' As her tears came the others materialized in the hall, their faces ablaze: Emmanuel from the study, Naomi from the kitchen, and Ruth on the stair.

'I've turned up, Esther, the bad penny safe and sound; not a scratch. Can't tell you much now. I'm at a military airport, but I'm home and I'll be with you soon. Can you put papa on? And then the little one?'

As Esther surrendered the phone to a father who could barely speak for emotion, she realized for certain that Sammy no longer belonged to her. Did she mind? As she mounted the stairs to her room she knew that she did – that it had been comforting to know she was the number-one woman in his life. But in asking to speak to Naomi he had shown where his heart lay and of whom he had been thinking, and she must find it in her to be glad.

In her room she sat down at her writing-desk and took out the letter Howard Brenton had sent to her in reply to her letter of sympathy about Rupert. She smoothed it out and read it again, and then took up her pen. '*Dear Howard*,' she began.

*

They were sitting either side of the fire, alone for once, for Stella had gone out in search of consolation and the other children were in bed.

'I don't care if it is wrong, Frank, it's what we're doing. Do you think I'm letting my first grandbairn be brought up God knows where, by strangers?' Anne was knitting, needles flying in and out of white wool.

'It won't be,' Frank insisted. 'It'll be with its mother.'

Anne sighed heavily and closed her eyes to indicate complete despair. 'Oh, Frank, our Stella's as likely to stick to that bairn as I am to sprout wings. I'm the only one that'll mother that child, and we both know it. So it's got to stay here in Belgate, or round about, so I can keep my eye on it.'

'That's as may be, Anne.' Frank was dogged. 'But think on this: what if it was our Joe's child and some woman somewhere was plotting not to let us know? How about that?' He was trying desperately to get the last gasp from his last fag end, and Anne would have mocked him for it at any other time but not now. This was too important.

'It's not our Joe's, is it, Frank? Our Joe wouldn't've got a girl into trouble. It's the fancy Brentons with their greedy ways that got us into this. Our Stella was a good girl till she took up with him –' Frank's eyes widened at this, but he did not contradict her. '– and they're not going to profit by it, not while I've got breath. And if you let on to Mr Brenton, Frank: well, I think you know what'll happen then.'

As Frank didn't speak, she continued: 'There's a few lads, nice lads…'

'They'll never take on another man's bairn,' he interrupted.

'They will if they think it's theirs,' Anne said triumphantly, too late realizing her mistake.

'Oh no,' Frank said, and this time he was adamant. 'We don't lie to any Belgate lad: not while I'm breathing. If Stella wants a husband, she gets one the decent way. And don't threaten me, Annie, because there's nothing – *nothing* that'll make me lie down to a bloody deception!'

Anne bent to her knitting, breathing easier now that there was no question of her own long-ago deception being revealed. She was furious at Frank's stubbornness and lost in admiration of his principles. He was too good for this world, but that didn't make him any less a husband to be proud of.

'Did you see that in the paper?' she said, when she could trust herself to speak. 'About morality squads? They're setting them up to deal with soldier-mad girls. I wonder what they'd make of our Stella? Still, she's had her wings clipped now and no mistake.'

It was weeks and weeks since Stella had seen Ricky but she meant to try to take up with him where she'd left off. When she arrived at the point in the wall of the camp where girls usually gathered, it was deserted, and the camp itself was eerily still.

'They're all gone, pet,' a passing policeman told her. 'I should run along home now, if I was you. The GIs are in the thick of the fighting by now, like as not.'

So they'd gone off to war. *Just my luck*! Stella thought, as she turned for home. Now her mother would force her to marry a Belgate lad and she'd be chained in Belgate for the rest of her life.

She was halfway home when she saw the three GIs, two of them elderly for fighting men, one the tubby little Eye-tie that Ricky had borrowed money from once, in a bar. He had peeled notes off a wad. What had his name been?

Marco? Mario? That was it! Stella tossed back her hair and smiled, the warmest, most welcoming smile she could summon up. 'Mario!' she said. 'What are you doing, still here?'

His moon-face beamed at this unexpected attention, and the two older men stepped aside as tactfully as they could. Mario transferred his gum from one cheek to the other, and stammered out a story about a twisted knee and a later embarkation.

'I was looking for Ricky,' Stella confided. 'Is he still here?'

She saw Mario swallow convulsively, and then the cap he had swept from his black curls began to twist in his pudgy fingers. He didn't answer.

'Well,' she repeated. 'Is he here?'

'He's dead, Stella,' Mario said. 'On Omaha Beach. We just heard: Ricky, and Joe Mazurkzi, and Lenny Brill – a whole heap of them didn't make it.'

Stella put a hand to her eyes and swayed. 'Oh God,' she said. 'Oh God, what am I going to do?'

And then Mario was taking her arm and pulling her gently against him. 'Let's find a bar,' he said. 'I don't know what's wrong, but I'm still here…'

On his way back from lunch with the young airman, Howard cut along Whitehorse Street, which leads from Piccadilly into Shepherd Market. Music was coming from the American Club, a radio blasting out The Marseillaise', and inside he could hear an excited buzz. Passers-by were stopping to listen. 'It's Paris,' someone called suddenly. 'They've liberated Paris!'

'That's nice,' the woman next to Howard said placidly, and went on her way.

When Howard reached the House he found it was true. At 2.30 that afternoon the German commander had surrendered to the French 2nd Armoured Division. German snipers were still active, but Charles de Gaulle was expected in the city at any moment.

'It's over now,' someone said. 'Or as good as over.'

That night Howard went by cab to Chester Square to collect Loelia who had come to London for a couple of days. They were dining together to talk about what Howard would do with his children when the war was over.

'Will we be safe tonight?' Loelia asked, as she came out to the cab, holding her long skirt in a gloved hand. There were diamonds at her wrist and ears, and she smelled of something exotic and very, very French.

'Of course,' he said, though he was far from certain. V1s could strike anyone, anywhere, but there was no point at all in telling that to Loelia. 'They're terribly good at stopping doodlebugs now,' he said as he handed her into the cab. 'As a matter of fact, I was talking to someone today who is in that sort of thing. He says they catch their wing and tip them into the sea.'

'How brave,' Loelia said. 'And how terribly dangerous.'

They dined at the Dorchester, cocooned in their own private island while hubbub went on all around them. Loelia bowed graciously to some friends as they went to their table, but once seated she gave Howard her undivided attention. 'I asked to come here because they say they get food on the black market. Quite wicked and probably untrue, but one does yearn for a decent entrée. I know it's been here for twelve or thirteen years, but I always think it looks like a glorified cinema organ: they built it for Americans, of course, and you know their taste for the vulgar. Not that I should say that, when my brother is married to one.'

'How is Laura?' Howard asked.

'Still skulking on the other side of the Atlantic. I expect she'll come back eventually, when she's sure it's safe.'

'And Max?'

Loelia looked at Howard and then lowered her eyes. 'Max, my dear Howard, is Max. We won't change him, any of us. I don't think about him too much now. I see him whenever he comes to Valesworth or I come to town, but I don't let him worry me any more. Do you know what I mean?'

'Yes,' Howard said. 'I know what you mean. Now, do tell me what you want from this wonderfully illegal menu.'

'Won't it be blissful when the war is over?' Loelia said as they sipped their aperitifs. 'The day after the armistice I shall set off for Cap Ferrat to lie in the sun like a lotus-eater. And then on to Nice. Do you remember the poppies, Howard? And the wisteria, wave upon wave of violet, and the irises, and the oleanders, and geraniums popping out everywhere? I can hardly wait.'

Howard did remember the Riviera, the scarlet splash of the poppies, the delicate lime of the euphorbia, the scent and sound of spring in one of the most beautiful places on earth. He had gone there with Diana, so how could he forget? But he very much doubted that it would have come through a world war unscathed.

'I don't think we'll be able to go there straightaway,' he said. 'There'll be a fair degree of chaos in Europe for a while.'

Loelia raised her brows in gentle disbelief. 'Oh, I expect it will settle down pretty quickly once we've won,' she said. 'We British are quite good at organizing that kind of thing. But of course the reason I most want peace is to have my son back home and out of uniform again.' Her eyes dropped then, as she remembered that his son would never return.

They talked of everything and nothing: of free Paris and the future of Europe and whether or not food could ever be the same again. And they talked of the dastardly German attempt to raze medieval Florence to the ground.

'At least the Ponte Vecchio survived,' Loelia said, 'but I hope they hang the man responsible. After all, history should be above warfare, or what's civilization for?'

After the coffee Loelia was ready to get down to business. 'Now,' she said, 'about the children. I want you to know that Henry and I will be happy to keep them with us for as long as you like. Forever, for that matter. Diana was my dearest friend, and Pamela is so very like her mother.'

'Do you think so?' Howard said. 'They might have the same looks, but temperamentally…'Did Loelia know that Pamela was her brother's child? Diana had never been sure, and neither was he.

'After all,' Loelia continued, 'she's fourteen now, and she needs a woman to turn to. The boys, well, perhaps you could manage them. They'll be going to school soon, I expect.'

She was avoiding his eye, and suddenly Howard knew that she did know the truth about Pamela: knew it, and wanted to keep her niece near her, without ever acknowledging her parentage.

'It's kind of you, Loelia, and I appreciate it very much, but I want my children back. All of them, as soon as possible. It's safe at the Scar now. As soon as I can arrange help I'm going to open up the house again. But until then, I'd be grateful if they could stay where they are.'

When he had dropped Loelia at Chester Square, Howard looked at the London skyline, wondering if he had done the right thing. Would Diana have wanted Pamela to be with the Dunanes? What would the child herself want? And then he remembered Pamela, her face alight as she looked out from the Scar at the Durham landscape. *She loves it there*, he thought. *Whatever her parentage that's where she belongs.*

29

October 1944

Sammy came home in August, thinner and older but recognizably the Sammy they loved. 'Give him time to tell us where he's been,' Esther urged them. 'He needs to do it his way.'

First though, there were old friends to greet and good wishes to receive from neighbours and friends and the Jewish community in Sunderland. Sammy marvelled at the state of the business until Esther felt she might burst with pride. But there were news items to tell him, the saddest being that of Joe's death on the Normandy beaches. 'So he's gone then, the *boyt'shikl*. He was a *mentsh*, Esther. I had plans for that boy.' There were tears in Sammy's eyes but he held them back, for Naomi watched him like a hawk, her face a barometer of how he was feeling, and his father had already wept for the death of the boy whose birth he had almost attended.

Naomi hangs on Sammy's every word, Esther thought and found herself smiling. When she looked up she met Sammy's eyes and saw that he knew what she was thinking. There was such warmth in his expression that she felt comforted. *He loves me,* she thought, *as I love him. As friends, as two people as close as friends can be.* But unless she was mistaken, Sammy loved Naomi, too – as a man loves a woman; as Philip had loved her. *I knew love like that once,* she thought. *I can't expect to know it again, but I can be glad for other lovers – especially when they are my friends.*

She left the room then and mounted the stairs, but as she looked back through the open door, she saw that Sammy had moved to Naomi and taken her face in his cupped hands. The girl was looking up at him with the eyes of love.

It was a week or more before Sammy got around to opening the pile of mail that had accumulated in his absence. Esther had dealt with business letters, Emmanuel had opened official letters 'just in case', but anything that looked personal had been put on one side. Esther was there when Sammy opened one letter, a bulky, over-sized envelope containing another envelope and two sheets of notepaper. It had been posted by Joe Maguire on 4 June 1944, two days before he left for France. Sammy laid the letter on the table and smoothed it out before he read it. '*Dear Sam,*' it began.

I suppose this is my last night of peace for a bit, so I thought I'd write while I had the chance. I listen to the news and it seems things are moving at last. So I'm off to war, without even knowing where you are, my best marrer. Up to no good, I'll be bound – at least I hope so, for your sake. It's funny how you adjust to things isn't it, Sam? And it's merciful really, because if we thought about what's going on and the awful things that are happening we'd go potty. Anyhow, I got a good mate out of the war, so it can't all be bad, and we have to be prepared to defend what's right. I'm enclosing a note for my mam and dad. Can you hold on to it till I come back, Sam? If I don't – well, you can guess what I want you to do with it.
The news is that Cogger has been invalided out – his piles, as you might guess, although the lads swear it's all my eye and Betty Martin. A huge Kraut bomber came down in the field behind camp. Two Spitfires got it, and down it came. We had a lucky escape, but the lads were all over it for souvenirs. It was nose down

in the bog and there was oil everywhere. I got a piece of fuselage, but someone pinched it – anything not nailed down, as you know. We are shipping out tomorrow, destination Berlin. Thanks for everything, mate. You are a good bloke. Take care of yourself, and my Auntie Es. And don't forget the letter for mam. If I make it, I'll buy the first pint. You can buy the rest, bloody plutocrat that you are.

Yours sincerely,
Joe

Sammy and Esther wept together, but then he dried his eyes. 'It doesn't make sense, Esther: a boy like that gone and a *shmuck* like me alive.' His voice was bitter.

Esther shook her head. 'It's not like that, Sammy. It's not a game: this counter or that. There has to be some reason to it, even if we can't see it. And saying life's not fair is pointless. Change things. That's the only way to make sense come out of it all.'

Sammy went to Belgate the following day, taking the letter for Anne and Frank. 'He sent it to me because he hoped you'd never get it,' he said, trying hard to keep his voice steady. 'It's late, because I was overseas and have only just got home. But here it is – and I'm sorry you ever needed to read it.'

They held the letter between them and read it together.

Dear mam and dad,
If you're reading this it means two things, one good, one bad. The bad one is that I bought it and you got that telegram. The good one is that Sammy made it. I expect you have had a lot of grief over me, and I'm sorry for that. It's very difficult to be writing this, thinking forward and back, so I think I'll stick to the

present tense. Tomorrow we go to – well, parts unknown. I expect I will survive and I mean to try because I like this life. I have had a good life so far, thanks to you two. A very good one in fact, with the best parents in the world. I want to live, but it is not what I want but what God wills. I'm not afraid of dying, as long as I don't show myself up. But I won't be dying for England because, quite honestly, I've hardly seen any of it so I don't know if it's worth it. But I remember home, mam, and what you made it… yes, the rules an' all, and the times you boxed my ears for my own good. And what we had there is worth fighting for: you two, and our house, and the rest of the family. So that's about it, except to say that if you cry and worry yourself sick, mam, you will do me no good and you'll spoil my picture of home. My one regret is that I haven't been able to do as much for you both as I would have liked, as I intend if I get through this. There's £37 10s in the post office, for what it's worth. Spend it on yourselves, and remember that wherever I am I am OK and if you are not working yourself up, mam, I will be happy.

Goodbye and thanks for everything. Kiss the girls and tell the lads I'm proud of them.

Yours,
Joe

P.S. Say ta to Sammy for delivering this. He's a good bloke, I hope you won't lose touch with him.

'I'll go,' Sammy said, awkwardly, seeing their faces but Anne held up a hand.

'Stay for a cup of tea, Mr Lansky. We need to get to know you.'

*

A month later, as the countryside turned gold and hedge-rows were bright with hips and haws, the Lanskys were preparing for a wedding. Tomorrow Samuel Lansky would be married to Naomi Guttman with all the solemnity of a Jewish ceremony. On the previous Sabbath he had been called to the Reading of the Law in the synagogue, and on the day before the wedding he moved into the flat above the Crowtree Road shop, for it was important that bride and groom did not meet for at least a day until they were re-united under the ceremonial *chuppah* that represented the home they would build together.

Now, Esther and Ruth helped adjust the white lace dress that had belonged to Sammy's mother, Cecelie. It fitted Naomi, thanks to Anne's frantic trips backwards and forwards to pin and tuck and hem. She and Frank would be coming to the reception after the ceremony, and they had bought a set of pillowcases as a present. 'Only utility', Anne said apologetically, 'but I've faggotted the edges and embroidered their initials. There they are, entwined.'

When Naomi was ready, Lansky came in to see her for he was her father in all but name. Cecelie's veil of Brussels lace covered her head, but the dark eyes, shining now with happiness, would have been ornament enough.

When Lansky had kissed her and embraced Ruth, he took Esther's hands in his. 'I thank you, my Esther, for keeping our home together for this day.'

Esther tut-tutted but he would not be put off. '*You* did it, Esther, you kept the faith for Sammy. I owe this day to you...' His eyes twinkled. 'And to Eli Cohen, my friend, who cannot tell boy children from girl children.'

And then the ceremony began. First Sammy came in to lower the veil over his bride's face, and then he returned to the synagogue to wait with the other men. The service would be in Hebrew, but he had painstakingly written it out for Esther, so that she would understand every word.

Emmanuel conducted Naomi into the synagogue, Ruth taking the place of the mother whom they might never see again. The *chazan* sang the welcome, the *baruch habo*: 'May He who is mighty, blessed and great, bless the bridegroom and the bride.' Then came the address, and after it the first blessing which was over wine, the symbol of joy. The second blessing praised God for his goodness in ordaining marriage and the home, and then bride and groom drank from the same cup to show that henceforth they would share the cup of life. Esther was suddenly, painfully aware that she was alone. In spite of all the love that surrounded her, from the Lanskys, from Anne and her children, from Ruth, there was no one at all for whom she came first. As light flooded the synagogue through the beautiful stained-glass windows, she schooled her face into a smile, but her heart ached.

Sammy slipped the plain gold ring on to the right index finger of Naomi's hand where it would remain until after the ceremony. 'Behold,' he said in a strangely boyish voice. 'Behold, thou art consecrated unto me by this ring, according to the law of Moses and of Israel.'

Then it was time for the *ketuba*, the marriage contract, and the seven marriage blessings were sung. Naomi and Sammy sipped wine, again from the same glass, and then Sammy was crushing it beneath his foot, and there were cries of '*Mazel tov*! from everyone, except Emmanuel, who could not speak for tears. The Rabbi spoke the familiar words: 'May the Lord bless you and keep you: may the Lord cause his face to shine upon you and be gracious unto you: may the Lord turn his face towards you and give you peace,' and, after the signing of the register, Sammy led Naomi to a private place to signify their newly acquired status as man and wife.

And then Lansky was beaming down on Esther, Ruth's eyes were signalling relief that all had gone well, and Eli Cohen and his wife were at her side, congratulating her on Naomi's appearance for all the world as though she were the mother of the bride. *I will be all right,* Esther thought. *I have friends and work and a home of my own – who could ask for more?*

Once she reached the Lansky house, however, there was no time to think of herself. They had made a feast, the best that could be arranged in wartime. 'Will there be enough?' Ruth asked anxiously. 'Yes,' Esther said lovingly, putting an arm round her. 'And let me tell you, in that blue dress you look *ba-tamt.*'

'Me? Delicious?' Ruth said. 'I'm the scholar.'

'You are a beauty today,' Esther said. 'A brainy beauty perhaps, but a beauty just the same.' She reached for a jug of fruit juice. 'And if you don't believe me, look at that boy in the corner: Eli Cohen's youngest. He can't keep his eyes off you.'

She had put Howard Brenton's gift together with the others. Sammy had insisted on inviting him, tapping his nose with his finger when Esther queried it. 'I have my reasons, and my spies.' Howard had not been able to come north, but he had sent a silver and crystal decanter and a note which spoke of his congratulations and his intention to visit them soon.

There had been a separate letter for Esther:

It has become second nature to write to you, Esther – I hope I don't bore you with my tarradiddle. The Belgate woman you told me of sounds excellent: if we can come to an agreement with her I will arrange for my brood to come home to the north again. There is so much to do, but I must face up to it. I will be in Sunderland next week – can we meet then? I so look forward to our meetings when I'm not dodging these wretched V2s.

The swell of laughter and gossip had begun to quieten down when Sammy whispered disappointedly in Esther's ear: 'She isn't here – your sister.'

Esther looked around. 'You're right,' she said. 'I can't think what would've stopped her. She was looking forward to it, and so was Frank.'

The Maguires had been ready to set off for Sunderland, Anne fussing over her hat and the set of Frank's tie, when a cab drew up at the door and Stella climbed out. 'Where's she been?' Anne said, peering through the net curtains.

'And who's that with her?' Frank said. 'It's never a Yank, is it?' He had not cared for the GIs, seeing them as an occupying army a million strong, swarming over Britain, which, they were fond of saying, was smaller than North Carolina. He saw and disapproved of their affluence, their posh uniforms, their over-familiarity with their officers, their constant gum-chewing, and their ability to have girls clustering round them like flies. 'They're always boasting,' his fellow miners said. 'And they're overpaid.'

But Frank had a deeper grievance against the US Army. No matter that they gave chocolate to children and seats on buses to any woman over thirty: they practised racial segregation, and for that he could not forgive them. Attempts by the US authorities to confine black troops to certain bars and pubs had led to an outcry in Britain and been hurriedly dropped – officially at least.

'It *is* a Yank,' Anne said, and let the curtain fall back into place. 'And our Stella's done up like a dog's dinner.' Her voice was full of foreboding.

Stella wore a new dress which strained slightly over her bulging stomach. When she entered the kitchen they saw that she also wore a ring on the third finger of her left hand.

'This is Mario, mam, Mario Dimambro. We got married

today. It's all above board. I would've told you but I didn't want a row.'

The boy – for if he was a day over eighteen Anne would eat her new wedding hat – stood looking nervously from one to another. Then he held out a pudgy hand to Anne. 'Hi, mom,' he said. It was the last straw.

'Get them out of here,' Anne roared. 'Get them out of my house!'

'My God,' Frank said bitterly to his daughter as he shooed her and her bridegroom towards the door. 'What will you do to us next?'

BOOK SIX

30

January 1945

'Mam, come quick!' Stella's voice was urgent, and Anne was out of bed and moving across the icy lino almost before the last word was uttered. Relations between the two had been strained over the last few months, but this was no time for recriminations.

'It's all right, pet. Your mam's here.' Anne held Stella's hand until the contraction passed, and then went to waken Frank to go for the doctor. 'Hurry up,' she said, as she pulled on some clothes. 'You can never tell with first bairns. And someone'll have to ring that Mario, not that it should be any concern of his.'

In the months since Stella had sprung her bombshell, Anne had remained unreconciled to the idea of her daughter marrying a Yank. She distrusted Yanks, who did nothing but splash their money about and ogle women. On the newsreel she had seen good-time girls flocking round Rainbow Corner off Leicester Square, which was a sink of iniquity by all accounts – not that the same scene wasn't repeated up and down the country. Stella's Yank was a mild-mannered Billy Bunter of a lad, but he was a foreigner, and all the tinned fruit in the world couldn't make up for that. True, he had bought her a ring the size of a pea, sent from America concealed in a box of soap, completely dwarfing the ring she had once received from Rupert Brenton, and which Anne had sold for her to a Sunderland jeweller. It was very nice, but could not affect the way Anne felt. All the same, Anne wasn't prepared to tell him the truth about the baby: not yet.

Frank fumed and fretted over the deception, taken aback by the fact that since Stella was already married, to be truthful now would be to condemn a marriage solemnized in church. *He's a Catholic,* he mused privately. *I suppose that's something* ... But he wondered how Stella had managed all the form-filling and the hurdles deliberately erected by the US authorities, who were no keener on fraternization than the British. She must have lied, that was all; God knows, she had been good at that since the pram.

Now, as the day of delivery wore on and Stella screamed and moaned in the room above, he remembered Anne's first labour, and Joe, red and wrinkled, looking up at his father in the oddly trusting way that babies have. And then his jubilant visit to the Scar to tell Esther; and Brenton, in the kitchen, cock-a-hoop about a son as well. Now both those boys were dead, and Brenton's grandchild was being born above, and it was his grandchild, too. Life was stranger than fiction.

When the deceived father arrived, Frank put his last drop of rum in a glass 'To wet the baby's head when it comes,' and then vanished to the Hall Moon, afraid he might give away secrets if he stayed.

Anne came downstairs to let in the midwife and fetch more hot water, and told Mario it wouldn't be long.

'Gee,' he said, twisting his cap in his hands. 'The baby's come awfully soon. Will it live?'

'Of course it will,' Anne said tartly, and went back upstairs. The boy was gormless but was even he daft enough to accept a full-term baby as being three months premature?

At eight o'clock that night Stella gave one last animal scream, the baby's head appeared, and then it slithered suddenly into view, dark mottled red and covered in blood and mucus. 'It's a boy,' the midwife said, and prepared to cut the cord while the doctor ran a finger round the tiny mouth and the baby gave a roar. The next moment, swaddled in a terry towel, it lay in Anne's arms. She looked down at it, seeing the bewildered little face which looked as though it had all the cares of the world on its shoulders.

'There, then,' she said, fingering the dark hair, 'there then: who's a granny's boy?' If only she had let Frank tell the Brentons; she had wanted to keep it from them, and in so doing she had turned her first grandchild over to an unknown family in a strange land. *But you shan't go,* she told the baby, silently, against its cheek. *You're stopping here with me.*

Emmanuel could not bear to read the newspapers nowadays, and yet he could not resist them. In December, during the first war-crimes trials, nine French Gestapo members had been sentenced to death in Paris. It was justice, but the court had heard horrifying stories of torture, murder and extortion. In Paris – the place of blossom and street music, of the smell of food and the sound of laughter; the place where Emmanuel had fallen in love, had wooed and won a bride, and been married, just as Samuel and Naomi had married, believing they would live happily ever after. He remembered the faces of his new wife's parents all those years ago, filled with sorrow that they were losing a daughter and joy at her happiness. *How had they died?*

And then, a few days ago, four young Soviet cavalrymen, guns at the ready, had moved cautiously down a road towards a barbed-wire encampment. Looking through the wire, they had seen a backdrop of corpses sprawled in snow, in front of which living skeletons moved slowly and painfully. The name of the place was Auschwitz-Birkenau. The SS had done their best to obliterate evidence and destroy documents, but sufficient remained to show that this had been the Nazis' biggest extermination camp.

How could God allow such horror? For the first time, Lansky felt shaken in his faith. What light, what hope was there for a world in which this thing, this desolation, could be?

He was seated in his chair, his newspaper discarded in front of him, when Naomi came in with tea and jam tarts on a tray. He smiled at her and peered at the tarts. 'Superb,' he said approvingly. But this time she did not beam with pleasure at his praise. Instead she poured out his tea and then sat opposite him, her hands folded in her lap.

'What would you like best in the world?' she said.

'Oho,' Lansky chuckled, anxious not to communicate his gloom to the young bride, for so he still thought of her. 'Best in the world? *Gefilte* fish, perhaps – or a strudel?'

No,' she was shaking her head, 'not food. Anything but food.'

Lansky perked up. Had she had a letter from Sammy, who had been back with his unit for a week now? 'Not food? So: my son to stop being a *leydigeyer* and come home to mind his business?'

'That would be nice,' Naomi said, 'but if we couldn't have that?'

He held up his hands in surrender. 'Let's save time. You tell me what I'd like most in the world.'

Naomi hesitated, and then drew a deep breath. 'How about a grandchild? In the summer. A girl or a boy.'

'It has to be one or the other,' Lansky said, trying to make a joke, in case his heart would burst. And then she was down on her knees and his hand was on the dark head, and a thousand prayers of thanksgiving were flooding through his mind.

Esther looked at the figures in front of her, projections for the next few months. They were very satisfactory, considering restrictions and shortages. When the war was over, business would be a piece of cake. Then she would have a cold store of their own as soon as building recommenced. The jam factory would convert into one – she'd already had it surveyed – but there was a bomb-site in Hendon that would be ideal. Plate-freezing equipment would come from Glasgow. Freezing was the future, according to Sammy, and he was usually right.

She looked up as Molly tapped at the door. The girl didn't speak, merely raised her eyes to heaven.

'No?' Esther said hopefully.

'Yes,' Molly said, and ushered Gallagher into the room.

Esther had dispensed with even the pretence of courtesy lately. Gallagher disgusted her, especially since she had heard how he had profited under Mrs Brenton's will. Today, however, there were none of the usual thinly veiled threats, the assumption that she would bend to his will. He looked around him, waiting for her to offer him a seat. When she did not, he eased on to a stool.

'Things are looking quite hopeful, aren't they, Miss Gulliver? I think we may see an end to this unhappy war and all its attendant inconveniences.' Esther smiled thinly but did not speak. 'Of course there'll be adjustments to be made,' Gallagher continued. Esther looked around her office, lined with files representing five years of form-filling. 'We'll all have to draw a line under things…'

He was hesitant now. What on earth was he getting at? 'Yes, a fresh start. No dredging up of…'

So that was it, Esther thought. Gallagher wanted to make sure the bodies stayed buried. She smiled.

'Oh, a fresh start, by all means, Mr Gallagher. But then, I always think you need to clear things up before you can start afresh, don't you? We'll need to look back at what's gone on, and see what can be learned. I've kept quite comprehensive notes. And then there are all the forms – you were so good about forms.'

She watched Gallagher go down the stairs, greyer in the face than she had ever seen him.

*

Sammy read the letter again, hardly seeing the paper for the words were imprinted on his mind.

> *The doctor says July. It's a good time to be born, with warm months ahead to grow strong before winter. I feel it will be a boy, Sammy, and I want a boy for Papa Lansky, but he says he wants a girl. He says this so as not to disappoint me, I think, or make me feel I must have a boy. If it is a girl, can we call it Cecelie for your mother, and Hannah for mine, and Esther, because I don't know what we'd do without our Esther, and they are all good names? If it is a boy, it will be Emmanuel Aaron Lansky for both papas. Can't you just see that name in the future? A great man, no less. I love you so much, Sammy. Papa says they will demobilize soon: will you be among the first? I know we must wait our turn, but I do so long to make a home for you. Which reminds me, my pastry was wonderful yesterday. Like a feather! Everyone said so.*

Sammy laughed then, remembering that less than a year ago he had cowered in one dark room in France after another, not daring to dream of a future. And soon he would have a child; boy or girl, it would be a *toyve*, no less. He buttoned the letter into his battle-dress and got ready for parade. Surely the ways of the Lord were wonderful. He had been a *shlemil* and a *shlubber*, and God had turned him into a family man.

They ate in the dining-room at the Scar, the house opened up now and prepared for the children's return. The harassed

Belgate woman who was the only staff they had at the moment had set a place for Howard at one end of the long table and for Esther at the opposite end, but Howard scooped up glasses and cutlery and set the two places side by side. 'It's nearer the fire,' he said in explanation, but Esther wondered if he was remembering Diana, who had always sat at the far end of the table when they dined together.

They talked of the progress of the war as they ate; of the future of Lanver Products; of Naomi's baby and of the imminent return of Howard's children. 'They'll be away at school for much of the year, of course, but holidays are a problem. The girl who was their nursery-maid for so long, left to go into munitions when they went to Valesworth. She's married now, with a child of her own, so there's no help there.'

'Lots of people will be looking for work once the war is over,' Esther offered. 'It's just the next few months that could be difficult.' She pondered. 'Why don't you ask Mary? She was always fond of the children and – well…' She plucked up her courage. 'Mary feels she owes you something.' It was difficult to say, and a relief when it was out. 'She'd want to help you, and so would Pat. Not forever – once he goes back into practice, she'll be a busy doctor's wife. But for now, for holiday times while he's still at the hospital and she's in Sunderland, I think she'd do it like a shot.'

'That would be perfect,' Howard said. His hand came out to cover hers, only in gratitude at first. But Esther did not take her hand away, and his felt oddly comfortable lying on hers.

At last Esther withdrew her hand and touched her napkin to her lips. 'That's settled then. You ask her, and I don't think she'll say no.' The housekeeper came in with coffee, and Esther rose to take the tray. 'I'll see to this. I expect you'll want to get away.'

'There's the dishes,' the woman said, casting an anxious eye at her master.

'We'll see to those,' Howard said. 'You get off to your family. And thank you for a lovely meal.' 'It wasn't much,' the woman said, 'but it was the best I could manage.'

It was delicious,' Esther said. 'And perfectly cooked. Now, off you go: we'll clear away.'

'Just leave them for the morning,' the housekeeper said, as she went, but when they carried the dishes out to the kitchen Esther donned an apron and began to fill the sink.

'You'll have to boil the kettle,' Howard said. 'We don't have hot water all day, to save fuel.'

'And you a coal baron!' Esther said, pretending to be scandalized. They laughed about the privations of war as they waited for the kettle to boil.

'Do you remember that night, in this kitchen…' Esther hesitated, wondering if she should remind Howard of Rupert's birth.

'The night we had Champagne?' he said gently. 'Of course. You were almost a child, still, and I was euphoric, and Maguire turned up at the door, equally proud.'

'You drank a toast to both the boys,' Esther said, lifting a plate from the suds and handing it to him to be dried.

'And now they're both dead. Was it a waste?'

'No,' Esther said slowly. 'It was a tragedy, but not a waste.' She saw his eyes were glittering and wished she could think of something comforting. But he smiled, and reached for another plate. 'You're right,' he said. 'Now tell me, how do you propose to celebrate peace?'

'With a rest,' she said fervently. 'Sammy is champing to take over the reins and I can't wait to lay them down.'

'You'll be bored,' Howard warned, but she shook her head.

'No, I won't. Do you know that I've never been out of Durham? Well, hardly ever.' She hesitated a little, and he wondered why. 'To Whitby once – and several times to meet Sammy on business in army garrisons: not exactly picturesque. But that's it. So when this war is over I'm going to see the world.'

'The world!' Howard said, smiling. 'That'll take time. But if you've never travelled, does that mean you've never been to London?'

'No. I've seen it at the pictures and in books, but that's all.'

'You must come to London, and come soon! We could put you up in Mount Street. I'd love to show you the city, even in its present battered state.'

'I'd like that,' Esther said. 'Then I can appreciate it when it's all rebuilt.'

She has courage, Howard thought. *And optimism. She does not think of the destruction, only of the rebuilding.*

He looked at the steady blue eyes, the firm chin, the resolute mouth. Where was the uncertain child he had known all those years ago? Now there was only a grace, a confidence that made him feel peaceful and yet stirred. *I want to take her in my arms,* he thought, suddenly confused. *I want to kiss her mouth, her eyes... I want to whisper to her and feel her heart beat close to mine.*

He remembered then what Lansky had once told him: 'She has *chen*, Mr Brenton. That is our word for a special quality. I saw it in the child; it blossoms in the woman.'

They walked out on to the Scar, and Esther unlocked the Hillman.

'Give my regards to your sister and Maguire,' Howard said. 'I hear they've had a wedding, too?'

'Yes,' Esther said. 'But it's a bit of a sore point: their new son-in-law's an American, and in Anne's eyes that means he has horns and a tail.'

'She's not alone in that view,' Howard said as Esther held out her hand.

'Thank you for a lovely evening – and I hope it works out with Mary.'

'Thank you for coming.' Howard held on to her hand.

'And for all your help. Drive carefully.' Then she was driving off down the hill, very competently for a woman. He watched her go, reflecting that he would have to buck up his ideas. Women could do anything, nowadays, and Esther was proof of it. After the war it would be useless to expect them to go back to being ornamental. As Howard went back into the house he was whistling, for some ridiculous reason 'The Marseillaise.' Esther must see Paris if she travelled. And Florence, and Amsterdam in tulip time.

Frank was whistling, too, as he sat up in bed, but under his breath. The house was asleep except for him and Anne and she was seeing to the baby. A grandson, and him only forty-six. It had been a hell of a day, and worse was to come if he was any judge. If Anne gave up that baby it would be a bigger miracle than water into wine – which was funny, because he'd never thought of her as the maternal type, all those years ago. If someone had said one of the Gulliver girls would be a tycoon, he'd've said Anne every time. But now she was a mother and grandmother, and Esther, a little mouse of a thing in those days, was riding round like Barbara Hutton.

Frank thought guiltily of the poor young GI. It wasn't right, what they were doing to him, but the boy had been as pleased as punch when he saw the bairn. He himself would never have fallen for a stroke like that, Frank reflected – not that Anne would've pulled one. It was only for her bairns that she was prepared to be unscrupulous. Though she hadn't wanted this: his grandson a Yankee! The boy was a Brenton, and blood would out in the long run.

He lay back on the pillow, thinking of the future. Everyone would have adjustments to make after the war, and Brenton more than most. He'd lose his seat when the election came, and if Gaffney retired and the Labour Party nomination came up, it would be his, Frank's. Was he up to going into Parliament? My God, it was a thought! But the Socialists had given a good account of themselves in government, Morrison and Bevin and Attlee, who had kept things ticking while Churchill rallied the troops.

Anne came into the bedroom, weariness etched on her face. 'Move over,' she said. 'I'm dropping.' She climbed in and lay down with a sigh. 'Thank God.'

'You can have a lie-in in the morning,' Frank said generously. 'I'll see to things.' They lay peaceably for a few moments, until the silence was broken by a sudden thin wail. 'That's the baby,' Frank said.

'Well, see to it,' Anne groaned, but she was already pulling herself up. 'I'm only joking, Frank. I'd no more let you loose on a newborn baby than I'd let pigs fly. Just keep the bed warm – it's about all you're good for.' But she turned in the doorway. 'Goodnight, grandpa,' she said and blew him a kiss as she went.

31

April 1945

Esther looked around at the white and gold eighteenth- century chapel. It had stone-flagged floors and plain dark pews, but she could see a tree in full leaf through the arched window behind the altar. The place was beautiful. She glanced at Howard Brenton in the front pew, staring steadfastly ahead. What must it be like to stand at a memorial service to a son killed in battle? She had thought of her own child, growing up somewhere and too young still, thank God, for war, when Howard's letter came.

We are having a memorial service for Rupert in the chapel in South Audley Street, near to us here in Mount Street. Perhaps you could time your visit to London for then? I begin to believe you will never keep your promise ... She had bought her train ticket the same day, and now she was here in a church full of well-dressed strangers, Howard's the only familiar face, and the street outside full of American soldiers.

She had turned down his invitation to stay in Mount Street. In spite of all her new-found assurance, she still felt a little in awe of 'Mr Howard.' She had been fifteen and thought him at least fifty when first they met. How old had he been then? How old was he now?

From time to time, as the service proceeded, she looked at him from under the brim of her navy straw hat. He looked sad, but more serene than she had expected; and when they sang 'I vow to thee my country' she saw his chin come up at the sound of the young voices around him in the pews. His children were there: Pamela, Ralph and Noel. He mentioned them often in his letters, and today she had been introduced to them. Other young people were in uniform or soberly dressed for the occasion: nieces and nephews, probably, or the children of friends.

She studied the older people. A woman next to Howard faintly resembled him, and dabbed her eyes a lot: his sister? Another woman, small and plump with red hair, with a man in uniform on one side of her, also red-headed, and another on her other side in a well-cut dark suit: that would be Loelia, who was keeping his children. She had a short veil over her face and wept freely, poking a wispy handkerchief up inside the mesh to dry her eyes. Her clothes were elegant, unmistakably expensive. 'Dearest Lee,' that's what Diana had called her all those years ago.

The service ended with a rousing anthem, and then they were outside the chapel and Howard was signalling with his eyes that Esther should join him.

'Loelia, may I introduce Esther Gulliver, a friend from the north?'

Loelia was smiling, extending a plump hand. 'How good of you to come all this way. This is my husband, Henry Colville – and my brother, Max Dunane.'

Esther smiled as she shook hands, but her mind was racing, Max Dunane: Max, the name on the letter on Diana's hospital bed. *My darling, darling Max, I am so lost without you.*

Anne was finding it hard to keep her son-in-law at arm's length, but she was determined to try. Her grandson, Francis Anthony, was *not* leaving Britain: on that she was determined. But the young American's easy ways and genuine delight in the baby were difficult to resist. He would coo into the cot as soon as he entered the kitchen, and carry the baby about in the crook of his arm, for all the world as though he had fathered a dozen before.

'He comes from a good Catholic family,' the priest told Anne approvingly, and she had no option but to look gratified. She knew that Stella was already dreaming of the Hollywood lifestyle she was sure awaited her; the house was littered with American magazines with pictures of pneumatic blondes and exotically coloured fruit salads splattered over them in extravagant fashion.

Certainly Mario was generous, showering them all with chocolate bars with daft names like Snickers and Lifesavers and Baby Ruth. He sometimes brought oranges, too, and bottles of Bourbon for Frank. 'Just like metal polish,' Frank pronounced, but in private. He liked the boy, and his warnings to Anne not to get up to tricks were delivered with monotonous regularity. Stella treated her husband with an almost contemptuous tolerance.

Today, Mario was full of the news of the mass surrender of German troops in the Ruhr. Two American armies had the industrial heartland of Germany in their grip, and Mario was proud of it. 'We'll have you Stateside by Christmas,' he told the baby as he teased its lips with the teat to encourage it to take the bottle.

Over my dead body, Anne thought, but she felt a gloomy certainty, now, that the war was coming to an end. She was pondering how and where to acquaint Mario with the facts of the baby's parentage when Frank came in at the kitchen door, his face sombre. He looked at Anne and then at the young soldier, happily feeding his son.

'You haven't heard, then?'

'Heard what?' Anne said sharply. Whatever it was it was bad, she could tell that from Frank's face.

'It's Roosevelt,' Frank said. 'He's dead, a heart-attack they say. He was only sixty-three.'

Mario's face had clouded, but to the men's amazement it

was Anne who burst into tears. 'Get off,' she said, when Frank offered clumsy comfort. 'There's too few good men in this world not to miss one when he goes.'

Emmanuel Lansky, too, was moved by news of the American president's death. He had been a friend to Britain in the darkest hours, and Churchill would feel the loss of an ally.

Naomi was coping well with her pregnancy, and Lansky watched over her like a mother hen, clucking with approval when she ate sensibly or drank milk; but they were both alert for news of the V2 rockets that were still landing in the south of England, perilously near the place where Sammy was now stationed, and directly on London, where Esther had gone by train against all their advice.

In vain, Sammy wrote to tell them he was safe. They had seen pictures of the huge craters the rockets made on landing; they had read the lists of the dead in the newspapers. When concern was expressed in the House of Commons about the Allied raid on Dresden, and church leaders offered protests about 'terror bombing', Lansky threw up his hands. 'So what are these rockets, if not terror bombing? They launch them to land who knows where? And this is civilized? Truly, we are all going mad!'

The day before Roosevelt's death, American troops had discovered Buchenwald, with piles of unburied corpses stacked more than head high, and 20,000 emaciated prisoners too weak to grasp that they were now free. Once these people had been Europe's intellectual élite; now they could scarcely take the food the weeping GIs pressed upon them.

An eye for an eye, Lansky thought. *That is just.*

But when he went up to his room, the sounds of Naomi's singing drifting up from the kitchen below, he prayed that God would cleanse him of his lust for vengeance.

*

The table at Mount Street gleamed with silver and glass, but the effect of the food shortages showed in the sparse buffet.

'Howard tells me you have a wholesale business, Miss Gulliver,' Loelia Colville said as they nibbled at canapés which tasted suspiciously like kipper. 'Have you always worked in that line of business?'

Esther saw Howard's eyes flicker as she smiled at Loelia. 'No, I was in service first, as a maid at the Scar. I helped in my father's shop before that, but it was hardly a job. I went into service when he died.'

'And now you're a tycoon,' Loelia said.

'I suppose I am,' Esther said graciously, and saw Howard stifle a grin.

As Loelia turned to have her glass refilled, he whispered in Esther's ear: 'I thought you might need a little protection, but I see you can fend very well for yourself. I'll attend to my other guests.'

The red-haired man came over then, to join his sister. 'You're from Belgate, I believe, Miss Gulliver?' There was something in his tone that made Esther long to tug her forelock. 'Do you come often to London?'

This is my first visit,' Esther said, and then, as he made a surprised face, 'I'm most impressed.'

'You see it in a sorry state. Still, some things remain, and once we have got rid of these wretched V2s...'

Esther had been appalled at the bomb damage. She had seen debris in Sunderland, but here in London it stretched for miles, and there seemed to be a greater acceptance of it than at home, where there was always a rush to tidy it away. But there was blossom here and there, and rose-bay willowherb gentling every bomb-site as though in defiance of the threat from the air – like the 'V for Victory' scrawled everywhere.

Pamela came up, carrying a tray. Esther had met her the

night before, and now the girl smiled a greeting. 'Daddy says you're going sightseeing tomorrow. May I come with you?'

'I shouldn't think Miss Gulliver has time, Pamela,' Max Dunane reproved.

'No, that would be lovely,' Esther said. 'I'm going back in the early evening, but I hope to see St Paul's and the Palace, and the House of Commons: I mustn't miss that.'

'Are you interested in politics?' Loelia said. 'Of course you're all terribly militant in the north, aren't you?'

'We take our politics seriously,' Esther said. 'But then it's important, isn't it?'

'The coalition will end soon,' Max offered, 'and not before time. That buffoon Bevin had the nerve to criticize Churchill last week.'

'I don't think that's quite true,' Esther argued. 'He expressed admiration for Churchill as a war-leader, and he spoke of his "unfettered loyalty" to him. He was simply emphasizing that his loyalty was to Churchill the man and not to his party. That's fair enough, surely?'

'My my, Esther – I may call you Esther, mayn't I?' Loelia said. 'You do keep abreast of affairs. I never imagined Ernest Bevin to be so profound.'

'Oh yes,' Esther said. 'I'm told he can read and write, too.' Max laughed but there was no real merriment in it.

'This area has become an American colony,' Loelia said, to change the subject. 'South Audley Street should be renamed Fifth Avenue, I think. And Grosvenor Square is simply one huge hostel.'

'They play baseball in Green Park,' Max said sourly. 'And their military police are called "snowdrops" – good God!'

'On account of the white helmets,' Loelia said. 'Or I suppose that's the reason.'

There was a polite titter, and then the talk turned to Truman, the new American President, whom Max proclaimed to be a 'hick'.

'Not only a hick, but a draper, I believe,' Esther said wickedly. 'Just like my father.'

There was a long silence, and then Loelia was chattering about the need to get back to Valesworth, and urging Pamela to collect her things.

Why was I so prickly? Esther wondered as they made their goodbyes to her. She was regretting her retaliation; it hadn't been ladylike. She moved away to the side of the double doors and stood, surveying the crowded room. It was then that she heard Loelia's voice on the other side of the door.

'I shouldn't worry about it, Max, she's no substitute for Diana. Besides, Howard will never marry out of his class.'

They mean me, Esther thought. At first the idea that they had imagined something more than friendship between her and Howard was amusing. Afterwards she wondered why either of the Dunanes should care.

Patrick carried Ben up to bed when they had eaten, and then he and Mary settled either side of the fire. 'No nice bottle of port from a grateful patient?'

'Nary a one,' Patrick said. 'There's some ginger wine though.' They drank the remains of the ginger wine from the church fête, and moved closer to one another a the hour grew late.

'I can't believe Ben is six,' Mary said.

Patrick nodded. 'Sometimes I feel the war has lasted forever; at other times, it seems you and I were married yesterday, and all of it has happened in a flash. We still have Ben, thanks to Diana Brenton – but I still grieve for young Joe. What a waste!'

'How much longer will it last, d'you think? And what will happen to Catherine and John when it's all over?'

'They'll come home – well, Catherine will. John will probably carry on where he is. They'll work, and eventually meet their fate, and marry, and make you a grandmother.'

'Thank you,' Mary said tartly, until Patrick leaned to kiss her in a most ungrandfatherly way. 'What about us?' she said, then. Will you leave the Emergency Unit?'

'As soon as I can,' Patrick said fervently. 'I have a few years left to practise medicine, and I want to treat grazed knees and wasp stings, bring babies into the world, and exult in my successes. I'm tired of death and failure.'

'So we'll go back to Durham?'

'We could. But I've been thinking: Belgate has no doctor of its own. How would you feel if...?'

He paused, trying to see whether or not the idea pleased Mary. She was silent for a long while, but he was patient.

'I think I'd like it,' she said at last. 'You'd be good for the place.'

'What about your memories?' Patrick asked anxiously.

'Of Stephen, you mean? They're mostly happy ones, Pat, in spite of the way he died. And it's all part of the plan, isn't it?' She did not say 'God's plan', for she knew he did not believe, and that was his right.

'Well, then,' he said. 'I'll arrange for the Belgate practice as soon as I can. Esther can have back her house, and we'll set up home again. In style. And before you mention the heart's-ease, Mary: if there's not room for your tub at the front door, we won't buy.'

The Dunanes had gone, taking the children, by the time Esther returned to Mount Street. She had gone back to her hotel to change and to lie on her bed for half an hour, digesting the day. Had she been too hard on the Dunanes?

Sammy would have said not but, looking back, Esther wished again that she had been more discreet. *Letting them know you weren't just a country bumpkin who never reads a paper*. But they had been patronizing. *To hell with them,*

Esther thought, and went to get washed. 'My darling, darling Max:' was that how you wrote to a friend, even a childhood friend? And why had Max Dunane bridled when Pamela asked if she could come sightseeing with her? In the end, she put the Dunanes out of her mind and went to rejoin Howard.

'I've booked a table for dinner at the Ritz,' he said. 'And while we eat, we must plan your day tomorrow.'

He handed her a glass of sherry and took up his own. 'To your visit,' he said. 'And may it be the first of many.'

His brow wrinkled as he saw she was laughing. 'What is it?'

'I'm just thinking of what my sister would say if she could see me now,' Esther answered. She saw he didn't fully comprehend. 'She thinks you're a – well, she doubts your integrity.'

His eyes crinkled in amusement – and then they heard the phut-phut of a rocket. Esther had only heard it on radio, and at the cinema on Pathé newsreels, but it could not be mistaken.

'Could I see it?' Howard shook his head at first, and then, seeing her curiosity, he switched out the light and opened the curtains. The dark shapes of the roofs opposite stood out against the pale evening sky. Searchlights were stabbing the sky, but there was no sign of the weapon, although the noise of its engine was louder and louder. Then suddenly it was absent.

'That's it,' Howard said, puffing the curtains back into place. She was about to protest when there was a thunderous roar and a shaking sensation that drove her forward into Howard's arms. 'Good,' he said when the tremor subsided. 'We still have windows.'

He twitched the curtains back open and Esther saw a column of flame behind the houses and black smoke billowing upwards into the sky. 'Near,' Howard commented. She was still within the circle of his arms and he made no move to let her go. 'That's your first real sight of London:

a doodlebug.' His voice was indulgent, even paternal, and Esther had the oddest sensation of wanting to close her eyes and relax against him. *It feels like coming home,* she thought.

She would have pulled away but he held her. 'Esther?' he said – and then again, 'Esther?' And then he was kissing her. Her mouth was firm at first and then melting, as he had always known a mouth should be.

At last he drew back. 'There now,' he said. 'You've seen your first rocket.'

'I'm glad I saw it,' Esther said, smiling, while her heart thudded uncomfortably. 'But once will be quite enough.'

32

May 1945

It had thundered in the night but Frank had been unable to sleep for excitement, so it didn't matter much. 'You can't really believe it's over, Anne, can you?' he had said once, and received an assenting grunt in reply.

'I suppose it was really over when Hitler killed himself,' she said, after a while. 'That'll mean perdition for him.'

'He'd've got perdition anyway,' Frank said. 'At least, I hope he would.'

He had not been able to believe the radio when the news came: '*The German radio has just announced that Hitler is dead. I'll repeat that.*' He had felt his knees go weak, and had to reach for a chair.

The total German surrender would come into force today, 8 May. The King was to speak, and so was Churchill, and church bells were to be rung, and bonfires lit, and no bugger was going to work – at least he wasn't.

'Is it time to get up?' Anne said, stirring, as early sunshine filtered through the curtains, and feeling him awake beside her. 'We've got a lot to do.'

Then, far off, they heard a ship's siren; just one at first, but then another, and another; until they were all blasting away. 'Yes, I think it's time to get up,' Frank said, and, as if on cue, the baby in the crib in the corner began to whimper for food.

Frank saw to the breakfast, while Anne gave the baby his bottle. 'Shall I shout for Stella?' he asked once, but Anne shook her head. When breakfast and bottle were done, she

tucked the baby in its pram, and took out her canvas shopping bag. 'Now you know what to do,' she said, 'and there's
plenty helpers. I'll get back as quick as I can, and I'm
expecting to find those tables up, Frank – from one end of
the street to the other. And decorated.'

'What with?'

'Use your imagination, Frank. Anything, as long as it's
red, white and blue. Set your mates to crayon on those plain
white serviettes.'

She pushed the pram to the cake shop, where she queued
alongside other women foraging for party goodies. 'You'd
think they'd make an effort today,' a woman said, 'seeing
the day it is. It wouldn't hurt them to give the stuff away.'

'Not the amount they've made out of us,' Anne agreed.
'But I've got her card marked.' The cake-shop woman had
enjoyed years of mastery, selling what she liked to whom she
liked. Now her days were numbered, but Anne still plastered
a smile on her face when her turn came. You couldn't show
your hand too soon.

'Bairn all right?' a woman asked as they went on to the
wet-fish shop, just in case of cod or whiting.

'Lovely,' Anne said, moving the pram cover aside to
give her a peep.

'She'll be going to America now, then, your Stella?' the
woman said. 'They say they're shipping them all out there
in liners. Very nice.'

'Nothing's settled yet,' Anne said firmly, fear clutching
at her heart. If the worst came to the worst she would tell
Howard Brenton the truth. He wouldn't let his grandchild
go across the Atlantic.

'It'll be good riddance to most of those soldiers,' the
woman said. 'Overpaid, over-sexed and over here. They've
taken advantage of us.'

'That's as may be,' Anne said. She couldn't really imagine
anyone getting the advantage of Stella. And besides, the

boy was her son-in-law, for better or worse, and not to be got at by outsiders.

In the fish queue there was general euphoria about victory in Europe. A girl expressed it for all of them: 'No more air raids, no more shortages, no more telegrams.' The woman in front turned round, her face sombre: 'You speak for yourself, madam. My man's in Changi. There'll be a lot more fighting before that lot's ower, and more telegrams too.' The queue went quiet, then, and Anne was pensive on the way home. If the war in the Far East dragged on, would it take Gerard, too?

She was almost at the gate when Esther's car drew up beside her, and her sister climbed out, carrying a cardboard box. 'I expect you're having a knees-up,' she said. 'This is odds and ends. It'll help a bit.'

Anne's eyes opened in amazement. There were biscuits, and sweets, and fruit, and tins galore.

'My God,' she said, and then again, 'My God! What about the coupons?'

But Esther was already back in the car. 'Anne,' she said, sticking her head out of the window, 'if I can't kick over the traces today, I never will!'

Howard went to St Paul's to give thanks. A service was in progress when he arrived, but another would soon begin. People were flocking in and out, the Lord Mayor in his glittering chain; a man and woman weeping both in mourning a mother with her child in her arms and a look of relief on her face. The choir sang the *Te Deum*, and then the congregation roared out the National Anthem until the rafters shook.

Howard walked down Ludgate Hill when he came out of the cathedral. It was strange to feel carefree after so many years of anxiety. Never again would he look anxiously at the sky, or listen in dread for the sudden cessation of engine noise. He walked on down to the Embankment and stood by the river, watching the passers-by, wondering what it was all like in Sunderland and in Belgate now.

Esther would be relieved. Sam Lansky would get early demobilization on account of his age and the need for his expertise at home, and then Esther would be free to travel. He thought of her embarking for foreign shores, eyes wide at the new and unexpected. How nice it would be to see the world again with someone who was not blasé about it all. In London she had been wide-eyed with wonder.

He went back to Whitehall in the early afternoon, to hear Churchill's voice broadcast to crowds fallen silent in the streets. Cars stopped, too, the riders on their bonnets suddenly still, to listen.

'The German war is at an end. Advance Britannia! Long live the cause of freedom! God save the King!' And then, as the great, sonorous voice died, people went mad, waving flags, blowing whistles, climbing lampposts, singing and dancing. Forms cascaded from office windows as though there were no longer any need for regulations.

'Let's go to the Palace,' someone shouted, and the crowd was moving, carrying Howard along with it until he could dodge into a side street and begin to make his way back towards the House of Commons.

He was there to see Churchill bow to the Chair: 'Mr Speaker, the German war is therefore at an end.' And then the Prime Minister, discarding notes and glasses, in a suddenly trembling voice said: 'Now, in two or three sentences, I will convey my deep gratitude to the House of Commons itself: the strongest foundation for waging war that has ever been seen in the whole of our history.'

Sammy went back to his bunk after listening to the Prime Minister's broadcast. So the war was over. He lay on his back, hands behind his head, wondering when he would get home. At least it was 'when' now, and not 'if'.

If the rumours were true, demob would begin any day, the older men going out first, and those without a special skill that the army needed. That fitted him on both counts. He had skills, but the army had never seen fit to use them – except once, and that was a secret. Still, he must be patient. There were plenty of men who would never go home again, men like Joe who had deserved to live. He could take a little more boredom if he had to. But he wanted to be with his wife, to put his hand on her belly and feel his child move. He wanted to be at his father's side, and send Esther off on her very first holiday – anywhere! After what she had done for him, the moon would not be too much.

Suddenly he remembered Paris, Roger and Martine and the gruff-voiced man who had stepped between him and an SS man on the journey to Falaise so that he would not be scrutinized too closely. How many of them had survived? He remembered, too, the gut-wrenching fear he had felt from start to finish of the whole operation. He had not told anyone about it for one simple reason: that he couldn't trust himself to speak of it without trembling.

Another man entered the hut, a lance-corporal with a loud mouth and a mean spirit.

'Lazing again, Lansky,' he said. 'You haven't struck a bat this whole fucking war.'

For a moment Sammy was tempted, but only for a moment. 'Jealousy gets you nowhere, Porter,' he said smoothly, and turned his head away.

Patrick Quinnell was celebrating today. The war was over. There would be no more dead and dying men carried into the nation's hospitals, and all the expertise, the equipment, the drugs and the buildings that had come into being to treat the casualties of war could now be turned against the diseases that afflicted people every day of their lives. Penicillin would prove a wonder-drug in the field of venereal disease; there would be no sad and terrible toll there, for year after year, after this war as there had been after the last.

On his way home, he called at an allotment where he had spotted tall white marguerites the other day, sprouting between the rows of vegetables. Now he bought up the lot, an armful, and carried them home to his wife. 'For you,' he said, 'on this very special day.'

Mary drew him over the threshold and shut the door behind him. 'Come here,' she said, 'you lovely man.' They stood in the hail embracing, holding the marguerites awkwardly for fear of crushing them. They went on kissing until a small voice piped up from the stairs.

'That's enough Hollywood,' Ben Quinnell said. 'Someone's got to get my tea.'

The Lansky household had listened to the Prime Minister's broadcast, for Esther had sent everyone home from the warehouse and shops at lunch-time and come home herself – 'To prepare the *simcha*.' Naomi was heavily pregnant now, her arms and legs stick-like, her face pale. According to the doctors all was well, but Lansky fretted over her constantly, asking Esther to procure all manner of vitamins and diet supplements. Esther firmly refused these suggestions. 'She's getting vitamins and milk, Mr Lansky, like every other expectant mother. Now, if you want to do something useful, eat your own meals so Naomi and I don't need to worry.'

Today he was smiling, as she and Naomi set out the best food they could muster. 'We'll have to start preparing for Sammy's homecoming,' Esther said, as they ate. 'It won't be long. I think he'll get an early demob.'

'In time?' Naomi said.

'Maybe.' Esther was reassuring. 'And if not, he'll get leave – you know Sammy.'

'Where *was* he all those months?' Lansky mused. 'He chooses not to tell – which makes me wonder all the more.'

'He'll tell us one day, when he's ready,' Esther said.

'And if he doesn't...' This was Naomi, vehement for once. 'If he doesn't, it's because he has good reasons.'

'Bravo,' Lansky said, his face alight. 'She fights for her man, this little one.'

They were about to raise their glasses when the phone rang. 'It's me: Ruth. Isn't it wonderful?' The others took turns to talk to her, exchanging news and congratulations. Then, as the receiver was replaced, it rang again.

'It's Sammy,' Naomi said, and all of a sudden her pale face was glowing, the eyes alight.

Back at the table, Esther raised her glass and the old Jew reciprocated. 'To the lovers,' she mouthed and they drank together. It was Lansky's turn then. 'To you, Esther,' he said. 'To your life, and the love you deserve: *lechayim*.'

They had left Stella and Mario in charge of the baby. Anne's list of instructions was so long that in the end Frank dragged her bodily out of the house. 'They've got to learn, Anne, it's *their* bairn – well, *hers*. By gum, we've got a tangled web there. That boy's a patsy: I think that's their word for it.'

'Behind the eight ball,' Anne said. 'That's what they say. "He's right behind the eight ball".' But she sounded abstracted, for she was thinking of Joe, who was not here on this supposedly joyful night.

They walked on, seeing the glow of bonfires to right and left, hearing the sounds of revelry, passing soldiers with girls on their arms and uniforms awry, and once seeing an effigy of Hitler hanging from a lamppost.

'Aye,' Frank said at last. 'It's really over. Although you can't quite take it in, not at first. When the –' He had been about to say, 'When the lads come back,' but he caught the words in time. Instead he said, 'Stella'll be making plans for her new life. They'll pull the Yanks out right away, I should think.'

'Maybe we should tell him the truth?' Anne said.

Frank gripped her arm and steered her into a shop doorway. 'Now listen here, Anne Maguire, I don't know who you think you are: God, most likely, the way you go on. You started this, not letting Howard Brenton know the truth about Rupert and Stella. And why? For your own ends. You told Stella to find a man, and she did. I didn't want her married to Mario any more than you did, but they were joined together in church and it's not up to us to split them. All we can do – and by God I am doing it – is pray that she pulls her socks up and makes him a good wife. If that happens, it'll be the best of a bad job. And if I find out you've done anything – *anything* – to sabotage that, I'll show you up in this village in a way you won't live down. Now believe me, Anne, because I mean it!'

Anne was taken aback at his passion – too taken aback to defy him.

They walked on until they were caught up in the laughter and gaiety around the bonfire. 'Give us a dance, missus,' a young Scots soldier said, and Anne was whirled away, screaming for mercy and loving every minute of it. But Frank, as he looked at the flickering flames, was remembering Howard Brenton, who had been robbed of a wife and a son, and now was being robbed of a grandson. There would be an election soon, and his seat in Parliament would be taken from him, and after that, with a Labour Government, his pits. *Poor bugger*, Frank thought. *He's going to be left with nothing.*

Except that Frank had heard rumours about Brenton and Esther. They had better not be true, or Anne would go mad!

*

Howard went back into the streets when he left the House, back to see the King appear bare-headed on the balcony with his wife and daughters, while the crowd sang 'For he's a jolly good fellow'. Every nationality was there; men and women who had heard their own national anthems only on British radio on Sunday nights for the last five years were singing the British anthem with gusto.

For some inexplicable reason he didn't want to go home to the empty house in Mount Street. He had telephoned Pamela and the boys at Valesworth. Soon they would all be together at the Scar, but now he had no one. All his friends would be with their families tonight.

He wandered on, sometimes carried along by the crowds, sometimes walking down almost deserted side streets. In one of these streets he heard the sound of weeping; it was a young black GI, in a shop doorway, his face in his hands.

'Can I help?' Howard asked.

The boy looked up, shame-faced. 'No, sir. There ain't nothing wrong... except that President Roosevelt should've been alive to see this day.'

Howard put out a hand to the boy's arm. 'Yes,' he said. 'His death was a loss to us all.'

As he walked on he remembered how the flags had hung at half-mast for the president, in the heat-haze above Piccadilly.

He found himself in Whitehall at last. Ahead of him, above a sea of faces, was the figure of Churchill on a balcony, waving his black Homburg and wearing his siren suit. He conducted the crowd as it sang 'Land of Hope and Glory' and then was cheered to the echo. 'This is your victory,' he told the crowd. 'In all our long history we have never seen a greater day than this.'

Then he was gone, and Howard turned away from the

lovers embracing all around him, lost in the exhilaration of this day of days.

A hand was tugging at his sleeve, and he turned to see a young Wren with an RAF pilot's arm protectively around her.

'Mr Brenton? It's me, Catherine Hardman.'

'Catherine!' Howard bent to kiss her cheek, and then stood back to study her. 'You look splendid. Wait till your mother hears I've seen you.' This was the girl he had once thought Rupert loved.

Catherine introduced him to her escort and then, plucking up courage, said, 'I wanted to tell you how sorry we were about Mrs Brenton. She saved my little brother's life, and we won't forget it. And about Rupert, too. He and I were such good friends...'

Howard saw her eyes fill, and bent forward.

'Not on such a night,' he said. 'No regrets. But come and see me when you can – here, in Mount Street, or at the Scar. We mustn't lose touch, Catherine. You are one of the keepers of my memories.'

As they went away, swallowed up in the crowds, Howard pondered his words. Where had they come from? 'The keeper of my memories'. Was that all there was to be in future: memories? A telephone box loomed up, and he levered open the door. A few moments later he heard the ringing tone. Let her be in!

'Esther? I had to telephone you, because this is such a wonderful night. When are you coming to London again?'

33

July 1945

Howard was awake at daybreak, foraging for himself in the Scar kitchen. There was little or nothing in the pantry; rations had been cut again as a result of the need to share food with the liberated European countries. He sat down at the table with bread and margarine and tea, and thought of the day ahead.

It was six weeks since Winston Churchill had resigned. Today Britain would go to the polls, but the result would not be known until the votes of servicemen overseas had also been counted. The Prime Minister had not wanted to go at this stage, with Japan undefeated, and nor had Attlee and Bevin, but they had been overruled by Labour's National Executive, who would only allow Attlee to carry on for a fixed term, until October. Churchill had refused this offer, on the grounds that it would mean uncertainty at a time when that could damage the war effort. So an election had been called, with Churchill certain that his war record would bring an easy victory.

Howard was less certain about it, but was sure his own seat would go. Belgate had waited a long time to have its say, and today it had its chance. Gaffney would achieve his ambition to go to Westminster, and after him, Maguire. *He understands Belgate*, Howard thought. *He will do very nicely when his time comes.*

The Conservative campaign had been built around a tour of the country by Churchill, who was seated in an open car.

The crowds were cheering him to the echo, but how much did this mean? Wives and sweethearts would be swayed by the preferences of their servicemen; and Labour was fielding more than a hundred returned officers, men who had seen action standing against dull local big-wigs. *Like me,* Howard thought wryly.

He was also dubious about his party's tactics. For five years the country had believed in the coalition: a group of men, Conservative and Labour, working together for their country. But in his first election broadcast, Churchill had accused his former colleagues of being ready to introduce 'some form of Gestapo' into Britain. Howard had thought that a colossal blunder, and Stretton agreed with him. 'Churchill's always been seen as a warmonger, Howard; remember the Thirties? Now he's declaring war on men who worked side by side with him, on quiet, clever, patient Attlee and Bevin who is patently as honest as the day is long. People won't like it; they want peace – they want reconstruction. They're tired of conflict.' The lights had blazed out once more all over Britain, and the nation was in the mood for gaiety.

Labour was not contesting Churchill's seat and had avoided personal attacks on him. Their slogan was 'Let us face the future', while Churchill's was 'Let me finish the job'. Churchill feared Russian domination, and he was probably right, but that was not what people wanted to hear. They wanted social reform, equality, and, above all, demobilization, which they believed would come more quickly under Attlee than Churchill.

Churchill will win, Howard thought as he finished his meagre breakfast, *but in the process a lot of Tories will say goodbye to Westminster, and I'll be one of them.*

He would be glad to be relieved of the burden of politics. He had done his share, and had never really enjoyed it, if he was truthful. He tried to imagine what it would have been like if there had been no war; if he had not lost a wife and a son; if all the legislation he had helped to see through had been concerned with peace rather than war. It was useless to speculate. For better or worse, his time in the House of Commons was over.

Howard collected the papers and letters from the front door and carried them back to the kitchen. Loelia wrote to wish him luck. *You must hang on to your seat, Howard. God help us all if Attlee gets his hands on the reins. This country will be on its knees at the war's end, and we must make sure the right men are in place to build it up again.* She ended with a PS: *Henry is thrilled about his baronetcy*.

Henry had received a knighthood in the Dissolution Honours for…? Howard pondered. For being Henry – that was the only conclusion he could come to. He had said the right thing at the right time, but never too vehemently nor for too long. And now he was to be rewarded, while other, braver men went unremarked.

He opened the local paper to see his own face smiling out at him, his hand tipping his hat. *Will he win?* ran the caption. His Labour opponent was old and ailing, and many people thought he had hung on too long. But the mood was for change – change at any price. The newspaper speculated that in a year or so there would be a new Labour nominee: young Gallagher or Frank Maguire. Howard frowned, remembering young Gallagher when he had been the Brenton office boy, and not much of a man of the people, then: punishing men for taking the makings of a fire. But Maguire was honest and strong. *He'll see Gallagher off,* Howard decided, and went to collect his car.

As he drove towards Belgate and the polling booths, his spirits rose. He would see Esther tonight, and he had other things for which to give thanks.

His relationship with Barbara had always troubled him. Had he used her? he wondered. He had done well by her financially, but was that enough? But then, as the election built up, he received a letter from her.

> *Dear Howard,*
> *I am writing to tell you of my forthcoming marriage. Alex is a friend and colleague of my late husband. They served together in the Hood, and he was invalided out in 1944. We met by chance at my son's school (he is an old boy), and found we had a lot in common. I feel this is what Ian would want. Richard needs a father, and Alex deserves a loving home. I wanted you to know this, because without your help in giving me this house I don't think it would have been possible for Alex and me to marry.*

Barbara went on to tell him of their preparations for the wedding, but Howard's one thought was a profound relief that his interference in her life had ultimately been for the good.

I send you both my heartiest congratulations, he wrote back; and, remembering her love of fine china, sent her a Crown Derby dinner and tea service from his own home, for the china available in the shops was scarce and unattractive. With the despatch of the gift, he felt as though a weight had been lifted from him. Once this election was over, he might begin again to feel a little like a free man.

Inevitably his thoughts turned to Esther: twelve hours before they were together. It would mean something to Belgate to see them so publicly side by side. What did it mean to him?

In the old days there would have been an impenetrable barrier of class between them, when King George V had spoken of his beloved people but in fact had been king of a divided realm. It had taken a savage war to make people realize that what divided them was as nothing compared to those values they shared.

Esther is my equal, Howard thought as he imagined her considering his words; challenging them if she disagreed; a smile lighting her face if he amused her with his tales of politics or war. *And even if she were not, I don't give a damn.*

Caroline would not approve the friendship, but he seldom saw his sister or her husband nowadays. And Loelia – he found he was chuckling aloud at the memory of Esther standing up to Loelia after Rupert's memorial service. She had looked every inch a lady that day – no, there it was: the prejudice that so damaged this country! She had not looked a lady, she *was* a lady: whatever 'being a lady' meant in the aftermath of Armageddon.

Esther was enjoying her first summer in her own home for five years. Mary and Patrick had gone back to Durham weeks before, but Esther had not deserted Emmanuel and Naomi until Ruth came home for the holidays and could care for them. And now Sammy was back home on leave.

Mary had cared for Esther's house; it was cleaned and polished and shining. But as soon as supplies were available Esther meant to refurbish it from front to back. 'Nest-building,' Ruth teased her. 'You are like a bright-eyed little sparrow, looking for twigs and sheep's wool.'

'Paper and paint in my case,' Esther said. 'And you can scoff – one day you'll have a home of your own, and I'll remind you how you tormented me.'

Ruth looked scandalized. 'I'll never leave here, Esther,' she said. 'Leave Papa Lansky and Naomi? Never! When I qualify I'll practise here, and care for Papa like he cared for me.'

Esther was about to say, 'One day you'll change your mind,' when she saw the concern on Ruth's face. *She doesn't want to think this won't last,* she thought. *She needs to think that what she has is permanent.* So she contented herself with a smile. But thinking of Ruth's future had brought a picture of Howard Brenton into her mind. That was strange. She dismissed it quickly. If she started thinking of Howard Brenton, she would go all moony and get nothing done. *We are different, she thought, and worlds apart. Even if he likes me, and even if I feel the same about him, it would never work.*

Esther looked back at the house as she left for the warehouse. There was no paint available at the moment, except for repairing war damage, and curtain material was non-existent. But shortages wouldn't last forever, so she happily designed and redesigned the whole house as she drove into Sunderland. She was choosing paint and locking the car when she heard the screech of tyres.

It was Sammy, dishevelled and wide-eyed, a camel overcoat over what looked like a pyjama jacket and the trousers of a suit.

'Esther! Thank God I found you! I rang but there was no answer –'

'It's not your father?' Esther said.

'No, but I've had to leave him alone. Naomi's time has come. I've taken her to the Infirmary, and Ruth is with her, but I've got to go back…'

'I'll go to your father,' Esther interrupted him. 'Now, you keep calm, Sammy Lansky. Where's the *chutzpah*? Where's the cool businessman?'

'Where's the gas and air?' Sammy said as he got back into his car. 'I want them to put me under and wake me when it's all done.'

Anne looked at the clock: nine-thirty. She had been up since six, feeding the baby and seeing Frank off to the hustings. If only old Gaffney had stood down before the election, then it would have been Frank's face on the posters and him in the limelight. She looked down at the sleeping baby, his mouth puckered where the teat had been.

At least she would be in Belgate while the baby needed her – not that she was planning to move to London when Frank went to Westminster; her place would be here, keeping the constituency warm. But there would have to be a bit of to-ing and fro-ing. Her first trip to London. My God!

Anne was roused from her wonder at the prospect by Mario coming in at the door, his face beaming, pulling tinned fruit and chocolate and butter from his uniform pockets like a conjurer with rabbits.

'Hi, mom,' he said, bending over his son to stroke the sleeping head. Anne was getting used to his greeting now.

'Put the kettle on,' she said, and watched him swing the kettle on to the coals. According to Stella, his family had an ice-cream parlour in New York and lived in the lap of luxury, but Mario seemed quite at home in Belgate.

'How's the boy?' he said when the kettle was hissing away.

'Fine. Here: take him. Your wife's in bed, if you want to go up.'

'Isn't she going to help out at the election?' Mario asked, as he gathered up the baby. 'I saw them all out at the school when I came by. Pop was there, shooing them in.'

'Our Stella help?' Anne said, scathingly. The boy had a lot to learn if he thought Stella capable of any action that wasn't in her own interest. 'No,' she said aloud, 'but I'll be out there if I get the chance.'

'Are you backing Churchill?' he asked, grinning because he already knew the answer.

'Not while he stands for the Tories,' Anne said. 'Any road, he's had his chance. We want a clean sweep, now, and no one in need any more, or frightened of doctor's bills. Now, get out of the way and I'll brew the tea. You can take a cup up to Fan Ann Tut, and see if she can bear to face daylight.'

*

Howard came back to the Scar at lunch-time to find a letter from his daughter. *This is to wish you luck, daddy, I hope it arrves in time. We will all be thinking of you today. I wrote to Noel and Ralph to remind them to keep fingers crossed.*

Howard smiled. Pamela was only fifteen but was already mothering her brothers. Her half-brothers. How strange that he felt closest to the child who had no part of him. When, if ever, should he tell her that? Tell anyone? In many ways it would be better if no one ever knew, but had he the right to keep the secret? And could he trust Max never to tell Loelia or Pamela – especially if things went wrong with Laura, and his other children were not returned to him? Howard read on:

I am simply longing to come home. Will we get the horses back straightaway? I'm not sure Blossom will take my weight now that I'm eight stone four, but it will be lovely just to kiss her funny old face again. And, if it won't upset you, I'd like to see to Blaze, for Rupert's sake. I miss Rupert, daddy. I know we used to row but we loved one another underneath. I'm going to try to make it up to you when I come home, and to learn about Belgate and the pits and everything. I want to help you.

I want to learn about Belgate – that's what Rupert had also said. Howard folded the letter and put it in his pocket, a talisman against the evils of the day. Then he put on his hat and went out to woo the electorate.

Frank had tramped the streets till his feet ached, exhorting, pleading, pointing out the importance of every single vote. Now he adjourned to the committee rooms in the Miners' Welfare hall.

'Sit yourself down, Frank,' a man said. 'Here's a mug. The tea's fresh.'

Young Stanley Gallagher lounged on a table, his red rosette in place, looking as smug as a well-fed tomcat. *By gum, I dislike you,* Frank thought. *And not just because you're after the nomination, too.* Stanley Gallagher lost no opportunity to oil his way into favour, even disowning his father when the elder Gallagher's depredations had become more or less public knowledge. Frank did not like a man who could rat on his own father. A son should not be blamed for a father's shortcomings, but a dignified silence would not have come amiss.

At first the men in the Labour group had been suspicious of Stanley Gallagher: even the name had been enough, for some. But he had boxed clever, no doubt about that. He was the first to call down wrath on the coal-owners and their henchmen, the agents. He espoused every Socialist cause, and was loud in his demands for nationalization. 'The people should control,' was his favourite phrase – but which people? He was gathering around him a bunch of cronies – *Arse-lickers*, Frank thought. Young Gallagher would have no chance of the nomination when the time came, for the pit vote would carry the day. All the same, he would bear watching.

With that, Frank put aside personal considerations and went back to the job of ensuring that Belgate would be represented in the new parliament by a man of the people.

Esther heard the phone ring as she sat by Lansky. She had never realized how gaunt the old man had become until she saw him laid back against the cushions, his eyes hooded as though he was too weary to open them fully.

'That may be news,' she said and got to her feet. As she crossed the hall she heard him speaking softly in the room behind her, and knew he was praying. Knew, too, that he dared not come to the phone for fear of bad news.

'It's a boy!' she cried, when she returned. 'You have a grandson: Aaron Emmanuel Lansky, seven pounds twelve ounces, and yelling at the top of his voice.'

Emmanuel smiled. 'Thank God,' he said. 'And the little *oytser*?'

'She's fine, too,' Esther said, and saw his eyes close.

She went upstairs then, to the drawer where she knew his *tefillin* and *tallis* were kept, took them out carefully and carried them downstairs. His eyes opened, and brightened at the sight of them.

'Thank you, Esther,' he said and smiled at her as she went to the door to leave him to his thanksgiving.

It was seven o'clock when Sammy and Ruth came home, wild-eyed and jubilant.

'What a boy, father! *This* big! A head like a god, and the eyes: so wise already.'

Emmanuel nodded. 'That's my Sammy, the father. Only the best!'

'All right, so I'm carried away a little. What's exaggeration on a night like this?'

'Here,' Esther said, bearing a tray. 'Let's wet Aaron's head.' They drank to the newborn child, and then Sammy raised his glass, carefully not looking towards Esther, for Ruth was there listening, but nevertheless aiming his words at her: 'To children everywhere, and the mothers who love them.'

He knows I have been thinking of my son today, Esther thought, and raised her glass to her lips.

Howard Brenton telephoned an hour later. 'Sammy has a son,' Esther told him. 'Born this afternoon!'

'That's wonderful. Give him my congratulations.' And then Sammy was wresting the phone from her.

'You've heard?' he said. 'Yes, very proud. There will be a *simcha* – a celebration, and you must be there.' Suddenly he pretended to shield the phone with a cupped hand.

'Esther would like you to be there. She will tell you differently, but I know my partner like a book.' He winked as Esther snatched the phone with one hand and put the other to her flaming cheek.

'I'll swing for you one day, Sammy Lansky,' she hissed. 'And that'll put an end to all your *plaplen*.'

'Don't be cross with him,' Howard said from the other end of the line and there was laughter in his voice. 'Now, you did mention you might keep me company at some stage of this election ordeal…'

Sammy was waiting when Esther came downstairs, buttoning her jacket and pulling on her gloves. 'It's good you go to him, for he won't win, I fear. You comfort him, Esther and don't hurry home. I will cover for you with papa and Ruth – for all the times you covered for me. Off you go, and don't do anything I wouldn't do.'

'*Oy vey*,' Esther said, smiling conspiratorially and rolling her eyes. 'Such scope he gives me!'

'I know what I saw, Anne,' Frank said two hours later. It was your Esther there with Howard Brenton, bold as brass.'

'Never,' Anne said firmly.

'I'm telling you. Ask her yourself. She didn't look ashamed of it – more like proud, if you ask me.'

'My God,' Anne said, 'the sooner we get rid of that lot, the better. I hope he realizes he's lost?'

'He's thick if he doesn't. Of course we won't know till the votes come in from the lads in the forces, but I reckon Brenton knows Gaffney's in and he's out.'

'What'll happen next?' Anne asked, sitting down once she had seen his supper and mended the fire.

'Attlee'll form a governments and we'll have the Welfare State and a nationalization bill by Christmas.'

'That quick? Who'll run the pit, then?'

'We will. There'll be a manager, but the men will appoint him. And there'll be fair play, and decent wages and conditions: no more bosses' men or backhanders. And there'll be new houses, Anne, and health schemes, and no more public assistance or the Guardians.'

'It sounds like Utopia to me,' Anne said doubtfully.

'Oh, there'll be hiccups, no doubt,' Frank said generously. 'But we fought for the new Jerusalem, Anne; we sacrificed for it. And now, by God, we're going to get it.'

His face was alight as Anne looked at him. *He's a dreamer*, she thought. *But he's a wonder, an' all.* She moved over to him, caressing his head roughly as though chastizing him. 'Come on, dafty,' she said. 'It's time to go to bed.'

They let themselves into the darkened house on the Scar, moving from room to room and switching on lights. 'When I came here,' Esther said, 'before you and Diana even moved in, I used to run from room to room clicking these switches. I couldn't get over it. It was like the illuminations.'

'So that's why we had such monstrous bills,' Howard said. He poured sherry and handed her a glass.

'Glad the election's all over?' she asked.

'Very. I've lost, I could see that tonight. I don't need to wait for the Service vote. But I'm not sorry; I'm not cut out for politics. I'm not quite sure what I *am* cut out for but, that's not it.'

Esther sensed he was flat and dispirited.

'There'll be lots to do when the war's finally over. And the children – when are they coming home?'

'The week after next. Loelia wanted to take them to Eastbourne, and I knew I'd be tied up here during the election.'

There was silence for a while, and then Howard sighed. 'I wish Sammy Lansky was here.'

'Sammy?' Esther was taken by surprise. 'Why Sammy?'

'He has a delightful way of getting to the nub of things.'

'You don't mean that nonsense on the phone?'

'Is it such nonsense?' Howard was looking directly at her now, and she felt suddenly unaccountably embarrassed. If they had been somewhere else, anywhere but here – this place held too many ghosts for both of them.

'Esther!' Howard was not going to let it go. '*Is* it such nonsense?'

She shook her head, unwilling to respond.

I'm waiting.' Howard felt suddenly more certain of what he should do than he had ever felt in his life. He remembered that day Stephen Hardman died on the Scar; and Trenchard standing in a sunlit street; the cogs of fate turning and his own feeling of impotence. But not this time.

'Please, Howard, don't spoil things. It wouldn't work, you and I.'

'It *is* working, Esther. And you know it.' He came to her, letting her put her face against his shoulder, saying and doing nothing for a long moment, until at last his lips brushed her hair. 'Do you want to go home now?'

There was a long silence, then a shake of her head.

'Does that mean "no"?'

She chuckled, then, and he felt her relax against him.

'Yes,' she said. 'I suppose it does mean "no". But are you sure?'

'I've never been more sure of anything in my life – and I don't need Sammy Lansky to tell me so.'

They stood for a while, kissing each other, content to be close; and then they went upstairs, switching out the lights in the hall, leaving the light on the landing to burn while they made gentle love.

Howard kissed her breasts, her stomach, her thighs, all the while her hands gentle upon his head, reassuring, guiding. And then he was entering her, terrified of giving her pain, relishing her acceptance of him, serene and totally unafraid. And as they rose to climax together the thought came to him, simple and yet a revelation: *This is love,* he thought. *Now I know.*

'Oh, Esther,' he said at last. 'I...' He was suddenly lost for words: this time not out of inadequacy, but in wonderment at the course his life was taking.

'Shush,' she said. 'No need to talk.' She held him in her arms, then, cradling his head, touching the familiar scar on his cheek with a gentle finger, wondering all the while how long it could continue, this feeling of having found peace at last.

34

August 1945

They sat round the table at the Scar, the children at first solemn, and then, as they got to know Esther, relaxing and teasing one another. She looked at them as they ate their pudding. Pamela was like her mother – perhaps not quite so beautiful, but with the same vivid colouring and well-defined features. But there was a serenity about the daughter that the mother had never possessed. Esther thought of Diana imperiously ruling this house, all those years ago. It was a different house now, shabbier and less stylish but somehow more at peace with itself. There had been a dozen staff in the old days; now there were three, and a part-time gardener. What would Diana have made of that?

'Did you enjoy London?'

Esther glanced up to find Pamela looking at her. 'Yes, it was wonderful. Most of the things I'd only heard of were still intact, thank goodness. But the bomb damage was awful. I was sorry you had to go back to Valesworth so soon; I was looking forward to seeing it with you.'

'Yes,' Pamela said. 'I was sorry, too, but Aunt Lee was in a hurry.'

'Do you like it at Valesworth?' Esther asked.

'Oh yes, it's lovely. But it will be good to be home.'

'Is Belgate home? I thought you might prefer London?'

Pamela looked faintly scandalized.

'Oh no, this is home. It always has been. It's fun to go to London sometimes, and shop and go to the zoo and things like that. But this is home. It was such fun in the old days, when Rupert was here…'

She fell silent then, and Esther let it go, getting on with her pudding and watching Howard sometimes as he talked with the boys. Tonight, unless she was much mistaken, he would ask her to marry him. She thought of his lovemaking, tender and complete, and yet with a sense almost of wonder about it. After all the years he had been married to Diana, a responsible husband, there was still a touch of boyishness about his ardour, and some of the vulnerability she had loved in Philip. She could love it in Howard, too, if she allowed herself to love. But it wouldn't work: that was the pity.

They both had so much history behind them; there was so much Howard didn't know about her and that she did not feel inclined to tell him. *I am too old for marriage*, Esther thought. *Too used to my own ways.*

'My mother loved London,' Pamela said, breaking into Esther's thoughts. Her voice was wistful. 'You knew her, didn't you? When she was very young?'

'Yes,' Esther said. At the other end of the table Howard was still listening to his son but she could tell that now he was aware of what was being said between daughter and guest. 'I came here when I was fifteen, the same age as you. I wasn't terribly good at being a maid, but your mother and I did have fun together, when she was expecting Rupert and when he was very small. And then I went off elsewhere.'

'To make your fortune,' Noel said, his eyes bright, and Esther laughed.

'To make a *living*,' she said. 'It's not quite a fortune yet'

'Dad says you're a very good businesswoman.' Ralph announced this as though what his father said was holy writ.

'Well, then, I must be,' Esther said, and smiled at Howard. 'Now, I'm going to clear these dishes and make some coffee. Any volunteers?' They carried the dishes into the kitchen and then Esther shooed them away. 'I'm only going to stack, while the coffee brews.'

But Pamela stayed behind. 'Will you tell me about my mother one day, when you have time? I don't really – well, we never got much time to talk, because of the war and being with Aunt Lee. She's told me quite a lot about mama in London, and when they were growing up together, but she doesn't know about here. About Belgate.'

'Of course I'll tell you,' Esther said. 'Perhaps we could go off together somewhere one day, just the two of us?'

'That would be very nice,' Pamela said. 'Could it be this week?'

They drank their coffee, the boys quieter now, Noel's eyes drooping slightly.

'I expect the war'll be over tomorrow,' Ralph said, trying to make conversation to stave off bedtime. 'Except that the Japs are awfully tough, and they don't believe in surrender.'

It was a week since the *Enola Gay* had dropped its cargo on Hiroshima. The world's most terrible weapon, the atomic bomb, had hit the Japanese city with a force equal to 20,000 tons of TNT. Birds had shrivelled in mid-air, people had burned to cinders standing up, but the Japanese hierarchy stood firm. Three days later a second bomb had wiped out Nagasaki. President Truman had called it 'an overwhelming influence towards world peace', but to the Japanese it was 'a diabolical weapon'. To the hundreds of families with soldiers in the Far East or in Japanese prison camps, it was the one thing that might shorten the war.

'They'll have to give in eventually,' Howard said. 'But it probably won't be for a while. Now, I think it's time you three were cutting off to bed. It's after ten.'

They all said their reluctant goodnights and went off, their good-natured wrangling dying away as they mounted the stairs.

'They're very nice children,' Esther said, in the pause that followed. 'More coffee?'

'Yes, please. It's awfully good – how did you get hold of it? We seem to have been drinking chicory for years.'

'It's better not to ask,' Esther said demurely. 'Sufficient to say I have my sources.'

'The children like you,' Howard said at last. 'Which makes it all the more sensible for us to – how do they put it? Legalize our situation?'

Esther moved to the fireplace and rested a hand on the mantel. 'I don't think it would work, Howard. I'm so used to being on my own, to making my own decisions, to having my own home – to being my own boss, if I'm truthful.'

'Is that all?' Howard rose to his feet. 'Esther, don't you realize how much the world has changed in the last few years? There are men and women coming back who have looked into hell. Do you really imagine they are going to meekly slip back into the old ways? We'll all have to change. If you marry me, I won't expect you to be anything else but what you are: your own woman.'

'There are so many things you don't know about me –' Esther began but he interrupted.

'I have my secrets, too. I might share them with you one day; I might not. But it's not your past I want, Esther. It's your future I'm interested in.' He remembered last night lying naked beside her in the wide bed. He had looked down at her face, and suddenly remembered some old, half-forgotten lesson in mythology. Someone, the Greeks, probably, had believed that each person was two halves, one male, one female. And the two halves were destined to search the earth until they found each other. Only then could they know perfect happiness. *I have found my other half,* Howard had thought wonderingly then. *After all this time, I am complete.*

There was, in Esther, that spirit of freedom, of independence, that he had loved in Diana, but in Esther it was coupled with a warmth and tranquillity that he had never before found in a woman. He did not ask her where she, a spinster, had learned to love as joyfully as she did; one day, if she chose, she would tell him. He knew only that he wanted to spend the rest of his life with this woman, who had come into his home as a child and grown into someone he admired as well as loved.

He would let the subject drop tonight, because he did not want to spoil a pleasant evening; but he would not let it go. He had loved Diana, he knew that now: he had admired her *joie de vivre*; he had been awed by her lust for life, her determination to do what she wanted, whatever the consequences. But he had not played a part in shaping their relationship and for that, at least, he felt ashamed. He would not make that mistake again. He went to Esther and took her in his arms.

'While we're all here,' Frank said, taking a paper from his pocket, 'I've got the list of names for the memorial.' The parish council meeting had closed, and his fellow members clustered round for a look.

There'll likely be one or two more,' someone said, 'before Japan's defeated.' There were murmurs of agreement and then Stanley Gallagher spoke.

'You've got Rupert Brenton's name there.'

'Yes,' Frank said.

'He's not a Belgate lad.' Gallagher licked his lips and looked around. 'He never came here unless he had to, or if he was after some girl. He has no right to be on that list. Anyway,' He produced his trump card. 'The Scar is outside the parish line.'

The men were looking from one to another. 'If he has no right to be on…' someone said doubtfully.

'We don't owe the Brentons anything,' another said. 'Cross his name off.'

'Hold on.' Frank knew he must act now or let them have their way. 'In case you buggers have forgotten, Brenton's lad died for his country, like the rest of those whose names are on there. He didn't witter on about parish lines or who owed who what; he went up in an aeroplane and copped it. I put him down, alongside my own lad, because he died like my lad: for what he believed in, for us, for our right to have sodding arguments about who goes on what list. Now, I say his name stays.' He looked around him at the men. Young Gallagher's eyes dropped, and Frank knew he had won.

He also knew he would pay for the victory. There were some eyes that did not meet his as he bade people goodnight, and groups were forming to murmur about it even as the men turned away. Frank trudged off towards Trenchard Street, trying not to mind about what he had just done – he had thrown away the nomination, probably. A light was still burning two doors down from his home; that couple had a son in the forces who was preparing now for the assault on Malaya. Now, that was real trouble. It would be dreadful if the lad died now, at the eleventh hour. But the Japs would never give in. They'd have to be picked off, one by one, or bombed out of existence. The victory bonfire was ready on the green. Please God they would light it soon.

Frank opened his gate, thinking that the atomic bomb had really obscured Labour's electoral triumph. Still, Attlee now had a landslide majority, and five members of Churchill's cabinet and thirty-two members of his government had been booted out. And the Liberals had fared even worse than the Conservatives. *We are the masters now,* Frank thought. And *Jerusalem's in sight, whether I'm in Parliament or not.*

He waited until Anne had brewed tea and carried it to the table, and they were sitting on either side with their cups.

'How did the meeting go?' Anne asked, reaching for the

sugar. He watched her put in the half-teaspoon that was all the ration allowed.

'All right,' he said carefully. And then, unable to hold back: 'I've probably buggered the nomination, Anne. I know you won't like it, but it can't be helped. I did what I knew was right, and I'm sorry if it brings your rag out, but I'd do it again.'

Anne had gone pale and her eyes glittered, but she didn't speak. She went on stirring her tea, round and round, as though she was churning butter, while he explained.

'We were talking about the arrangements for the war memorial, and all the names. Then someone said, "Why is Brenton's lad on? They live outside the parish line." And someone else…'

'Who said that?' Anne interrupted.

'Stanley Gallagher,' he answered. 'And Jimmy Coxon backed him up. So I said, "He's on because he's a Belgate lad and he died the same way as the rest. That's why he's on." And then they argy-bargied, but I held on… so his name stays. But I've got a feeling I'll pay for it in the long run.'

He had expected a tirade. Instead, Anne took a long sip of her tea and wiped her mouth with the back of her hand,

'Well,' she said at last, resignedly, 'that's Westminster up the spout.' Frank was taken aback by her calm. 'Don't you mind?'

Anne shook her head ruefully. 'Sometimes, Frank, you are dimmer than a Toc H lamp. Of course I mind; I'm full, if you must know. Choked. But you didn't have any option. Rupert's dead, God love him, and he's the father of your grandbairn. If he was good enough to die for sods like Gallagher, I dare say he needs to be remembered somewhere.'

As Frank raised his cup in hands that trembled slightly he gave thanks that life with Anne was never dull. Every time you thought you'd worked her out she bowled you a bouncer. And that was a fact.

'I'm going up to bed now,' she said. 'I'm dog-tired.'

She could not tell him how heavy her heart was; not after what had happened at the meeting. She would have to keep it to herself. Tonight she had used her secret weapon. 'It's not your bairn,' she had said to Mario, when Stella was upstairs and Mario broached the subject of their leaving for America. She had expected disbelief, fury, renunciation, but Mario had simply held up his hand, palm out.

'I know that, momma. And I know whose child he is. Enough!' And there had been something in his face that silenced her. She had lost Joe; now she was to lose her grandbairn. It wasn't fair.

Mario, watching her, had seen the consternation on her face when he had silenced her. Surely she had realized he knew the baby was not his, but Ricky's? He had wondered if he should tell her about Ricky, but in the end he had held his peace.

Stella was sound asleep in her bedroom, dreaming of the Statue of Liberty and the lady's life that awaited her in the United States. It was Anne who tucked in the baby and smoothed the dark fuzz of hair that crowned his brow. That had come from the Brentons, for his mother was fair as a lily. *Unless it came from me,* Anne thought, fingering her greying hair that had once been black. She turned, sensing Frank behind her.

'Isn't he lovely?'

'Lovely, Anne. Now get to bed before you drop. I'll be joining you in a minute, when I've wound down.'

He always liked to sit for a while, to clear his mind of the turmoil of the meeting and catch up on the news. He boiled the kettle again, and watered the pot, then he turned on the wireless for the last news of the day. But it was not the cut-glass tones of the newsreader he heard; it was the quiet, precise voice of Clement Attlee, telling the nation that Japan had surrendered unconditionally, and the world was at peace.

Frank wanted to tell someone – anyone. But Anne might be asleep by now. Then he remembered the light two doors up – they might not have the wireless on, they might not know. He ran out into the street, forgetting he was in his stockinged feet, cursing when he trod on a pebble, but not turning back.

The door was opened almost as soon as he knocked, and he babbled out his good news: 'It's over, Lettie: all over! Your lad's coming home!'

Emmanuel Lansky, lying in bed in the dark, had listened to the wailing of the baby below until it ended. Now all was silent again. He had a son and a grandson; the chain endured. And the boy Aaron would grow up in a world without fear. He thought of the grey old men now in the dock in Nuremberg, the city where they had staged their torch-lit rallies and proclaimed a master race. Soon they must listen to the recital of their crimes – mass murder, atrocities, genocide – and accept the revulsion of the entire world. But Lansky had lost his thirst for vengeance. All he wanted now was peace.

'Papa?' It was Sammy, cautiously pushing open the door.

'Sammy?' Lansky struggled up in the bed. 'Put the light on, I'm not asleep.'

As light flooded the room he saw Sammy had his son in his arms.

'Does he sleep now, the *boyt'shikl*?'

Sammy looked down at the baby. 'He's full. He always sleeps when he's full.' He moved to the bed and laid the shawl-wrapped baby at his father's side. 'I came to tell you the news, papa. The war is over. There's total surrender. I've just heard it on the wireless, and from the Prime Minister, no less. Tomorrow is to be a day of rejoicing.'

Lansky looked down at the sleeping child. 'Thank God,' he said.

'Papa...' Sammy was sitting at the foot of the bed, as he had done when he was a child. 'Remember when I was away? The time when you got the postcards?' Emmanuel nodded. 'I wrote them but I didn't post them. I was in Paris, and someone posted them for me, to keep you happy.'

'Paris?'

'Yes. I went there for a purpose, to do something I knew how to do, in the family home. The Germans had put it to a bad use. I – I evened things up a bit.'

'It was dangerous! How could you do such a thing?'

'Because I had to, papa. And I was careful – oh boy, was I careful! And I'm here now, and it's over. I wanted you to know because I don't keep things from you, but please don't tell Naomi – not yet. When she is old and grey and fat, I'll tell her. For now, she has trouble enough with this one.' He looked down at Aaron, lying in the crook of his grandfather's arm.

'If it had gone wrong,' Lansky said, 'there would have been no son, no Aaron. You're a fool, Sammy: *der ferd*. But I'm proud of you.'

'Not half as proud as you will be, papa. I'm going to make things hum, you'll see. The sky's the limit.'

'*Oy vey*,' Lansky said wearily, looking down at the sleeping baby. 'Here we go again!'

'I ought to go home,' Esther said, not wanting to break away but mindful of the need to get up for work in the morning. 'It's half-past twelve. I won't be home before one.'

Howard walked out to the car with her, holding her arm, wishing with all his heart that she was mistress of his house with no need ever to go again.

'There's a light on down there,' Esther said suddenly, looking down on Belgate.

'It's a fire,' Howard said, and Esther anxiously picked out first Anne's roof, then the detached house on the village edge where Patrick was to set up his practice and he and Mary would live. Both were dark and safe.

'It's a bonfire,' Howard said, 'in the vicarage grounds. No, on the green. It's the VJ bonfire! There are people round it… and that's a crake they're sounding.' A rocket whooshed suddenly into the air and exploded into a luminous haze.

'The war's over!' Esther said. 'It must be over!'

Howard let out his breath. 'Thank God.' No more homes to visit, no more death.

They stood for a while, watching the crowd grow, the fire take hold.

'Things won't be easy,' Esther said at last. She had moved into his arms, both of them staring fascinated at the scene below. 'They all think it's going to be a land of milk and honey now: Jerusalem, Frank calls it. And I'm not sure that's possible.'

'No.' Howard's voice was sombre. This country has almost bankrupted itself to win the war, and there'll be little or no gratitude from the countries we reprieved. As for America, they'll stop lend-lease now. We'll have to cut down on imports of food, cotton, petrol, everything; and what we make we'll have to export. I pity my successor, Esther – pity all politicians. In London alone there are 700,000 houses to repair. Multiply that by all the towns and cities which suffered, and it's an impossible task. Men will come home in their brand-new suits to find they have no roof over their heads. They'll find children who don't remember them, and employers who don't choose to remember them. It was like that last time. We mustn't let it happen again; not in Belgate, anyway. They'll nationalize the pits, but before they do I want to make that huddle of houses down there as near to a new Jerusalem as I can. Does that sound pious?'

'No,' Esther said. 'Idealistic, perhaps, but not in the least pious.'

Howard was turning her round now, gripping her arms in

his desire to impress his words upon her. 'Help me, Esther! You'll have to work like you never worked before if people are to have even a sniff of milk and honey. Let's work together. Marry me, Esther, for God's sake.'

Esther stepped back a little and looked at him, wrinkling her brow. For what seemed to Howard an eternity.

Suddenly she smiled. 'Well, it can't be this week,' she said in matter-of-fact tones. 'We'll have to make it the end of the month.'

It is 1945: Britain is still struggling with post-war rationing but there's an exhilerating sense that the country is building a 'new Jerusalem', as Belgate coalminer Frank Maguire puts it. Under brand-new Labour government, nationalization will soon hand the pits to the miners. And many barriers have been shattered by the war. Esther Gulliver, once in service at the big house on the scar, is marrying coal-owner Howard Brenton.

As much as she loves Howard, Esther is anxious: his aristocratic friends disapprove; his teenage daughter Pamela needs guiding in a world of manners and court debuts of which Esther knows nothing - and there's the secret from her past that she doesn't dare tell him...

Denise Robertson's large, warm-hearted novel, sweeping from Durham to London and back again with its diverse cast of characters, captures the growing confidence of Britain in the prospering fifties and sixties.

Coming soon from Little Books,
the story continues in:
Towards Jerusalem